BLOOD ROSE

1980s Vampire Ballerina Paranormal Romance (Cursed Winds Book 1)

Kesha D Ely

ISBN: 9798218764135

Library of Congress Control Number: 2311419
Printed in the United States of America

for Twilight, Vampire Diaries,
and Mortal Instruments fans

Contents

PROLOGUE

I tire of my soul regressing to a shell. Every day brings nonstop regret and self-hatred. Why didn't I do more to protect myself? Living with this curse is punishment for my lack of courage. My fear of fighting back. But…how could I have??! The thing wasn't human. I don't know what it was! How it soared in the air. How red its eyes were. The way it drank blood, as if it were a natural food source.

Humans don't feed on each other! What was it? It seemed to be a boy, just as I am… but the motion of its limbs proved otherwise. The monster moved with the wind. It defied gravity. It broke the laws of physics! WHAT WAS IT???!! Why did it doom me with death???!

My life source has faded to nothingness. My soul is a lifeless void. My heart is gone… it no longer operates! My eyes are colorless! My reflection has vanished! I should've fought for my life! I should've defended my mortal soul! Even if that meant dying… at least I'd actually be dead, and not a reanimated corpse existing solely for the blood of others.

*I wouldn't be a beast capable of brutal measures. A hellish monster that disregards the virtue of human life. The mortal spirit is a sacred gift. I've always known this. In the teachings passed down to me, the Ani-Yunwiya—my Cherokee people—honor the Great Spirit, Unetlanvhi, the Creator of all things. Life, in every form, is a blessing. Our stories teach that harmony—***ᎤᏃᎴᎲᎥᏫᏯ*** (***ᎤᏃᎴᎲᎥᏫᏯ, unolevhvwiya***) *is what the Creator intended for us. Balance with the land. Respect for life. Reverence for the spirit.*

I was raised to know the sacredness of breath. The sacredness of being. And still—I took life. I severed what Unetlanvhi had given. I shattered the harmony. I went against everything I was meant to protect. Against the old ways. Against the teachings of my ancestors.

I carry this burden now. The weight of broken balance. My hands—bloodied and stained—are no longer clean in the eyes of my people, or my Creator. I've dishonored the sacred trust. I've turned my back on the path. I feel unworthy of calling myself Cherokee. Not while the echoes of the dead cling to me.

My family fears me… so does my tribe. My humanity grows lesser and lesser second by second. My taste for violence won't decrease. All seems to be hopeless. I seem to be trapped with this evil mark for all eternity. Or so I thought. Of course, magic is real in a world of vampires. Maybe this source could present a cure. A cure would offer an escape from this inferno. Guidance back into the light.

This girl, Kayla Harris, has a bright aura. I've never seen a human contain such a shine. White fire lives within her. I believe she is the path to heal my cold heart... and broken eyes. I believe in her. A Spell Bender, a sorceress of unlimited power. She will aid my redemption.

My faith stands with her. Even if all fails, I've prepared for that outcome. If there is no cure, I'll accept that truth as long as I have her near me. The glow within her... the brightness of her soul... would be close enough to peace.

CHAPTER 1: HOME

1983

KOTA

Kota Ahoka, a toffee-skinned boy with silky black hair, opens a locker. The hall is crowded with students. Some listen to cassettes while swapping books from their lockers, while others chat. The Native boy grabs a workshop book and slams his locker. His long hair hangs past his sharp jaws, and his big brown eyes shine under the sunlight. He strides the noisy hall. Groups of teenage girls stare after him, starstruck.

Many boys glare at him jealously, hating how his flowy hair surfs the air. His sight is set on a door at the end of the hall. The mixed looks continue as he walks. Kota grins. *Should I say I can't help being cursed with beauty? Or will those words make the jocks jump me?* He soaks up the attention. A cute girl blocks his path before he can reach the door.

"Hi, Kota." She smiles. "Do you have a date for the dance?"

Kota attempts to respond, but another girl hustles over angrily. "Hey! I was going to ask him!" A tall girl comes along, bumping the other to the side. "Wanna go with me?" "I asked first!" the other argues.

"Well, I'm asking now." The two face-off like batty cats.

Uh oh. I hope they don't fight over me. I should put an end to this before it gets ugly. "I appreciate you two asking, but I'm going with my crew. Sorry."

The two girls' boiling expressions switch to dreamy awe in a flash. Kota's native accent is light and soothing, so much that it ends their spat. "Oh…" The first one stares at his mouth in a daze.

"Maybe next time." He grins.

"Okay… next time." The tall one speaks serenely.

The bell rings. Everyone in the hallway scatters to classrooms like a swarm of bees. Kota makes it to the door. Two boys wait there, shaking their heads. Mike is dark-toned with jerry curls. Jimmy is ginger-haired with blue eyes.

"Wow!" Jimmy starts. "You just keep turning them down."

"Seven total, counting those two."

"We already planned to go together." Kota clarifies.

"So…" Mike scoffs at this. "You should ditch us for a babe."

"Whatever happened to loyalty?" Kota goes into a loud classroom.

"It doesn't apply here."

"Why not?"

"You already have a cheat code. Why not use it to land a chick?" Jimmy uses animated hand gestures to convey his confusion.

"I don't have a cheat code."

Mike laughs as the three take seats at workstations full of wood slabs. "Dude?"

"I'm serious. I don't know what you guys are talking about."

"Your voice… you lighten it to lure girls in. Just admit it." Jimmy squints. "You know they love it."

"No, I don't. For the last time, this is how I talk!" Kota stresses.

"Hmm, mmm… right." Mike doubtfully eyes him.

"Good afternoon, class." The teacher greets his students. "Today, we're going to build a candleholder." The man uncovers a cloth to showcase a block of stained wood mounted on legs. It's shaped like a horseshoe. "This is the subject that you all will be replicating. You have thirty-five minutes." The man winds up a clock on his desk. It ticks like a bomb. A clunking noise. All the students pick up the wood pieces.

Kota opens a drawer to unload the needed tools: a saw, drill, nails, hammer, and stainer. *I still can't believe that after three months, these two think I fake my voice. If I deepen it, I'll sound like Darth Vader… not even a cool version of him. It's silly… I can't help how I sound. Making girls swoon isn't done on purpose.* He saws the wood block into a shorter shape, since it isn't as defined as the teacher's. Mike and Jimmy chuckle while sawing. This distracts him, so he stops and looks their way.

"Guys…stop…"

Jimmy cheeses. "Hi, I'm Kota." His voice is higher pitched to mock. "I'm a flower child." The two burst into laughter.

"Quit it!" His cheeks heat up.

"I'm a Casanova." Mike jabs, using the same tone.

He huffs, continuing to cut through the wood. "I'm not."

"All girls want me… even the queen bee."

Kota halts and glances over at Jimmy, speechless. "Wait… Macy Hart?"

He nods. "The word around is that she wrote you a note and tried sticking it into your locker. Her boyfriend caught her, though. I'd steer clear of the jock king if I were you."

"When did this happen?"

"Last week. You didn't hear?"

"No…"

"You would have rejected her, anyway."

"Boys!" the teacher yells. "The clock is ticking. Get to work!" The three end their chat. They slice the wood, then wipe it clean. Dust particles float in the air as the class shape their pieces.

Wow… the queen bee was at my locker… with a note for a date? That's insane! She's the most beautiful girl in school, with the toughest boyfriend. That's her type. Why is she interested in me? He ponders while dividing the sides of the wood chunk into a sharp cut. He does this with ease. *Mike is wrong. I would have said yes if I ever got the note. Macy has flawless handwriting. Teachers dote on it for how traced out it looks. Angelic cursive.; I would have realized it was her asking. WHOA… THE QUEEN BEE WAS AT MY LOCKER! SO NEAT!*

The coloring stage is next. The dull wood is shaded cherry with a paintbrush. The process of hammering the legs on comes next. Kota bangs in four nails on each side, then mounts the finished product. He eyes the timer—ten minutes to go. Everyone else is still working. *Hmm… I just don't want to sit here doing nothing. Maybe I could add a few mods. My dad taught me handy work; we built our garage last summer break. So, I know what I'm doing.*

He takes a stencil blade from the drawer and begins carving a large dreamcatcher on the side. The wood sheds, dropping curled pieces to the table. Kota is sure to keep the depth of the design at two centimeters, so as not to crack the old wood. *It's a lot more delicate than a new slab. That's something else my father taught me.*

The circular shape and hanging feathers are easy to complete. But the webbing star symbol inside takes about five minutes. Once done, he repeats the mark on the other side. He's only able to complete half of it before the timer goes off; rattling atop the desk.

"Time!" Most of his peers haven't finished the project yet. Jimmy and Mike have just begun painting the wood dark. The teacher patrols the desks, surveying each assignment. Five are to his liking. The stern man shares approving glances. When he reaches Kota, he frowns. "Mr. Ahoka. Your duty was to create a replica, not to dirty it with graffiti! That's a C minus!"

"Graffiti???"

"Yes. Is that symbol not illicitly drawn on your assignment?"

"Yes, but—"

"No excuses. Keep your symbols away from art! You've been here long enough to adapt, so do so. And you two," he sets his sight on Kota's friends, "D minus."

Kota gawks at the teacher, who presses onward down the aisle.

"What did he mean by adapt?" "Just ignore it," Mike grumbles.

"Well… you defaced it, dude."

"I finished early and was bored. This isn't graffiti." Jimmy shrugs just as the bell rings. "I didn't deserve a C minus…"

The three pile into a line leading to the door. A girl taps Kota's shoulder. He spins to find a lime-eyed redhead. "I thought it was cool. Mr. Boone overreacted. That symbol is art." She whispers supportively. "Umm… anyway, I was wondering if you had a—"

"I'm sorry, but I'm not going with a date."

The girl's humiliation is clear as day. "Oh, okay…" Her eyes jump to the side. "I hope you have fun."

"Likewise." She blushes shyly before shuffling off.

"That's eight." Mike uses his fingers to count.

"You're a natural heartbreaker, Ahoka." *These two are getting on my nerves. Do they want me to bail on them?*

A green-haired girl dressed in leather awaits them in the hall. "Hey, dweebs, ready for tonight?"

"Sup, Liz." Kota greets with a jerk of his chin. "Yep, so ready. I got the drinks."

"I'll buy the pizza," Jimmy adds.

Mike drapes his arms around her shoulders. "And I'll supply the kissing."

"You wish." Liz shoves him away and starts down the hall. The boys flock after her. Blue banners hang from the ceiling, promoting the Under the Sea dance. Fizzy bubbles and seashells decorate the backdrop. Liz rolls her eyes. "We should ditch the dance. Why do you guys insist on going to a cheese fest? Y'all can't even get dates."

"Hey!" Mike's mouth drops. "Yes, I can!"

"We all can. Especially Kota. He gets tallies every day," Jimmy defends his friend.

"Those bozos only crush on you, then go on to the next. Trust me."

Kota shakes his head at Liz. "Nope. I could pull all of them if I wanted. Even the top girl. Macy Hart is into me." He gloats.

"You're shitting." Her flat tone is dismissive.

"I'm not." He squabbles with her. "Tell her, guys."

"It's true." Jimmy beams. "It was hot gossip last week while you were despising human life."

"Ha ha, very funny." Liz fakes amusement. "And who cares? Macy Hart is a snooze. You're better off dating a grandma. She's so vanilla."

"She's won Most Beautiful three years in a row." Kota admires the queen bee's status.

"Those contests are rigged… plus she uses boob tissue."

Kota playfully bumps her shoulder. "Sounds like someone has a green monster on their shoulder."

"I'm not jealous of the plastic queen."

"Don't worry, I'll dance with you." Mike reaches for her hand.

"You're going to lose that hand if you touch me, and that's sad. Cus, it's your girlfriend."

"Why so cruel?"

"Oh, Mike, why would you think that?" she exclaims sarcastically, as if a sweetheart.

"You're so mean."

"No, I'm a ray of sunshine." She smirks. "What time is this dumb dance?"

"6." Kota scrolls his locker combination in. "We'll show at 6:30 and leave at 8."

"And stay out till midnight!" Liz replies enthusiastically. "Now…that's a real party."

"You sure you can be out that late, K-Man?" Mike asks, concerned. "Isn't the rez strict on curfew?"

"Yeah… but I have a secret way out." He pops the book inside his locker and shuts it.

"You're gonna get busted. What punishment would your parents give you?" Liz cocks her head to the side.

"I'd probably have to cook dinner until my hands go sore."

Her eyes widen. "That's it?"

"Yeah."

"That's not punishment…"

"Yes, it is; hand cramps are the worst!"

"Can we switch houses?"

"Depends on if y'all eat poyha."

"P-what??"

"Poyha… deer meat and wild berries."

"That sounds nasty."

"Oh, trust me, it's the best."

"Kota." Mike tilts his head forward. "One more coming in, hotshot."

Uh oh… I'm sure the last girl went to cry. I'd rather not do that again. I should be flattered by the attempts; instead, they're causing anxiety. I want to run away. I want to flee outside, but that'll be rude. I don't enjoy being mean. I honestly want to keep my word to my gang.

Kota's thoughts are transparent enough for Liz to get a read. She marches ahead to meet the girl, who rocks a chic fairy style, short olive dress with loose sleeves. The flower headband she wears has veiny roots covered in green leaves.

Aww… she looks so sweet. Meaning she's going to crash hard over what she's about to hear. He gives a regretful gaze as the wistful teen stops in her tracks.

Liz crosses her arms. "Kota isn't accepting dates; he's going with us. Try someone else. Sorry, hon."

Kota cringes as her face droops into a grimace. All her confidence fades. The girl doesn't speak; she just goes back the way she came at a hasty pace. *Great… now I'm a bully. Maybe I should skip the dance to avoid facing the girls I rejected. That's if they're still going. I should apologize again to ease the pity I feel.* "I'll meet you guys at the bus stop at five."

"Fine. I guess I'll wear a nice dress." Liz drones drearily.

"You mean a black dress?" Jimmy cracks. "As always."

"For your information, I have different shades in my closet. Ink. Spider. Coal. Oil."

"Could you wear something pink?" Liz prods her elbow into Mike's side. He groans and hunches over in a painful howl.

"See ya, guys." Kota chuckles.

CHAPTER 2: LIFE

Kota exits the window-filled hall and out into a manicured courtyard. He opens the Wood Shop book as he paces along ultragreen nature. Autumn trees contrast with the garden covered in yellow and orange leaves. The wind twirls the colorful leaves in a scurry. His hair ripples in the wind, catching the attention of a group of girls who pass by.

"Hey, Kota." The clique says in unison, giggling softly.

"Hey." Kota looks up briefly, smirking charmingly, then returns to reading the book. He skips to page 45, where a porch mailbox is displayed. *I'm almost done with this one. It's a gift for Mom. I should work on one for my sister, Dyani. Maybe a doghouse as her birthday present? A puppy? I'll have to hide it somewhere so the surprise isn't ruined. I believe that's on page 105.*

Kota glides along a leaf-infested sidewalk, his shoes crunching on the shriveled leaves. He nears a bus stop where other teens wait. The designation set in his mind is the Ozark Mountains—Tahlequah, where the Cherokee tribe resides. A town with a population of 1,482. Unfortunately, it's too overpopulated to the point that the reservation had no openings. So, he had to transfer to another school district.

He boards the bus, going to the middle to sit. The town of Tahlequah is located at the foot of a vibrant mountain. The crummy town doesn't match the beauty of the surrounding hills. The place is in need of funding to demolish abandoned buildings and increase property value. Most citizens ride bikes since cars are too expensive. *Our family car has been around for forty years. Grandad worked on it until his knees went bad; now Dad does all of the repairs. It's a sturdy Volkswagen.*

The bus arrives at the main entrance of the reservation. The tribe officers wave to Kota. He returns the kind gesture. "I'm awaiting the Pow-Wow for your agitsi's (mother's) pudding," one rez officer states eagerly.

"Me too! She's making a bunch, so we can gorge out."

"Good to know!"

Past the rez gates are cracked sidewalks and small ranch houses. The lawns are covered in vibrant leaves, giving the area an appeal despite the poorly constructed homes. The neighborhood is quiet and almost vacant. A few people occupy the park at the end of the street. He nears a one-story house paneled with white siding. Kota raises his hand above the doorframe to the ledge to retrieve a house key.

Inside, loud music bumps; *Witch Queen of New Orleans* by Redbone. He closes the door and goes to the kitchen. His sister washes dishes, swinging her short hair side to side to the beat. Her bronze skin and defined cheeks resemble his. "Hey."

Dyani glances sideways at him and stops her dancing. "You saw nothing!"

"5 bucks and I'll wipe my mind clean of it." He pokes. "Is Mom in?"

"No. She went shopping for the Pow-Wow. Dad said to put away his tools. For some reason, he thinks if I touch them, I'll end up in the hospital."

"You do trip while you walk."

"That was one time! My pants were too long!" She cups bubbly water in her palm and tosses it his way.

Kota dodges the foamy streak, using his book as a shield. "Hmm…I'm gonna side with Dad, *kamama* (butterfly)."

"Asdudi galvladitlv." *(Shut up.)*

"Tla." *(No.)*

"Go do what Dad wants!" "I will… when I want to."

"You keep forgetting I'm older. That means I hold authority when Mom and Dad are out."

"Does that mean I can go to the dance?"

"No… you're too annoying."

"I think that's a yes."

Dy goes back to scrubbing dishes. "Why do you want to go, anyway? Once a spot opens here, you'll be gone from that school."

"That's a big if. The rez doesn't even have a spare desk."

"For now."

"I doubt the classrooms will get roomier."

She dries a stack of plates one at a time, placing each in a cabinet bearing rose wallpaper. "Still… you shouldn't get attached. You'll be where you belong soon."

"I have no issues fitting in. I'm pretty popular."

Dyani rolls her eyes. "If you say so." "I am!" he defends himself while laughing.

"Even if you are, I don't want you there."

"Why not?" His soft voice drags out the question.

"Have you ever heard of bigots?" Dy asks while lathering cups with a sponge.

"It's not that bad. One teacher is rude… a few guys glare. Other than that, everyone else is nice."

"Or they're pretending nice when you're around."

Hmm… is that true? Kota ponders, then shrugs. "My friends don't. That's all that counts. We're partying tonight."

"A school dance is nowhere near a party." She snickers.

Should I tell Dy about the bonfire? Or would she rat me out? I'm not sure if I can trust her. My sis usually gets payback when I annoy her. "Depends on who you go with, clumsy."

"Okay… you're getting on my nerves!" Dy dunks a cup into the bubbly water and charges at her brother.

Kota jets from the kitchen, hackling like a hyena. He makes it outside and swings the door shut just as the liquid splats it. He paces to the garage with a big, goofy smile. The unit is compact, big enough for one car and tiny storage shelves. He reminisces, remembering him and his dad placing the shingled roof and molding the windows to their panes. The interior holds oak walls and a concrete floor. There are tools on the counter, far from their shelves. Kota goes to collect them and pack them back where they belong.

Dad finally fixed that grandfather clock. It took him ages. Now I can finally get around to finishing the mailbox since the workspace is clear. He opens a cabinet below the shelves and pulls out a letterbox with the name *Ahoka* engraved on its front. He uses a screwdriver to twist hinges onto the back, then sets a flap of wood atop it to connect the piece. After the roof of the mailbox is complete, Kota spray paints it pure white. The chemical dye mists the air.

At 6:00 p.m., he goes to his room…gray walls and a blue twin bed. A narrow closet is his destination. Kota browses for a casual outfit, believing a formal suit would be over the top. He decides on a simple style with a hint of class: a dress shirt with buttons undone, dark denim flare pants, and a jacket. The last accessory is mid-rise boots. On his way out, he writes a note and pins it to the letterbox: **Nasginai Unitsi** (*For Mother*). He treks down the block to the park. Kota lifts the flimsy gate and crawls underneath to escape.

The school's gymnasium is covered in blue and white streamers. Paper-mâché balls hang from the ceiling. The same banners from the hallway also drape, only this time, there are tons of them. Tacky fish stickers sprinkle the floor, glowing neon under the dim blue lighting. A long food table holds pizza, nachos, punch bowls, and cake. The squad makes their way to it. Liz is in a smoky babydoll dress and platforms. Jimmy and Mike are in graphic T's and blazers. Kota is the fanciest of the bunch.

The song *Mr. Roboto* circulates the gym room. Teachers patrol the sidelines of the court, surveying students in flashy attire, puff dresses, pastel suits, and varsity jackets. The jock king bullies drinks from geeks. He invades their personal space with a menacing demeanor. The boys bail under pressure and forfeit their punch, speeding away. The douche is an evil version of Prince Charming. He and Kota lock eyes. His blue ones scowl from across the room at him. The big blond guy steps toward Macy, a chocolate-haired, silver-eyed girl, and seizes her by the waist, treating her as if she's an object to be claimed.

Really?? That's a desperate move; the guy needs to chill. Kota eyes the football jerk from across the jammed dance floor, aware that he's watching him like a territorial lion. *I get that they're dating, but he needs to switch it down a notch. Does he think I'm going to yank her away?? Although that is tempting. Macy is a peculiar beauty; her eyes alone draw people in. Crystal irises. She's a cheerleader…the team captain, to be exact. It's as if being with a jock was written into her life's coding. I'm still surprised that she likes me. I'm not the athletic type. Why is she into me?*

The crew scoops juice into red cups and linger around the table with others. Teens break out the moonwalk, adding too much friction to the foot slide; the dance isn't seamless. The sprinkler is goofy and forceful. The partiers appear in need of psychological assistance. The robot dance is embarrassing enough for a seconddegree burn.

"Eww…" Liz rips her gaze from the disastrous scene. "I'm counting the seconds."

"It's not that bad," Jimmy quarrels. "You can't possibly hate fun."

"I don't hate fun. I just prefer smaller crowds."

"Are we going to see a different side of you tonight?" Kota grins to one side.

"Oh, yeah… you guys won't recognize me."

"Why not?"

"I'm kina wild… but only when I'm comfortable." "Aww, was that a compliment?" Kota teases.

"No, it wasn't."

Mike nods. "Yeah, it was. You love being around us. Admit it." He beams.

"I think someone's a teddy bear, all fluff on the inside." Kota singsongs.

"Shut up! I hate you guys…"

"Uh oh…" Jimmy snickers. "We're on her bad side… for the hundredth time."

"Sorry, we're just not used to you being nice."

"Yeah… well, don't get used to it."

Kota spots Macy gazing at him from across the room. Her curious pale eyes burn into his. The blue light highlights her slim face and tiny features. The girl's olive skin glows. The peach dress she wears contrasts well with her eyeshadow and pink cheeks. *Whoa… she's so beautiful…too bad she's taken.* Her boy toy blocks her from view like a colossal statue. The football player shoots another warning glare his way. He flexes the collar of his varsity jacket as a means of intimidation.

"Don't start any drama, man." Jimmy moves to hide Kota from the jock's line of sight. "Unless you can fight."

"No…he's too smart to dumb himself down." Kota is taken aback by her statement. *Oh wow, two compliments in one night. Is the world upside down?* His mouth hangs. Her eyes hesitantly dart to the side. "I'm gonna go to the restroom," Liz blurts, taking off fast through the crowd.

Jimmy gawks after her. "No way…" "What?"

Mike cocks his head to the side.

"Liz is crushing on Mr. Dreamboat here," Jim jabs a finger at him. "How did we count Liz out as a chick?"

"Maybe because she doesn't act like one… more like a Grinch."

"Or a negative Nancy," Kota adds.

"Great… now you're even more annoying." Jim scoffs. "You got the most difficult girl in your pocket, too?? Show off."

"Maybe a little…"

"A little??"

"You have another thing you do with your hair." Mike points to his long, lush mane.

"My what?"

"You do something extra to it, so it's super bouncy."

"Wow… you're reaching with that one! I just use shampoo."

Jimmy analyzes his lavish mane of dark hair. "And a conditioner."

"No."

"A native kind that makes you one with the wind." "With herbs and shit in it," Mike seconds.

They have to be kidding! A secret native conditioner??? Kota titters. "You two are something else…but I accept your envy." He remarks, drinking from his cup.

When Liz returns, the boys stand in awkward silence, not wanting to address her being sweet on Kota. She looks between the three, skeptical of their quietness. "What are you guys up to?"

"Nothing."

"Just chilling."

"Yeah, we're up to nothing," Kota seconds swiftly.

"Sure… I totally buy that." Liz tightens her lips. "What were y'all talking about when I was gone?" "Nothing," Jimmy lies.

"So, none of you spoke a word; you just stood here like creeps?"

Jimmy bobs his head up and down. "Yep, we were total creeps the whole time."

The current song fades out. *Holy Diver* by Dio blasts the speakers. This rock song stirs up a rave concert. All the teachers march over to the pit forming on the dance floor. The crowd rapidly grows in size.

"Wow, they're actually playing a good song??" Liz is impressed.

"Wanna head bang? We can't be wallflowers," Kota suggests.

"Sure… but we're the only two with long hair." She pokes.

"There's no ban against us short-haired participating."

"YEAH, WHAT HE SAID!" Mike backs up Jim with a warrior shout.

"Alright, let's go then." Kota gestures to the dance floor.

"I guess I can mingle with the goofies…" Liz huffs.

The four place their cups down and join rowdy teens in the middle of the floor. The adults find it hard to de-escalate the wild students, who hop aggressively to the music. Most give their best impression of the seizure dance.

Mike and Jim break into crazed neck movements since they lack long hair, while Liz and Kota headbang properly. "Race for the morning. You can hide in the sun till you see the light," she sings along with the track.

The other three join in. "Oh, we will pray it's all right!"

The crowd around shouts, "Gotta get away, get away!! Holy diver, yeah!!" The teachers throw ridiculing looks, covering their ears because of the hollering.

"Got shiny diamonds like the eyes of a cat in the black and blue. Something's coming for you!!! LOOK OUT!! Race for the morning. You can hide in the sun till you see the light!!" The teens distort their voices as the singer does. Everyone jumps and rocks their heads. Mike almost falls; Liz points at him and laughs hard. When the solo slices through the speakers in distortion, the crew mimics air guitars, continuing their hostile head jerks.

"Gotta get away, get away!! Holy diver, yeah!!!" the youth bellow out the lyrics.

The principal, a tall man, stomps to the DJ, jabbing his finger. The music host leans to hear what the man is saying. The principal points to their Numark mixer, stressing his words. The music cuts.

"What? Seriously??!!" Liz throws her hands into the air.

"Behave yourselves!!" the principal shouts into a microphone. "That behavior isn't allowed here!! The DJ will play something slow."

"Aww!" all of the teens groan. The song *On the Wings of Love* mellows out the rocker mood. The romantic piano and air strings course through the gym.

Liz pushes her hair from her face. "Of course, something slow and safe. Gag." She imitates a puke noise.

Kota swipes his hair to the side; she studies his hands. A sudden softness in her eyes catch him off guard. *Oh… are we having a moment?* He freezes. The affectionate lyrics sound from all around them. A fluttering sensation vibrates his stomach. Liz's caramel eyes are so delicate as she focuses on him, blinking slowly. Kota notices her chest pumping faster than it was before.

"You are the sunshine that lights my heart within. I'm sure that you're an angel in disguise. Come, take my hand, and together, we will rise." The lyrics of the track are sung with passion.

Liz's pale cheeks blotch red. She drops her gaze from his. "We can head out early…" She hurries toward the exit.

Kota is astounded. He stares at where she just was… at the blank space. *Did that just happen???* He turns to the guys, who are just as surprised as he is. "You can't say no to her," Jimmy gapes. "You'll end up ten feet under without a trace."

"No… she'll do worse than that," Mike debates this seriously…not joking at all.

"It was the song, guys. It's all mushy and crap." "No…it wasn't." Jim disagrees.

"Come on, let's get to the woods," Kota treks to the exit.

It was the song. Liz wasn't being weird before. Well… maybe a little. She did say I was too smart to dumb myself down; that was new. I'm still processing that. I honestly think what just happened was because of the love song. If Liz wanted more than friendship, she would have said so by now. Right?

CHAPTER 3: UNHOLY

Liz leans against the side of the brick building. She limits her eye contact to small peeks. The night wind blows her green hair all over her face, but she doesn't care to fix it. "You lames ready?"

"Yeah," Jimmy oddly examines her. "I just need to grab the pizza."

"I stashed the drinks in a bush." Kota adds.

"Isn't your dad gonna realize his drinks are missing?" Mike wonders.

"No. I bought the pack myself." Kota brags like a badass.

"You're not 21, though. How'd you do it?"

"I may or may not have done identity theft."

"What???" Liz probes him. "That's not like you...I don't believe it."

"Well, I did it. I swiped my dad's ID. We're practically twins, so the clerk didn't investigate. Plus, he has no signs of aging, so that helped."

"But your name and age aren't the same..."

"I held the ID far."

"Hmmm… shocking." She straightens from the wall.

"I can be a rebel when I need to."

"Well, let's hope your criminal activity paid off. Hopefully, the drinks are still there."

"They should be. No one was around to spot me hiding the pack."

"Hot beer… yummy," Mike says satirically.

"I chose good shading…a bush under the growth. So, they'll be cool, not hot."

"And music? We can't have a shindig without it."

"I stored my satellite radio there, too." Kota brags cooly. "I thought of everything." "Good,"

Mike is relieved.

Liz strolls to the pavement; her dark boots flatten the maroon leaves. "The bus is coming."

Kota follows her…so do the other two. The bus stop is just down the street. The vehicle's tires are plastered with yellow leaves. The driver is considerate enough to hiss to a halt and wait for the squad. No one else is aboard the bus, so the seating is free range; yet they still sit with each other. Kota pairs with Mike, Jim with Liz. Pizza Hut is five minutes away, so the stop is quick.

Jimmy gets out and power walks into the dome roofed restaurant. They watch him through the window as he nears the check-in counter. The place is empty. Jim receives service right off. About seven minutes later, he returns with three boxes. The bus hisses forward. The tires roll on gravel for the next four miles. Liz pulls the string when she spots the forest sign.

The bus driver swerves to the curb and pauses the vehicle. "You kids be safe; it's late," the man cautions.

"Don't worry, my house is close by." Kota lies, sharing a malicious grin with his peeps.

"Have a good night."

"You too."

"Thanks, dude." Liz winks at the driver as they dismount. Mike's eyes double in size. "I want a wink too." "I'll give you one later." She flirts smoothly.

They wait for the bus to depart so they're not spotted going into the forest so late at night. When it shifts to make a left turn, the squad moves. Kota glances over his shoulder at an empty road. "The coast is clear." The entrance gate is a few yards away. When there, Kota goes to a bush, removing an 8-pack of beer and the satellite radio from its depths.

Liz leads the way into the woods. There's a campsite not too far. Jimmy sets the pizza boxes on a boulder, then lights a match. The orange aura aids with visibility. The forest is pitch black beyond the flame.

"Help me find wood for the fire." The other three assist Kota, scouring the area. Mike picks out a large log and carries it to a fire pit made of stone. Kota knocks on a log. It's mushy. He frowns. "Make sure none are soggy. It won't light if it is."

Mike taps his finger on the wood. "No, it's solid." A total of four logs are brought to the fire spot. He and Kota collect leaves and twigs to spark the bonfire.

Jimmy lights a row of matches, then tosses them atop the gathered weeds, which sets aflame. "We have fire!!" he sings.

"And now let's get music because your singing sucks." Liz mocks him.

Mike extends the radio antenna for a signal. He presses the power button. "Hello, late-nighters," a station host speaks. "I hope you're ready for fiery tracks. Our callers have voted for this week's hottest release and narrowed it down to a winning tune. Dio's Rainbow in the Dark!" The heavy rock song streams. Guitar, piano, strings, and drums clash in harmony.

"BUMP IT!!" Jimmy opens the pack of beers. Mike turns the volume knob all the way up. Jim tosses a bottled beverage to everyone. The wind increases, and the fire swells, flickering embers into the darkness.

"When there's lightning, you know it always brings me down." The group howls. "Cuz it's free, and I see that it's me who's lost and never found!! I cry out for magic. I feel it dancing in the light. It was cold. Lost my hold to the shadows of the night!!"

Liz downs her beer in a few gulps, then hand gestures to Jim for another one. She does a sexy finger nudge; her feistiness baffles him. "Who are you right now??" He throws her another bottle.

"I'm the funnest girl you'll ever meet." She winks as she catches it.

"Ooo!" Kota exclaims like an impressed little kid.

She sways to the music. A sexy enchantress performing a slithering dance. "Do your demons. Do they ever let you go?" Liz's light voice is flawless with the melody. "When you try, do they hide deep inside? Is it someone that you know?!!"

The boys bellow, "You're just a picture; you're an image caught in time. We're a lie. You and I, we're words without a rhyme! There's no sign of the morning coming. You've been left on your own. Like a rainbow in the dark. Just a rainbow in the dark. Yeah!!!" The scaling guitar overloads the song with a sporadic solo. The teens circle-dance around the raging fire, casting long shadows. Head banging madly. Kota swings his hair from side to side. Jimmy punches the air to the beat. The gang from a carousel around the campfire, high on joy.

Liz continues her sensual dance; she beckons Mike with a finger. He stops his drummer impression and follows her command. Liz tugs him closer to make out. The wind gusts her hair. Strains of green swipe across his face. The color is striking against his chocolate skin. She sucks at his mouth, switching her neck from side to side.

"HOLY SHIT!!" Jimmy laughs.

Kota holds his beer up for a toast. "To the best night ever." Their bottles tap together in a clink. He gulps his drink, then tosses it. The glass bottle shatters on the ground. Kota imitates the main singer, faking as if he's holding a microphone. "Feel the magic. I feel it floating in the air. But it's fear, and you'll hear it calling you. Beware. Look out!"

Liz ends her spicy make-out session with Mike. Her gaze falls on Kota. The same gentle look they shared returns. *No way… is she about to...?* Liz clears the distance between them and plants her mouth on his. Her glossy lips are slippery. His gut electrifies; his heart speeds. Kota kisses her back, matching her rough motion. Their breaths tangle. Liz claws her neon green nails through his black hair. Kota's palms latch to her elbows. He dives into her mouth. Her lip gloss tastes like coconut; he devours the flavor with delight.

Jimmy clears his throat loudly. "Am I included in this lip train?"

Liz gives one last peck to Kota's plump lips before breaking from the smooch. "Of course." She trails her hand down his cheek. "I'll be back."

Liz struts to Jim. Kota evil-eyes him. "You couldn't wait, dude?"

"Nope," Jimmy grins at Liz, who entraps his mouth with hers. Mike chuckles. He opens a pizza box and chomps on a slice. The music blares on. Kota goes for another beer, still irritated by the interruption. *Jim saw we were into it...that was a jerk move.*

A gushing noise sounds from ahead of him. His tan eyes stare ahead, perplexed. *What's that?* Kota listens for it again. It's gone now. *Hmm... it must be a bird or something.* He leans to get another beer. The swooshing noise reoccurs. Only it's at his side. Closer. Kota slowly straightens from the crouch.

A surveillance sensation causes the hair on the back of his neck to rise. *Swoosh.* The noise is behind him now. He turns fast. A blurry figure dashes toward the fire. Fully blacked out. He can't distinguish what it is in the night's shade... *but his instinct warns him of danger.* Icy fear floods every vein in his body.

"GUYS, WATCH OUT!!" His alerting words are too late.

The odd figure jumps high, soaring abnormally. It lands atop the fire. This catches the gang's attention. Someone who's unfazed by burning flames surveys the group. Liz backs away, her legs shaking with fright. Jimmy and Mike are frozen in place. The figure is of a man, but his eyes shine through the shade of night. Rosier than the fire. Kota's forehead numbs. He's horrified by the unnatural irises of the being.

The demon darts toward his friends. Its hands bare long talons. The talons slice the necks of Mike and Jimmy. Squirts of crimson splatter the air as a broken water hose would. The two boys drop to the ground. Dead.

"AHHH!!!" Liz screams and flees. She doesn't make it far. The thing sails after her, flying after Liz, as an eagle does its prey.

"NOOO!!!" Kota screams. The creature bites her neck. The chomping sound is grotesque. Her bones crush under the weight of its razor-sharp teeth. "LIZ!!" Kota runs ahead, his heart hammering. "NOO!" He hyperventilates while racing toward her.

The vampire pulls fleshy chunks out of Liz's neck. The outpour of blood spills onto the leafy ground, coating it red. Kota halts and exhales all the air from his lungs. His heart ceases to beat due to utter disbelief. The monster swallows the fluid of her neck like a fish does water.

Liz's eyes go motionless from the pain. They shut off due to shock. The veins of her neck protrude squiggly lines. The vampire groans in pleasure; the sound is throaty and savage. *It's a human… but it's not. WHAT IS IT??!!* Kota is dizzy from lack of oxygen to the brain, so he forcefully inhales.

The vampire menacingly twists its head his way. Its scarlet eyes burn into Kota's frightened ones. The thing drops Liz's body to the ground; she hits the concrete like a rag doll. Limbs flopping like jelly.

NO! NOO! SHE'S NOT MOVING! LIZ!!!

Lines of blood seep down the predator's mouth, trickling down to its pale neck in a haunted dance. The immortal man lunges for Kota, gliding the air… a bat out of hell. Claws…razor-sharp teeth…and blonde hair are the last things he sees.

CHAPTER 4: CARNAGE

The glint of dawn shines over the campsite. The teens lay unconscious on the ground; their clothing stained with gore. Their ghastly necks simmer in the low sun, now dried black. Kota's hair is bathed with plasma and mud. His eyes flutter. The dim sun painfully sizzles his eyelids. The strange sensation wakes him.

Kota's eyes open, but they're no longer chocolate. A pale tint replaces the warm color. He slowly sits up, holding the back of his pounding head. *What did I dream last night??! That was insane! A demon man with scarlet eyes. I guess I can't hold beer.* He pulls his hand away from the nape of his neck… and is stunned by the blood. His eyes pop out of their sockets.

NOO… NO! THAT WASN'T A NIGHTMARE?? Kota stares across the campsite; shaded ashy blue. He peers through the sheer light. His friends rest in puddles of crimson. Lifeless, with chalky skin. *NO… THIS CAN'T BE REAL!* Kota shouts internally, scooting across the leafy ground, scared. "NO, NOOO!!!" He hyperventilates as if suffocating… yet his chest doesn't rise. His lungs don't extend. His heart is soundless.

THIS CAN'T BE! It can't! These aren't my friends dead on the ground!! THESE AREN'T THEIR BODIES!!!!! CAN'T BE!!! Kota sobs at the sight of Jimmy, Mike, and Liz's startled eyes… the windows to their souls are empty. Heaps of tears stream down his numb cheeks.

Kota crawls to Liz. "LIZ??" he cries. "LIZ… WAKE UP!" He shakes her, only to gasp and withdraw his hand. Her skin is ice cold. *She's dead… they're all dead!* Kota glances at Mike and Jimmy. "NO, NO… GUYS, GET UP!!!" He gawks at the gruesome gashes on their necks, recalling the attack.

IT WAS ALL REAL??? THE CLAWS? THE BITING? THE IMPOSSIBLE SPEED? THE BLOOD?? THE BEAST??? His hand darts to his neck, finding an identical wound there. *That thing bit me. But… why am I still alive?* Kota's eyes sting from rushing tears.

I want to be dead! He buries his head in his hands. *I froze in place when I should have fought… I'm the reason they're dead. Why… why didn't I fight? Why didn't I hold the thing back so they could escape?! So, they could've lived??!* His gut plummets to an endless pit. Survivor's guilt eats him. Sun rays illuminate the lower half of the trees circling the campground. Kota's ears twitch. His hands fly there, feeling the movement repeat.

What is that? White noise fills his eardrums, ringing loudly.

His gaze jets to the sun. An impending doom shivers his bones.

GET AWAY FROM THE SUN!

Kota stumbles to his feet, startled by the inner voice that isn't his. Its tone is frantic and devilish. *None of this makes sense,* his clueless mind replies.

GET AWAY FROM THE SUN!! The warning comes again, now desperate. **IT WILL KILL YOU!!!**

Kota squints at the low-hanging orb. The sizzling noise increases. His legs backpedal against his will. The ball of light buzzes on like a whizzing rocket. *Why is it making that sound??* Kota watches it in confusion. *The sun flashes, turning the whole sky pure white.*

RUN!!!

The inner survival instinct leads him off into the woods, panicked and fearful. His boots crunch on twigs, leaping over boulders at incredible speed. The sunrise hisses behind him like a gigantic serpent, morphing from dim to starburst orange. Kota increase his pace; his joints fluctuate as if not connected to bone. He flees in an unnatural motion.

The blood that stains his skin intensifies, developing to a mouth-watering tease. *That smell.* Kota wipes his fingers across his cheek, collecting the fluid. *That smell is so… so…sweet.* He sniffs the liquid like an addict, then moves his fingers to his mouth.

NO! STOP! RUN!!! the deep voice snarls.

Kota stares over his shoulder at the sun, mortified enough to fight the thirst. The ball of light ascends the sky. His skin particles flare as if little fires are growing from within the cells. A flaming burn comes next. He yells. Smoke rises from his body. His feet blur as his skin steams, leaving a trail of hazy mist behind. Kota's visualization enhances, zooming in on a crevice beneath a hill. The sun blazes, humming as if about to explode.

Kota dives there, to the cave under the hill. His boots catch fire as he reaches the shade. "Ahh!!" Kota pats away the flames with his hands, extinguishing his boots. His palms blacken from the contact, yet no pain is felt. To his amazement, the burnt skin heals, sealing away the second-degree scorch within moments. Kota stares in disbelief. "How…?" He studies his hands, then the daylight beyond the cave. Pillars of sunlight reach in, bustling at high volume. So many questions rattle his mind.

How is this possible? What am I? Am I what that thing was? Am I a monster??

He sits in the dark hole for hours, cringing from the sun whenever it peeks into the crevice. He finds himself at the back wall once noon comes along.

Kota hugs himself. "No… I'm not that thing. I can't be! This is a bad dream. That's all," he speaks hoarsely. "That's all." When a blanket of light splits one side of the cave, Kota scampers to a corner to evade it. This repeats for hours—him fleeting from the sun while his mind tries contemplating what's wrong. Wondering why sunlight is his enemy all of a sudden.

I remember riding horses on sunny days. Remember the beams of warm light covering every inch of my skin. I loved galloping through the open fields. Loved being bathed in the sunshine that poked through the mountains. I loved being bathed by Mother Nature. Now I'm afraid of it. None of this makes sense. He's relieved when night falls. "Good. I can go home. I have to get home."

Kota zooms from the cave like a human race car. Once again, the effortless running returns. He blasts from the forest, past bus stops and gas stations, streaking down bare roads. When he bypasses the school, he slows. Flashbacks of him and his squad. The dance floor, the loud music. The crowd. All of them head banging and jumping. Liz giggling at Mike falling. Jimmy's ginger hair beating the air. Kota stops in his tracks.

I have to go back for them. But what will I do with their bodies?? Take them to their parents? That's the right thing to do. If I can stomach carrying their corpses. I don't think I can. The image of their dull skin and empty eyes haunt him. The wounds on their necks sicken him. *I can't.* Kota rips his gaze from the building and presses on.

There are Rez cops at the front gate. He smells the metallic scent of their blood; hears it rushing in their veins, pumping their vessels. Chittering a song of lust. The desire to taste the liquid reoccurs. *NO… I CAN'T HURT THEM!!!* Kota races around the reservation to avoid attacking the guards.

I've known Bly all my life. He's looking forward to my mom's pudding. He has two kids he's taking to the Pow-Wow. I can't harm him.

He uses his secret way in…the loose gate. He walks a street of gloom, glad because no one will see that he's covered in blood. His hole ridden, charred shoes step cracked sidewalks. Kota is almost home.

Everything will be alright when I get inside. I'll feel better. The street is usually silent, but now it blares with the noises within houses. Whirling microwaves. TV broadcasts. Snoring neighbors. Each noise is crisp, as if right beside him. Kota climbs the stairs, reaching for the knob. His hand meets an invisible force field.

NO... NOO! I NEED TO GET INSIDE; LET ME INSIDE! "DYANI! OPEN THE DOOR!!" Kota yells drastically, his light tone rooted with strain. He tries to reach for the knob again...with no luck. The hidden barrier between the door prevents him from making contact. Footsteps from beyond the door pound like a hammer. Kota covers his ears and winces. The chain and the main lock click before the door opens.

"Where have you been? Mom and Dad are out looking for you!" Dyani inspects his clothes. "ARE YOU OKAY? THAT'S BLOOD!!!"

"I don't know what's happening..."

Her hand drops from the knob. She eases to the door's threshold. "You're scaring me."

"I need help!" he sobs. "HELP ME!!"

"I will...come in; we'll figure this out." Her voice trembles.

"I can't." He puts his hand out, going a few inches, only to snag. He tries to place his shoe past the frame; it meets an invisible barrier.

"Stop joking around!" His sister takes him by the arm and tugs. His body slams as if there's glass before the door. Kota grunts from the impact and frees himself from his sister's hold. Dyani is shocked. "What the...??!!" She tries to pull him inside again but loses against the unseeable force.

Kota scans the archway in doom. *This is my home. I belong here. I was born here... and now I can't step inside??? Home is what I need. I HAVE TO GET INSIDE!* "Help me... please!" He drops to his knees.

Dyani passes the archway to console her little brother. She kneels and wraps her arms around him. Only to immediately hiss and recoil from his frigid touch. "YOU'RE FREEZING!!!" "I don't know what's happening!!" Kota wails.

She covers her mouth with her hands. "I...I...I don't know what to do... Kota. What's wrong with you??!!"

A motorcycle speeds down the street. Kota covers his ears, shouting at the discomfort the roaring engine brings. His eardrums violently throb. He swears they're bleeding from the inside.

Dyani runs in and slams the door, holding her chest. "WHAT THE HELL?!!" His screaming ends once the bike is far in the distance. Dyani cracks the door to find that her brother is gone. "Kota..." she mutters unevenly, peeking down the barren street. She jets to the kitchen. A green phone hangs on the wall. She holds the receiver to her ear and dials 918-456, using a rotary spinner. Dy paces back and forth, her hands quivering anxiously.

The front door opens. She drops the phone and runs to it. A man and woman in their forties survey her. Mato, her father, is tall and short-haired. Her mother, Odina, is short with back-length hair. "Has your brother come back?" Odina interrogates; her long face is grief stricken.

Mato's chest heaves. "Please say yes."

"He did... but something is wrong." Their daughter twiddles her thumbs, her neck tightens, showing her veins.

"What do you mean?" Her father's chiseled face is tense.

A gate swings open beyond the back door. The creaking, rustic sound catches all of their attention. Dyani steps away as her mother nears the back door to view the swinging gate.

"Dyani? Tell us," Mato presses his daughter for information.

She clutches her fingers through her long hair in panic. "Kota isn't okay! He's ice-cold and can't come into the house!" Dy eyes the back door. Her mother follows her daughter's gaze.... landing on the back door. Odina goes to open it, not at all afraid of the cryptic warning. There's a yard beyond where the moonlight illuminates the tall grass.

Mato furiously gazes at her. "Whatever game this is, end it now!"

Odina spots Kota at the back gate. "He needs to be inside; it's freezing." She paces to the gate. Kota sits outside it, his head hung low. "Son...?" His mom exits the gate to him. The wind blows heavily, flowing her thick hair forward. This motion exposes the veins of her neck. Kota's head straightens like a whip at the smell of copper. "Honey, come inside and tell us where you've been." She grips her coat to her chest. "You'll catch a cold. Come on inside."

Her son stand and turns to face her, zeroing in on the veins of her neck. *I NEED BLOOD!* The dark voice in his head demands. Odina notices his eyes...terrified at the sight of how devilish they are. Kota looks to her neck, where blood swishes and chitters. "BLOOD!!" he shrieks. His mouth extends, revealing sharp, pearly teeth that reflect the moonlight. His mother screams. Mato races outside.

"NO, DON'T GO OUT!!" Dyani squeals.

Mato examines his son's demon eyes and sharp teeth. His mouth hangs wide. "No... it can't be," a chilled whisper escapes him.

Kota growls longingly. Their son's mouth stretches abnormally, exposing rows of canine teeth. He charges at his parents, ready to kill… ready to feed. Mato pushes his wife behind him. He mimics an arrow symbol using his hands to mark the shape mid-air. The floating shape outlines the air in a white tint. Much like an archer, Mato aims the symbol at his son.

The magic sign bursts white. Kota drops to the ground like a ton of bricks, releasing an animalistic screech. He squirms in agony. His skin smokes as it did in the forest. Mato grabs his wife and rushes her to the door.

"NOO!!" she protests.

Dyani grabs her mother, who tries to wiggle free, but fails. Dy pulls her inside. Mato backs away, alarmed. Kota hollers on the ground like an injured beast. The monstrous howls echo the block. His father hurries inside and closes the door.

Kota fights to stand. The magic rune his father used binds him to the ground. His arms are restrained; he flings them high to break free. But his limbs bang back down to the ground. The white outline of the rune cages his body in place. *Dad used a protection symbol. I need to use the one for freedom. I WON'T KILL MY FAMILY!*

Gloominess clouds his mind. *BUT YOU MUST FEED, OR YOU WILL DIE!*

NO, NOT MY FAMILY!!

Kota tries to raise his hands to trace the freedom symbol into the air, but he can't lift far. Instead, he carves it into the stone ground with his sharp nails. The concrete splits from the pressure he uses to slice in the sign; a drawing similar to bird wings. Once completely etched, the shape blazes white. The energy that entrapped him disappears. Allowing Kota to flee.

CHAPTER 5: MIRROR

He stops at a river; the swelling water thrashes along submerged boulders. Kota sits beside it, realizing he has no reflection within the ripples. *Am I what that thing was? I'm a demon???* He touches his spiky teeth; each one molds into points at the end. Kota senses heat within his irises. His fingers trace his eyelids. *What's wrong with my eyes??!* He squeezes them shut as tight as he can.

What's wrong with me?!! I tried to kill my parents! Why did I do that? I need their help!! My dad warded me off like an animal. My mom… and my sister are frightened of me. My family… my blood! Kota digs his hands into soggy dirt, shaking uncontrollably. *Who will help me if they won't?* Tears stream from his devilish eyes. *Who?*

I will help; the inner fiend comforts him. **All you must do is listen to what I say.**

"I won't!"

To survive, do as I say.

"No... you made me this way! This isn't me. You did this!! GO AWAY!!"

You will lose; the lack of blood will defeat you.

"I don't care…"

Good…rid yourself of emotion. Feel less to have desire. This life requires that. Let go of all the care you have.

Humans are for food and pleasure. I will show you.

A beating heart fills his ears. The chambers of the organ pulse and chitter. The delicious scent of sweet plasma hypnotizes him. The taste of desire…his mouth overflows with saliva. He gulps to ease his fiery throat. The pulsing heart is full of stocked veins. The swishing liquid traps Kota's mind.

The smell is just as great as the taste. The devil within persuades him: **Have a drink.**

Kota's eyes dilute black, a colorless pit. He's puppeteer'd ahead by the evil influence. "I will have a drink," he says in a zombie trance. Kota's legs whip the air. He utilizes the sound of the heart to track down his meal.

Downtown Tahlequah has many storefront shops. A man enters an ice cream shop. The bell attached to the door rings. Kota shivers at the chiming, shielding his ears. He observes the man chatting with the cashier while pointing to the vanilla flavor. Kota smells the creamy dessert, but it doesn't compare to the blood. He takes a big whiff, savoring the tantalizing aroma.

Look to the car. The dark voice instructs him.

Kota does so. There's a sedan parked on the curb. A woman and two children are within. The man exits the shop with four vanilla cones. "Alright, off to the movies we go." The father opens the driver's door. "This means no asking for candy once we're there. Alright?"

"Okay!" The little boys say in unison as they hang from the window.

Their father hands them the ice cream, then gets in, closing the door. He hands his wife the other cones. "Sit back and buckle up."

Kota zeros in on the green veins bulging from their hands. A sloshing river of desire flows through each vessel. He takes a long sniff. The delicious flavor of their plasma attracts him. He zips toward the car, not caring that the shop worker inside can see him. Kota rips off the side door where the mother is. The woman squeals, horrified. The father reaches for the glove compartment. The children scream.

He goes for the mother's neck, sinking his razor teeth into her hot skin. The father pulls out a .45 handgun but pauses to ogle in fright. His wife is being fed on. The gun shakes in his palms. Kota sucks her blood. The liquid electrifies his tongue. He groans in delight, craving more. The father shoots three times. Kota is unfazed by the bullets. The rounds rip through his clothes instead of his skin. There's no pain. Kota withdraws. Blood splashes the white ice cream.

SLICE THEIR NECKS!!

Kota obeys his dark half and preys on the father, slicing his throat. The man chokes on his own blood. The kids drop the gory cones and pull at the door handles. Kota's nails grow into claws. The two boys pause and watch the talons grow. He cuts their throats. The children slump unconscious. Kota slurps on the father's neck, tearing the flesh to shreds with his jagged teeth. The long gulps of blood lubricate his lungs. His dead, flat organs bulge wide.

Every ounce of red is drained within minutes. When no more red ooze exits, Kota climbs back to the children. Just as he's about to consume the little ones, whiteness blinds the car. On the window is a symbol: two arrows facing a circle in the middle. This mark brightens the car's interior. Odina and Mato swipe the glass windows, duplicating the drawing on each. Their son's eyes flicker from black to white.

NOOO! LOOK AWAY!! The demon warns him.

It detests the rune, which wards off evil. Kota, its host, is hypnotized by the brightness from all four windows. The menacing presence evaporates from his mind. The black eyes fade away. Kota falls unconscious.

Thank the Creator for allowing silence. Finally, I'm away from that beast! That awful devil! I thought I'd never be myself again. I was wrong. My parents came for me. I thought they left me for good… wrote me off as bad. I'm glad they haven't. They will help me.

Mom knows many healing treatments; she'll fix my condition. I guess she knows magic too, just as Dad does. I never knew native signs were enchantments. I always thought they held the ideals of our ancestors, nothing more. I'm glad the signs have more meaning. If not for that, I'd have no hope. I would have kept killing… kept submitting to the bad inside me.

It told me to drink from that poor family, and I did. It possessed me… crippled me… used me for its own merit. I disappeared. My heart did too. My morals were dismissed as if I weren't human. I KILLED A FAMILY! HOW COULD I DO THAT???!!

The scorching vibration of the sun jerks him awake. Kota lies on the floor of his home. In a small living room. The curtains are closed; their backdrops lit orange. The dim room is quiet despite his family's presence. Dyani is on the sofa; the bags under her eyes are intense. Mato and Odina kneel on the floor.

Herbal leaves surround him in a perfect oval. Inside the circle, the herbs form symbols for protection and evil spirits—a three-arrow design. Kota hoists himself onto his elbows. His sister flinches at the motion, scared that he'll attack. His parents are calm.

Odina sadly stares at her son. "How do you feel?"

"I feel…better," he replies lowly.

"Good," She sulks. "The castings are working."

Mato stands; his expression very stern. "Son…you need to tell us what happened."

The image of the being in the woods blooms before him. The red eyes. The rapid speed. "Something attacked us. It killed my friends." His voice cracks. "They're dead… in the woods." Tears drip from his eyes.

"Oh, no…!" Odina covers her mouth, her eyes now glossy.

"Their parents were out searching… same as we were for you," Mato speaks sorrowfully. "Those poor folks will lose their hearts from this news." He huffs dismally.

"May the Great Spirit guide the young souls to peace," Odina prays mournfully.

Mato shares a heartbreaking glance with his wife. "Yes, the Creator will rest their souls." He looks at Kota with weakened eyes. "I wish you hadn't witnessed such violence." He steps into the circle to rest a firm hand on his shoulder. "Your friends are in a place of no pain… and their parents will meet closure soon."

His mother is distraught by her tear-ridden son. She enters the circle to give him a tight hug. Her hands rub the back of his head. "It's alright, *walela* (hummingbird)."

"No… it's not." His father breathes. "I know what attacked him. As insane as it sounds, it's the truth, dear…"

"I don't think so… this has to be dark magic."

"Dina, he feeds on blood!"

"No… he's not that!" she argues, trembling hard. He's never seen his mom so unnerved in his entire life. "He's still my boy… I can fix this!" Odina's hands tremble. "I *will* fix this!"

What can't I be? What are they talking about? Dad knows about this creature inside me. He says, "It can't be," when he saw my eyes. He looks to his father. "What am I?"

Mato sighs roughly. "My father told me tales of blood demons. I always thought these were bedtime stories to scare me asleep. Until last night. I wish the creature stayed a story to spare you of this fate. If only I could take on the burden."

"Blood demon??!" Dyani croaks from the couch, her hands grasping the armrests. "What is that?!"

"Your father believes Kota is a vampire."

He blinks rapidly, baffled. "VAMPIRE??!!"

"Yes, son. The thirst, the eyes… your teeth. If this was dark magic, as your mother believes, our charms would have healed you. They haven't… meaning your soul is damned, not corrupted."

"NO! I DON'T WANT TO BE THAT! Please fix it! I can't keep killing!" Kota pleads. "I'm not in control. SOMETHING IS MAKING ME KILL, MAKE IT GO AWAY!!!"

"Son, we're going to help the best we can… but you cannot be saved. You're cursed. The best your mother and I can do is conceal your hunger, so you don't harm anyone. We can handle this creature. Tell us exactly how it looked and where it fled."

Kota covers his eyes, sniffling. "It had blonde hair and ruby eyes… it moved like the wind. I'm not sure where it went. I blacked out."

"In the woods? Where exactly?"

"Ummm." He rakes his brain for a moment to remember. "The campsite at the third entrance."

"Dina, can you conduct a location spell?"

"Yes…but it'll take a few days. I need artifacts from the scene to draw energy."

Mato grimaces. "Let's go."

Odina fidgets her fingers, her sight darts between Dyani, who's pale, and her nervy son. "You two should rest."

"Your mother's right."

Kota drops his hands from his eyes. "But… what if it kills you both?!"

"It won't… now get some sleep." Mato and Odina leave the circle.

"IT'S TOO FAST, IT'LL GET YOU!! Please don't go!" Kota gets up to follow them. He face-plants into an invisible barrier that prohibits him from exiting. "What?" He bangs his hand against it.

"A blockade… for safety. You'll be confined until your thirst is cleansed," His mother explains.

"Cleansed?? Meaning it'll be gone for good?" Dy is hopeful for this outcome.

"No… a temporary cleanse until there's another solution. Now, no more questions. Rest, the both of you."

"How can I do that?" Dyani shivers. "My brother is a blood demon!"

"Ease your mind, *kamama* (butterfly). Trust in me and your father."

Mato shares a tight grin with her and Kota. "Listen and rest; you've been through enough for one day. We'll handle this." Their parents leave, stepping out hastily. The thud of the door and jiggling keys follow after.

Kota vigorously massages his temples; a hard pressure is there. Dyani gets up from the sofa in defense mode. "What's wrong?!! Are you hungry?!"

"No… it's not that."

"Are you sure?!" Her voice goes up in octave.

"I am." He lowers his hands. She inches into a corner. "I won't attack you; I promise."

"I don't believe you… you tried to hurt Mom and Dad."

"That wasn't me."

"It was…" Her throat strains into wiry veins. "You heard Dad… he said you're damned. Cursed. Nothing possesses you."

"Dyani, I'm not a killer!"

His sister jumps, half scared yet stubborn enough to hold her ground. "But you killed, brother! That means you are!"

The bloody ice cream reemerge in his mind. The screams of his victims. His throbbing temples force him to squeeze his eyes shut. "I didn't want to. Please believe me. I never hurt anyone in my life, you know this. I would've never done it if the demon wasn't there. Please believe me, Dy!" He begs. Her brows furrow emotionally. She bites her bottom lip, torn between disgust and pity. "There has to be a spell. A cure," Kota whispers shakily. "There has to be."

CHAPTER 6: HOPE

KAYLA

Kayla Harris, a dark-toned girl with yaki hair, plucks a book from a case. A thirteen-star symbol designs the black book, pure white—a witchcraft grimoire titled *Spell Benders: Runes and Incantations.* Kay observes the hardcover, trailing her finger across the star. *My mom is one weird collector. I never asked why she has these. I guess because I've seen them all my life. They're so familiar… yet I don't understand why we have them.*

Kay looks over the bookcase enclosed in the wall. The shelves are full of hardcovers; the only difference is the year editions. The oldest one dates to 400 B.C. The latest stops in the year 1931. They are sixty in total.

I never asked what this literature means. I assume that my mom is superstitious. Kay slips the grimoire back into its slot on the case. *Anyway, where's that Chanel perfume? That's why I'm snooping in Mom's room.* She maneuvers through a pale pink bedroom. Its walls are paneled and trimmed gold. The floor is padded with thick, fluffy carpet. Kay goes to a vanity table with a heart-shaped mirror. It's full of makeup, perfume, and lipstick.

All accessories are in a sorter, organized into categories. Kay leans to pick a fragrance from the back row; a bulky glass bottle full of gold liquid: *Coco Eau De Parfum. Chanel Paris.* She pops off the diamond cap and squirts her neck. The citrus blossom scent is dreamy.

She sniffs the air. "Ahh!" She spritzes her hair, which drops past her shoulders. The ends are curled, and the color is black as night. She returns the fancy bottle to its spot and treks from the room, her curls bouncing above her shoulders.

Kayla passes a massive bed cluttered with pillows. Wedding pictures frame each nightstand. Her mom glows in a white gown, and her dad is tall and handsome in a classic tuxedo suit. Kayla grins at the candid photos on her way out.

The hallway is grand, just as the bedroom, only it bears crown molding. Many doors line the corridor; labeled as if in a hotel. Plaques caption the doors: *Bathroom, Powder Room, Office, Guest Room, Kayla's Bedroom.* She nears the end of the hall to the living room.

Luxurious wall-length windows view the city of downtown Chicago. The ceilings are high and beamed. Off to the side, a spiral glass staircase leads to a second level. Her feet tap up the stairs to a rustic art studio caged in by long French windows. Many art easels are aligned in a row…each one hold canvas full of ballerina dance sketches. Kay retrieves a purple bookbag beside one of the easels. As she bends for it, she eyes one of her sketches.

A figure posed like a teapot, wearing a cream leotard and tutu…just like Kay. She picks up a pencil from the easel tray and streaks it down from the hips of the dancer, drawing lines for legs and feet. *I have a solo audition coming up. I need to complete my sequence.* She lifts the large board to view the drawings underneath.

Kay swipes through the many illustrations. Each of the models display different ballet positions; waltz, pirouette, plié, twirl, wide lunge, fouettés, arabesque, assemblé, attitude, and penché. *Hmm, that's less than a minute. I need more than that if I want to dominate tryouts. My instructor will expect a show-stopping performance. I'll have to work on choreography.*

She arches the ends of the tutu, then drops the pencil. She returns downstairs and nears an industrial elevator. Kay quickly checks herself out in a mirror, running her hands down the leotard. *Okay… I look fine enough.* She leaves the sunny penthouse.

Outside the high-rise, Darius, a chestnut-skinned boy, awaits her. His kinky hair is brown in the sunlight. When he sees her, he beams widely. "Morning, cutie."

Kay blushes. "Morning." She smooches him. Darius grabs her hand and strolls with her past side shops. The towering skyscrapers above them cut out the sun, inviting great shade. The glass surface of the towers sparkle. Noisy traffic booms from all directions; vehicles jam up at traffic lights as far as the eye can see, puffing out gas from exhaust pipes.

The two walk along the pavement. "How'd you sleep?"

"Like a baby, thanks to your mixtape. I loved the city ambiance one you did. Especially the piano." Kay compliments. "I'm glad… that one took forever. I need a studio. That way, it won't take as long."

"Maybe that can be a birthday present?" Kay pokes his nose, grinning wide.

"You'd be the best girlfriend if you manage to fit a studio in my place."

"Or I can have my parents buy you a new place." She boasts.

"Show off." He rolls his eyes.

"You know you love it." Her light voice teases.

Darius pulls her to his side. "I do."

Kayla stares at her feet, overwhelmed by his affectionate gaze. *I know it may be too soon… but I think I don't just like my boyfriend. I think it's the other L word.* Kay shyly tucks her hair behind her ears, glancing up with heavy eyes. Time stands still. The tunnel vision is intense; the two don't break contact. Pedestrians bypass them, veering to avoid a collision; some even throw them looks of irritation their way.

The two don't notice this at all; they're locked into each other. He takes in her adorable, small features while she explores his hazel eyes. *Her heart flutters. I have to tell him the other L word. I have to say it. If I can. My bashfulness always gets the best of me.*

A blaring horn breaks their concentration. Darius shields Kay from the crosswalk, placing a hand before her. Vintage cars rush by, whizzing the air. "Oops." He chuckles. "We should do that somewhere safer."

"Agreed," Kay nods, giggling. "Did you study for the chemistry test?"

He grits his teeth. "A little… I kind of nodded off."

I hate it when he does this; doesn't he care about his grades?? She fusses internally. "Uh oh."

"It's fine. I remember the topic. I'll get a good enough score," he states confidently.

Kayla grimaces. "Hopefully. We'll be a cute valedictorian couple."

"We would." He pulls her close to his side. "Maybe I can come over tonight to study?"

"I wish you could…my parents won't be home. So that's a no."

"They're busy again?"

The traffic sign turns red; a walking figure glows. They cross with dozens of others. "Dad has new cases, and Mom is closing on condos. They're going to make it up to me. It's no big deal." She spots his mind calculating. Darius's handsome face is displeased. *Here he goes with his anxiety; he needs to relax. There's no need for the lines wedging his forehead.* "I'll be okay, don't worry."

"Just because it's downtown doesn't mean it's safe."

"I have pepper spray."

Darius laughs. "What? It's a weapon; the police use it."

"Ahh…" He groans, concerned. "Okay, how about I check the rooms?"

Kayla kisses his cheek. "Deal."

"Since you don't want me over." Darius pouts.

"It's not that…" she sighs, rolling her eyes.

"Then what is it?"

"I'm a bad liar. If I make up a story, my mom will see right through it. You're only supposed to be over when they are, remember?"

"They won't find out if I leave before they get home…."

"You're a bad influence, sir." She pokes in a British accent. The couple reach an all-glass dance studio. The main door is etched with silver letters, which read: *STUDIO DOLL*. Darius opens it for her. "Why, thank you, good sir." She continues to mock the London regal accent.

Inside are grand hallways of crown molding and white walls. Kay and Darius venture past empty ballrooms. The white floors glimmer like fire. The ballroom is full of wall mirrors. The golden hue from the skylight above gives a dreamy effect. *I love this place. It's my second home. Most days I'm here prepping for the stage. It's overkill, but practice makes perfect.* Kay presses down the needle of a record player. A lovely string instrumental circulates the fancy room. Her cream ballet shoes prance across the floor, flightlessly maneuvering.

The tips of her shoes swirl, straight as a brick. Her lean body churns with a wide wingspan. Her tiny hands rest on her waist, intensely. Kay's brows crease while holding the position. She breathes deeply. *Okay, keep a straight back, low shoulders, and relaxed muscles,* the teen reminds herself. *Don't lose your footing!*

Darius chuckles. "Smile. You have to do that for the crowd."

"I know." A frown plasters her heart-shaped face. "I'm focusing…." She waltzes in a three-step stride, brushing pretty shoes over the floor with ease before extending a leg. *Steady stride, stay on beat. One, two, three,* she mentally instructs. Next is a pirouette. Heel to the opposite toe in an X shape, arms arched at her side, stretching out one leg, then her arms. Now with the opposite leg bent, one arm curved and the other out straight. This forms into a plié, a bend of both legs leading to a spin, landing in a wide lunge.

Her tutu floats majestically. Kayla prances, floating on air, performing a music box dancer move. Toes high against a straight leg, one arm posted above her head and the other resting near her chest. She pauses, breathing deeply. Her shoulder, abdominal, calf, and hamstrings overwork. *Good, keep going!*

She shifts her body into five fouettés, kicking a leg out with each full circle. Kay breezes on, completing a choreography segment:

arabesque, assemblé, attitude, penché. Her shadow marks the floor with glides, twists, and poses. There's no ice below, yet she skates. The duplicate in the mirror is right on her tail.

The instrumental wraps to an end; the only sound within the room are her shoes tapping. She disapproves of how late her left foot is, so she tries again, sure to have a firmer hold. By the time she's done, the room spins, and she's wobbling.

Darius stands to steady her. "Whoa, whoa, don't turn into a merry-go-round."

"He he he… don't tempt me." Kay flashes a big smile.

"Is that the full routine?"

"No… just the beginning. I need ten more minutes of choreography." She sighs drastically.

"You'll figure it out." Darius smooches her hand. "You're amazing."

"Aww!" She kisses him. "You're being super sweet."

"It's the truth…you are." He brushes his nose against hers. "Sounds like I'm the best boyfriend in the world."

"Number 1."

"You too…"

"Hey, I'm not a boy!" She snorts cunningly.

"No… you're too pretty to be one." He plays with her fluffy tutu, curling the hem around his fingertips.

Kay flips her hair behind her back. "I know."

"Don't get big-headed."

"Too late." She eyes a clock above the door. "Oh, crap!"

Kay tugs him toward the exit. "Let's get to school."

Outside, the sidewalks are hectic. Many students wait for the green light. The girls rock preppy skirts and big, tazed hair. The boys sport leather jackets and band T-shirts; Eurythmics, Dexys Midnight Runner, Taco, DIO, Naked Eyes. All decorated in neon splash art; similar to Picasso.

When the light changes, the group hustles alongside business folk. Buses hiss and rumble, their tires rolling harshly on gravel. A brush of summer air ripples everyone's hair. Kayla sniffs the air while crossing a corner bakery. Fresh doughnuts, cookies, and tea seep from the open doors.

Blue tents drape from the tops of shop windows, allowing protection from the sun. The buildings around are a mixture of old school and modern…brick high-rises versus steel ones pillared to the ground. The group passes an alley, looking both ways before stepping toward the modern area. Dozens of banners promote a

Theatre show; each one wrapped from street poles like flags. The upcoming ballet show.

Kayla points to it enthusiastically. "Two weeks! I can't wait!"

"You'll steal the show."

"Wish me luck." She adores how her boyfriend crosses his fingers in support.

Jones College Prep comes into view—a steel high-rise sealed to the sidewalk by round columns. Darius sweetly pecks his lips to Kayla's. "See you later."

"See you later."

When he turns to walk off, her eyes gloss over with tears. Kayla blinks rapidly to fend off the waterworks. Her stomach knots up. *If only we were at the same school, this limb-ripping moment wouldn't happen. I asked my parents to transfer me, but they're paying high tuition to broaden my future. I wish they had listened. I'll still have a bright path regardless of which school I go to. I need to see my boyfriend every second of the day.*

Kayla pouts. She joins behind a clique of girls in pink, who bully others by shoving them out of their way. The snobbish manner at which they hold their bags above their shoulders annoys Kay. *Vanessa Skye and her minions. The Plastic Pinks. These girls always show off and make us feel like trash. I can't wait for someone to give them a wake-up call.* The clique pushes on with no regard for students who stumble to the floor. Kayla makes her way over to help one of them up.

A mousy girl with bangs collects her books from the floor. Kayla helps her gather her belongings. "Thank you," the girl mutters in a whisper before speeding off. Kayla glares after the pompous clan, glad she has friends who are sweethearts.

CHAPTER 7: ORDINARY

Within the juggernaut school, light blue and gray shade the walls. Many teens chat while sitting on the window ledges. Heaps of book bags sprinkle the floor. A logo in the center showcases an eagle, shaded black on gray. On the second level, there are banisters of clear glass. The ceiling reaches seven floors. Endless windows showcase the city's glam. Elevators, staircases, and escalators. All this luxury for a thousand students who flood the halls.

Kayla removes a lacy yellow tank and white jeans from her bag. "HEY KAY!" two girls shout obnoxiously, causing their friend to almost stumble into her locker. They giggle. One has a caramel complexion with a kinky ginger mane, and the other is tan with sleek brown hair. Both carry clear bags full of school supplies.

"Hey," Kayla grins ear to ear while opening her locker to grab school supplies.

"I wish we could stay in that?" Jia gestures to Kay's ballet uniform with a gentle Korean accent.

"We can lie and say our schedules changed and we have no time to swap outfits." Mya shrugs with a tenor tone.

Kayla closes the locker and heads down the hall; the two follow after like ducks. "Maybe." She frowns. "It would be cool to make our mark off the stage. But at least we can wear dresses." Kay eyes the clear bags that her friends carry. "Aww, I forgot my bag! Sorry, guys, I was rushing. Darius…"

"Was outside!" they complete her sentence with teasing giggles. The crew enter the girls' restroom.

"Hey, don't make fun of me!" Kay cackles, entering a stall. "I don't see him enough."

"You're holding out. So, you're telling me you never snuck him in your room?" Mya interrogates.

"No," Kay says from the stall.

"I call bull." Mya's mouth drops. "No way, you haven't!"

"You know my parents—no boys unless they're at home."

"It's good to obey the rules." Jia supports her. "I have the same law. My mom's new motto is: 'No boys after 8.' I'm not even dating. She's losing her marbles!"

Kayla exits the stall, wrapping her bag around her arm. The bright outfit compliments her cocoa skin. "Our moms had to be separated at birth. I got the same curfew."

Mya's eyes fill with disbelief. "My parents gave me rules too, but I don't follow them. There's more to dating than kissing. My advice is to sneak off and have fun." She winks.

"That works… for someone without anxiety." Kayla points out. "I'm fine with the pace we're at."

"At least mess around; doesn't it get boring?" Mya is skeptical.

"No…"

"I bet it does for him… it's been months. I'm sure he's tired of waiting."

"My dad courted my mom for a year. The right guy will wait." Jia states wisely.

"Exactly." Kay jams her dance outfit into the gym bag.

When the bell rings, they all exit the restroom, parting ways. Mya strolls down the hall, joining a maze of students. "We'll continue our chat at lunch!" Her words irritate Kay, yet she doesn't show it. *I don't know what there is to continue. Darius and I are fine going slow. Sometimes Mya digs farther than she should.*

Jia and Kayla line up behind students who smell of heavy cologne and fruity perfume. Their first period is photography. The classroom has rows of desks pressed together into pairs. Floor-toceiling windows preview the lively city. Vents whoosh out air conditioning.

Their teacher, a tall woman in her mid-thirties, wears a yellow dress, her hair in a bun. She draws a smiley face onto the green chalkboard. "Good morning, class!" she sings, all chipper.

"Good morning, Ms. Ruby," her students respond, taking their seats.

"Today, we will add the 294th photo to our year collage. Remember to capture something different." Ms. Ruby carries a tray of Polaroid cameras, handing out one to each student. "Go and explore!"

The teens chatter amongst one another. One boy with an afro groans, "I forgot my skateboard! I gotta choose something else now."

Kayla, who shares a desk with Jia, accepts the camera from Ms. Ruby. She powers it on, draping her bag across her chair. A list of photos buffer on the tiny screen. Some display clouds, automobiles, rain droplets, concrete, snow, and multicolored butterflies.

"Hmm… I can snap a pic of a bee…. then run." Jia jokes, mortified by the thought.

"I'm out of ideas." Kay places the camera down, resting her chin in her hands, all discouraged. "Maybe…"

"The hem of your tutu?"

"I already did that."

Jia leans onto the desk, her lips perched. "The terrace on the roof. We can try that." All the students pile out of the room. Some flash their devices at wall banners, doorknobs, handles, and restroom signs.

"Oh… good thinking!" The two leave for the hall, passing a tiny girl with orange hair who aims her camera at a fire hydrant.

The friends ring the elevator, hitting the button together, their hands sandwiched as one. When the lift arrives, many teachers step off. "Hello." A tall, dark-haired man eyes the camera. "Off to add to your portfolio?" The girls nod. "There's a family of birds on the fifth floor, the third water fountain, on the windowpane." "AWW!" the two gasp.

"Oh, perfect, thank you!" Kayla takes Jia by the arm, leading the way into the elevator.

"You're welcome." The doors close.

"That's better than the terrace."

"That can be our 295th addition." Jia presses the fifth-floor button. The elevator travels upwards, passing floors hidden behind its doors.

"Now, all we need are seventy-one more. I wonder what the final project is?" Kay muses.

"Probably a paper… or a poster."

"Some poster that'll be." Kayla gives an uneasy expression.

"Or paper."

"I hope not… I suck at essays."

"You're better at them than me. I gotta start days ahead to get it done." Jia complains. The elevator doors slide open; she leaps out of her skeleton. Kay bursts into uncontrollable snorts. "Eww, stop!"

"I can't!" She snorts like a pig. They chuckle while wandering an empty hall, locating the third fountain's windowpane, where four birds are seated.

"Shh…we might scare them off." Jia places a finger to her lips. Kayla covers her mouth, still releasing little sniggers of amusement. She aims the camera, centering the family of birds into frame, and clicks the capture button.

Pre-Law, second period. Kayla sits in a courtroom of dark wood paneling. A judge's podium stands at the head of the court.

The seating arrangements are accurate and separate the crowd with a swinging door. There's a mock case reporter, a typewriter, and a Bailiff. The students sit in the crowd section, chattering. The guard steps beside the Judge's podium. "All rise." The class stands, now quiet as mice. "This court is now in session."

The teacher, in judge attire, takes a seat—a man in his forties with a long, uncompromising expression. The Judge sits. "Be seated." Extremely quiet teens take their seats. "Good morning." "Good morning, Judge Smith," the class sings.

"I'm assuming you all are prepared for the mock trial." Everyone nods. "Lawyers and defendants, gather yourselves."

"Which one are we doing?" Chester, a long-haired boy, enquires between the group.

"The cow one, I think….. ask Fred." Kayla inclines her head to a ginger-haired, freckled boy who passes through the swinging door.

"I don't want to get yelled at…could we choose something else?" Chester eyes the Judge with utter dread.

I thought I had bad anxiety. I wonder why he's so scared of Smith. I mean, Smith is strict but not terrifying. Chester doesn't want to do this; I should swap places. There's no need for a meltdown today.

Kayla shares an empathetic glance with him, then eyes her group. "What was agreed on? There was the cow, the traffic accident, and domestic violence."

"I think it's the domestic one. HEY FRED!" Izzy, an emo girl, shouts out to him.

Judge Smith stands, his presence now ridiculing. "No shouting, Izzy! You would be deemed unprofessional in a real trial and threatened with dismissal. ADJUST YOURSELF! Walk to Fred and ask what you need of him!" The teacher rubs his forehead harshly before sitting.

She does what he commands. At the podium, Izzy mutters something to Fred, who responds quietly. When she returns to the group, she clarifies the case. "He says the cow one." The group snickers.

"You guys are gonna get us in trouble." Chester shakes his head, leaning back on the bench dejectedly. "We need to take this seriously."

Izzy rolls her eyes. "It's too early to be a killjoy." "Kay, can you please go? I can't." He pleads.

"Teacher's pet." Izzy jabs.

"Don't tease." Kay stands. "I'll do it."

Relief fills Chester's face. "Thanks, I owe you."

"Don't worry about it." She reassures him with a smile, then beckons to Izzy. The teens near the podium. The wood door swings behind them. Izzy takes a seat while Kay goes up.

Judge Smith bangs a gavel. Fred clears his throat. "Good morning, Your Honor. My name is Xavier, first initial F. Your Honor, this is a case of tragedy. My client, Mr. Boone, suffered a great loss last week and is set on reparations."

"Please state the loss."

Fred holds back a laugh, fighting to keep a straight face. "A cow." The room roars with laughter; some students clutch their stomachs in response.

Smith sighs longingly, unamused. "ORDER!" He beats the gavel down. The room falls silent. "Proceed."

"Last week, Mr. Boone let his cows out on a hot Sunday." Fred's voice changes to a southern drawl. The room uproars, same as a comedy show. Kayla fights off titters, trying hard to remain serious. Struggling. "When that woman!" He shouts in a convincing country accent, pointing at Izzy. "Ran over poor old Spotty on a devil motorcycle, going well past 55." He delivers each word dramatically. "Her reckless behavior requires punishment!" Fred bangs his hands on the podium.

"Mr. Xavier, correct yourself; this isn't drama class!" Smith hits the gavel down once more. "ORDER!!"

Sniffles escape Fred, who animatedly wipes his eyes, acting emotionally overwhelmed. "I'm sorry, Your Honor. My emotions got the best of me."

"Allow the plaintiff to the podium; you may be seated."

Fred shares a competitive glance with Kayla as he departs, whispering the words: *"You're going down, missy."*

Kay coughs to hide a laugh. Mr. Boone steps to the podium. He hesitantly eyes her; she gives him a thumbs-up, urging him to continue the fun. The boy locks eyes with the judge. "Hello, Your Honor."

"Hello, Mr. Boone. Please state the events to your best ability."

"It was early, around 10 a.m., when I went to the barn to let my cows flock." Boone puts on an odd rural accent, an awful country hillbilly tone.

"NO MORE VOICE ACTING, OR YOU ALL WILL

RECEIVE F'S!" Smith growls, banging the gavel down three times.

"Uh oh…" Kay turns to Izzy. "The fun is dead." "Crap."

The emo girl slumps in her chair.

Come lunchtime, the trio meets up at the food line. The girls pack their plates with tuna wheat wraps, kettle chips, and water. Kayla surveys the alternatives: pizza, fries, hot dogs, chips, soda, and cookies.

"Let's make it a junk day."

Jia fixates on the steamy apple pies; the aroma is so tempting. She reaches for one, holding it over her plate. "Maybe just one cheat day."

"We have a show. Anyway, I can't have sugar… my mom always knows. I break out really bad." Mya sighs.

Jia gives Kay a puppy dog peer, still holding the apple pie. "The sodium will bloat my feet, sorry. We have to tough it out." Jia drops the pie back into the tray, moping.

The three walk to the back of the lunchroom. Table after table, teens chomp on junk food. A few students gulp down soda in a drinking contest. Some plates are loaded to the max.

Fred has four slices of pepperoni pizza, two bags of chips, and extra dipping sauce. "We'll get Smith next time." He speaks with a full mouth. "There's no way that man doesn't have a funny bone." "It's a lost cause; he's a robot." Kay cracks.

There's a bench that looks out at the busy lanes of downtown; this is where the friends sit. Mya runs her hands through her kinky red hair and leans forward. "Back to boy talk. Now, what time do your parents get home tonight?"

I should lie to avoid the chat. Kayla thinks fast, her eyes shifting a bit. "5 p.m."

"Oh… that won't work. We can try some other time." She nibbles on her tuna wrap.

Good, she didn't notice I lied. I would be a laughingstock if she realized I did. I'm not as outgoing as Mya, who has had three boyfriends. I've only had one. Darius. Making out is all I'm ready for. She needs to butt out. Again, Kayla hides her frustration, being too kind to hurt her friend's feelings.

"How about you, Jia?" Mya delves on, drinking her water. "I know you're crushing on Fred." Jia blushes, shushing her fast. "Don't be shy; share your hot dreams about him."

A long beep comes from Kayla's bookbag; she unzips it, pulling out a Motorola pager. Darius sent her a message. A row of black digital hearts post across the screen. Her chest flutters. Kay flashes her teeth, her irises now wide and high on love. *Does that mean he loves me? Is that his way of saying so?*

Kay closely examines the bedazzled device. "What does it mean when a boy sends you hearts?"

"Is that why you're glowing right now?" Mya singsongs.

"Maybe…"

She leans forward with a large smile. "It means he doesn't just like you. If you catch my drift."

"I've been thinking about saying it."

"Go for it."

"But Teen Magazine says the guy has to do that."

Jia nods in agreement with Kay. "True… it's not very ladylike to say it first."

"Stop listening to that trash." Mya scorns. "Girls can cut to the chase; guys prefer it over getting their egos hurt. Trust me."

CHAPTER 8: HOLLOW

In history class, a big-bellied man rolls down a projector. The out-of-range screen is illuminated by a lamp. The teacher moves the projector box to clear up the image. On the screen is a lengthy video. "Pay attention." The man says, pressing a button on the wall near his desk; automatically shutting the shades on the large windows. Darkness falls. A documentary plays. The caption reads:

The Lost WWI Vampire Dugout
The Underground War.

"VAMPIRE?!" a student yells, perplexed.

"It's a figure of speech, referring to the dead below the trench." The teacher clarifies. "Now quiet; eyes on the screen."

The documentary displays grainy footage of WWI. "It was a secret war, a clandestine war, a barbaric war." A man in a tunneling suit states gravely as old battleground footage plays. Students recite word for word into their notebooks, Kayla amongst them. She writes fast, as if a transcriber, finishing words as they are said. Diggers on the screen use hammering drones on solid stone. The machinery chips away on domed sections of concrete.

"It's like breaking into an Egyptian tomb or something. This thing's been sealed since the First World War." Another explorer says, geeking out.

Kayla and her classmates perform jumping jacks on a glossy floor. The gym room is full of teens who appreciate the refreshing breeze from the windows. Fred shoots hoops with a tall girl, defending the ball. His stance is wider than his shoulder-width, knees bent, all weight is on the balls of his feet. The girl dribbles, blocking Fred's hands, which are out to his side. He does a shuffling sort of dance. He tries to swipe the ball from the girl's grasp; she blocks this by tugging it to her chest.

Kayla stops her jumping jacks to jog over to join them. The girl passes the ball to Kay, who easily catches it, wiping sweat from her forehead. Fred traces the ball; his eyes find it in her hands. "Nice dancing; maybe you should do ballet."

"I wouldn't want to steal your spotlight." He dives for the ball. Kay evades the attack, dribbling and striding the court. "But then again… I'll look good in a tutu."

Kayla buckles to her knees, cackling hysterically. Fred steals the ball and runs it to the basket to dunk. "That's not fair… you cheated!"

He reverse runs past her. "Basketball 101." His maroon hair gleams in the sunlight as fire would. "Let's go again. Marla, you wanna tag team?"

Marla, a tall girl, shakes her racer-back shirt to fan herself. "Sure… but we need someone else to even it out. 2 on 2."

Fred examines the gym room, his eyes landing on a quiet boy at the top of the bleachers. This teen holds his backpack close to his body with a dismal expression. "We can ask the new kid?" He suggests. "That'll get him out of his shell."

"True." Kayla treks to the bleachers. *I'll be back. Okay, how should I introduce myself? Hello, I'm Kayla. Or, Hey, I'm Kayla? I don't want to sound too formal. I think I'll stick with the last one.* She decides, stepping up the stairs and to the aisle the boy is in. She waves at him. "Hey, I'm Kayla."

"Oh… hey." The chubby boy says guardedly, not sure why she's talking to him. "I'm Luke."

Kay sits beside him. "Hi, Luke. So… we want to invite you to play ball." She points to Marla and Fred, who use the cue to wave. Fred does this obnoxiously, much like a wacky inflatable man. "It'll be fun."

Luke's eyes lower. "I don't know how to play. I'll just stay here."

"Don't worry; we won't judge."

"But everyone else will…" he whispers solemnly.

"Ignore them." She beckons to Luke, offering her hand. He's hesitant for a few seconds before accepting her kind gesture.

After school, yellow buses line the curb, waiting for students to pile aboard. Kayla, Jia, and Mya stroll the sidewalk. Rush hour crams vehicles into tight lines. The sun scorches, revealing the girls' impeccable skin. It's crystal clear due to good food hygiene and restful sleep. No dark spots and minimal acne, thanks to expensive diet. The ballerinas must be flawless for every show and appear as a fantasy. Which they are. The majority of their peers have typical teen acne, while they show like airbrushed celebrities.

Ahead is a busy Starbucks; the line bends around the corner. The baristas prepare drinks beyond the windows, adding cream and sugar to steaming cups. "Why is there sugar everywhere?" Kayla grumbles, upping her pace to a power walk, too seduced to trust herself from the urge.

They meet up with Darius, who awaits them on the corner. He hugs his girlfriend firmly. She locks her arms around his neck. "Hey you."

"Hey, you."

Darius nods to her girls. "What's up?"

"Same old, just tons of homework." Jia shrugs.

"Sup, lover boy." Mya ups her chin coolly. "She's all yours. See you tomorrow, Kay." She retreats down the stairway with Jia.

Darius and Kayla remain embraced; he kisses her nose. "How was school?"

"Boring. How about you?"

"Fun… and sweet. Some boy sent me hearts."

"I bet it was a boy you really like."

"Hmm…maybe." Kayla stares at her boyfriend with a penetrating gaze.

Okay, here it goes. I gotta tell him. Anxiety eats at her stomach. Her eyes go hesitant; bouncing in every direction as she tries to prepare her confession. *Oh, I can't! Oh yes, I can! Get it together!*

She searches her mind for a different language—one she began learning at eight years old. "Je vous aime." Kayla speaks fluid French; the words romantically roll off her tongue.

This catches her boyfriend off guard. "Huh?" Darius is clueless. "What does that mean?"

"Nothing." Kay simpers while strolling on. The traffic sign changes to a walking figure, guiding them safely across.

"Was that French? What does that mean?" She inverts her lips, hiding them completely. "Was it something sweet?"

"I can't say."

"It sounded sweet."

The couple arrives at the towering skyscraper. "Still coming in?"

"Of course, I need to make sure you're safe." The vintage wood elevator lets out to the chic penthouse. "Wait here." His protective mode activates. Darius drops her bookbag and leaves, scanning the living and dining room as he heads down the long hall. He searches the office for any intruders. Next are the closets— nothing but clothes hang within. In the bedroom, he does a 360sweep before exiting.

The two bathrooms are inspected. He checks behind each door. The kitchen is enclosed by elongated windows, which peer down to stuffed streets. Upstairs, he scans the art studio, then goes out to a balcony where furniture and a firepit are. No one is there.

Darius descends the staircase. "All is good."

"I told you; I'll be okay."

He exhales hard. "Still, you shouldn't be here by yourself."

Kayla stares at her feet, shifting her weight from side to side. "I know… but it's okay." She gives a shaky grin. "I'm used to it."

Darius cups her chin into his palm. "I'll call you when I get home, okay?"

"Okay."

His lips pleasantly brush her forehead. "I love you." Kayla swallows hard. Her shoulders strain. Her eyes reluctantly drop to the floor. He caresses his fingers through her textured hair. "You don't have to say it back." Darius comforts her, sensing her nerves skyrocketing. "Bye."

"Bye," she murmurs.

Her boo boards the elevator. Kayla turns to watch him, still nervous. She musters enough courage now that he's not facing her. Her cupid bow lips mouth the words: *I love you.* When the lift opens, Darius waves. She waves back as the elevator doors close.

She observes the quiet penthouse, her hands beating at the sides of her legs. She's lonely and bored without his company. *I wish he could have stayed, but I'd rather not get in trouble. Darius is right. I shouldn't be here alone. Yes, this place is a fairytale; I love it… but the home part is missing.*

Her heart sinks. She goes to the kitchen, to the fridge, sliding out strawberry yogurt. Kay snatches a spoon and hops onto a barstool. Her shoulders droop as she twists side to side on the stool, rubbing the back of her neck.

I know Mom and Dad love me, but couldn't they call off sometimes?? I hate being in a ghost town. Do they care how I feel? I feel meaningless. Kayla allows her eyes to water. She unwraps the yogurt, dumps the spoon into it, pulling it out repeatedly, not caring to eat it. It's only a distraction. The droopy spoon plunges in and out of the pink slop.

Why can't they be here? Tears trail down her cheeks. Kayla wipes them away fast. *I guess I have to deal with it. As always.* A wall clock ticks, echoing the mini mansion. The sound reveals how empty the penthouse is. How hollow. Kay stares out of the tall windows at a plane. Her gloomy eyes fixate on the aircraft sailing the wide sky…all by itself. *I guess I gotta deal with it,* she repeats, forcing the words to ease her mood.

Kayla awaits her boyfriend's call, knowing his voice will end her need for attention. *I don't think he knows how much he helps me when*

I'm here alone. Or maybe he does? Darius always calls to soothe me. She watches the wall phone, yearning for conversation. When it rings, she sprints to it.

"Hey, beautiful." His warm voice banishes her sadness.

In the morning, she posts to a beam with other ballerinas. All the girls wear white leotards. Each member holds onto bars with one hand, with the free one outward. The heels of their feet face in, while the toes extend forward.

Standing before the group is a dance instructor, Isabell; a woman in her early thirties dressed in all black, her blonde hair in a ponytail. She holds the same position as the class.

"Demi. Demi." The girls follow the instructor; her free hand sways outward, bends, then goes forward. Grand plié," her demeanor is similar to a boarding schoolteacher…firm. She dips low with her toes pointed. "Six, seven, eight, parallel." The instructor straightens her arm outward, legs spread, and hands crossed behind her back in a low bow. "Eight counts, turn in." Isabell returns to the starting position. "Demi. Demi." The moves repeat.

Kayla zones out, gazing at the studio windows at fluffy clouds. *I have to say I love you… I can't mouth it when he turns away! Why am I so scared? Why? I'm a wimp. I know how Darius feels…it's clear as day. So, what's the issue? What's in the way? I know my feelings aren't the culprit. Whatever it is…it needs to stop.*

After practice, the dancers retire to a sunny locker room, sitting on benches to untie their lacy shoes. Some bend over while others cross their knees to reach without leaning.

Mya examines her friend. "You zoned out. What's up?" The three untie their ballet shoes, beginning with the lace at the top, roped around their ankles.

"Nothing." Kayla avoids eye contact, angrily untying her shoes, upset that she can't say three simple words.

Jia eyes her with understanding. "She's probably just tired, Mya."

"Kayla," Isabell summons her from the doorway. "Your mom is on the line."

Kayla goes to the hall, wondering why her mom is using the car phone. She only uses it for business. Kay spots the corded phone. The receiver lies atop a bulky wall base. She picks it up and instantly hears car windows muffled by wind. "Hey, Mom." She pictures her mother's short, coily hair blowing wildly. *I bet she's driving somewhere immaculate. Probably on her way to close on another mansion or condo. Whichever one it is, I imagine it's a glamorous property.*

"Hey, sweetie! So, your dad and I are free tonight. I'm so sorry about yesterday. I'm making chili con carne. We can catch up, okay?"

"Sure, that sounds fun. Can Darius come?"

"Yes, he can. Great, okay, that's a plan! See you later. Bye, honey."

"Goodb-" The call ends as Kay begins to say goodbye. She holds the phone to her ear, hoping the buzzing line was still her mom's voice. *I want to talk more. Doesn't she?* Kayla hangs up, half happy about tonight but irritated over the rushed chat.

At home, she bathes in a luxurious platform tub. The cold water frosts up the knobs. She adds bath bombs, which fizz green in underwater explosions. Kay undresses and gets in, releasing satisfying sighs. Her muscles de-stress as she soaks in icy water. Ahhh…" Her brown eyes peer at the Chicago skyline. A cloudedout sun dims the autumn afternoon.

Her mind returns to analyzing why she couldn't say the three words. Maybe I'm just not there yet.

When Kay is done bathing, she wraps herself in a robe. Her bare feet graze the spacious penthouse carpet, to the glass staircase. She works on a canvas in the art studio. The ballet positions are all captioned. She uses a pencil, Prismacolor Ebony: **model 14420,** and sketches tutu figures in various postures.

I need this solo. If I fail to win it, someone else will take the spotlight. I can't afford to lose. That's the only way my parents will spend time with me. If I'm in the spotlight…that's the only time they reschedule their work. I need this!

CHAPTER 9: UNVEILED

Nighttime falls. Darius and Kayla cuddle on the sofa in the living room. A horror movie plays on a thirty-inch big-back TV. The aroma of spice and sauce flows from the kitchen.

Kayla sniffs the air, picking out beans and garlic. "Hmmm… it smells so good!"

"You're lucky… my dad cooked homemade pizza yesterday. It was terrible! Can I stay here tonight?" He jokes, beaming enormously.

Kayla blushes. "What is it?"

"Nothing."

Darius squints. "No, it's something. Tell me."

"I don't think I should. It's not like it's going to happen anyway…" she retorts miserably, knowing her boyfriend can't sleep over without a huge dilemma from her folks.

"Can I take a guess?"

"No." A ghost pops up on the screen with sunken eyes and a mouth that drops past its neck. She jumps. "Let's choose something else!"

"No way, you haven't grabbed me out of fear yet." He flirts.

Kay snickers, wringing her arms around his waist. Darius trails his hand through her thick hair, down her cheeks, then to her neck. Someone clears their throat. The two separate from their embrace in compete dread.

At the hall, a middle-aged man crosses his arms with a demanding expression. James, Kayla's dad. His afro is short; he's dressed in casual attire; sweater and slacks. "Thank you." His formidable tone corrects the situation.

"Sorry, Mr. Harris." Darius composes himself, keeping his distance. James turns away and steps down the hall in extravagant dress shoes.

Kayla waits until her dad's office door shuts before reaching for his hand. "Busted." She huffs. Darius glances to the hallway before pulling Kayla to his side and wrapping his arms around her waist. She rests her head on his chest, shielding her eyes from the bloody scene in the movie.

Her arms hug around his stomach and squeeze like a snake. "There, I grabbed you. Now change it to something else… please!"

"Okay, we can try a romance one."

"Aww." Kayla swoons hard, holding a hand to her heart.

He ventures to a rack of VHS tapes, sorting through the options. Which one?" Darius rotates the massive display that belong in a Video Store…not in a home.

"Gone With the Wind." She points to the bottom.

Darius bends to pluck out the VHS. "Isn't this a sad one?"

"It's bittersweet."

"Why not a happy one?"

Kay shrugs. "I'm in love with all the ball dresses."

Darius plucks out the bulky tape and ejects the old tape from the player. The screen goes dark. He inserts the second one. The player whirls and spins. The opening credits play. He heads back to the couch to embrace her by the waist. Kay rubs his palms, enjoying the heat burning from them.

Footsteps sound from down the hallway again. For the second time, they quickly scoot apart. James briefly observes the two before returning down the hall. Darius and Kayla eye each other, grinning mischievously.

The long dining table is set for four. Large serving bowls line the center; bread, greens, crackers, and sauce. Kayla's mom serves chili. Everyone gets two scoops. Mary makes to sit the bowl down, only to halt and add another scoop to Darius's.

"Why'd you do that?" James is puzzled.

"Teen boys have a huge appetite." Her mom explains.

"Thank you." Darius grins.

"She's trying to fatten you up; watch out," James pokes.

"Am not! Look, my brother vents about how much his sons eat. One ate a whole pizza…by themselves. It's because of their growth spurt." She places down the serving bowl.

Kayla tilts her head to the side. "How do you know that?"

"From Doctors Magazine." Mary adds garlic bread and greens to their plates. "It makes me wonder if I really wanted a boy like I thought. I can't imagine how much more I would be shopping."

"Yeah… my dad said I'll have to get a job with how much I eat." Darius agrees while chomping on the spicy beans.

Kayla frowns, taking in new information she never knew. "I didn't know you wanted a son."

"Well, you were about two years old," James dips his garlic bread into the sauce. "We weren't in the best circumstances. So, we decided not to."

"Oh…" Kayla accepts the answer, reaching to fill a cup with juice.

"Besides, I'm happy with what we have. A beautiful, talented girl." Mary gushes at Kayla with great accomplishment.

"Mom… stop…." Kay groans, embarrassed.

"What's wrong with saying that; baby?"

"You're being too sentimental; that's not cool with the youth." James guffaws, observing his daughter's uncomfortable expression.

"Oops, sorry, honey… but it's all true." Mary winks, taking a seat.

"It is." Her dad adds.

"I say, take the compliment and run with it," Darius comments.

Kayla gives a crooked grin and shoves away the mushy moment. "So, where are you taking me, Dad? Mom has the mall planned for Saturday."

"Oh, right, the makeup day. I was thinking of the skating rink. I thought it would go hand in hand with ballet…it beats your mom's idea."

Mary throws him a competitive glance. "We'll see."

"We will." James retorts in a challenge. "I even got rhymes ready."

"Oh, no!" Kayla sinks into her chair. "Dad… don't."

"No, you'll like them, trust me."

Her boyfriend's eyes light up at the subject. "I could mix a track for you." Kayla gives an incredulous gaze to him, much like an angry cat.

"Hmm, good idea. Maybe the DJ will play it for a few bucks." Her mouth drops, and her brows shoot up. Everyone laughs at her dramatic expression. Kayla attempts to stay serious but loses to the amusement.

After dinner, the lovebirds return to the sofa, savoring their last cuddle before 8 p.m. The two snuggle, keeping a lookout in case James does another security sweep. *I wish he could stay the night, but that's not happening. Ever.* Kayla sulks while watching the old-timey movie.

Scarlet and Rhett's love story makes me wonder. Darius rarely argues with me. I wonder why. I mean, he is around my parents most of the time, so he must behave. I can't even imagine us getting mad at each other. Of course, we bicker, but that's it. I think that's a good sign.

"You okay?" Darius lifts her chin to dissect her face.

"Yeah…" Kay mumbles.

A long inhale travels his chest. "You're hiding something."

"I don't want to talk about it." She broods. A clock above the fireplace chimes, announcing that 8 p.m. has arrived. The noise rattles her ribcage. *NOO! THAT DIDN'T FEEL LIKE TEN MINUTES. UGH!*

"Goodnight." Darius strokes her hand before leaving for the door. There's a tingling burn where his fingers just were. A static heat. A token of his effect on her body. She scowls, not saying it back because it'll make her cry. Her already watery eyes would leak.

In the morning, Kay wakes in a yellow bed, yawning and stretching. There's discomfort from her back; tight muscles. *Oh, no! I gotta get rid of that! I can't have that!! Not with auditions coming up.* She gets out of a fairytale bed. A glittery headboard paired with a sparkly canopy. There are dollhouse dressers set in each corner, high from the floor. A real-life playset for a little princess.

An almost risen sun showers the lower half of the room, while the top half is still darkened. Kayla's nightgown flows behind her as a princess's would. She takes a green smoothie from the fridge, bananas, strawberries, and spinach, and sips it on her way upstairs.

There's a balcony off her art studio. The city beyond the glass is windy. A perfect fall day for multicolored leaves to blow in the wind. She stretches her legs one by one, using patio furniture as a workout bench. The rigid muscles are concerning; her legs aren't awake enough to be flexible. So, she performs slow back kicks to activate them. *I have to be careful...I can't push myself too much.* The workout session doesn't last long; all she does is prep her muscles a bit to encourage faster repair time.

Later on, she goes to the kitchen for a quick breakfast. Almond milk and Cheerios, not the honey nut kind...that would be too sweet for her health. *God forbid I have a sugary breakfast, like every other girl my age. No...I have 1 gram of sugar, toasted oat flavor, unsweetened, whole grain, the health-conscious option.* "Time to eat cardboard...yippie!" Her sarcasm is professional as she hops atop a stool with a wide rimmed bowl.

Her eyes go to the empty dining room table....to the 8 chairs that host ghosts instead of her parents. While pouring the gold oval loops, she plays pretend...plays house...with the vacant table. "School was fun...glad you asked. But I wish I could see my boyfriend more. Can I switch to his school? This is dumb...dad...can you fix it?" The clattering oats cease hitting the bowl. Then comes the splash of the milk. "Why can't I have Fruit Loops?? These taste like wood, Mom." She huffs and slumps over, propping her elbows on the pristine island counter.

The place is so clean…so…untouched. No different than a model in a department store. Nothing in the house is lived in…or shows wear and tear. No different than a bomb test home….full of manikin humans, fake harmony.. fake furniture. The ultimate clean.

Kay chews, munching loudly in the graveyard house. The noise is too uncivilized to bounce off the spotless walls and impeccable windows. "We should have pancakes…with loads of syrup! And let the syrup spill all over…!" This excites her more than it should; the idea of being silly with them…enthuses her. "Who cares if we make a mess…it'll be fun." Kay laughs roughly, knowing this will never come true…knowing that the house will always be…picturesque and unblemished. She goes back to eating, yet her eyes are still on the dining table. "Good talk….it's nice to catch up."

Kay's pager beeps from her gown pocket. The bedazzled device reads: 15. *That's Darius. He'll be here soon; I need to get ready.*

She chooses a polka-dot dress. Kay slides into powder blue flats and then hustles into Mom's room to spray on Chanel perfume. An odd sensation overcomes her. An ominous one. She slowly glances over at the bookshelf. Her blinking slows to a hypnotic speed… her hefty lips part. The shaded room darkens more than it already is. She sets down the bottle, unsure of the sudden draw to the dark literature.

A cryptic hum attracts her like a magnet; her feet move forward with a drag, hesitant yet curious. Her cocoa eyes lock onto a book at the top. The one from 400 B.C. She slides it out. "I should get ready for school." Kay hastily returns the magical book to its spot… and backs away. But the peculiar hum returns, this time causing her to swallow hard. "I could take a peek…real quick." She plucks it back out, scrolling to the first page, which holds bizarre chants:

INITIATION SPELL - Enrus De Cov.
A 13-pointed star illustrates this spell.

WATER SUMMANCE - Aqwav coum.
A parting sea illustrates this spell.

AIR SUMMANCE - Wina coum–
Floating airwaves illustrates this spell.

EARTH SUMMANCE - Grroc Coum.

A cracking cave illustrates this spell.

"Hmm... I wonder what would happen if I said one? I doubt any of this is real, the same as the Ouija board."

I used one before on Halloween, and nothing happened. These things are all for fun. My mom has them, the same as people who collect action figures or artifacts. It's just a hobby. The feeling I had before was just curiosity... nothing more. I need to quench it and move on.

"Now, which one should I say?" Her eyes scan the mantras. "It would be nice to have more wind. I'll say that one." Kay clears her throat. "Wina coum." She darts to the window, throwing back the thick curtains. Her gaze travels over the autumn trees. They're motionless. Kay waits a few more seconds, hoping a leaf will blow. Nothing occurs.

"I knew it! That was silly. These are just joke spells...pranks...nothing else." She steps back to the bookcase. *But still... why did I expect the trees to move? And why did I buy that Ouija board? I think my mom's oddness is rubbing off on me. That has to be it. Well... my curiosity is quenched. That's the end of that...*

A pounding arises from the window. The striking force jolts her enough to drop the book. Kay covers her mouth and recoils, eyes widening in panic. The glass behind the curtains vibrate. The noise grows in volume, hurting her eardrums. She winces and covers them. A whooshing sound convinces her that there's a tornado outside. The walls shake. Wind sweeps in from the vents on the ceiling, whipping her hair all over her face. The strength of the air pushes her entire body backwards, a tornado's intensity.

"NOOO! STOP. STOP. STOP!!!"

The whirling goes to a rest...so abruptly. Now there's complete silence. The walls halt shaking. The vents cease their gushing. Kayla's heart pumps hard. Her sight drops to the spell book on the floor. The star symbol wakes the dread in her. *What in the world?? What just happened??! NO! NO, WAY! NO WAY!!!*

CHAPTER 10: UNMASKED

KOTA

The living room is touched by dim sunlight. The lack of buzzing assures him that the sun hasn't risen yet. He sits in the oval, watching his parents sweep away leaves. *I don't know if I should leave the circle. Did the cleansing work? What if I get the urge to taste blood? What if I become a demon again? I can't hurt anyone else. I wonder if my folks figured out a solution.*

"Is there any hope?" he asks his mother.

Odina gives a grin. "Yes, my walela (hummingbird). You are free of the blood curse for a little while."

Her son gives out a relieved sigh. "Does this mean I can go to the Pow-Wow?"

"Yes… but don't roam too far just in case the spell doesn't hold," Mato warns.

He smiles. "I won't."

Yes! I want to get out of the house and be normal… not locked up in a circle scaring my family. I want to get past that phase. It's been two days. I could use a distraction… and some fun. This year's Pow-Wow will be the biggest one yet. All the love will aid my dark soul. I always feel safe at the celebration. The excited smile fades from his face. *But… then I don't want to be out; that vampire is around. No one is safe… no one should be out.*

"What about the vampire? Should anyone be going to the Pow-Wow? It's not safe."

Odina shakes her head. "All is fine. The creature is no longer in range, according to my locator spell. It has left. Everyone here is safe. Come…" She holds out her hand. "Everything is alright."

Kota grasps his mother's hand. "What about school?"

Mato grimaces. "We decided you shouldn't return."

"Why not? Mom said I have a few days…"

"I know… but you're still dangerous… you're not a normal teenager. If you have a mood swing, who knows what you'll do? Your strength is dangerous."

"Plus… school will only remind you of your friends," Odina chimes in gravely. "It's all too soon."

Kota sulks. "Do their parents know?"

"I gave an anonymous call to the police. I thought I'd spare them of hanging missing posters."

"Has anything been arranged? A service of some kind?" He wonders.

"Not that I know of. I'll ask around." *If there are burials planned, I hope they're closed casket for their parents' sake.* He blocks out the image of their mutilated bodies. "Let's not dwell on it. Come help me with the pudding." His mom leads him to the kitchen. The shades are drawn to protect him from the daylight.

Kota studies the buzzing from the window. "How long until I can be in the sun?"

"I called your grandad. He says it'll have to be something you wear… jewelry of some sort. I'll do some reading on hexing."

Odina plugs up an industrial mixer. She collects ingredients from the fridge. Cornstarch, sugar, baking soda, salt, chocolate soy milk, and vanilla extract.

Kota helps her pour tablespoons into the mixer. Dyani passes the archway. He notes how fast she zooms by and huffs miserably. "Dy hates me."

"She doesn't… this is just an adjustment. She'll come around." Odina powers on the mixer and sets it on the third speed limit.

He flinches at the sound. The machine motor is beyond loud. A chainsaw in his head. He muffles a yell of anguish, yet a groan still escapes. His mother realizes his discomfort and switches it off. "Oh, my dear, I'm sorry. I'll ask Grandad how to ease your senses." She gathers two whisks and lifts the top of the mixer. They use the tools to hand churn the liquid.

My ears are too sensitive… that means the Pow-Wow music won't be enjoyable. The vital part of the celebration is the live band. "How will I enjoy the music?"

"We…can sit farther away, or in the car. Whatever is best for you."

"But we'll miss the show… we always sit close."

"Rest your mind."

Kota slumps his head in pity. "I'm ruining everything.."

"Shh…stop with that, the night will be fun."

"No, he's right," Dyani utters from the hall. "How will we enjoy the show?"

"We'll manage."

"Will we also manage to arrive late? The sun is an issue for Kota, not the rest of us. The introduction will be over by the time we get there."

"We'll make the grand entry."

"Barely." Dy snickers violently. "We might as well not go!"

"HOLD YOUR TONGUE!" Dyani sighs and stomps away. Odina annoyingly peers after her daughter.

Kota's sight lowers; he focuses on mixing the pudding. *Tensions are high… all because of me. My sister isn't wrong. I'm complicating everything. Why can't I just walk in the sun? Why does sound hurt me? Are there more vampires out there besides the evil one? There has to be others. There has to be vampires who know how to live with the sun. Who know how to comfort the pain of noise.*

Within an hour, five bowls of pudding are placed into a deep freezer. Kota finds a casual outfit; only the performers wear ceremonial garments. *I wish I could wear headpieces and feathers.* Instead, he chooses brown pants and a shirt with hanging fringe. His mother wears earth tones as well, a dark green dress lined with yellow. His father is in all black, a loose-fitting top and flare jeans. Dyani chose a simple blue dress, only it's made of rugged suede. *She looks like she's from another century…one where hand sown gowns are the only fashion.*

The family gathers in the living room. Dy still has a temper; she watches the curtains, irritated that the sun is out and high. *It's only noon. My sister can't handle waiting for sundown.*

"Let her go."

Dyani hops from the couch. "Wado, Adadoda (Thank you, Father)." Her restlessness is cured. Dy hustles out the door as fast as a wild horse.

"I wish you hadn't done that; she has to be here for support."

"Why ruin her day?"

The green wall phone rings from the kitchen. His wife gives him an annoyed glance, disappearing with his parental guiding. Odina shakes her head disappointedly while making her way to pick up the phone. ""Hello?…yes." There's a brief pause. "It's your father," she informs her husband. "Yes, the sunlight hex. I have the manuscripts; I just need to study."

Mato focuses on his son. "How are you feeling?"

"Bad…I ruined Dy's day."

"Your sister will recover. Is there any thirst?"

"No. Just the buzzing…my hearing is amplified."

"How so?"

"The mixer is a chainsaw."

Mato broods. "I'm sure my father will sort out these mishaps. He's a caster…but his magic isn't as strong as it used to be."

"Are there others out there who cast?"

"I'm sure there are… your mom and I will do our best to locate one for help. You have our word."

"Dear, your grandfather wishes to speak to you." His mom calls him over to the phone. "Hold it far, in case it's too loud."

He does as his mother recommends. "Osiyo, Ududu (Hello, Grandfather)."

"Osiyo, Kota." An elderly voice chimes; calming and sweet. "How are you?"

His grandfather's tone is high in volume through the receiver, so he holds it at an awkward distance. "I'm still adjusting." He ups the volume of his voice, since the old man isn't superhuman.

"I assume your hearing is catastrophic?"

"Yes…"

"I have remedies for that as well. I'll forge a necklace for all the issues. The thirst, sun, and senses will be put at ease. But not cured. You'll never be able to remove the locket. Understood?"

"Understood." Kota nods. "When will it be ready?"

"I will begin carving tonight. As for the spelling, that will take a while. I wish I could have done it sooner, but my strength has lessened over the years. But I will gift you this blessing. There is still hope. These horrid days will soon be in the past."

Kota can't help but allow his emotions to stir. His eyes water up a bit…he blinks the droplets away. "Wado (Thank you)."

"Of course, walela (hummingbird)."

He wipes his eyes, perplexed that such a human quality can still belong to him. *Aren't tears a sign of being alive?? A sign of being human? I thought I was dead. Why would the devil allow me to pose as human? Is it to mock…or is it for balance? Even animals feel. When thrown from heaven, even Satan felt emotion. I guess this life comes with a double-edged sword.*

Once the sun sets, the family goes out to the porch. "We can stay here if you'd like." His mother consoles, holding jumbo containers of pudding.

"I think we should join the crowd."

"But the discomfort?"

"I'll handle it… Dy was right, we can't enjoy the show from here."

Mato grins proudly at him. "Yes, you'll handle this."

The park is where the town's Pow-Wows are always hosted. The fire staffs mounted in the soil of the ground; take him back to his childhood. *I remember my 5-year-old self wearing a headdress too large, which kept slipping down past my eyes. I remember being fascinated by the flaming staffs waved by the dancers. I still am.* A flutter of honor consumes him.

Kota's lifeless eyes burst with color. Fireworks scatter the sky in orange and yellow explosions, representing the Cherokee Nation. Tiki torches circle the entire park, ten feet high. Flags hang, rippling gracefully. The Great Seal at the center; surrounded by seven yellow stars. Each positioned towards the middle, paying tribute to the seven clans.

Drumming, flutes, and chants resonate the neighborhood. He endures the blasting music, not caring that his ears feel as if they're bleeding from the inside. The pulsing is crucifying. *But the pain is worth it...* He smiles so big that Odina giggles happily. The three enter the park, mingling in with the mass. All members of the community are present, well over a thousand. Kota tiptoes to see over the shoulder of those ahead of them; they're at the back of the crowd.

An assembly of performers prance in the center of the park; moving as one in a flawless circle dance. Their beaded moccasins, ankle-high footwear, and pucker-styled toes glide in unison. Their head-dressings bounce; the eagle feathers are colored black and white. The entertainers bear long, braided hair with otter ties.

Both men and women wear vibrant costumes complete with dangling fringe. The artists grip flaming staffs. Rattles are tied, which twirl and shake to add flair. Women sway their shawls in a breathtaking motion, resembling huge, colorful birds flapping their wings. He cheers with the crowd, clapping up a storm.

Orange, yellow, blue, green, purple, gold. The traditional costumes are mesmerizing. Kota appreciates the singers who all communicate a sacred rhythm on a gigantic drum. Their beating hands and chanting vocals warm his heart. His eyes gloss up. *It's so beautiful. Life is still beautiful despite the darkness inside. All I need is my tribe to remind me where I belong. I belong here. We are strong as one.*

"Let's get closer!" Kota grazes through the crowd.

A few in the audience notice his appearance. Pale skin and even paler eyes. This makes many double-take. Kota is surprised that people he's known since childhood are flinching away from him. Fleeing. Terror waves over the crowd, an uproar of hectic screams. One man holds his arms out to protect those behind him. The defensive grimace he gives is soul-shattering.

Oh, no... Kota's eyes sweep those around him.

They all back away, no longer enjoying the show. The yells of children pierce the air. He's seen as a horrendous monster in their eyes. A devil. The band's music stops. The singing fades. The entertainers slow their dancing. The joyful festival dies. The mob clears further and further away, isolating Kota into a lonely circle. Many attendees exclaim in long gasps…others are too speechless to make a noise…or to even move.

There are rez officers here….and Bly is amongst them. A friendly face that now holds hostility. *What? Why? I know Bly… he knows me too. I don't understand! Am I that menacing?? Is my appearance that chilling?* The officers march their way.

Mato and Odina rush to shield their son. The audience part ways for the cops. "Mato… what do we do?!" Odina panics.

"Stay calm."

Bly studies Kota's ashy skin. It's no longer brown as his is. He gawks at the creepy eyes and the ghastly soul in front of him. A shiver overtakes his body. "It's true… you fed on the Waya family!! You killed them!"

CHAPTER 11: FRACTURE

"Bly… listen." Mato begins.

"YOUR SON IS A KILLER!"

"Please let me explain."

"There's nothing to explain!! Jacy saw the slaughter outside his shop. Kota is evil!"

"MY SON ISN'T EVIL!!"

"Tell that to the chief!" Bly presses a button on a CB radio clipped to his belt. "Chief, you're needed at the Pow-Wow. It's the Ahoka kid."

The radio emits static before the commander replies, "Are the allegations true?" A bassy voice asks.

"Yes."

There's a long pause. Everyone scans Kota for the beast he is. Fright consumes the crowd. Children gawk at him as if a boogeyman brought to life.

"Clear the park." The chief orders from the radio.

"Everyone, disperse." Bly instructs the audience. "Escort everyone away." His cop crew approaches the guests, handgesturing to the street. The crowd follows the directions, murmuring as they depart. The cops form a line behind the guests, guiding them to the street.

"Contain the Ahoka family, I'll arrive shortly."

"Will do, Chief." Bly scans the area. "Where is Dyani?"

Odina searches the crowd like a hawk. "Dyani?!!" She examines the street twice before locating her daughter. Dy watches from the sidewalk with the rest of the party. Frightened. Her mother offers her hand. "Come, please." Dy debates staying with the crowd or standing with her family. The struggle is evident in her shifty eyes.

Kota gives a begging glance, one only a little brother in need can give. Helpless for her. "Please. Dy." His voice trembles.

Her lips quiver, she glimpse at the audience, mortified by their critical glares. Dismay and embarrassment taint her.

Mato holds his hand out. "Kamama (butterfly)." He speaks warmly. "Come."

Dy exhales and lowers her head in shame. She treads over, taking her father's hand. Ignoring Kota.

Why is she being so heartless?? I told her the truth. I don't want to be this way. How could she abandon me when I need her??! I need my family. I won't survive without them. Kota's heart drops to the pits. He stares at his big sister, wounded.

It doesn't take the chief long to arrive. Ridge, a tall, broad man, dismounts a Jeep. Dressed in a brown uniform. The mountains of Tahlequah design the sigil on both his badge and uniform. The street is still occupied by citizens.

Ridge does a shooing motion with his hands, beckoning them away. "Clear the premises. Goodnight to all!"

The townsfolk shuffle off, leaving the street to the sidewalk. Ridge watches them pace the pavement. Some turn the corner, while others enter their homes. The chief doesn't glance away until all are out of sight.

He gives a hard gaze to the Ahoka family, his green eyes linger on Kota, astonished by his appearance. "How could you become this?! I've known you since the bassinet. How could you kill so gruesomely???"

"My son was attacked by a creature!" Mato steams. "He didn't choose to kill!"

"A creature??" Ridge's wonder gets the best of him.

"A blood demon."

"Blood demon??!!" Bly exclaims.

"Impossible, there hasn't been an encounter in centuries." Chief Ridge is skeptical.

"I'm telling the truth! It was alone; it passed through Tahlequah. The three teens in the woods were its victims… so was Kota."

"Or your son interfered with ᎤᏞᏙᎱᏬᎫ (witchcraft) and now suffers the consequences! He's already killed innocence. He did the same with those teenagers!"

"My son was attacked! I'm no liar!"

"I conducted a locator spell. The animal fled far enough to escape the charm. The beast is most likely underground. We can hunt it together." Odina offers a solution.

"So… you've utilized sorcery on sacred soil?!" She closes her mouth, ashamed. "That is forbidden!" Ridge boils. "For that, the Ahoka family pays the ultimate price." "NO…

DON'T!!" Mato's eyes bulge.

"There is no other choice."

Kota is lost as to what the ultimate price is. Mato steps to the chief, the officers swarm to form a protective barrier between the two. "Chief… my boy has gone through enough. Please… jail would be kinder."

"No… his soul is gone. His presence on Tahlequah will taint the land and summon death. My words are final!"

Mato drops to his knees, his voice trembling with urgency.

"ᏣᎳᎩ (Cherokee) would not cast out one of its own without first seeking harmony," he pleads, his hands pressed together in reverence. "I, Mato Ahoka, call upon the Creator—ᎤᏅᏓᏳᎦᎲ (The Great Spirit) — to bless us with ceremony for a soul gone astray." He bows his head in solemn prayer, whispering. "ᎤᏅᏓᏳᎦᎲ, ᏙᏍᏗᏎᎣᏗᏏ ᎤᏟᎹᎠᏫ, (Creator, restore balance to the wandering soul)."

Chief Ridge stands still, the weight of law pressing against the pull of tradition. He exhales, his shoulders softening, and slowly bows his head as well. "May the Creator grant balance," he murmurs. Then, he eyes his staff. "Ready their dwelling for the ritual." They're escorted down the road by the sheriffs and chief. Residents peek from the front windows of their houses. The way back is similar to a walk of shame. The harsh eyes from the curtains follow them all the way back to their home. Their lifelong neighbors frown upon them.

Kota sulks at people he's known since preschool; their cruelty is beyond intense. *They all hate me… just as my sister does.* He looks to Dyani; she stares ahead, dodging his eye contact.

Mato climbs the porch stairs and opens the door for everyone. "Gather the bundle," the chief orders. Odina nods and disappears into the kitchen, returning moments later with a woven pouch filled with sacred herbs—white sage, sweetgrass, cedar, and small river stones. She hands it to Ridge.

"This space must breathe, so that which does not belong may leave." He turns his head. "Dyani, open the windows."

She boosts up each of the six, allowing the cool night wind to sweep the room. The curtains stir. Odina kneels at the center of the living room, laying down a hand-carved smudge bowl and placing the herbs inside. She and Mato arrange eagle feathers wrapped in red thread, facing four directions—north, south, east, and west.

Kota lingers at the archway—shoulders tight, palms clenched at his sides. His eyes move across the scene: the smoke bowl, the feathers, the waiting circle. It's all very scary….and dooming to him.

Bly approaches him. "Come, Kota." He places a hand on his back. "This is not punishment. This is your way back to balance." They walk together to the center. Kota is positioned just beyond the smudge bowl—between the feathers. His chest rises and falls, full of apprehension.

Bly hands him a river stone. "It'll keep you steady."

His mother meets Kota's eyes, offering him an eagle feather. "For prayers," she whispers. "You don't have to speak them aloud; the Creator already hears."

Chief Ridge lights the herbs in the smudge bowl. Wisps of white smoke float slowly, curling like breath patterns in the air. The scent of cedar and sweetgrass is thick. He removes his hat, bowing his head as the circle begins to form. "ᎤᏁᎳᏅᎯ, let this child return to harmony."

What if the Great Spirit judges me? What if I mess this up? I did kill…killing is a sin…a dark mark. I'm no longer pure. Maybe the Creator is mean. Maybe… it doesn't want me whole again. Kota hyperventilates, losing his nerve to hopelessness.

His father places a steady hand on his shoulder. "Breathe, son. The Creator listens—not with anger, but with knowing. There is no judgment, only the path back to balance."

Everyone speaks low and rhythmic: **"Udalvltanv tsusquaganasdi."** (Balance…bring balance to the one who walks in shadow)." Odina fans the smoke with a feather, directing it toward her son. Kota stands still, too worried to move while the ritual is taking place. The others pass the feather in gentle, clockwise motions, sharing the piece and repeating the words.

Ridge holds the feather near Kota's chest, waving the smoke gently upward. "Let the old fall away. Let the spirit breathe clean. Cleanse the body. Restore the spirit. Call the soul back to center."

Kota rests his eyes, his hands shaking, but he doesn't step away. He doesn't run from fear. He needs help. He relaxes his worries. Taking in the warm smells of cedar and sweetgrass. All is tranquil…even the odd chanting…everything is steady. But….not for long.

The windows start to rattle. Booming wind pounds in. The chief flinches from the sound, bewildered by the belligerence outside. The curtains ripple flaring inward. A massive gust of air. The drapes rip from the rods and flatten to the walls. Strikes of lightning wash over the house. Pure white blazes through the clouds; unnatural and vigorous. The ground quakes.

Kota's eyes blacken. Ridge shudders, dropping the bowl to the floor. All of the sheriffs, including Bly, out their handguns from their belts.

Mato panics. "NOO!!" The guns fire. The bullets blast the air, zipping Kota's way. Mato rushes forward. His hands write across the air, carving a glowing spiral shield. The radiant mark pulses wide, protecting not just Kota, but Dy and his wife too.

The bullets collide midair. **POP; CRACK!** Sparks scatter as each metal round ricochets on the magic barrier. Each round deflects in a burst of white until silence drops like a hammer.

"STOP THIS!!" Odina shouts. "PLEASE!!"

"The Creator has abandoned him! Has abandoned you all!!!" Bly hollers. Kota's pitch-black pupils remain intact, not converting back to normal. Frozen in place. "Look at his eyes!!! Tsul '**Kalu** has taken him!!" The Cherokee Devil. "He'll bring curses upon us all!" The lightning blinds the room, accompanied by chaotic thunder. The storm outside rages on, something deadly. "We must kill him!"

"Killing will release the evil on this land!" Ridge contends. "I obeyed the right of ritual. It has been denied by the Spirit. Your boy is no longer of our kind." His ruthless eyes fall onto Mato and Odina. "Leave Tahlequah and never return. You have until midnight."

KAYLA

She sits on the balcony in the dead of night. There are bags under her eyes. Kay is rattled; her hands tremble. Her mind recalls the odd encounter in her parents' room. Flashbacks of the wind, the shaking windows… the vibrating glass. She tugs a blanket closer to her chest. Her complexion is dull.

I had to imagine it. My imagination got the best of me, that's all. No way in the world did that actually happen. She hugs herself, staring at the half-moon. *But if it didn't occur, why am I acting this way? I've been distant ever since. I've been acting bizarre the whole day. Darius noticed something was off.* She recalls meeting him outside the penthouse:

"Hey beautiful."

"Hey." Kay replies unenthusiastically.

This troubles Darius. "What's wrong?" "Nothing…"

Her tone is one note and shaky.

"Are you sure?" He pulls her into an embrace.

"Yeah, I'm sure… I just had a bad dream, that's all."

"Aww. It's okay. I'm here now."

Kay smiles. "My savior."

"Do you want to talk about it?"

How would I even begin to explain? My mom has freaky books in her room full of spells. I said one, thinking it was meaningless, but ended up summoning wind. Yeah… he'll totally believe that! Darius will think it's a joke. If only it was April Fools. "No… I don't want to. Let's head to school."

"We're not going to the studio?"

She shakes her head. "My body needs to recover; I overworked myself."

"Oh, alright." His hazel eyes study her back side. "You forgot your bookbag."

"It's fine, I don't need it." *The last thing she wants is to go back up. The thought of passing the bedroom has her skin crawling.*

The whole day is off… her energy isn't as vibrant. In Photography, Jia noticed that Kay was withdrawn. She's the type to give space instead of prying. Although Kay felt her observing her the whole class.

Mya, on the other hand, investigated between the bell. "Did you and Darius fight? Or are you mad at your parents?"

"No… it's just a bad day." She gets that Mya is worried, but feels her friend needs to know when to leave people alone with their thoughts.

Chester and Izzy are respectful during Pre Law. Kay is glad that they're more like Jia. They give empathetic stares and uplifting smiles every time she met their eye sight. In PE, she tries sitting out on the bench to gather her thoughts, but Fred is too lively to have a mopey friend. His enthusiasm rubbed off. He didn't dig for info; he only got Kay up and moving.

"Let's turn that frown upside down, Missy. Try to beat me… I doubt you can."

That got me in a combative mood and made me forget for a short while. Today might be better. But who am I kidding? I barely slept. I need coffee. Kay leaves the balcony, a long blanket dragging behind her. In the kitchen, she locates a kettle and fills it with water. Next, she flicks on a stove eye and sets it there. As she waits for it to heat, she peers out at the city. Dawn is approaching. Kay huffs and rubs the back of her neck.

Does Mom know what the books can do? Has she ever said any of the incantations? I want to ask her… but I don't want to seem insane. I should start with simple questions. Why does she collect them? And for how long have they been a part of her life?

When the kettle whistles, Kay removes it. She adds coffee powder to a cup and pours. No cream or sugar. She drinks it black.

The healthiest way to consume the hot cup of joe. Her pager, which is wrapped in the blanket, beeps.

Darius paged her: **14.** Kay turns it upside down to properly read it. The number 14 now translates to *Hi.* She goes to the wall phone and dials the number 12, then the last four digits of Darius's number. She selects 406: which will translate to **XOXO** on her boyfriend's pager. Kay sips the coffee, waiting for her pager to go off. After a few seconds it does: **XOXO**.

"You're up early." Her dad says from the archway.

"I couldn't sleep."

"Why not?"

"I had a nightmare." "Wow…

you still have those?" "Not

really…" She rubs her eyes.

"Was it the squirrel monkey?"

"DAD! DON'T TALK IT UP!" Kayla covers her ears. *Why would he speak of it? That monster haunted me all my childhood!*

James chuckles. "Sorry." He walks to the kettle.

"I add enough water for you a cup." "Of

course you did, you're a daddy's girl."

"Maybe a little." She hangs up the phone.

The sound of heels announce that her mom is awake. Mary rocks a grape-colored flare suit, very 70s chic. "Nope, she's a mommy's girl all the way."

"It's always a competition with you."

"You know you love that about me." Mary analyzes her daughter. "Honey, you look sick. What's the matter?"

"She had a bad dream."

"About what?" The mother-bear within her activates; she coddles Kayla.

Can I tell the truth? If I told them that I had a nightmare about the magic books, they wouldn't judge me as much. This is a perfect opportunity. "It was about the grimoires in your room."

James makes a cup of coffee. "It's good to know I'm not the only one who's freaked out."

"They're not freaky; don't listen to your dad. They were handed down from your grandmother; the grimoires are family history."

Family history??? Handed down from grandma? Does that mean the casting I did was normal? I work on phrasing my words into subtle curiosity. "Are the spells real?"

"No…" Mary caresses Kay's curly hair. "I thought they were when I was younger. I even recited one. Those are just words dressed up to seem magical. Although your grandmother says otherwise. She claims witchcraft is real. My mom held a séance once, but it was just a prank."

"So… none of it is real?"

"Not at all." Mary comforts her daughter. "Forget about the dream; it's just your imagination getting the best of you."

Was it? Or do I want to believe it was? My eyes know what they saw. My mind just can't comprehend it. I can't deny how the environment shifted from calm to chaotic. I can't deny how it all ceased when I shouted, stop. There was a presence in the room… that listened to me. I'm not insane. Maybe Grandma isn't either.

CHAPTER 12: DISPLACED

Kay showers and dresses for school. Black leggings, a pink T with a thick, buckle-belt at the waist. An outfit she ordered from the Seventeen magazine catalog. She's somewhat energetic on the walk to school. Kay tries to appear as normal as possible, but the small talk is short.

Darius takes note of this. "Are you mad at me?"

Kayla gasps. "No! Why would you think that?!"

"It's just… you're not talking as much."

"I just got a lot on my mind…that's all."

"Tell me."

She contemplates, staring ahead as her tiny feet cover the sidewalk of yellow leaves. *He'll think he's dating a psycho if I tell the truth.* "It's nothing."

"Is that dream still bothering you?"

"A little… it's nothing. I just need a few days. I promise I'm not mad at you." *Now would be the perfect time to mention that I love him. But I'm a chicken.*

In history, the class opens a book full of the wars of the world. The WWI dugout is still the topic. The robust teacher writes page numbers on the blackboard with chalk. *Read Page 55 and 67. No Talking. Quiet Zone.* Kayla flips to page 55:

The Vampire dugout (known locally in Belgium as the Vampyr dugout) is a First World War underground shelter located near the Belgian village of Zonnebeke. It was created as a British brigade headquarters in early 1918. The 171st Tunneling Company of the Royal Engineers mined it after the Third Battle of Ypres/Battle of Passchendaele.

The same student who exclaimed the word "vampire" leans to whisper to a fellow peer. "What if they're down there for real??"

"Huh?" a frizzy-haired girl retorts in a hushed tone.

"What if there are vamp—"

"MR. CLIFF! EYES ON THE PAGE!" the teacher barks. Cliff leans back to his desk and reads on.

It is an odd name. Why vampire? Why not the dead dugout or the fallen dugout. Either phrasing would have summed up the soldiers who were killed. Cliff's questioning is right when it comes to the title, but he lost me at the end. There's no such thing as vampires. Dracula is a fictional story that spun nothing but nonsense. He's being dumb. Kayla continues reading:

Vampire became operational from early April 1918, housing the 100th Brigade of the British 33rd Division, the 16th King's Royal Rifle Corps and the 9th Battalion Highland Light Infantry Regiment. But after only a few weeks, the dugout was lost when the Germans undertook the Battle of the Lys in April 1918. It was recaptured in September 1918, when its last occupants became the 2nd Battalion of the Worcestershire Regiment.

By lunch, Kay has some clarity about the encounter. *Mom is probably right. None of it is true. It was just an extremely windy day. If magic is real, why hasn't anyone seen it? I should dismiss it as I did the existence of vampires.*

Jia and Mya join her at the designated lunch table. Each of them have salads and water. "Are you better?" Jia asks, hoping that she is. Her kind, pie face lifts Kay's spirit.

She takes a deep, cleansing breath, then smiles. "I am."

"What was up anyway? Is it your period?" Mya snoops.

"I don't act weird on my cycle." Kay titters.

"So, what was your deal?"

"Mya!" Jia groans. "Stop, just be happy she's better."

"It's fine, I can tell her." *It's best that I give in now, or she'll nag me forever. Mya is just worried and shows it in a different way. An annoying way.* "I had a bad dream." She repeats the lie.

"Oh… that's it?" Mya laughs.

"Was it the squirrel monkey?" Jia's voice is therapeutic, as if she has a degree in evaluating trauma.

"Oh my God, why did I tell y'all about that!"

"I hope it wasn't too bad." Jia hugs her. "I'll pray for you tonight to keep it away."

"It wasn't that."

"I bet it was." Mya deduces. "You said it was big as a beast and chased you. That would scare the shit out of anyone."

"The dream wasn't that scary." Kay rolls her eyes. "It was about my mom's witch books."

Jia gulps, covering her mouth. "Oh, no! Did they haunt you!"

"Kinda…" *I think I can tell my girls. Besides, we already use the Ouija board on Halloween just for kicks. We've been down a superstitious path already. So, what's the problem? I think I can reveal what happened.* "I said one of the spells…and it worked." Kay clenches her teeth, awaiting their reactions.

Mya cackles like a witch. "Really, Kay??! If you're trying to prank us for Halloween, it's not working."

"I don't think she is… she's just saying her dream." Jia quarrels.

"No…she's trying to pull one over. You can't get me with this. Spells are not real, girl."

"So why do you talk to a Ouija board every Halloween?" Kay starts up a banter.

"For fun... it's the spookiest time of the year for a reason." She answers frankly.

"What if we do it this year and something happens?"

"It's not real, Kay."

How is she so confident? And why can't I be the same? I'd love to have her mindset in this circumstance. I don't even buy my own lies. It wasn't a dream. No matter how many times I tell myself, it won't be true. "Can I be honest?"

Mya eats her salad. "Here she goes again, trying to fool us."

Her smug demeanor irritates Kay, who seethes with frustration. "I'M NOT JOKING!!" For the first time ever, she has enough courage to snap back. "JUST LISTEN TO ME!!"

Mya flinches back... befuddled that her friend is yelling. Her mouth drops. So does Jia's. The buzzing tables around suddenly go silent. The cafeteria is soundless for a few seconds. All eyes are on them.

I didn't mean to get that loud, but Mya is getting on my nerves. She thinks she knows everything! Kay puffs out air. "I'm trying to tell the truth here!"

"Okay... okay... I'm sorry." Mya's meek voice proves she means it. She's never seen her friend speak so feebly. "I'm listening." "Me too." Jia's brows shoot up to her forehead.

Kayla leans forward, beckoning them to do the same. Aware that everyone's attention is still on their table. "I don't think it was a dream..." she admits in a muted tone.

KOTA

The Ahoka family gather what they can. Furniture and appliances are left in place. The Ford wagon can only hold so much. Only sentimental items are packed into the vehicle. Dy silently cries while carrying jewelry boxes and a bag of clothes. She mean-mugs Kota on her way out the front door. Her brother mopes.

This is all my fault. If I hadn't ventured through the crowd and exposed myself, we'd still be living here. I know Mom and Dad are thinking the same.

"Help your mother, Kota." Mato directs him while carrying picture frames.

Odina is in the kitchen. Her teary eyes reminisce memories within the wallpaper. Kota also recalls the good days. He revisits the time he spent in this kitchen as a kid. He always helped his mother with baking. His chubby face covered in flour. How he snuck fingerfuls of chocolate, how he stole peaches from the cobbler.

He even recalls him and Dy strapping on their bookbags for school. The two were two peas in a pot, they always packed lunch together. Their happy, chipmunk giggles haunt his ears in an eerie echo. Odina sniffles and wipes her eyes. His mother turns away, grief stricken.

"Uyoayelvdi, Unistsi," *(Sorry, Mother).*

"No… don't be. None of this is your fault. Life is unpredictable." She cuddles him. "There comes a time when goodbyes aren't pleasant. But new beginnings are welcomed."

Is this truly what she wants to say? Is my mother this calm on the inside?? Or is she hiding behind a shield to spare me? There's no way everyone isn't thinking the same. We're a tribeless family because of me. We have no clan, no people. Now… we have no land. No community. Our home is gone forever.

She breaks from the embrace. "The dishware and jars are going with us." Kota nods, making his way to pack the pieces into a cardboard box. Odina goes to unhook pictures from the wall. She muffles a sob. *Mom is trying to be stronger than she actually is.*

"My father might have a solution for the sun predicament." Mato marches to the wall phone. "There's no way he'll be safe in the car for 12 hours."

Kota stops packing the box. "12 hours?" He wonders. "Where are we going?"

"Your Grandad offered us shelter in Chicago." Mato dials numbers into the phone.

"Oh…"

His father places the receiver to his ear. "We have little time to pack, so please hurry."

Kota picks up his speed, moving faster than a normal human. The countertops are cleared within seconds. So are the walls. Odina shrieks, holding her chest. He regrets this reckless choice. His mother is disturbed by his inhuman motions. "I didn't mean to… I'm sorry."

"It's fine." She lies, composing her terror. "This is the last box. You can begin packing your room."

He hoists the box and walks normally to the front door. The rez officers survey the house from their cruisers. Bly's eyes burn into Kota's with much distrust. Five cop cars line the side of the street. Neighbors sit on their porches, watching the Ahoka house.

Dyani is in the car with her head in her hands, weeping. Kota stacks the box in the trunk, then approaches the back door of the wagon. "Are you alright…?"

"Just get away from me!!" Her eyes shoot daggers at him. "You ruined everything!!"

The words wound his soul; he winces as an abused puppy would. He slinks away, returning inside with his shoulders slumped. His bedroom is where he goes. Kota views a closet full of clothes. His bed, then his dresser; full of peg dolls, painted warriors, and chiefs. Horse figurines, wooden flutes, dream catchers, handmade pottery, feather headdresses. His brows knit together. He caresses the pottery bowls he created.

I shouldn't pack these. Or anything in the room. That'll only bring aching memories. Memories of belonging somewhere I can't reach anymore.

Kota fixes the bedsheets and tidies up the floor. He packs nothing. His pale eyes mournfully sweep over the room before closing the door.

His parents hustle out of the house with boxes. Kota helps. This time he's sure to avoid using his speed abilities. The living room and dining room are full of taped boxes. He hoists three with ease. Once the house is cleared, he and his father head to the garage.

The doghouse that he wanted to craft for Dyani is there. A work in progress, only an outline of planks, no base or coloring. The wood shop textbook lies on the counter, opened on page *105*.

"You should give it to your sister; it may brighten her mood."

"I'll leave it…"

"Are you sure?" Mato frets. "It'll be a nice gift for her?"

"I'm sure."

His father's light brown eyes drop to the floor. "Remember this?" He stares over the tiny garage. "Yeah… it took five days."

"Only because you complained about hand cramps." Mato sniggers.

Kota eyes the shelves full of tools. "I wish we didn't have to leave… I wish none of this happened."

Mato hugs him. "I do too… we all do. But we'll overcome this. Home is where the family is, not where the land resides."

"How can you be so sure there's hope?"

His father breaks away, resting his hands on his son's shoulders. "Because you're not a lost cause… you're just lost. We'll find a solution. Your mother and I promise you this. So does your granddad."

"I'll never belong anywhere… no matter where we go, people will react the same way."

"As long as you have us, you'll have normalcy." His dad declares with certainty. "Speaking of normalcy. We have an answer for the sun. An emblem. Once we're done clearing the garage, the mark will be placed on your skin."

It doesn't take long to clean up, since only tools are within. They load each into a large box, then tape it up. Kota tapes sideways as his father does the middle. This is the last package to hit the trunk. Dyani still pines in the backseat, wiping her inflamed eyes.

The cops examine him from their jeeps, keeping note of Kota's actions as if he's a bear ready to pounce. They watch from the windows as if hunting in the woods; cautious and alert. The officers trace his every step. A few hold shotguns across their laps. Kota eyes the hair-triggers…where their fingers rest.

Odina follows his line of sight, noticing the violent switches. "Come, walela (hummingbird)." She calls for her child. He joins her on the porch. "Aren't you taking this?" She points at the mailbox he crafted. "I'm sure it took hours. We could hang it at Grandad's."

"We could." Mato agrees. Kota grins faintly. His mother removes it from the porch wall and hands it to him.

"Let's begin the marking. Come inside." His Mom leads him to the dining room. There are smudge bowls on the table, full of crushed herbs and dark liquid. "Have a seat." Kota sits. The clinking from the bowls fills the room; the gentle sound eases him.

I wonder what the symbol will consist of. I've seen sun markings before. I'm not sure if a normal one will aid my skin. Wouldn't it just draw more sun??? I hope this goes to plan. I trust Grandad. After all, he was once a Speller…meaning he has great knowledge.

The touch of the dark liquid on his skin is cooling, not painful. He's thankful for this; the last time it burned him badly. Kota breathes softly. The ringing and the cold massage on his skin are comforting.

Mato and Odina use their fingertips to paint a complex sign upon his skin. A bold circle marks the center; from it, an array of uneven lines expand. The art resembles a cross with jagged spikes. The cutoff design is clean and bold.

CHAPTER 13: SHIFT

Come midnight, they leave their home. Mato shuts the door, locking it. He lingers for a good while; separation anxiety devours him. He blinks away tears before turning away. Odina and Kota buckle into the wagon while he steps to a cop car. Bly rolls down the window. Mato hands over the house key.

"The spare is—"

"On the third windowpane… I haven't forgotten."

"Right…" He gives a long face. "I guess this is farewell, brother."

"It is…" Bly rolls up the window. "Farewell."

Mato glides to the wagon and straps in. The street is touched by hazy moonlight. The roofs of the cop cars glisten under the pale shine. Mato adjusts the rearview mirror, then reverses from the driveway.

The tires roll on the gravel towards the street. The five officer cruisers whirl the sirens twice before the engines are revved up. Mato steers the wagon ahead, his chin held high. The neighbors exit their houses to watch the exile. Elders, adults, teens, and children. They all bear the protective arrow symbol on their faces, jaws, foreheads, and noses. The quiet is forsaken. Their disgust is immovable and crippling.

One police car swerves around the wagon. The chief drives with his partner. He bans the family with a scowl, then speeds ahead to lead the way. The other four cars cage the wagon like a box. Odina takes hold of her husband's hand as he guides the car forward. Dy cries, hugging her arms around her legs.

Kota catches sight of the residents through the side mirror. All of them linger into the street, surveying their departure through the peak of the midnight moon. The small mountain town fades away in the distance, swallowed by farmland.

The cops trigger the siren lights, which strobe the wagon in red, white, and blue. His father keeps his chin high to appear tough. Kota knows he's just as emotional as his mother. Especially when the car passes a horse field. The majestic animals graze the grass in dim moonlight.

All of their attention go to the galloping animals, recalling all the riding games. *It all seems to appear vividly before Kota. Capturing the flag from one another while on horseback. His human days. When his skin was as it should be… not comatose. When his sister loved him. When his mother wasn't weeping. When his father wasn't scared. How the flag waved through the wind. How it was passed between their hands in competition. How warm their hands were.*

He stares down at his cold ones. Tears drip past his porcelain cheeks. The plain fields stretch as far as the eye can see. *There's no escape from how he and his family ran through the tall weeds, playing hide and seek. Or the picnics they hosted in the tall grass. The fun. The joy. The sense of belonging.*

Kota shuts his eyes to end the memories playing out before him. Droplets of tears continue to fall. The ride is quiet all the way to the state line. The chief's car circles around to join the other four. Each car shields the border, uniting side by side to show force. Mato inspects the vehicles through the rearview. A frown is present on his handsome face. His brown eyes reveal how forlorn he truly is. He inhales roughly…deep…to the core.

The wagon passes through a lonely country road. Odina looks back at Kota, concerned. She reaches a hand back to hold his. His mother doesn't jump from the iciness of his skin. She tolerates it.

Hours pass. The wagon travels through open fields. The sun grows high. Kota opens his eyes to view it. The golden rays no longer buzz violently or set him aflame. The voice is no longer present. He hears nothing from the fiend that once corrupted him. The marking worked. He's bathed in sunlight without any discomfort. The paleness of his skin glimmers instead of burning. He almost looks human. Almost. The orange lighting gives the illusion of his normal complexion.

"Any pain?" His father peeps back at him.

"No… there's no pain."

"Good." Mato is relieved. His mother's hand still embraces his, although she's asleep. Dyani is resting too. He attempts to place his hand atop hers, yearning for sisterly affection. But halts. *My temperature will only scare her awake.* He withdraws his hand regrettably. "Give her time."

His son sighs. "How much?"

"As much as she needs… and take as much as you need. That's all we can do." His father eyes the divided sky, half dawn, half night. The stars are still visible. "Remember our game?"

"How many stars."

"Count as many as you can."

This was the way his dad got him to fall asleep as a kid. He'd tuck him into bed, then open his bedroom window. Kota recalls this as if a movie rolling on a screen. His father always said, *tell me how many there are in the morning.* He starts counting in his head… knowing now that he's older that it's impossible to get to the end. There are billions of stars in the galaxy.

He uses this game to rest his mind. *The white dots distract him.* 1. 2. 3. 4. 5. 6. 7. 8. 9. 10. 11. 12. 13. 14. 15.16.17.18.19.20.

Kota rests his eyes again. He doesn't sleep; he just sees darkness. No dreams. Only the wind rushing against the metal frame of the car. He reflects on the sound. Hoping to find balance, all he finds is his stomach sinking into an endless pit.

By sundown, the farmlands are gone. The skyline of Chicago engulfs the horizon. Towering skyscrapers made of white lights. Yellow streetlamps. The fresh scent of Lake Michigan. The expressway guides them past congested buildings. The streets are compact. There's little nature. Concrete blocks out the ground where there should be grass. The trees are skinny and frail. The trash-filled pavements show no unity.

This place is colder than his dead soul. I don't like how dangerous it feels. Or the depressing atmosphere. There's no community like back home. Everyone here are strangers…nothing more. There's no harmony… the littering is proof of this.

The homeless camping on the sidewalk stings his heart. The sight is never-ending. Each corner hosts those who are down on their luck. *This is a prison.* The air smells of coal, most likely from the nearby factories off-loading toxins. He activates his super hearing to isolate the sound of machines hissing fumes from factory pipes.

The dark city is barely illuminated. Shadowy side roads and alleys line the way. Glass shards shatter the asphalt of the street. Burned-down apartment complexes. Torn-down brick buildings. Abandoned churches with boarded-up windows. Kota eyes the stained glass. The multicolored hue portrays artwork of angels.

I guess their god has forsaken them the same as mine did me. This is where the hopeless end up. A hell on earth. His sight goes to the electrical lines stretching from pole to pole. The static noise pricks his ears, zapping.

Where are the stars? In Oklahoma, the night sky is a firefly show. This place…is a void. How can that be? Even the moon is foggy, instead of clear.

A brick home is where the car pauses. Mato parks the wagon on the petite street and powers off the vehicle. The headlights fizz off, surrounding them in darkness. "Wake your sister."

Kota decides he can't do the same. Dyani will hate his touch, so he speaks instead. "Dy, wake up. We're here." She mumbles awake, wiping her eyes.

The front door of the house opens. Kota looks to find his grandfather stepping on the porch in an orange poncho, which is just as cheerful as his grin.

KAYLA

The girls eye the bookshelf full of grimoires. They're spooked by the literature. Jia is pale as a sheet. Mya is trying to keep it together, but anxiety overtakes her voice. "So… your mom said they are just prank books, right?"

"Yes…but my grandma has been passing them down forever. I think that's a bit too much for a prank."

"Which one did you read?" Jia's voice is wobbly.

"The one from 400 B.C."

"Halloween is tomorrow…you're just getting into the spirit. That explains the dream." Mya concludes to ease her own nerves.

The trio gaze at the first book atop the shelf. The binding on the side reads: **Spell Benders: Runes and Incantations**.
"What's a Spell Bender?" Jia questions.

"I have no clue…" Kay exhales slowly, trying to steady her breath. The walls feel tighter, the air heavier. Her heart pounds like a warning drum in her chest. The room presses in with a silent weight, crawling under her skin. Every instinct in her body screams to run—but her legs stay frozen. "I didn't ask my mom about that yet."

"Have you called your granny?"

"No."

"You should."

"Jia, stop, it's just a joke."

"We don't know that for sure."

"I'm not pulling a joke, Mya! I know the difference between a dream and the real world!"

"Okay, okay, fine. But I don't buy it until I see it."

"I'm not saying another spell! It's too scary!"

"I'm not suggesting that." Mya breathes. "Where's the Ouija board? If there is a presence, we can call on it."

"That's not smart." Kayla turns away from them to hide her panic. "Whatever is in these books is evil…" The stillness of the room is eerie. Even the motion outside fails to penetrate the windows. Usually there's the sound of city ambience…but there's nothing. Kayla clears her throat to add a disturbance to atmosphere. "Maybe it was a dream. Just forget it."

Jia walks to lay a hand on Kayla's back. "Yeah…that's probably the best thing to do. Forget about it. We can focus on something else."

"Like shopping for our costumes." Mya suggests. "We could go to the cinema and see *Never Cry Wolf.* Then sneak to party."

"I'm not sure about sneaking out."

"Me either." Kay agrees with Jia. "Let's go shopping. I don't like being in this room!!" The menacing atmosphere returns to attack her nerves. Her skin tightens with goosebumps. Her breaths labor with her heart. Kay flees from the bedroom and into the powder room. She closes the door and locks it. Her shaky hands twist the cold-water faucet. She douses her face in the icy liquid.

Louds knocking from the door startles her. "KAYLA??! KAYLA???!!" Her friends shout. Their fists banging on the wood.

Kay hyperventilates. The wind encounter revisits her mind. *The hammering breeze. The trembling glass. The roaring tornado outside. The shuddering walls and overflowing vents. The creepy humming, in a language she doesn't understand. The spell book spoke to me?! Why?? It was very delicate. The force could have easily harmed me, but it didn't. Did it want me to listen… just as it listened to me?? I ordered it to stop, and it did. The entity seemed conscious.*

A knife is stuck through the side of the door to pry it open.. Kayla stops drowning her face and towels it dry. Her girls stumble in, almost falling over one another.

"You scared the hell out of us!! Why did you do that?!" Mya snaps.

"I'm fine."

"Are you sure??!!" Jia is out of breath.

"Yeah… I'm sure." Kay hangs up the towel. "Let's head to the mall." She hustles out of the restroom to the elevator.

Kay is as quiet as a church mouse on the bus. She sits at the back; her crew follows after her. Their eyes never leaving her alarmed face. Kayla spots the two whispering something, but she pays them no mind.

Maybe I should call Grandma? What if she can explain what was in the room with me? Or what if she tells me it's a load of crap? I don't know what to do. Do I avoid it? Then again, how can I? I'll always pass the room and see the bookcase. There's no avoiding it.

The mall is full. It's Thursday. Everyone is here since it's the usual hot spot hangout. The only differences are the attire and the music. *Monster Mash* blasts from the ceiling speakers. It's Halloween Eve. Many wear costumes. Skeletons, clowns. Magicians.

Witches. Skater kids roll their boards down stair railings, dressed as prison inmates in striped jumpsuits.

Children race through play bins dressed as cowboys, cowgirls, Barbie dolls, and stormtroopers. Many bungee-jump from the ceiling, dressed as vampires. Their flowy capes ripple the air. Their sharp teeth and blood-stained clothing complete the look. The food court tables are full. Kayla spies many *Lord of the Rings* characters. She's surprised by a group of Archangels. The white wings attached to their backs are impressive and mechanical as they waver the air.

The three ascend the escalators. Upstairs is smoky and full of thick cobwebs. A man dressed as a spider startles them by jumping from behind a corner. Jia squeaks. Mya shudders from the eight wiggling legs. Kayla covers her eyes due to a bug phobia. A clan of women dressed as cheerleaders cartwheel past them.

Kayla laughs, cheering them on. "We need to learn how to do that!" Her glum mood loosens up enough that she can interact normally.

"Deal, let's master cartwheels by New Year's." Mya holds her hand out to pinky swear. Jia and Kayla close the swear with their pinkies.

"Now, what are we going as tomorrow?"

"We can buy the blue dresses and get tiaras."

"No, that's so typical." Mya scoffs. "We can do better than that."

The girls pass by storefronts full of Halloween costumes and masks. Kayla observes a fairy one. It's green and shiny. The dress has puffy sleeves and wings attached to the backside. It's regal and otherworldly. Something Tinkerbell would wear. "How about fairies?"

"Not bad." Mya inspects the dress from top to bottom. "We'll have to cut the hem. It's too long. We want to look hot…not like Mormons."

After buying the fairy outfits, the trio hit the food court for burgers and milkshakes. Kay relaxes her mind over the spell, convincing herself it's nothing. She chooses to be silly instead of scared of the unknown. She lives in the moment with her friends. Kayla cover her mouth with an ice cream mustache.

"Ahh…my skills of art have reached their peak!" Kay deepens her voice to sound like a wise old man. "I shall retire the craft!"

"BRAVO. BRAVO!" Jia claps her on. "Great guru

"stache…however did you get so grand??"

"I was born this way, my dear summer child!" Kay adds more ice cream to her mustache, creating curling ends like a comic book villain.

Mya cackles at the nonsense. "I am the only grand artist here!" She dips her finger into her shake to scoop up enough cream to draw a fluffy beard on her chin. "Beards hold the highest power…now bow to me!" She roleplays an epic voice.

"Oh, no…a battle!" Jia throws up dramatic hands. "Whatever shall we do??"

"A BATTLE IT IS!" Kay stands from her seat.

"Yes…I duel you…" Mya hops up to, grabbing her milkshake straw to use it as a sword. "Grab your sword."

Kayla roughly yanks her straw from her shake, slopping cream all over, splashing her friends face and her own. Jia falls to the floor in gut wrenching giggles. Mya wiggles her straw at Kay, beginning a play fight.

If the night had said this way. If only a nightmare didn't ruin the joy of the night.

At the stroke of midnight, Kayla experiences the scariest dream of her life. She finds herself in a black void. The sound of wind rush her way, yet she can't see anything. The darkness is absolute. Her hands and body aren't visible. The rolling wave booms her way.

Kay flees from the thrashing air, running as fast as she can down the sightless abyss. The *Spell Bender* book glows on a white pedestal in the distance. Kayla's feet pound towards it. The book soars above the shining pedestal and floats mid-air. The sound of the heavy wind behind her now travels above her head. Kay looks up… finding the impossible.

A figure made of complete air flies above her. Kay is awestruck; her feet pause as she gawks at the entity. The graceful manner in which it glides the air is fascinating. The humming carol from before returns. She didn't understand the words when she first heard them. Now they are clear as day. The foreign language emitting from the being is translated to English.

"Spell Bender 13. The time has come to metamorph." The transparent being lands beside the opened spell book. Its glowing eyes fixate on her chocolate ones. She swears its irises are made of white fire. The sizzling brightness of its eyes blaze out the darkness. The surroundings burst with whiteness.

Kayla jerks awake in her princess bed, holding her pounding chest. Kay gulps, wrestling crazed gasping. The moonlight sparkles across her bedroom, casting diamond patterns along the walls. She leaves the bed, going to a window to open it for fresh air. Kay chokes on the cold breeze, noticing that she's sweating. Her trembling hands wipe her wet forehead.

What in the world was that dream? And what did the air spirit mean by "Spell Bender 13??" There was a message to the nightmare. A meaning behind the word metamorph. But what am I supposed to change into? Kay stares at the moon… confused.

CHAPTER 14: THE VEIL

KOTA

Kota observes the moon from a tiny bedroom. He wasn't able to sleep… since he's dead. Rest isn't needed. Although his family begs to differ. His parents and sister are resting from the long drive. Nothing much has happened concerning his condition. His grandfather is still spelling the necklace. Kota hears him chanting in Cherokee from the kitchen.

I'm glad I can be somewhat normal. It's not a permanent change, but it's close enough. I can never remove the pendant. I can't morph into a demon again. I can't kill again. There's no need for my hands to be bloodier than they already are.

He leaves the windowpane, deciding to go see his grandfather so his thoughts don't depress him. The pleasant old man sits at the kitchen table, clutching the necklace in both hands while reciting. His eyes are closed as he cites an incantation on repeat. Kota doesn't understand most of it. It sounds ethereal. Ancient. The words *Great Spirit* is recognized amongst the elegant gibberish. His grandson remains silent, not wanting to interrupt. He listens to his sleeping sister, hoping she won't hate him after the pendant is around his neck. *Will she ever trust me again? Am I still her little brother?*

"There is no need to stress, Kota." His grandad's wispy voice interrupts his inner monologue.

"I'm not." He lies.

"I know how to read energy." The elder says, with his eyes still shut. "I see through senses, not just my eyes. Thanks to my connection to the spirit world."

"Spirit world??"

"Yes… there are many entities in this universe. Mostly consisting of natural elements and senses. Sight, Sound. Touch. Earth, Fire, Water… and air. Each one visits me in my dreams."

"They visit you??"

"Yes." The calm old man nods. "Us spellers draw from each source to harness power." The necklace glows white in his hands. Grandad opens his gray stone eyes. "And now our collaboration is done." He stands, wobbling a bit, so he grips the table.

Kota dashes over with the speed of light to steady the elder. "Wado, (Thank you)."

"Gvlielitseha, (You're welcome)."

"I enchanted it to para-bond to your skin, so it'll never slip off or part from your flesh." His Grandfather raises the wooden jewelry. The centerpiece displays a three-arrow symbol. Two for evil spirits and one for protection. He drapes it over his grandson's neck. The white glow gives off a warm heat signature onto his skin.

Kota analyze as the light parts into lines. The pale lines travel down his chest in unison. They squiggle and swerve to the middle and stop. The pattern of each is just as artistic as a Picasso painting. Abstract artwork in motion. He gawks. Even when the brightness disappears from his chest, he still gapes in astonishment.

"Wow!"

"That is the easy part."

"What's the hard part?"

His Grandfather cleans wooden scraps from the table, using his hand to scoop the mess from the surface and into his palm. The pieces blaze into white fire, then incinerate. "The hard part is locating another speller. I hope I am not the only one in this region."

"What if you are?"

"Then… I'll have to search beyond to find one. I can only offer the easing of your senses. A more powerful speller could possibly uncover a cure."

"A cure?? You think there's one out there?!"

"Nature always has a balance. Light and dark. Evil and pure. Every illness has a medicine… be it from the earth's soil or the doings of a celestial deity." Grandfather beams at him with all the positivity in the world. "There is always hope."

"How fast can it get here?"

"Once your parents are well rested, we will perform the incantation. It will take all three of our energies. We will have to bind our blood in order to discover another speller."

"How long does that take?"

"That depends on how far the person is. It may take hours… or minutes. Unfortunately, geography is an issue in this world as well as in the realm." He jokes with a chuckle.

"I didn't know there was another realm."

"Yes… as above…so below. A carbon copy of this world…only enhanced by spirits. It lives in those who share a bloodline with the first immortals…as our family does."

"But Dyani and I aren't magical…"

"The ability to cast is available to your sister if she activates it. As for you… I fear the dead cannot summon." He grimaces.

"If there is a cure… can I?"

"Yes... but the path to rejuvenation is never as easy as it sounds. There are more of your kind roaming this planet. Who wish to purge darkness from their soul just as you do. Hypothetically, if there is a cure, there will be a hunt for it."

Is Grandad right? Are there more like me? I've pondered this before. I'm sure I'm not the only vampire besides the one who turned me. And I'm sure I'm not the only one wishing for mortality to return. I wonder if those vampires can be located. There must be a way to pinpoint like-minded souls. I'd rather not journey on my own for the cure. A team would be better. But I'm getting ahead of myself. As Grandad said... this is all hypothetical.

I need to focus on now... not a what if scenario. Once my parents are awake, they'll find someone to help me further. Someone who can give me more than supped jewelry. I just hope it doesn't take long. I'm restless. Great Spirit, if you still care for me, please make this speedy. I know I'm lost to you, but as a parting gift, please bless me with the key to all of this.

KAYLA

Kayla twirls the cord of the wall phone. She wraps her fingers in and out of the loops. The receiver hums. It's 6 a.m. She's been up since midnight debating if she should make this call. Her drowsy eyes are skittish. The rustling wind outside scares her. She jumps and covers her mouth to muffle a scream. *Yeah... I need to make this call. I hope she's awake. My grandma is an early bird. Whenever she visits, she's up at 5 a.m. sharp. I'm sure she's awake.*

The line clicks. "Good morning, Mary." Her grandma has a raspy voice. She could be a jazz singer.

"It's not Mom, it's me."

"Hi, Kayla. Are you calling to add to your Christmas list?"

"No... it's about something else."

"What is it, sweet child?"

I should just spit it out. Why am I trying to rephrase my thoughts? If anyone will believe me, it'll be her. "I had an encounter with Mom's spell book. I think I'm going crazy. I had a nightmare about an air spirit." Her words rush out. "It called me a Spell Bender. Mom told me the books were collected by you. That's why I'm calling. I don't know who else to tell. Mom thinks it's a joke. My friends don't know how to help." Kay's breathing hitches in her throat, suffocating her. The phone line is quiet for some time. She side-eyes the receiver, afraid of what her grandmother will say.

Does she even believe in this? Did I make a fool of myself?

"IT HAS HAPPENED!!" Her grandma celebrates. "Your mother never unlocked the gene; that's why she said it's a joke. OH, MY SWEETHEART, WELCOME TO OUR LEGACY! ASK ME ANYTHING!"

She squints at the phone, bewildered by what she's just heard. "What do you mean by 'our legacy??"

"I'll fly in next week to guide you through this. You should be full of pride, not fear. We've had magic coursing through our veins for centuries! We're one with the first immortals."

Kay tightly massages her forehead; her temples crease from the tautness of her fingertips. "What are you talking about? Immortal beings?"

"Spell Benders. Lycans…Vampires!"

Kayla's mind flashes back to history class. To Cliff… who she assumed was silly. *"VAMPIRE?!"* His stunned voice rings her ears. The title of the assignment resurfaces: **THE LOST WWI VAMPIRE DUGOUT /THE UNDERGROUND WAR.**

The phone drops from her hands, banging to the floor. Kayla's eyes widen. The sight of sharp teeth dripping with blood. A revelation of hellfire eyes peering out of darkness. Of an inhuman figure soaring the air. She makes out blonde hair. Kay wedges her hands against her eyes, pressing down hard. Hard enough that her eyelids are spotted with silvery pressure.

WHAT IS THAT?? WHAT AM I SEEING??! She backs away from the wall phone. *NO WAY!! THERE'S NO SUCH THING AS VAMPIRES!!!*

Kay runs to the restroom to drown her face in chilly water, fighting for air. "No… that's not possible. Vampires are fake. People dress up as them on Halloween." She recalls the costume goers from the mall. The bungee jumping crew free-falling from the ceiling. Their flowy capes rippling behind them. Their sharp teeth bloodstained. "No… it's made up. It's all made up…" Kay mutters, convincing her mind to disregard what her grandmother just tells her. *But what was that vision? Was it another nightmare happening outside my sleep??*

I think it was a man… but he had red eyes and was flying through the air. Humans don't do that. She sits on the cool bathroom floor, her head in her hands. Her mind whirl pooling. *What if it's true? I don't understand why Grandma would lie; she's not the type to enjoy scaring people. Halloween isn't even her favorite holiday.*

Is it true? Are there really vampires?? Are there really werewolves?? Are there really Spell Benders??

The school hour approaches, so Kay gets up from the floor and goes to shower. The icy cold water relaxes her tense shoulders. But her mind is still erratic. *Am I part of a legacy?? That would explain how I was able to summon air. Why did that wind entity visit my dream? What if I'm just losing my mind? No one has witnessed paranormal activity but me. Not my parents, or my friends. Could it all be in my head?? I guess there's only one way to find out.*

Tonight, my girls and I will use the Ouija board. If nothing occurs when I'm around them… it means I need psychological assistance. If something does…then I'll finally have a solid answer.

Photography class is full of teens in scary costumes. Zombies, Grim Reapers, Devils, Witches… and of course, Vampires. Kayla inches to her desk, scared of the fake bloody teeth. Her green fairy costume contrasts lovely on her dark skin. Her face of glitter and sparkling wings shine in the sunny classroom. Jia sports the same look, only her tan skin is sprinkled with gold glitter instead of white.

Ms. Ruby chose to be Morticia from the Addams Family. Although her bubbly demeanor offsets the character. She's too down to earth to be evil. She uses orange chalk to draw a huge smiley face on the blackboard. "Good morning, Class!" she sings in an eerie tone.

"Good morning, Ms. Ruby!" The class matches her spookiness.

"Happy Halloween. Today we'll be capturing a picture of something unusual."

One girl raises her hand. "What do you mean by unusual?"

"Out of the ordinary… or bizarre. Think of it as a scavenger hunt. I've hidden figurines. Locate them to complete today's assignment."

Jia claps enthusiastically and peers at Kayla. "Yay!! Come on!" She springs from her chair, looping her arm into Kay's. "Time for a scavenger hunt!" Jia skips over to collect their camera from a tray. Then she springs out into the hall, forcing Kayla to do the same. "What's wrong? You're so quiet."

"I didn't get much sleep."

"Was it another bad dream?" Her friend grimaces.

"Yeah…"

"Hmmm… I wonder what it means?"

The truth will definitely make her burst out in laughter. I wouldn't even be able to say it with a straight face. I'll be too embarrassed. No one will believe that I'm part of a supernatural legacy. I barely believe it myself. "Anyway… let's search for the figurines."

"Okay." Jia releases Kay's arm, heading to a fire extinguisher.

Kayla checks behind bulletin boards and underneath rugs. Finding nothing. She continues hunting. Behind water fountains. In between the cracks of lockers. Underneath classroom doors… and atop door ledges. The two meet up to scour the girl's restroom. The sinks and stalls are clear of any figurines. The paper towel machine as well.

Hmm… Ms. Ruby hid it well. "It must be in the hall… but I don't know where else to look."

"Me either." Jia sighs. "This is a tough cookie!" The girls go back to the hallway to examine it. Kayla eyes the windows… the panes are spotless, empty. Jia follows her line of sight, gasping. "You found one!" She races to the window.

Kay is clueless by what she means… until Jia's fingers pry a silver ornament from the lining of the window. It's a creepy character. One Kayla seems to be haunted by today. A vampire figurine. The jagged ends of the cape cover its feet; the rest of the cloak spans out as bat wings would. The mouth is carved like razors. Its eyes are dotted red.

Kay's forehead prickles; a cold sweat lathers it. Her temperature drops. Her heart wreaks havoc on her ribcage. Jia doesn't notice any of this because she's too busy framing the item into the camera. When she snaps the picture, the devil eyes on the figurine flicker back in response.

Law class brings on even more ghastly costumes. Mummies. Pirates. The Joker. Aliens. Bigfoot. The Exorcist. Frankenstein. Kayla is thankful that there aren't any vampires in this period. Still, she's unhinged. Her skin is clammy. *I must look sick… or do I look as if I added makeup to moisten my face?? Is the sheen on my forehead disturbing anyone? Or is it assumed to be part of my costume?*

Izzy is Snow White with a gothic twist. Her pale skin and black hair is uncanny; she looks just like the Disney Princess. A carbon copy… only with navy blue eyes instead of brown. The blue dress is a corset with mixtures of black lace, crocheted into spiderweb patterns. Even the ruby-colored bow headpiece features knitted designs. "Hey fairy girl, where's your wand?"

"I don't think fairies have wands." Kay corrects her.

"But they have magic… unless it comes out of your hands." Izzy ponders. "Like Tinkerbell and her pixie dust."

Fred howls deafeningly from behind Kay, who yelps and slips out of her chair to the floor. "WHOA… SORRY!" His hairy arms hoist her back into her seat. He's a red-haired werewolf; the fur on the outfit covers every inch of his body. He sports an X-Men Wolverine-Esque beard. His olive skin is painted gray, yet his freckles are still visible. "I'll howl softer next time."

"No… don't worry about it." Kay giggles haphazardly. "Nice jump scare."

"Thanks, hon."

Chester cosplays Gene Simmons from KISS. His long hair is tazed to look frizzy and puffy. The black and white face paint creates bat wings across his dark eyes. The leather, spiky getup is spot on, complete with metal beading.

Judge Smith sits at the podium. He wears no costume, just his normal law attire. He's strict as usual as he bangs the gavel. "Since it is Halloween, I will construct a scenario that is fitting. You all will state the crime and jail time."

"Is today actually going to be good??" Fred whispers to Kay. "Maybe he has a funny bone after all."

"Ehh… I still think he's a robot." She shrugs… then her bones go stiff. *Is there such a thing as a cyborg in the immortal world? Or does it draw the line there? Or is everything from the movies real?* She dismisses the topic, sensing goosebumps forming on her arms.

"That's amazing FX makeup!!" Chester inspects her bumpy arms, unaware that they're from the coldness submerging her body.

Judge Smith bangs his gavel. "Silence! Listen!" His intimidating tone booms the room. "Here is the scenario. You are all in the point of view of the judge. The trial consists of a stolen body from a graveyard. The plaintiff is seeking reparations for corruption of company property and justice for the affected family. How will the defendant be charged?"

Kayla browses her mind, trying to work out an answer. *We've studied this before… a while back. What were the crime and jail time? I need to remember.*

"Indecent activity?" Chester gives an unsure estimate.

"No."

Izzy squints. Her rosy cheeks are dimpled due to her pouting her lips. "There's no jail time…the company can sue for tampering, though."

"Incorrect."

Fred grumbles to himself. "It's a felony…"

"A felony of what class act?" One student tries opening their book, hiding it beneath their desk. Smith catches this. "No cheating…books down!" The student snaps it shut and sits straight in their chair.

Kayla rummages her mind. *Come on… I can remember this! THINK. THINK! I can't give the wrong answer. I'll hate myself for it. I'm top of the class… Smith expects better from me… just as my parents do. I can't be a disappointment.* She flexes her brain's cortex, forcing a memory to come back. "Body snatching would be the crime." She begins, still turning the wheels of her brain for the rest of the answer.

"Correct… now what is the felony class and jail sentence?"

Come on, mind… third eye… or whatever. REMEMBER!! An old foresight of a textbook page surfaces in her mind. Black words on white read: class 4 felony. Her mind's eye scrolls down to read the rest of the page. Penalty of 1 to 2 years. She recites from memory, "Class 4 felony… with a sentence of 1 to 2 years."

Smith grins slightly…this simple motion shocks the whole class. Their flabbergasted expressions are priceless. "Correct, Ms. Harris. Congratulations. You've won the class candy." He stands from the podium with a jumbo cauldron of sweets. "Happy Halloween, come get your sweets!"

Everyone applauds Kayla. She blushes from the attention. Izzy winks at her. Fred howls. Chester plays an air guitar.

Wow, that was cool. I was worried I wouldn't remember. My photographic memory came in handy. Although it felt as if I was revisiting the past more than a memory. My mind's eye was actively reading the page…in real time. Is the third eye a true ability? Did I just use it to travel backwards?

CHAPTER 15: SACRAMENTAL

In the lunchroom, Kayla receives a standing ovation. "SHE CRACKED THE ROBOT!!!" Fred screeches. "WE'VE FINALLY BROKE SMITH!!" He escorts her through the lunch line as if she's a celebrity, holding his hands out. "Sorry, no pictures. Kayla Harris has no comment on the matter."

"You're dumb." She chuckles.

"I accept that label, superstar." "What's all the ruckus?" Mya asks.

"Your girl here made Smith smile… although it was very Mona Lisa. Still, it counts as a win."

"I won candy for the class."

"You guys are lying… that guy is incapable of emotion."

"Crap… we should have taken a picture." Fred places his hands on his hips. "Quick, let's go back and act it out!"

"Why didn't you cut it??" Mya stares at the long hem on Kay's dress. The hem on hers is cut into a diamond pattern, aesthetically jagged. "Let's go to the restroom." "Can I watch?" Fred flirts.

"In your dreams." Mya scoffs with disgust.

"So, you're saying there's a chance when I'm sleep tonight?" Mya takes Kay by the hand and steers her through the crowd.

In History, the class drafts a paper on the dugout. Each of them read from the textbook while taking notes:

After November 1918, all deep dugouts, including Vampire, were abandoned. When the troops left, the subterranean structures slowly submerged. After the removal of weaponry by military clean-up teams, the Belgian locals recovered the dugout and reverted it for farming.

This information eases her mind. *Okay, so the place isn't full of vampires, just locals who profit from the landmark. I can rest my mind now. The dugout doesn't hold any paranormal beasts below the surface.*

KOTA

Mom and Dad woke early this morning. Unfortunately, they have to prepare for the casting… meaning I must wait longer. They aren't as strong as Grandad, so they have to link to him. He described it as para-bonding, this time with humans, not an object. I wonder how attached they will become. My necklace is welded to my skin… latched on like glue. Will their energies mash to mine like second skin?

The three of them huddle on the floor in a circle of herbs. There is no symbol on the wood flow this time; instead, the mark is on their foreheads. A looping sign with two points on each end. The sign for energy in Cherokee. The color against their brown skin is charcoal black.

He and his sister watch the ritual. Dyani's heart is speeding so fast. *Is this scaring her? Are the chants freaking her out? I guess she's still getting used to magic. This is new for both of us. Something we assumed was made up for fairytales and Halloween. Which is today. Today is Halloween. Out of all the days for a séance to take place, it must be today. The evilest day there is.*

Our household never celebrates it. The Great Spirit is the only thing we worship. A spirit of purity. Halloween is about darkness being idolized by humans. The glorification of death it brings is disgusting. Even more now than ever. I guess because I'm part of the dead cult now.

By sundown, the refrain is done. Grandad retrieves a map of downtown Chicago, laying it across the floor. "Now for the drawing of blood."

"Look away..." Mato cautions Kota, who does so.

He doesn't trust that the necklace will stop me from craving blood. I'm a creature who lives for it. The slicing of the knife on their palms is detailed. The ripping of their skin… the blood oozing from their wounds. The sizzling. The mouthwatering tease. The sweet…tantalizing aroma is irresistible. Kota strains to subdue himself. He stops inhaling air… although his pupils dilate.

"Kota??!" Dy croaks.

"I'm fine…!" He replies with forced obedience. *I won't hurt my family.* The dripping blood on the map is arousing. It dries out his throat, like sandpaper. Kota squeezes his eyes shut to block out the taboo request. *Humans don't feast on humans…I must keep training myself to believe this. I must…in case there is a cure.*

"You can look now." His father states.

He turns around, discovering that the blood is no more… now the trails are white fire. The flaming lines travel the map in unison, curving along the paper in a hive mind. The inferno browses the map… searching for another speller. Spanning from the west side, where they are, to the east. Downtown.

Kota dissects the motion of the white inferno maneuvering past streets, parking lots, and skyscrapers. Nearing the lake. It seems as if the flames will never halt…the speed doesn't slow. Grandad collects the herbs to light them aflame in his bare hands. The fire on the map pause its path to circle a skyscraper. The blaze burns out…

leaving a ring of ash. Grandad spreads the fiery leaves mid-air. The heated leaves float, painting a portrait of a human. Each piece arranges into facial features. Aligning to form a heart-shaped face profile, button nose, almond eyes, and bushy hair with curls on the ends.

Kayla Harris.

KAYLA

"I thought you wanted to forget this?" Mya bickers with Kay, who lays a Ouija board on the floor of her parents' bedroom.

"I changed my mind."

"Why?"

"Yeah... you told us it was too scary."

"I know... but I've been seeing things." Kayla admits, taking a seat on the floor. "Crazy things... not just in my sleep. I'm having visions."

"Visions??" Jia joins her on the floor, sitting beside her.

"Can we just get on with this?" Mya checks out her makeup in a mirror; the green glitter is still spotted all over her body. "You had a bad dream, big deal..."

"No... I saw this when I was awake."

"That's not possible."

"Mya, listen to her!" Jia scowls.

She huffs heavily. "Some dreams are vivid. Like the ones where you think you're falling."

"I called my grandma this morning, and she confirmed that this is real.. She's flying out next week to help me." Mya has no retort. It's obvious that she's freaked out by how her arms hug her body. Even her shoulders are hunched now. Kay finds this odd since she was the one who suggested using the board. "You were the one who said: if there is a presence, we can call it."

"I did."

"So, what's the problem?"

"Nothing..." Mya hurries over to sit cross-legged next to Jia. She tries her best to collect her wits. "Let's just get this over with. We're supposed to be out trick-or-treating. Then off to the movies."

"Which movie?" Jia attempts to have a normal conversation, but her jittery voice exposes her anxiety. "Never Cry Wolf?"

"That's not a horror… it looks like a snooze-fest. *Eyes of Fire* seems like the best option. But it plays in 30 minutes…we'll miss the showing."

"It'll be quick." Kay holds her hands out so her friends can take one each.

The trio lock hands and peer down at the rugged Ouija board. The oak wood is thicker than an inch. The bold letters gleam under the dim lighting of the room. Beyond the window is darkness. Kay goes to open it. As she returns, she grabs the first book on the shelf, flipping to the page that has the summon incantations:

INITIATION SPELL – ENRUS DE COV
WATER SUMMANCE – AQWAV COUM AIR
SUMMANCE – WINA COUM
EARTH SUMMANCE – GRROC COUM

Her friends read the page, wondering if any of this is real. *Who would put so much effort into a prank book? The detailing, the language, the descriptions. The dated binding. The thirteen-star symbol. The thickness of the literature…hundreds of pages long.*

"Which one did you say?" Jia asks, all petrified. Her tan skin has a hint of pale.

"The air summance."

"Not the initiation one?"

"No."

"How were you able to cast without initiating?"

"I'm not sure…my gran said something about our bloodline. Maybe I don't have to speak it."

"Say it… and see what happens." Jia squeaks with curiosity.

Kay clears her throat. *Okay, here it goes. I hope it works so I don't seem like a lunatic. Or do I want it to not work?? I'm so… confused.* She shushes her racing thoughts. "Enrus De Cov."

The book before them combusts with blinding light. The room bleaches over. Pure white. The girls scream. There's nothing but brightness. The room disappears. The walls, floor, and ceiling are engulfed in burning flames. A white inferno roars and sizzles, same as the flames of hell.

"WHERE ARE WE??" Mya shrills.

"KAYLA??!! WHAT'S HAPPENING???!!!" Jia yelps.

Her ragged breaths catch in her lungs. The flaming room astonishes her. *How is this possible?? Where did my parents' bedroom go?* Kay's amazement transforms to trepidation. Prickling needles form down her arms. Dizziness follows… along with a headache. Shortness of breath. Heart palpitations. Kay almost faints. Her eyes

105

droop weakly. She's close to passing out, yet she musters enough strength to shriek, "TAKE US BACK!!!!"

The roaring fire ceases its sizzling. The brightness disappears, converting the room back to normal. The floor, ceiling, and walls morph back to reality. As soon as the whiteness is gone, her girls run for the door. Jia's sleek, brown hair flows fast behind her, same as Mya's curly mane.

"DON'T LEAVE ME!" Kay whimpers. "COME BACK!"

The bedroom door slams shut. Her besties try opening it, but the handle doesn't budge. It's frozen to the door frame. No matter how hard they pull down on the lever, it doesn't move an inch.

"I DON'T WANT TO DO THIS ANYMORE!!" Jia sobs. "LET US OUT!!!"

"DON'T LEAVE ME! I'M SCARED!" Kay's arms quiver at her sides, twitchy with apprehension.

"Then throw away the book!"

"I still have questions…I need to know why I'm number 13. I need to know if vampires are real!"

"VAMPIRES??! What the hell are you talking about??!!!" Mya quarrels. "You're being silly!!"

"I need to speak with the air god from my dream."

"Air god???" Jia shakes her head. "Okay…I tried to support you, but now you're talking nonsense!!"

Kay looks down at the book; inhaling all the oxygen she can, holding it in until her arms stop quaking. "I'm not going insane." She shuts her eyes and speaks the wind summance. "Wina Coum."

The same experience from before reoccurs. A tornado force pounds from outside the window. The glass of it thumps deafeningly, seizing their eardrums with numbness. The wind blows fiercely through the vents. The walls earthquake. This time, Kay braces herself for the intensity, so it doesn't thrust her back with its might.

The gushing air slices the room, sounding of a hurricane. The screeches from her friends are buried by the storming wind. She opens her eyes and places her finger on the indicator. A triangular piece of wood with a glass center. "Air spirit, answer me." The howling wind amplifies, debilitating the sense of sound. A whitenoise bustle, resembling that of a television. "Why am I number 13?" The indicator hovers over the bold letters, spelling out:

Y O U
A R E

T H E
K E Y
"Key to what??"
The piece floats across the Ouija board:
T O
P O W E R
"That doesn't make sense…what power??"
O F
T H E
E L E M E N T S
A N D
S E N S E S
I still don't understand what that means. Whatever, I'll ask my grandmother for better elaboration. On to the next question. "Do vampires exist?" Her cocoa eyes eagerly follow the triangle as it spells out the next answer through letters.
Y E S
Her breaths deepen, yet this realization doesn't halt her mission. She has one last question. "Are there any in Belgian, Zonnebeke? In the WWI dugout?"
B E L O W
T H E
S U R F A C E
The same prophecy from before invades her mind. Crimson eyes. A blonde-haired vampire… lunging through the air. Only there are new additions. The surroundings aren't covered in darkness this time. It's dawn. There's a burnt-out campfire. Dead teenagers lay on the ground in pools of gore. One of them has a neck gash…Kota catches her attention.

Kota Ahoka.

She revels in his magnetic beauty… his long, coal-colored hair. His brown skin and curved cheekbones. Kay assumes he's dead as the others, judging by how much the boy is bleeding. Only she is shown that he's not. When his eyes open…they are porcelain. As dazzling as the blaze from her dream. As pearly-white as the dimension, the bedroom entered.

KOTA

The Ahoka family surveys the scorched circle on the map. Kota's attention goes between it and the floating portrait of Kayla.

The artwork of leaves still hover mid-air, shimmering brightly. He can't help but revel in her attractiveness.

This girl is a Disney princess. Her angelic face is bewitching. The small nose and heart-shaped face. The pointed chin. The doe eyes. I wonder what color they are. He's compelled by her graceful presence. Although it's just an illusion of Kayla, he latches onto her essence.

"Are you certain?" Mato converses with his father.

"Yes... the address is correct. Yet I am not sure of the unit number. The location is a penthouse…not a stand-alone home. I regret that this is as much information the force can give."

"How far?" Kota asks. His eyes rip away from the holographic sketch of Kayla.

"12 miles." His grandfather answers. "I think it will be best to orchestrate what will be said."

"How come?" Dyani pinches her lips. "She's magical, and we need her help. That's all we need to say."

"It is possible that she knows nothing of this world. Her life may be ordinary… we must prepare for that outcome."

"Meaning there's a chance she'll be useless, and this was all for nothing?"

"Dyani!" Odina scolds her daughter. "What has gotten into you?!"

"I'm just saying what you all are thinking."

Her father throws her a silencing stare. "ENOUGH!"

Could my sister be right? Could the ritual have been a waste? "How likely is it that she knows nothing?"

"Let's be optimistic until proven otherwise." Mato declares rationally.

"Maybe you and I should talk with her." Odina suggests to her husband.

"That will be tricky. The girl may panic at the mention of a vampire."

"We have to approach her with reason… and place care into our wording."

"Mato is not wrong. Vampires are known to the outsiders as lore from movies." Grandad's voice falters… he's drained.

"Father, you should rest."

"Yes…" He nods, catching his breath. "I should."

Kota and Mato help him from the floor, escorting him to a small bedroom. His grandson adjusts his pillow, and his son lays him down. Grandad's frailty has multiplied. Although he's an elderly man, he's usually a bit spry for his age. Kota doesn't like how weakened he is. *Not one bit.* "I'll stay with him. While you and Mom work out a plan."

"Wado, uwetsi (Thank you, son)." His father departs.

"No need to worry… rest will rejuvenate me," the old man says stubbornly. "You can go."

"I'm staying." His grandad drifts into a slumber as easily as a newborn. Kota kneels at the bedside to monitor him.

I can't lose anyone else. I already lost three friends… I can't imagine losing a relative. I hope my folks brainstorm an idea. I hope this wasn't all for nothing. What if this human girl is a dead end? How will I react if she knows nothing of the supernatural world? Would I hate myself…? Would I beat myself up because I weakened Grandfather? Would I feel selfish?

CHAPTER 16: UNNATURAL

KAYLA

The girls remain silent. Kayla doesn't know for how long. She lost track of time… and of reality. The world is not what she thought it was. The dimension shifting… the vampires. The otherworldly entity. The insights that were gifted to her. The universe is nothing as she was taught.

An eruption of fireworks breaks the silence. The explosion shockwaves through their bones. They all jolt and eye the window. Orange and green blast the night sky. Kayla collects the book, returning it back to the case.

"What was talking to you??!! On the board??!!" Mya squawks. "ANSWER ME, KAYLA!! WHAT WAS SPEAKING TO YOU?!"

"And where did we go??? That… place. Where was that?!" Jia is frantic.

"I don't know… but I dreamed it before." "What was moving the board?!" Mya shrieks.

"I'm not sure… but I call it an air god. That's what it seems like."

"No…you said the words, and it obeyed you." Jia shakes her head. "HOW???"

Kayla turns to face them. She's more level-headed now. Her voice doesn't waver as she replies. "It's my legacy." Kay accepts everything that her grandmother told her…now that she has proof. She doubts nothing. Questions nothing. "It's all true… everything my gran told me is true."

"Let us out of this room!!" Mya screams.

Kay goes to the door and simply opens it, facing no struggle with the handle. Her peeps sprint out, their dresses fluttering fast behind them. The two press the elevator button, ringing it up. The kitchen phone warbles just as more fireworks pop off in the sky yet again. Her companions squeal in response.

Kayla, who is done being petrified, barely flinches. *There's no need to be skittish… I'm a part of this peculiar world now.* She goes to answer the phone. It's Darius. "I'll be over soon. I checked with Izzy, Fred, and Chester. They should be there. Time to raid for candy!" he exclaims, all stoked up.

"Perfect! Can't wait. I'll see you soon."

"Bye, baby."

"I love you." Her newfound confidence gives her enough courage to say the 3 words.

Darius sucks in a breath, staggered. "You….said it…?" Her boyfriend gives a harsh laugh. "Wow… I love you, too." She cheeses hard. "Hurry over, so we can say it in person."

"Will do, superstar." He hangs up.

Kay returns the receiver to the holder. Her clique is gone. They fled. She summons the elevator. Once downstairs, in a shiny lobby, she marches outside where her classmates mingle with her girls. *I hope they don't sense anything odd. I don't think they'll be easily convinced that I'm somewhat of a witch.* Jia and Mya play calm as best as they can. Kayla sees through their faulty façade. The shuddering of their hands and uneven breathing. Even their dull eyes… eyes that have seen the unbelievable.

"But I thought we were all going? That blows!" Fred protests. "But you guys got all dressed up. Why the change of mind?" He eyes the two.

Kay jets over before her friends can speak. *There's no telling what Mya will say… she might actually spill the beans. Jia, on the other hand, might make up a better excuse. At least that's what she guesses. Kayla has no clue how her friends will function after being shown a new side of the world.*

"They're joking!" She lies.

"Are we still on?" Izzy asks.

"Yes." Kay says anything to forward the conversation. *My classmates don't need to know… because they won't believe it without seeing it. My confession will be coined as an attempt to creep them out on Halloween.*

"Cool." Chester imitates the KISS singer's deep voice. "Let's rock and roll!" This time he actually strums an electric guitar, not an imaginary one.

"But… your girls said there's been a change of plans." Fred isn't buying my lie; he's skeptical.

Kay shares a pleading look with her besties, knowing they need normalcy to keep them sane. *They can't go home and sink deeper into madness. I have to keep an eye on them. They might lose their wits.* "Please, come out with us… going home will only make the night worse."

"Worse?" Izzy probes. "Is there something we're missing?"

"It's… related to ballet." Kay comes up with another lie. "We're trying to get past a bad patch." She mixes a bit of truth in.

"Oh…" Izzy believes it.

"So… are we going or what?" Fred examines Jia and Mya. They have no choice but to nod.

"I'll guitar the way!" Chester continues the deep voice. He strums the electric guitar, which sounds like acoustic strumming because there's no amp connected.

The bunch venture along the sidewalk; their destination is the bus station. Darius runs into them on the way there. He's a knight in shining armor, complete with a chain-link shirt, silver breastplate, and helmet. The sword across his back looks real like a real blade.

"Sup, dudes." He greets Chester and Fred.

"I only answer to rocker dude." Chester goes on acting as a metal icon.

"Sorry, rocker dude." His sweet eyes land on his girlfriend. "Hello, my fairy princess." He puts on an epic voice, forcefully rounding his syllables. Darius bows low to her like a true knight. "I've come to rescue you from the beast of loneliness!" "My hero!" Kay jumps into his arms.

"Eww… get a room." Izzy fakes a gagging motion with her hand.

"We shall get a room!" Darius goes on with a heroic voice.

Kayla giggles. The others walk ahead. The two are given privacy. More than they've ever gotten. This is new; Kay doesn't know how to act. *Do I jump for joy that I'm finally seeing my boyfriend after hours…without my dad intervening? This is the first time we've truly embraced. I love being unsupervised. I love not having a care in the world about my shyness. My life has a new meaning. I'm changing to adapt to who I am now.*

She peers up with eyes of burning need. "I love you."

"And I love you…" He returns the entranced look.

Kayla plants her lips to his. The butterflies in her stomach multiply, adding pressure to her abdomen. She dotes on the fluttering sensation. *Wow… I was able to say it out loud without chickening out?? I guess tonight is revolutionary.*

The lovebirds file after their posse, preparing to trick or treat. Instead of scourging homes for sweets, the crew hops from shop to shop. The storefronts are decorated with cobwebs, skeletons, spiders, and bats. The bakery passes out large Hershey bars. Starbucks hands out orange-striped cookies. The flower shop distributes candy cane-shaped daisies. The city sidewalks are bombarded by kids and teens.

The squad don't use pumpkin baskets; instead, Fred tallies all the goodies into his bookbag. Darius scopes this out suspiciously. "I'm watching you, Sir Fred…" He outs his sword and does a half prance forward. "YOU SHALL NOT STEAL THE BOOTY!" The warrior voice returns.

Fred howls, stretching his neck to the moon. The hairy fibers on the costume fan out in the moonlight; imitating porcupine spikes. "I will skin your flesh with my canine teeth!" he growls. "Try as you might, beast! You will lose your head!" "FIGHT FIGHT!" Izzy eggs them on.

Kayla cracks up... expecting her besties to join. But they can't seem to recover enough to enjoy humor. *Maybe they'll lighten up soon. I just need to give them time to normalize. Everything will go back to how it was.*

The gang racks up goodies for the next two blocks. To the point that Fred's backpack can barely zip up. Chester assists him in squeezing it against a wall to get it shut. Kay finds his black, swinging hair very comical. It's a bushy nest... Chester really worked hard on it. The two boys manage to get it zipped.

Fred wipes his forehead and huffs. "Phew!!" "I thought werewolves were strong?" Kay probes.

"And I thought fairies were tiny?"

"We are tiny." Mya sounds a bit normal. The fearfulness is nearly gone from her tone. "Ballerinas are real-life fairies. Take it back, or you won't come to our show."

Fred holds his hands up. "Sorry, sorry..."

Mya simpers. "So, off to the movies now?"

Izzy rolls her eyes. "Lame. Let's go party. The football captain is throwing a rager at his mansion."

"That sounds fun!" Mya regains some of her spunk.

"But... we planned to go to the movies." Jia is not on board. "Plus, parties have alcohol and other... things going on." She innocently hints at sex.

"So what? That's what makes it fun." Izzy places her hands on her hips. "You guys down?"

Kay bites her bottom lip. "Umm... I don't think that's a good idea. I have a curfew..."

"Just say you lost track of time."

"I don't know..."

"You can't obey rules forever. We're young and free, why not enjoy it?"

"It's a yes for me." Mya sides with Izzy.

"Let's rock!!" Chester sings in a demon voice. Fred nods to agree.

Darius doesn't want Kayla to be uncomfortable... or to get in trouble. "I can take the blame for you, so your rents don't lose it."

"That's silly of you to do."

"It's not… come on, let's be spontaneous." "Free
and young!" Izzy sings in a falsetto.

"FREE AND YOUNG!!!" Those who agree to be rebels
sing along with Izzy in the same high-pitched tone.

Jia and Kay glimpse at one another. They're so alike…both
of them fear getting in trouble. But the rest don't care. They run to
the bus stop, leaving the two who are undecided racing after. The
back is the only free place; the rest of the bus is loaded up. Every
seat is occupied.

Kayla takes hold of a pole, gripping it. She can't hide the
apprehension on her face. Darius kisses her and strokes her cheek.
"It's alright… you're only scared because this is new. New things are
intimidating at first. Then it gets easy."

His silky voice soothes her, as it always does. But there's
more impact to his words. It correlates with what transpired in the
bedroom. The intimidating thing being her powers… and how it
became easy to accept. *If I can conquer my new abilities… I should be able
to do the same with lying. I said before that tonight is revolutionary. I need to
keep it that way.*

Since Izzy knows the address, the gang waits on her move.
The bus travels from the city to a suburb. This is the first time Kayla
has ever seen a dark community. The streets are lit by Halloween
lights. No streetlamps… just the moon and orange bulbs. Even the
bus stop is dark.

The team dismounts and follows Izzy's lead. Her goth dress
sways in the autumn breeze, blending in well with the dark orange
leaves littering the ground. The mansion takes up the entire side
road. It's the biggest house Kay has ever seen.

The front yard is massive; staged with ten-foot-tall ghosts.
There's so much fog. Strobing lights are seen from within the
juggernaut palace. There's a crackling on the pavement leading to the
front door. *Are those beads? Or tiny firecrackers?* The mystery doesn't
end there. The grand door opens by itself. There's no one there.

Trance-like rave music bumps from inside. It's so dark. The
strobing disco balls provide little exposure to the void. The slow-
motion, techno wave music adds suspense and adrenaline. All of the
dancers inside form a pit, hopping, gyrating, head banging. The club
aesthetic is titillating.

Kayla has always been so tamed. Never being allowed to be
involved in rebel activities. Always being a goody two-shoes. For
once in her life, she lets loose and goes with the flow. She takes

Darius by the hand and steers the way to the dance floor. The bass
drowns out all sound. All Kay can hear is her heartbeat.

*So many school peers are here. The loners. The nerdy. The popular.
Everyone mixes in.* The couples dance so close. Closer than she's ever
seen. The singing is sensual and defiant. The words are unfamiliar,
but their meaning is well known. Craving freedom.

Kayla grows curious of the lust. The couples here don't
mind PDAs. They make out, slither their bodies together, and even
grope each other. Her wonder overtakes her rationality. *I want to be
close like that with Darius. I should do it.* Her palms trail down his chest
to his waist. She sways her hips side to side, puzzling her body to his.
Darius is caught off-guard by her newfound confidence. The racy
dancing pleases him; the joyful jeer on his lips speaks volumes. His
hands latch onto her hips, drawing her close.

The erotic singing blasts the room. Every vibration of the
bassy music is felt. Kay and Darius make out... not caring that
everyone sees. *I don't care what anyone thinks. I finally feel alive... free...
powerful.* Their hungry mouths devour one another. Their hands slide
down each other's bodies. The world disappears. The music
submerges their veins. The flickering lights highlight their starstruck
irises. The thirst excels. Kayla wants to lose herself in him. But she'd
prefer privacy.

Mya's words echo her mind. *"There's more to dating than
kissing. My advice is to sneak off and have fun."*

Many of the couples head upstairs to the bedrooms. *I'm not
sure we should do that. Maybe the backyard would be better. I'm not ready for
the big step... but Mya was right. There's more than kissing.* Kayla escorts
her boo out back to the large, landscaped yard. Away from the party.
The fresh air makes has her realizing just how smoky the house is.
Her lungs free themselves of the smoky fumes.

Darius grins to one side. "You're different tonight."

"You're the one who wants me to be spontaneous."

"I did... but I didn't expect this."

Kayla presses him against the wall. "Maybe I did change...
a little."

"What brought it on?"

"You wouldn't believe me."

"Try me."

Kayla nibbles on his earlobe with much feistiness.
"Promise you won't be afraid?" She whispers into his ear.

"I won't."

"Something happened tonight…" Kay begins… only to halt.

A strange incantation immerses her eardrums. A foreign chant in a different language. She's unaware that Kota's parents are attempting to locate her. The native words are mystifying to her. Her eyes locate the sound, following the source of the noise. Ahead of her is a holographic apparition of Mato and Odina. Hovering midair… is a portal. Kayla squints, perplexed. She notices the pointed symbols on their foreheads…same as the 13-edged star on the grimoire.

She doesn't wince. Instead, she advances to the portal. *What is that? Who are those people? What am I seeing?? What in the world is going on???* Her feet stagger… she's disturbed by this strange ripple in reality. Kay has never seen a dimensional gateway. Or witnessed people within one… staring right at her.

CHAPTER 17: TETHER

KOTA

"Her location has changed," His mother states from the living room.

Kota retreats from his grandfather's bedside. His attention is on the portal that spawned there. The view is very hazy; Kayla can't be seen accurately. Although she saw them as clear as day, their visuals aren't as fortunate.

"Why has it changed…?" Dyani wonders.

"Maybe she sensed us."

"Meaning she ran away?"

"That's possible." Mato stares ahead at the blurry view of Kayla.

"She's too young to be on her own. She must have parents." His mother disagrees with her husband. "I think she'll return home."

Kota eyes his father. "Maybe Mom is right."

"There's no way to know for sure. There has to be a reason the girl jumped from 13 miles away to 34."

"We should visit in the morning… her parents may know where she's gone."

Mato looks to his wife with brooding eyes. "There's a flaw in that. We don't have her name."

"We have a fine enough description from the first encounter. I'll sketch a drawing."

Mato ponders, holding his chin. "That would be wise." "I'll go too," Kota announces.

"No… your mother and I will handle this."

"I don't think she'll help if I'm not there."

Dy nods in agreement with her little brother. "He's right. He has to be there, so she knows he's a vampire."

Odina glances between her children, somewhat swayed by their reasoning. "They're not wrong, Mato."

"We'll do this our way."

"Please, Father… can I go? This is too important to sit out."

Mato gives a long sigh, debating his answer. "I'll stay in the car, I promise."

"Stay with your grandfather; watch after him. The spell was strong." He advises Dyani. "I'll allow you to come along."

Kota is thankful for this permission… and for his grandad being monitored. *My mind will be eased if he's watched after. My dread of losing him is greater than tagging along. Dyani is pissed; I guess she wants to go too instead of babysitting. This is a huge update; we'll finally have answers. My sis is just as anxious for a solution as I am. I hope she doesn't get mad over this. She may get over it. Same as how she got over hating me.*

It seems she's coming around. This is the first time my big sis supported me since the change. Same with her siding with me…this has me hopeful of restoring our bond. Tonight, will be a good night. We have a Spell Bender. Now, all we have to do is prepare for the morning.

Kota doesn't sleep. Everyone else does. He roams the house, finding himself examining where the portal once hovered. *It's a shame I couldn't see her face. The gateway was all fuzzy. Could she see me? I hope so. That'll make tomorrow a success. If she knows my appearance beforehand, maybe she'll see my truth. That I'm not human.*

Green and orange fireworks pop the dark city sky. The spooky holiday ends at midnight… yet it still has a lingering presence. *Why is that? Is it true that the day holds supernatural energy?*

The sun rises at dawn. Kota will never get used to the feel of it on his flesh. The traumatic boiling he endured before will always haunt him. He watches the lines of light dance across his forearms. He raises his fingers to absorb the hotness of the glowing rays.

Kota's happy to have some normalcy… regardless of being a monster. *I can still live… even if the cure is a dead end. Magic has helped me so far. Maybe I should drop the wish to be mortal… and go after the vampire who's done this to me. I could channel this depression into revenge. That would help. I could kill the red-eyed devil who cursed me. That could be my closure.*

It's smart to have a backup plan. This girl could choose not to help me…she could be a stranger to this all and say no. Say no to fixing me. Kayla could turn me down and go on with her life. I must prepare myself for that outcome.

His grandfather wakes at 8 a.m. "Osda sanalei (Good morning)."

"Osda sanalei."

"I assume there is a plan?"

"Yes." Kota recaps what happened last night. He leaves out nothing. The portal. The concerning distance Kayla traveled. The choice to involve her parents into the mix. The plan to visit.

"Will you go along?"

"Yes, I'm going."

"I agree with my son. Your appearance may frighten her. You must view the world from normal eyes. Seeing a vampire may be too distressing for her."

"I understand…I'll stay in the car. I promise."

"I will sit this one out…to recover."

By noon, they're dressed to go. Dyani is sour; she pouts as they leave. Mato drives using the marked map for instructions. The streets are semi-crowded. The horror of rush hour hasn't begun yet. The bummy, dilapidated neighborhoods are miserable. The cracked pavements; boarded up buildings, and foul air quality darkens the day. The sun is blocked, a gray orb. The leafless trees are dismaying; their naked roots hang in a sickly manner.

The homeless beg for money on the roads, going from car to car; holding cardboard signs reading: **Change for food. Help. 5 days of an empty stomach.** Odina rolls down the window to give coins to the lost souls. Their grateful smiles brighten the bleak morning.

Kota grins at the feeling of hope radiating from their spirits. This is the first time he's felt the emotions of others so vividly. Before, it was a subtle overheating in the gut. Now…deep waves in the stomach; a spark rumbles his core. A tingling of his spine and heart. *Wow. My bones are shivering… but in a good way. As if the Holy Ghost has entered me.*

The shift from the destitute region to the high-class district is cataclysmic. The charming, old-school Chicago truly conveys the essence of the 1960s. The tall skyscrapers are pure stone. The colossal size takes him and his parents by surprise. Luxurious storefront restaurants are shaded by huge umbrellas.

Designer store fronts, jewelry, perfume, cologne, suits. Businessmen and women. Street artists. A pianist performs on a grand piano in the park. Others paint canvases for their audience, gaining a few coins for their service. There are no homeless souls in sight. The endless sea of expensive is marvelous. Their crappy car trails the drawbridge, passing the lake.

His father monitors the map. Kota sees it as if he's not in the backseat. The way he can zoom in his view is God-like. *We have one more turn… and we're there.* Kota counts down the seconds to speed up time. *1.2.3.4.5.6.7.8.9.10. Here is the moment of truth. The shot in the dark. The final solution to my torment.*

The Volkswagen parks on the curb, in front of the glamorous penthouse. There's a bellboy at the spinning lobby doors.

His father twists off the ignition and peers back at his son. "Stay put."

Kota's parents step out of the car. He stares after them, full of angst. *I can't go inside… but I can use my advanced hearing range. I can hear the rustling of the picture my mother drew. If I focus hard enough, I can isolate noise.* He engages his ears to pinpoint his mother's footsteps. Little by little, he distinguishes her motion from the roaring city. Until the ruckus of commotion and traffic fades to an inaudible frequency.

"Hello, good noon." Her footsteps pause.

"Good noon! How may I help you?" The receptionist greets kindly.

"I'm looking for this girl. I was told she resides here?"

"Miss Kayla Harris. Yes, she does. Unfortunately, she has left for the day."

Kota's heart drops to the floor of his stomach. Unlike the glorious sensation from before, this one is bone-crushing.

"Could I speak with her parents? Could you ring them down?"

"I'm afraid her parents have stepped out for the day as well…on business. I'm sorry. You may leave a message." The woman grabs a pen and notepad. "To whom should I say it's from?"

"The Ahoka family."

KAYLA

Kayla stretches over a ballet barre. The glamorous dance studio is empty. Only her and the sun rays mark the room. She…a ballerina in a cream-colored leotard and tutu. She flexes her arm and leg muscles to loosen the tightness. Her mind revisits last night.

Who were those people? They looked similar to the guy I saw. Although their skin is brown, his was extremely pale. I'm guessing he once had the same complexion. Maybe they were his parents?? But why would they call on me? They opened a portal. I wasn't expecting that. I thought I had all of this under control, but I don't.

I left the party as if a boogeyman was chasing after my life. Darius rode back home with me. We left the others partying at the mansion. I'll have to apologize for ditching them. I had to get away from the insanity. Kay recalls the bus ride home:

"What's going on??" Darius is alarmed by her change in character.

"I'm just worried about getting in trouble." Kayla lied.

"It looked like you saw a ghost! Are you that terrified?"

"Yes..." She grips the pole as the bus comes to a stop. Her deadpan, shocked expression has him wrapping his arms around her.

"It's alright. I told you I'll take the blame."

Kayla lengthens her back on the barre, remembering what happened next. The nightmare she found at home. Red, white, and blue siren lights. A cop car outside the penthouse. Kay didn't think twice about it. Chicago is an aggressive city… police cars are normal. The cops are always around. But once on the 17th floor, she found the true meaning:

As soon as the elevator opened, she and Darius spotted a police officer. A uniformed man jotting down information in a notepad.

"Her middle name is Aria, born November 30th, 1967. Her height is 5'6. I called her friends' parents. Their children haven't returned home either." *Her mom doesn't notice that the elevator has opened. She was too full of anguish…same as her husband. Mary clasped James as if too weak to stand on her own two feet.*

James spied her exiting the lift. "KAYLA! You had us worried sick! Where have you been?!"

"Oh, thank God…" *Mary is so relieved that she holds her forehead.*

"Abort the search." *The officer reported into his walkie.* *"The teen just walked in."*

"Copy that." *A woman responded from the static radio.*

The cop looked at James and Mary. *"Your daughter won't be filed in the system as a runaway. I hope this gets sorted out."*

"It will. Thank you for all your help, officer." *James walked the man to the elevator.*

"Please don't scare your parents like that again, kid." *The cop warned her.*

James glowered at Darius, who left the elevator to allow the officer inside. Her Dad held in his anger, bottling it up until the metal cage closed. The tension was thick. The silence was menacing.

Once it was closed, he exploded. *"EXPLAIN YOURSELVES!!"*

An icy hot sweat worked Kay's forehead. *"Dad, I'm sorry!"*

"It's my fault, sir. I lost track of time. It won't happen again."

Mary wiped her teary face. *"You know your curfew…still you broke it!"*

"I'm sorry, Mom."

"Sorry doesn't cut it, missy!" *James roared.*

"It's past midnight!" Mary scowled; scared and angry at the same time.

"Mr. and Mrs. Harris, please don't blame her. I was irresponsible with her curfew."

James folded his arms. "Thank you for getting her home. We'll handle it from here. Goodnight, Darius."

"I'll see you tomorrow." Kay flashed him a quick grin.

"We'll see about that..." James retorted.

"Get home to your mother. She's just as petrified as I am." Mary escorted him to the elevator.

Her dad analyzed her very harshly. His rage built more and more by the second. The only thing that was missing was the steam from his ears. It took a few seconds for the metal carriage to arrive to pick up Darius. Once again, there was an intense silence until the elevator door closed. James stared down his daughter. Kayla was too ashamed to combat his chiding glare. She eyed the floor in humiliation.

"Do you have any idea how many kids go missing on Halloween??! How many get harmed?? We thought the worst! You worked your mother into a panic attack and had me ready to hunt you down!"

"Where were you?!" Mary grabbed her daughter and shook her. "Where were you?! At a party?! We drove around for miles. You weren't out trick-or-treating!"

"You weren't at the theater or the mall; we checked. She was definitely at a party. Darius is starting to be a bad influence."

"No, he's not, Dad!"

"You think I don't know what goes on there??!!" James yelled, every vein in his forehead protruded, ready to pop.

"Why are you behaving this way?! You always follow the rules!!"

I shouldn't be judged for having fun, for once in my life! I can't always follow their law like the perfect child!! Kayla huffed and puffed. Her eyes sizzled with resentment. She shoved her mother's arms away. "Maybe that's the problem!"

"Excuse me??" Mary sneered. "Watch your tone!"

"Maybe if you two didn't lie about spending time together, I wouldn't break the rules. You both promised to make up for all the late nights. YOU LIED! What happened to the make-up days?! All you two care about are your jobs!! All you do is lie!!!"

"You're grounded... and you're not seeing Darius until we decide you can." Her father flared his nostrils. "You owe both me and your mother an apology."

"No, you owe me one!!" She stomped her feet all the way to her room.

James attempted to march after her, but Mary stopped him. *"Let her cool down."*

"Not until she apologizes!"

"Let's not escalate this anymore, dear."

Kayla slammed her bedroom door and ran to her bed, burying her watery face into the pillow.

I haven't apologized yet. I woke up this morning and snuck out to practice. I don't care if they're mad at me. They can't ground me from the ballet show.

CHAPTER 18: PATIENCE

Kayla returns to the present, letting the flashbacks remain in the past. She runs through her solo choreography—waltz, pirouette, plié, twirl, wide lunge, fouettés, arabesque, assemblé, attitude, penché, battement, jeté, relevé, tendu. Then she freestyles the rest with long jumps, high spins, lengthy twirls, elegant poses, and spread-eagle lunges.

The fabric of the tutu breathes in the air of the room, flowing as clouds do. Surfing. Kayla creates poise art in a fluid dance. Her body is a well-oiled machine. A force of pure frustration. An outlet of artistic angst. As if made of clay, her limbs form complex tangles, shapeshifting into remarkable figures. The styles of modern and classic ballet merge as one.

She ends the choreography by sticking the landing with one-pointed foot on the floor while the other reaches far behind her. Kay holds the pose, keeping as still as possible. She doesn't move an inch.

The sound of capping interrupts her. It's coming from the doorway. Isabell is there. Her blonde hair in a high ponytail. "You're beginning to dance with emotion… not as someone following a lesson."

Kayla ends the stance, relaxing her limbs from the rigorous workout. "I thought we're supposed to follow the lessons."

"Not when on the stage. The best dancers morph into their craft… without restraint. Without fretting over the mathematics. Ballet is more than forcing demands. It's about soul. Passion. Your practice is the first I've seen where my lessons are dismissed." "Thank you." Kayla bows gracefully.

"Your drive has improved. What has changed?"

"My dreams showed me my true path."

"Which is?"

Kay chooses to be honest. "That I have power within…and that it's time to wield it."

"Indeed, you do." She walks off. "The solo is yours. Prepare yourself for tomorrow's show."

Kayla's mouth drops to the floor. All the craziness of yesterday disappears, now buried under excitement. Winning the solo trumps the horrors of last night. She's ecstatic. Thrilled. Kay hops up and down, squealing. She dashes to the hall phone to dial Darius's number. As soon as he answers, she blurts, "I WON THE SOLO!!"

"Yes! I knew you would. Congratulations!"

"I can't believe it!"

"Maybe your parents will lessen the punishment."

"I'll just apologize; I don't care. Today is the best day ever!" she singsongs. "I'll call you later; I gotta tell them the news." Kayla swoops up her bookbag and runs all the way home. *THIS IS THE BEST DAY OF MY LIFE!!!*

When home, she finds her mother flipping pancakes in the kitchen. James sorts through folders at the kitchen's island. Kay jets out of the elevator. "When did you leave the house??!!" James roars.

"I'm sorry, I went to the studio to work on choreography. I should have asked first."

"YES, YOU SHOULD HAVE!!" He places down the folders and marches her way.

"I'm sorry about last night. I'm sorry for yelling. Can we just forget it?"

"No, we can't. You're not supposed to go out, you're grounded!"

"But I won the solo…" Kay clenches her teeth. "Isabell said so. Please… can we celebrate??" She twiddles her thumbs, peering at her father with precious puppy dog eyes. "Please, Daddy. I'm sorry about everything."

James tries his best to resist the adorable stare. The pouty lips and big sad eyes. But the power of his baby girl wins against his fierceness. James cracks a grin. "You know I can't say no to that look."

"She knows." Mary chortles.

"You're still grounded…."

"I know."

James sighs…then shrugs it off. "Congratulations! That's my girl!"

Mary spins around with Kayla like a little kid on the playground. "You'll be in the *Chicago Tribune!*"

"Joffrey Ballet is in the bag." Her dad is proud. Let's drink!" James browses a walk-in wine cellar. He shakes up a bottle of sparkling cider.

"No, don't!" Mary flees the foamy spray, fearing getting soaked by the hose like outburst. Kayla stays put as her dad uncaps the bottle. The fake alcohol hoses her down. She sniggers goofily, twirling around in pure bliss.

KOTA

The Ahokas inspect the kitchen phone. Odina bites her nails. Mato paces back and forth. Kota sits at the table with Grandad and Dy. "The day is still young; they may call by noon." His Grandad is optimistic.

"Hopefully," Mato mutters.

"The girl returned home… we should take that as a good sign. Our summons didn't scare her away."

"So… does that mean she knows of the supernatural?" Dyani ponders.

"I hope so…" Odina goes to the sink to tidy up the dishes. "Should we have left more than our name and telephone number? Something to place urgency?"

"The key is avoiding being overbearing," her husband counsels her.

"What if they think we're salespeople? Mom may be right," Dy says.

"Another visit will clear any confusion," Grandad advises.

"Are you sure you're strong enough?" Kota frets. He's on guard with his grandfather due to his all-knowing abilities. As a mortal, he wasn't able to sense how slow blood flows when someone is exhausted. Now he can. The reduced twittering in his veins is worrying. Grandad's body is running low on resources. *I have to convince him to stay home.* "Maybe you shouldn't ride along."

"I am fine." He pats Kota's hand and stubbornly shakes his head. "Shall we go at noon?"

Mato halts pacing to eye the phone. "Let's give them more time before being too hasty."

"What will you say?" Dy peers between her parents.

"The truth… that we need their daughter's help."

"And… if they ask what the help is for?"

"We'll tell the truth. If we're believed to be insane, so be it. This is our only chance."

She doesn't combat her father. But Kota is aware of why his sister is asking this. Saying a vampire needs help from their daughter would sound like a prank. A joke. A late Halloween hoax.

I need to be visible… because I'll be the proof of the truth. My appearance will end all of their disbelief. One look at me will awaken shock in their souls. Same as with my tribe. My lost tribe… who damned me because of my dead skin and tainted eyes. My unholy mark on the universe is hard to miss. I know my folks want to try the easy way. The safe way. The plan that's best for not inciting terror. But that is the only way to convert nonbelievers. How can someone believe what they don't see??

They stare at the phone until noon. No one speaks until the clock strikes 12. Mato sighs. "No one may be home."

"Saturday is usually a relaxed day," his wife contends. "Or maybe the receptionist forgot to deliver the message."

"Maybe." He shakes his head. "This may be a shot in the dark. We have to consider other options."

Grandad is deep in thought; his wrinkled face is all bunched up. "I doubt there are more Spell Benders. We are only a few in number. The last gathering only held 10 total…and that was decades ago…"

"Do you still have contact with and of them?" His son eagerly locks eyes with him.

"No…our last discussion was a disbandment."

"Disbandment?"

"Yes…"

"Why?"

"For our survival." He responds drearily. "There are those who seek to use magic as a weapon. For selfish gain. Our power is unlimited once we group as one. The true demise of our kind was corruption. I've seen many fall to the dark side for their captors."

"How can that be?" Kota is dazzled. "If your powers are unlimited, how can someone hold you captive??"

Grandad grimaces wearily. "Vampires have compulsion and can control you…as if a puppet-master. Many Benders had no choice. We fled to preserve the legacy. This girl is the only one who is not hiding…most likely because she is unaware of the risks. Which means she may be of little help." His ominous voice discourages everyone in the room. The small shed of hope fades away. The optimism is drained by the words. Grandad notices this. "Do not worry." He grins pleasantly to cheer them up. "Patience is key."

I don't think we'll get a call from the Harris family. The realistic outcome is that they didn't receive the message. Or they did and chose to pay it no mind. After all, we're strangers. They know nothing of us. Our name is meaningless. I want to believe this Kayla girl is my savior. I want to believe… but these circumstances are breaking my spirit. Is faith blocking my path to her? Are these obstacles meant to be? Is this a sign that she cannot help me?? His pale eyes never leave the clock.

The second hand drags on for hours. Kota examines it… even when everyone disperses. He barely hears them bid him goodnight. His attention is locked in on time, as if it still dictates his life. *Time is for mortals. A way to measure their existence. What good does it do me now that my existence is never-ending? Why do I care for the meaningless milliseconds? The meaningless strokes?*

Come midnight, he decides to leave the empty kitchen for the backyard. A tiny plot of land compared to their home in Oklahoma. Everything here is compact. The buildings are so cramped. The grass isn't as green. The dirt is poisonous. He bends down to take a handful of the cold, hard soil. The dirt grains sprinkle to the ground as if made of pebbles.

His artistic eyes shoot to the murky sky. Another night with no stars. *This dismal atmosphere is a sign. I'm just as trapped as the stars and as hard as the soil. I should accept this life… just as the environment has.*

The trill of police sirens blare from down the street. The whistling of a train resounds the air. Kota sits on a bench. He buries his head into his hands. The brisk wind of autumn mushes his hair, tossing it wildly. The black strands cut across his zombie complexion.

His eyes are far away. He focuses on the gravity of the wind. The particles are visible. Air… an element unseen by the naked eye is clearly detectable. The mist is not the same as fog… or as thick as a cloud. The air particles are slightly masked; yet outlined in a strange haze. If he wasn't concentrating on the spot, this discovery would've been lost to him. Kota tracks the gush as it journeys through the trees.

The importance of patience dawns on him. *I could be like the wind. Patient and constant. Assured and steady. Being trapped and hardened isn't my only option. Grandad was right. Patience is key… tomorrow is a new day.*

KAYLA

TODAY IS THE BIG DAY! I'LL BE SOLOING TONIGHT! ME??!! WOW! I STILL CAN'T BELIEVE IT!!

Kayla packs her bookbag with her stage wardrobe. The beam on her face is a mile long. She zips her bookbag and slings it across her shoulder. Her bare feet dash up the stairs to the rustic art studio. Pure sunlight beams through the windows. She grabs a pencil and goes to the canvas to draw the rest of her routine. Sketching the last of the ballerina figures in tutus. When done, the canvas is full and her smile is overflowing.

"Yes!" She clasps her hands together.

Her legs dart down the glass staircase, hurrying into her room. She changes from her robe. Her ballet crew is on the way.

Even though it's only 12 p.m. and the show isn't until 6, they still have to prep. Meal prep, stage arrangements, practice, and stretching. There's a charter bus outside; she peeps it from the bathroom window.

Kayla dresses in leggings and a baggy off-the-shoulder shirt. Her feet slip into sneakers and trace to the door. "See you later!" she yells to her rents, who sip on coffee. Kay doesn't hear their response because she boards the elevator and presses the button.

The white charter bus is glamorous. It's the limo of all buses; so large and shiny. The wheels are gigantic. She takes her time climbing the jumbo steps, so she doesn't fall.

"READY FOR TONIGHT!" Mya screams from the back of the bus, cupping her hands over her mouth.

"YES!!"

Jia gives her a massive hug. "Congrats on the solo!!"

"Thank you!" Kay squeals. From the corner of her eye, she spots a blonde girl mugging her down. *I expected some jealousy. All of us here were competing for the spot. Most of the girls are definitely upset at me over winning.* The blonde girl leans to whisper into her friend's ear. Both of them maliciously scowl at her. *Their thoughts are so easily translated to:*

Why you? I deserved the solo. BITCH!

Isabell detects their rudeness. She waves her finger side to side. "Behave yourselves! Today is the same as any; we're a team! No ugliness is allowed." The instructor singles out the two, who hurriedly fix their bitter expressions. "ALRIGHT, ARE MY GIRLS READY?!" Isabell acts as a hype man.

"YES!" they all cheer.

"ONE MORE TIME WITH ATTITUDE!"

"YESSSSS!!!!"

"THERE WE GO!" She applauds. "Now be seated; we'll be there soon." She strolls to the front of the bus to a food stand. The table is full of protein shakes; wheat toast covered in avocado.

Kay and Jia head Mya's way. Kayla can't help but stare at the back of the blonde girl's head. *Raven is top 5 in the class. She felt she deserved the title. Deserved the spotlight. I would be upset too, if I lost the shot... especially with how hard I worked. She'll get it next time... hopefully she won't hate me forever this.*

We all want to impress our parents. We're all banking on the solo, so they pay us more attention. She must feel like a disappointment. I know I would feel that way too. I do feel that way...all the time.

Kay takes the middle seat, sandwiched between her besties. They hold hands, giggling cheerfully. For the first time ever, she detects an enchanted atmosphere. The thrill of each dancer is easy to read. Hints of yellow silhouettes all of the girls. The ultimate aura for joy etches from the borders of their skin. *There's a sisterhood. We may not be friends, but dedication connects us as one. As one dream. We'll kill it tonight!*

Isabell hands out the healthy treats so her girls can munch. The dancers need a hefty dose of protein to rile up their muscles.

The ride is thirty minutes…traffic is heavy. The theater is only three blocks away. Most people are on lunch break. Their stylish cars confirm the wealth of their professions. This little moment reminds her of her parents. They'll be at her show. Being her biggest fans… her personal cheerleaders. Kayla is stoked.

She easily visualizes the Harris Theatre; a square building made completely of black-lined windows. All of a sudden, her mind is photorealistic, as if standing before the art center at this very moment.

My mind is doing the time travel thing again. Same as in law class when I reversed the past. I wonder how far back I can go. Days? Months? Years? Centuries?

CHAPTER 19: FINALE

KOTA

We have a new location on Kayla Harris. Grandad surprised us with the report this morning. He did a summoning song, knowing he shouldn't have. He needs to recover. But what's done is done. He saw where Kayla is heading. The girl is on her way to Harris Theatre for some sort of show. She has a performance tonight.

I'm glad it's a place where we can actually go…not a private domicile. This is the update we needed. Another shot. One last attempt to discover if there is a cure. I have to keep positive that she can locate one. Grandfather said it best. Nature always has a balance in place. Natural cures are in most plant life on Earth. There are floras that cure deadly poisons. Maybe it'll be some strange herb that'll cure me. Or a special kind of liquid. Maybe magic won't be my savior?

The Ahoka family pile into the wagon. Grandad and Dyani join them this time. "Remember, you three…you'll remain in the crowd. We'll handle the conversation," Mato orders. "The objective is to blend in."

I want to ask, "how can I blend in?", but the pendant has restored a hint of my normal complexion. I'm still ashy… but not as much as I was before. I was white as a ghost when I first changed. My tan skin was gone completely. At least now there's a glimpse of the tint. A somewhat silvery-brown hue. As for my eyes… the honey color will never return.

The wagon rolls down a single road. The drive is long due to them living on the west side, not the east. The same drastic transition from poverty to worthiness bothers him yet again.

I always heard how bad cities are. I never thought there could be such separation. Back home, my town was one. No one lived better or worse. No one laughed in the face of the lessor, with lavish houses and fancy cars. We were a community. This city is far from that.

It's hard to not dwell on his hometown. The deep cut is still present in his soul. The coldness of this environment reminds him of how much he loved Tahlequah. My forever home will always plague me. So will the reason we fled. I'm the problem… even now, I'm something to be fixed. Just as this city.

Kota gazes at his hands as the car steers. He ignores the window and the giant buildings whizzing by. He's thinking ahead now. To the theater. To finally seeing Kayla in person—not through a layer of magic. Her charming face and doe eyes. The swirling curls of her bushy hair. *I can't wait to see the colors she possesses.*

Grandad functions as their map—he has the dwelling memorized. Mato swerves the corner streets of downtown Chicago, peering through the rearview mirror at his father. "Are we close? Do you see the place?"

"Yes." Grandfather's eyes glow white under the sun, similar to a cat's night vision. Eerie and jarring. He's accessing the surroundings. Stretching his third eye further to see. "Three roads. Keep straight," the old man directs with certainty. He views the exact building. "A theater full of black-lined windows." He describes. "Her thoughts are vivid. The child must have opened her mind. I can see through her this time."

Mato keeps straight as commanded. The theater is hard to miss. A new addition to the older buildings lining the streets. Modern and edgy. An artsy, box structure—five level high compound. He flips on the turning signal and parks on the curb.

Kota is suddenly cynical. The weight of realism warps his mind. *What if this goes badly? What if she says no?*

"Rest your mind," Grandad reads him. "She will help. Trust my intuition…" He reassures his grandson.

Mato and Odina leave the car first. Dyani follows after. Kota aids his grandfather getting out of the back seat. *Will I be able to walk through? This is a public domain… right? I guess I'll find out.* His shoes near the threshold. Although his heart is dead, he witnesses it imitate pounding—only the organ doesn't pump.

The surrounding blood does. The relief of passing through with no complications eases him. Inside, the walls are neon colored: pink, yellow, orange. White banisters cage a three-tier staircase in extravagant taste.

His parents approach the box office booth. He's never seen them prioritize a task this way before. They're on a mission. Mato and Odina have a fair in their stride similar to sharks out for blood. "Which show stars Kayla Harris?" his is mother urgent. "That'll be LUNA. An original narrative by Studio Doll. Kayla Harris will be soloing."

"Perfect. We'll take five tickets."

KAYLA

A buzzing frequency needles Kayla's ears. The noise rattles her teeth and needles her spine. She stops stretching her leg to cover her earlobes. "What is that noise?!"

Jia pauses mid-stretch, resembling a flapping bird. "What noise?"

"Is there a speaker on... or something?"

Isabell, who strolls past the balancing bars, shrugs. "It must be a sound test."

Kayla uncaps her ears a little, then winces and covers them again. "I can't concentrate...it's too loud!"

Isabell stops to listen hard... confused by the silence. "I hear nothing."

Kayla looks down the rows, where her classmates bend their bodies to perfection. "No one else hears that??" She's stunned when everyone shakes their head "no".

Mya listens: she even strains her neck. "No...maybe it's stress."

"I don't think stress messes with your hearing." Kayla scoffs.

"Well... what else can it be?"

It could be that man and woman trying to reach out to me. The ones from Halloween night. I heard a similar buzz... only this one is severe. Once again, she keeps this to herself. *No one will believe that I saw two people open a portal right in front of me.* Kayla lowers her leg. "I need water, Ms. Hayle."

"Make it quick, or your muscles will go lazy."

"Yes, ma'am." Kay hustles out, leaving backstage, which is cluttered with ladders, tall light poles, and hanging costumes from previous shows. The last performance was *Sleeping Beauty.* Aurora's glittery blue dress and Maleficent's black and purple cloak hang near the door. She nears a drinking fountain, gulping down the water. It's cold enough to calm her ears some. But not completely. So, she keeps drinking until the humming subsides.

Are those people back? But why? What do they want? Is the boy I saw before connected to them? She recalls the night she used the Ouija board. A burnt-out campfire. Dead teenagers on the ground. The one with the neck gash. His unbelievable gorgeousness. His long, dark hair and rugged, soft features. His pale eyes...and how they matched the pastel flames from the strange dimension.

The boy isn't human. The air spirit showed me the truth. He's a vampire. His unbelievable appearance proves that this is true. I assume the man and woman are related to him. Possibly his parents. She leaves the fountain to carry on with the stretching exercise. The chiming tone is a little better. It doesn't hurt as much anymore. *I hope this doesn't ruin my solo.*

This is the biggest night of my life; nothing should ruin it. Kayla posts to the barre and follows along with the class.

Isabell demonstrates before her students, bending one leg to the side of her head. Then, holds this spot for ten seconds before switching. Next is a low dip leg split. They all reach the floor without ruining their straight postures. The praying mantis pose is next. Their legs create a perfect square while on tiptoe. The stick insect position is held for twenty seconds, while they arc their arms. Their core muscles heating up like a furnace.

Afterwards, ballet shoes are broken in. The girls unwrap new slippers. "Ahh…" Kayla sniffs the pleasant smell of brand-new fabric, recalling her 5-year-old self sliding her small feet into the shoes.

The group uses a tool, similar to a food grater, to scrape the bottom of the stiff shoes, shredding the material into falling dust. Then they bang the ballet shoes on the floor, focusing on the tip; whacking the area repeatedly.

Once done, the class bends them back to the front. A popping sound follows. The same is done to the shank—the middle of the slippers—until more popping occurs. The ballet slippers are banged on the floor a few more times. Until they flex back and forth with ease.

Okay, done. Perfect. My arch will be one with the footwear. I won't slip or sound too loud on stage.

"Remember, the scouts will be front and center," Isabel announces.

"How many are coming?" Kay is curious.

"5 total…all from New York." Exclaims of disbelief escape the girls, who stare at each other in astonishment. "This show will write the history of our studio. Tonight, opens the path to nationals. So, bring your best."

There has never been 5… one or two at most. This means Studio Doll is gaining a reputation. "WOW!" Kay gasps. *Good thing I finished my routine! Usually, our shows draw in less talent scouts. This will be a huge win for us!*

"Alright, gather around." Her class huddles in a circle, laying their hands atop each other. "On three, one, two, three! STUDIO DOLL!!" they yell, throwing their hands up.

KOTA

Time is speeding up instead of slowing down. *I thought when anticipating something; the seconds mock you by going slow. That must be a myth… because the minutes sprint.* The Ahoka family enter the auditorium at 5 p.m. The crowd is massive… so is the stadium. Hundreds of rows of seats start from the very front and end three stories high…on balconies.

He avoids eye contact, knowing people are wondering why he's so colorless. *Maybe their first thought isn't a vampire… they could think I'm sickly. But still, my eyes are a mystery. It's best I look away and hope the attendees assume I'm wearing outrageous contact lenses.*

Kota reads the program packet. The cover showcases each of the members of Studio Doll. His eyes eagerly searches for Kayla, but all of the ballerinas are turned away in the image. This was done to showcase their blue costumes and how they tie in the back like medieval corsets.

So, she's a ballerina? A good one too, if she's soloing. Kayla must be an immaculate dancer. It appears she's a triple threat. A talented performer…a Spell Bender… and a beauty queen. I can't wait to see what she does on stage. I doubt she anticipates seeing me as much as I do her. Can I even exist in her world? Does she know what I am? How I look? Will her heavenly eyes sweep past me as they would a stranger?

His mother escorts them to the 8th row to their assigned seats. Grandad wobbles. Kota steadies him. "You shouldn't have done the spell…"

"Maybe so…" He inhales hard, finally admitting he was reckless to use so much power by himself. Kota assists him in sitting down.

Mato is wary of his father's loss of energy. "You need to eat…to fuel your strength. He makes his way to the main doors, excusing himself to bypass the large crowd.

"I will untap from her mind… now that I am certain."

"Yes… please take it easy." Kota can't help but be intrigued by the mind link. "How certain are you?"

"Completely."

"Do you know what she's thinking?"

"Yes… but only in fragments," he answers frailly.

"Does she know about my kind?"

"She knows of vampires… particularly a red-eyed, blonde one. Kayla has seen your transition."

Red-eyed blonde one??? That sounds like the vampire that plagued me and my friends! Who killed my crew… who trapped me in this life of hell! Kota is too rocked by this information to say anything. He witnesses flashbacks of the vampire above the campfire. *How it preyed for fun…for pleasure.* The joy of the game is evident now that he's experienced the taste of hunger. *That demon enjoyed the chaos it wielded. It deserves to pay for its actions.*

Odina sighs in relief. "Good to know. That's one less thing to worry about. The talk will go smoothly for us."

"Fingers crossed, little brother." Dy grins.

Kota snaps out of his brooding and gives a wide smile to his big sister. "Thank you, kamama (butterfly)."

"You're welcome, walela (hummingbird)."

Mato returns with two soup bowls and crackers. "Please eat."

Grandfather accepts the warm meal. "Wado, uwetsi (Thank you, son)."

No one is left standing; every guest is seated. Each row is a sea of endless heads. The live orchestra is set up on a designated platform before the stage. The violinists are the first to strum their instruments, although the chattering of the crowd drowns most of the tune out.

CHAPTER 20: HOURGLASS

KAYLA

In the dressing room, vanity tables and changing curtains await them all. The team drape their costumes on a rack—glittery blue leotards and tutus. The girls burst into jumping jacks, high knees, and bicycle crunches. Another warmup before the big performance. Then, finally, the teens slip into the outfits.

Each ballet dancer applies sticky gel squares to their big toes, then in between. The elastic bands of their shoes are strapped on. The ballerinas place on the molded shoes, testing the elasticity.

Kayla, as well as the rest, stands on their tiptoes, raising up and down as if connected to a spring. This satisfies them enough to go on. The teens tie the lacy shoes into bows. Then the performers pile to the vanity tables. It's time for makeup. The ballerinas apply silver eyeshadow and sheer blush to their cheeks, pinning their hair into high buns.

Mya pulls open a drawer to her table to sort through makeup. She finds one close to her skin tone…a primer liquid foundation. "I need to be flawless," she pines, even though her skin is perfection.

Jia looks in her drawer as well. "I need some too…just in case."

From down the way, Kayla spies her friends patting on the foundation. She judges her skin in the mirror, running her fingertips over her pores. *I wish they were smaller. Maybe I'll add just a little makeup.* She opens her drawer and selects the second darkest shade—mocha. Kay dabs a few dots on, using her fingers to beat the liquid in.

When done, she outlines her eyes with a gel pen, swooping a wing to both ends. Dramatic black is the shade of choice. Kayla lengthens her lashes with mascara, then spreads pink lipstick on. The last thing the girls do is roll on sheer tights. The beauty queens line up once they're all gussied up. Each of them are a different shade, from light to tan, brown to dark.

Isabell looks them over. "4 minutes. Breathe deeply. Don't look at the crowd. Remember to never pay attention to their faces— that's only a distraction. Always look above at the lights." An orchestra of piano, strings, and drums sounds from the stage. "You're all beautiful as swans. Now be just as graceful." Isabell steps on stage behind the dark curtain.

Kayla leans to the side, sticking out from the straight line.

"Raven."

Raven leans her head of blonde hair sideways. "What do you want?!!" she says with harsh annoyance.

"Good luck." Kay raises her thumbs to be nice. Raven keeps a smile off her face. The girl is still sore about losing and doesn't accept her niceness.

The curtains lift, reeling above Isabell's head. Their instructor doesn't move until the drapes are to the top of the stage. Isa moves forward, holding a microphone. "Hello and good evening ladies and gentlemen." The crowd applauds in a rumble which rolls over the entire theater. "Tonight, Studio Doll has an original: *LUNA*! Enjoy the show." The instructor exits the stage.

The audience quiets down as the music swells, now featuring divine vocalizations. The teens take to the stage. A spotlight falls on each of them, giving a dreamy illusion to their sparkling costumes. The music shifts to cheery. The vocalist sings a playful tune. The dancers join hands, spinning, before branching off across the stage in a magnetic fashion. High on their toes one second, leaping the next. Twirling, impersonating a Ferris wheel.

The stage props come into play. A cardboard moon lowers from the ceiling, along with dangling stars. The artwork is amateur; yet appealing enough to convey the scene. Roses shoot from a hidden compartment on the stage. The crowd mumbles at this addition. The girls effortlessly catch the flowers. The ballerinas float across the stage, gesturing to the moon, bowing, and blowing kisses.

Each ballerina attach strings to the back of their dresses. Once attached, they are flung upwards to the moon. One by one, the prima donnas slip the roses into tiny holes in the glowing prop.

By Act Two, the music transitions to sinister. The singer wails in distress. The stage props advance to factories and city buildings. The hanging stars are gone; now the backdrop displays a murky sky full of clouds. The moon is hazy... no longer clear. The ballerinas prance hectically, in distress. Their feet stir in unity. Pirouettes. Jumping twirls. Graceful struts. High lunges. All while floating on strings, generating poses meant for goddesses. Smoke seeps from the ceiling. The spotlights turn black, hiding the sparkle of the costumes.

Kayla's solo begins. She acts dramatically, weeping, as all the others fall to the floor, becoming motionless. With a single spotlight on her, she gains momentum from the edge of the stage. Her tutu flares as her body is risen mid-air. Kay's hands reach for the moon. But she drops, falling, only to land with crisscrossed legs. The audience cheers. Kayla glides across the stage, much like a skater. She attempts to soar to the moon again…but falls once more, creating a U shape with her entire body.

The tune grows somber. More fog fills the stage. Kayla elegantly shifts her body into configurations. Plié. Wide lunge. Fouettés. Waltz. Arabesque. The crowd roars for the fluidness of her limbs. Kay presents the next movement with undying passion. Assemblé. Attitude. Penché. Grand jeté. Grand adage. En pointe. Then twenty pirouettes without breaking formation. Her body is in God mode. Invincibility and ultimate power charge her up.

She sails to the moon…successful this time. Now face-toface with the blurry light. She waves away the fog, finding dead roses behind the mist. Her dramatic portrayal expresses her anguish. She weeps theatrically.

The orchestra mirrors the emotion with a scaling violin note. The vocalization slows as the singer can express lyrics. "Spirit of earth. Heart of the core. Forgive our transgressions to right our wrongs. Come heal all the trouble… rewrite the stars. Come heal the vessel once loved by gods. Rewrite our danger. Rewrite our harm. Forgive all wreckage, for we are lost. Forgive our sins upon the stars!"

Kay air dances: her feet give the illusion of an invisible floor, mimicking rope walking.

"Dear moonlight, the stars are fading. The moon will meet the same fate. Please give your children another try…to clear the poison which marks the sky!" The vocalist escalates.

The stage combusts with vibrant illumination. A blaze from the moon flashes as the music culminates. The stage backdrop returns to its original state…the clear view of the stars and moon. The live band quiets down…now only the piano plays.

The ballerinas on the floor slowly float midair, no longer stiff of movement. They soar, air dancing and swirling above the stage. The music surges to a happy harmony, drawing out its ending. Piano, strings, drums, and vocals mesh triumphantly. The orchestra reaches the Coda, an epic culmination.. The audience stands and praises the show with an ovation. The Studio Doll members gather at the center of the stage, bowing in unison.

Upon rising, Kayla's ears vibrate violently. Her hazel eyes seek to discover the source. But there are too many faces in the cluster of people. She and her ballet company wave to the crowd as the Queen of England would, elegant and poised.

As they exit the stage, Kay continues trying to pinpoint where the mental disturbance is coming from. Her dark eyes sweep the audience. To her surprise, her sight lands on the fifth row. On the Ahoka family. The parents catch her attention first… then Kota.

THE BOY FROM MY DREAM!! Is that what I'm hearing? Is he the source?

KOTA

Her eyes are earthy. A pleasing mahogany tint… same as her radiant skin. There's a cast of light bordering her body, as if she's a fallen angel with a halo. How does she possess this shine? Is she a divine goddess in human form? Is that possible? Then again, the world I'm in now is impossible. The stage lighting and glittery costumes have nothing to do with her twinkle. It's as if she carries the essence of the burning herbs that my parents ignited. As if she walks with a light source.

She saw me. She looked my way. I wonder what Kayla thinks of me. Do I frighten her?

"Stay here; we'll go backstage." Mato leaves his seat, his wife trailing after him.

Kota taps on his long-range hearing to eavesdrop. He clearly distinguishes his parents' footsteps. This time it's easier to block out all other commotion. His folks exit the stadium and circle around the lobby. There's a narrow hallway; his parents footsteps bounce from the walls almost immediately. The tight hall leads backstage. Kota's ears bend backwards to tune in all noises.

"You were incredible, baby doll!"

"Thanks, Dad!"

"Brava, you shined so bright up there!" Mary kisses her cheeks.

"Mom… stop… don't embarrass me!"

"I'm sorry… I'm just proud!"

"KAY! YOU MURDERED IT!!" Mya sings.

A heavy knock lands on the door. It's too strong to be his mother's. "Who could that be?" Jia contemplates.

"Maybe talent scouts. There's 5 in the crowd!" Mya brags.

"5???!" Mary blurts, amazed. "Oh wow, that's insane!!"

"Answer it, Kayla. I bet it's for you!"

She must have listened to her friend because she approaches the door. Kota knows it's her. He feels the light of her body. A gentle frequency. The vibration is familiar… *as if I've heard it all my life. As if it's a token of my childhood. Why is that?*

He wants to know why she sounds different from other humans. But he has no time to brainstorm. The door opens. She sucks in a breath. *Is she frightened??* He detects Kayla's heart quaking in her chest. Her breathing is shallow. Her lungs are tight. The pressure on her organs worries him. *Oh, no...*

"May we have a word?" Mato begins.

Kay quickly closes the door. *I'm guessing that she's paranoid about being overheard.* She leads my parents down the hall. "I've seen you... both of you...in a portal!"

"We've been trying to connect with you for assistance. Our son is struggling with a curse. Being that you're a Spell Bender, we believe you could help. Of course, we'll have to ask your parents' permission before anything is agreed on."

Her heart rate doubles. "My... my parents don't know what I am," she says in a stuttering whisper. "I don't know how to tell them. So...let's leave this between us. Just for now?"

"Of course... we understand."

"Is that a yes? Will you help us?" Odina impatiently awaits the answer.

"I'm sorry... I have no clue how to help. I don't think I can...I'm sorry."

"Oh..." Odina tries hiding her distress, but her voice is too bleak to conceal her crushed hopes.

"I'm new to this...but my grandmother isn't. She's a Spell Bender. She knows more than I do."

"Your grandmother is like you??" Mato asks in utter disbelief.

"Yes."

KAYLA

Mr. and Mrs. Ahoka share a profound glimpse. "Your father said they're in hiding."

"He must have been wrong..."

Kay is bewildered. "What do you mean by in hiding?" The dressing room door opens. Mary and James. They look the opposite way for their daughter. "They can't know yet..." Kayla whispers in haste.

"We left our phone number with your receptionist. Call us as soon as you can," Odina murmurs.

Her parents notice her with Mr. and Mrs. Ahoka. They walk over. Kayla fixes her anxious expression. "Hello, we're the parents of this talented young lady," He boasts. "I'm James; this is my wife, Mary."

"Lovely to make your acquaintance." Odina shakes Mary's hand.

"Likewise."

"I'm Odina."

"Mato." The dads exchange handshakes as well.

"We don't mean to be brash... but did our daughter surprise you enough to sign her?" Mary believes that they're actual talent scouts.

"Mom... they don't operate that fast." Kayla plays along. Mato goes along with it as well. "Yes... that is true. But we'll keep Ms. Harris on the top of our list and reach out at the proper time." *Wow... he really made that sound certified. Kayla is impressed.*

"Until then, have a wonderful night. Enjoy your celebration."

"Thank you." James nods. Odina and Mato grin pleasantly before departing down the hallway.

That was a close one! I'm glad nothing was exposed. It's not as if I want to hide this from my mom and dad. It's just that I don't know how to address it. Maybe Grandma will expose the truth to them.

Mary wiggles her eyebrows. "That's a good sign that they'll choose you."

"Hopefully. Anyway... are we going out for dinner?"

James shakes his head. "No... we're going home."

"I thought we were going to party?"

"You're still grounded."

She puffs out air from her cheeks. "Fine..."

"KAYLA!!!" Fred howls from behind her. Once again, he causes her to leap out of her skeleton.

"FRED!!" She shrieks. "Why do you do that??"

"Because it's too easy, superstar." He winks. "You owned the stage. I'm so proud of you!"

"Aww, thanks."

Chester and Izzy make their way down the hall. Kay jets over to embrace them. "I'm so sorry about ditching the party." "Don't fret it. We know how harsh your parents are." Izzy shrugs.

"Yeah. We get it, all is good, man." Chester waves his hand nonchalantly.

"We'll...not really. It's not all good. I'm grounded until further notice."

"Damn... that blows!" Izzy grits her teeth.

"Yeah." Kayla stares past their shoulders, expecting to see her boyfriend. Her eyes droop when she doesn't spot him.

"Let me guess... you can't see Darius either?"

Kay grimaces. "Yep...this blows big time."

"Time to head home, sweetie." Mary beckons her over.

"I gotta go... I'll see you guys at school."

"Bye, rockstar."

"Catch you later, dazzle queen." Izzy gives her a wave. Kayla waves goodbye to both them and Fred. Her girls enter the hall.

"Aww, leaving already?" Jia mopes.

"Yeah....I'm grounded."

"Oh, no!"

"Geez, really??" Mya gawks.

"Yeah... really. Let's do walkie-talkies." She huddles with her besties to whisper, "Something else happened...you wouldn't believe it!" When she pulls away, her girls are lost.

Mya strains her eyes, stunned, but keeps herself composed. "Okay...talk later."

"Later."

"Night." As she strolls with her parents, Kay's mind is on Odina and Mato. *I wonder what they meant about Spell Benders being in hiding?? Is that true? If so... what are they hiding from??*

CHAPTER 21: MYSTIFY

KOTA

"There's good and bad news," Mato declares once in the car. He looks to the rearview mirror at the three in the back. "Kayla isn't sure she can aid us... but her grandmother is a Spell Bender." Kota was made aware of this due to his special hearing, but his sister and Grandfather are oblivious.

The old man sucks in a breath. "Her grandmother?!" He's speechless. "Did the child mention a name?"

"No."

The tension lines of his forehead express his brooding. "Very... strange! Two of my kind actively practicing, when there is a pact to remain isolated."

"That's what I assumed," Odina states.

"As you said, this is great news." He beams at his grandson. "We are close to an answer."

"How close?" Kota asks his father through the mirror.

"The girl will call soon...just have patience."

It feels as if I've been waiting forever to receive a solid answer. It seems I'm always waiting. Maybe restlessness is getting the best of me. The fact that I'm so close to the finish line is torture. Kota takes a slow breath and accepts that he has to hold on a little longer. *Kayla can't fulfill my tribulations in one night. Especially with her being new to spelling.*

I wish I could have been there, speaking with her. Hearing her voice without seeing the magnificent face it belongs to….bothers me. Kayla is a reallife princess. Someone meant to be explored in artwork. A goddess of angelic beauty. Even the way she dances. She creates her own wind. The motion of her tutu. An angel in action. I doubt she'll ever see me this way. The look on her face when noticing me in the crowd was... doom. I can't get my hopes up thinking she's just as infatuated as I am with her.

KAYLA

I've never seen such a dazzling guy before. Maybe the fact that he's a vampire amplifies his beauty. I wonder how he looked as a human. It couldn't have been a huge change. Could it? The ashy skin of his has a hint of dark silver... his pale eyes aren't dead. There is life to them, despite him being deceased. *There's a softness... a kindness.* Kayla admires his uncanny good looks, wondering how his voice sounds. *Is it dark or light? Angelic? Or demonic?* She debates while rummaging through her dresser drawer for a pink walkie-talkie. It's bedazzled, same as her pager.

Kay holds the button. Static emits from the radio. "Triplet squad unite. Copy?" She sits on the fluffy carpet of her bedroom floor.

"Copy," Mya replies first.

"Yep, that's a copy."

"There's so much to tell!"

"I don't know... how freaky is it? Because last time was..." Mya's voice trails off.

"Yeah... last time was too much!"

"It's not as weird," Kay assures them. Her eyes are glued to the bedroom door. "I left the party because of what I saw." She mumbles low.

"What did you see?" Jia squeaks.

"Please don't say a monster... I'll have to sleep with my night light on," Mya laughs nervously.

"No... it's nothing like that. It's more bizarre than anything. There was a portal...at the party. That's why I left."

"Portal???"

"To where?!"

"I'm not sure," she answers them both. "But... there was a man and woman on the other end."

"NOO!! This is creepy! Why did you lie and say it wasn't!" Mya shivers.

"As opposed to entering another dimension?" Kay stabs. "How is this creepier?" "It just is!"

"What did they want??" Jia is obviously biting her nails.

Should I creep them out even more by mentioning that vampires are real? That the people I saw need my help with their immortal son? "They..." She monitors her words so she won't give the two a heart attack. "Need my help with something."

"So, they're good guys? Not evil?" Jia's voice trembles.

"No... they're not evil."

"What do they need help with?" Mya stammers.

Once again, Kayla struggles to address the existence of vampires. "I'm guessing something from the world of strange. What else could it be?" She plays dumb to spare sending her girls into hysteria.

Last time my crew got so distressed. I'm not sure if they can handle the word vampire. These beings are considered bloodsucking demons. Although their son didn't appear vicious. Or wicked. Is the evil label just a bad stereotype? Are all vampires bad?? Are they all horrible sins of Satan?

"You still there?" Mya whispers.

"Yeah... I'm still here." "Why did you get so quiet?" "No reason," she says too quickly.

"There's something you're not telling us!" "No." She lies, holding the back of her nape.

"You're a bad liar. I bet you're holding your neck." Kayla quickly drops her hand. "Am not!" "What aren't you telling us??" Jia is frazzled.

"It's been a long day." "Tell us!" Mya emphasizes.

"I scared you two enough for one night."

"I thought you said it wasn't as bizarre. Why are you avoiding it?"

"I'll tell you the rest at school, I promise. We can meet on the roof. Deal?"

"Deal."

"Okay... deal," Mya says in a ghostly monotone.

The pack meets on the roof terrace of the lavish school. The garden is bright green, complete with benches and stone ponds, and the pathway is pebbled with white marble. Kayla peeks out of the door, checking the stairway in case someone tailed them. No one did. They snuck away as everyone went for breakfast in the cafeteria.

She huddles with them around the pond. "We weren't followed."

"Why are you being so secretive?" Mya's eyes size her up.

I should just spit it out... so I can express the dilemma I'm in. "Don't scream... don't run." Jia holds her breath. Mya goes still as a statue. "Nod once to agree..." They do so without speaking. Kay's warning riddles them incapable of forming words. "Okay... so." She clenches her shoulders to her neck. "Vampires are real... I've seen one... well, two, actually. One in a vision and... one last night. In the audience. I think he's our age. The man and woman I saw in the portal were his parents. They need my help....and gave me their number to call." She holds up the note with ten digits on it...one she asks the receptionist for on her way out. "I'm going to call."

Neither Jia nor Mya blinks...or breathe. *This is worse than Halloween night. At least they were responsive. They ran and screamed. Now my girls are silent as corpses... and just as motionless. I hope they don't get sick to their stomachs.* Mya is on the verge of vomiting. Jia's teeth rattle aggressively.

"I don't think all vampires are evil." Kay lightens her voice to somewhat baby-talk the two into a comfort zone.

"Those don't exist..." Jia debates.

Mya is in so much shock that she can't form words. Her mouth opens and shuts as if she's a malfunctioning robot.

"I thought that too... but I've seen them with my own eyes."

"This could all be in your head," Jia croaks.

"Then how did you two see the dimension??"

"Maybe we're all crazy..." she goes on with utter denial.

"No... the Spell Bender books date back to B.C. My gran is flying in to train me; she's one too. My ancestors were the same, so they can't all be insane." This silences them both. Kayla twiddles her thumbs. "I know how it sounds... but our reality is a lie. For all we know, everything from stories is true. It might help if you assume fairytales are real." Kay hopes this solution will break her friends out of the comatose state they're in. "Look... I can't do this alone. I need my girls with me on the call. Please?"

KOTA

The kitchen phone trills. He's the only one in the room and see this as an opportunity. *I want to talk to her. I still feel that we should meet. Hiding me from her is a bad choice. She has no idea who she's helping. Or how much I appreciate it.* Kota moves in on the phone, only for his father to round the corner.

"Everyone to the kitchen, now!" He summons the household. Kota conceals his urge...the enthusiasm he had to pick up the phone is dead now. Mato answers the call that his son wants to take. Those without special hearing hunch their ears to the speaker to make out the words.

"Hello, Mr. and Mrs. Ahoka," Kayla greets formally.

A hotness ruptures his dead heart. As if it has a temperature. As if it is living again. The symphony of her voice awakens a whirlpool in the gloomy tissue. *Huh? What??? How is that possible?? I'm dead... What is happening?*

"I would love if more was explained so I can understand." The sharp frequency of hers is hard for Kota to disregard. His heart inhales every musical note escaping her mouth.

147

"Share any questions you have. We will answer all," Grandad says tenderly.

"What exactly do you need help with?"

"We're hoping to locate a cure..."

"A cure?"

"Yes."

"For vampires?"

"Yes."

"Is that even possible?"

"The earth provides natural cures. Our hope clings to this option," Grandfather enlightens her. "This is the best way, since Kota is new and has not completely lost his humanity."

"Our son hasn't always been this way. This curse is very current," Mato notifies her.

"How current?"

"He was human two weeks ago."

"Oh..." Kayla mutters sullenly. "I'm sorry to hear that."

"Thank you, dear," Odina says with gratitude. "Not just for calling, but for wanting to help as much as you can. We appreciate you involving your grandmother."

"You're welcome."

"When can we arrange a meeting?" Mato asks.

"She flies here in two days. We can meet then."

"Please share her name." Grandad is curious about this.

"Gloria."

"Hmmm..." He knits his gray brows together. "I recall the name..."

"Huh??" Kayla is lost. "How do you know her?"

"I am also a Spell Bender."

"You are?!"

"Yes."

"Wow... there must be loads of us, then?!"

"No... unfortunately, our coven is small."

"Oh..." she mumbles. "Still... it'll be so cool to meet you just to know more of my kind. My grandma will be happy too."

"Please arrange a time as soon as possible." Odina pleads. "We'll host the meeting at our place."

"I will...I promise."

"Do you have any more questions for us, Miss Harris?" "Yes... who are Spell Benders hiding from?"

Grandad responds to this one since Odina is uncertain. "You've seen him in your mind. The blonde demon with red eyes."

Once again, he pieces together the riddle. His grandfather mentioned this before. He thought maybe it was a coincidence. This time, he doesn't keep quiet. "That sounds like the one who attacked me!" he exclaims, staring at his parents, who seem to have forgotten the description their son gave them. They tried to hunt the animal down and failed. So naturally, they forgot the details.

Grandad grimaces. "The possibility is slim..."

"What if it isn't? What if we can locate him using Kayla?" Kota speaks her name for the first time. There's a tone of attachment in the depth of his gentle voice. A sliver of admiration leaks through. "She's seen him!" A hint of vengeance fuels his thirst.
His eyes glint ruby, stirring the fiend inside to wake up.

"This isn't about revenge, son."

"This isn't revenge... it's justice." Kota combats his father.

"Sometimes both blur into one..."

"THAT THING IS A MURDERER!!"

"Calm yourself!" Mato chastises him with a hard glare.

Kota stews in anger. *Why won't he hear me out? Even if the description is a coincidence, he should be on my side. Helping me!! Why can't my father support me?!*

Odina rummages through a kitchen drawer, retrieving a pen and paper. "Maybe we should listen, dear." She hands him the items. "Draw what you remember of the creature...that way Kayla can confirm the truth." This eases him a bit. He appreciates that his mother is with him on this... yet he's still wounded that his father isn't. Odina stares at the phone. "Miss Harris. Do you have any more questions?"

KAYLA

She's too distracted by what has just been said. She can't fathom another question. *I guess that's all for now. Our next meeting will be another chance for me to take the floor. Plus, the bell has just rung. I have to go to first period.* "None that I can think of. I'll let you know If I have more questions. Goodbye for now."

"Yes... goodbye for now," Mrs. Ahoka replies. The line ticks off.

The trio stands inside a gray phone booth of the curb, their ears around the speaker. Kayla gapes at the receiver, wondering if Kota is right. *I did see him and the other vampire in exact order. As if the sequences were linked. Was that more than a coincidence??* She hangs up the phone and turns to her posse. "Thank you. I owe you guys big time."

"Yeah, you do...the nightmares are on the way," Mya is as stiff as a board.

"I can't believe this!" Jia teeth still rattles, they haven't stopped since the rooftop.

"I know... me too. I questioned my sanity, too. But it's true... and I think this is only the beginning." Mya blows out jagged breaths. Kay assumes her heart is attacking her...that she's having an anxiety outbreak. Her breathing is hoarse and fast. "Deep breaths in and out, it's okay, " Kayla coaches, same as a therapist does.

"NO!" Her raspy growl is strained. "No...none of this is okay! It's not okay!!" Mya flees from the phone booth to panic in private...away from them...away from the truth. Jia hurries after Mya to console her, although she needs emotional assistance too. Her hand clutch at her collarbone, digging into the flesh until it's pitted white. They leave her by herself in the booth.

Kayla cradles her head in her hands, distraught. *I wish this was easier for my girls. I wish they could adapt to this odd universe like I have. I was scared for a bit... before adjusting myself. Was that because I decided to ignore it and press on? Or because my bloodline has been exposed to it for centuries?? Strangeness is part of my history.*

In history class, the topic remains the same. *I guess The Vampire Dugout is the assigned subject for this month too.* She bets there will be some huge final assignment to sum up the studying. Kayla finds herself more and more intrigued by it, now that she knows the truth. Today, the class utilize VCN ExecuVision, a computer presentation software. The students work in the library on white, hump-backed computers, using slideshow tools and text to sum up their assignments.

The chalkboard reads:

**PREPARE A NEWS REPORT SCENARIO.
CHOOSE THREE TOPICS TO DISCUSS ON CAMERA.**

Cliff raises his hand. "What is it, Mr. Cliff?" the plump man breathes out firmly.

"A news report? Why are we doing that?"

"To place yourselves in the past. You'll also dress accordingly and speak in 1918 dialect. But you'll have plenty of time before the video is due. As of now, I'm arranging an educational trip to Belgium."

Kayla tugs her mouth to one side. *A trip to Belgium? To a place lurking with immortal creatures???* The Ouija board revealed what was beneath the surface. The scarlet-eyed, blonde villain that banished Spell Benders. *Kota's conclusion wasn't wrong. I've seen who killed him... and possibly know where the beast is.*

I can't wait for our next meeting so I can confirm this. I don't need a picture drawn to verify the truth. The only issue is how my words will promote danger. The fury and pain Kota has will lead to a fight. This vampire murdered him and damned his soul forever…why wouldn't he want to get even?

CHAPTER 22: BITTERSWEET

KOTA

I tap into my past memory…which I didn't know I could do. I guess my rage has a strong will. I revisit the campsite and apply my enhanced senses. My human eyes were too low-grade to peer beyond the darkness. The firelight had glared brighter in my mortal phase. In my immortal phase, I see through all the blackness of the night. Crystal clear.

The face of my enemy is just as I would've imagined—snarled and vicious. There's a glint of joy hiding in his smile. His pure, bloody eyes burn as flames of hell would. The smirk of dominance. The complete disregard for human life. As if we were just packs of food. I don't choose to kill... but this devilish man does.

Kota fixates on the drawing he produced. Now he has a face to place to his suffering. A face to target his wrath on. Since he cannot sleep as a vampire, he spends the night glaring at the drawing in his bedroom. There's no light on in the tiny space; only the source of the moon shines in.

Kayla must be able to give me a location on this beast. It'll be difficult to ask since we're not allowed to be alone. Father still feels that it'll be too overwhelming for her. And my dad always sticks to his word...which is annoying. I have to speak with her...alone.

The sound of digging breaks his attention. It's dawn now. Kota realizes how long he's been evil-eyeing the paper. Time got away from him. He speeds to the window. Odina is digging up dirt and dumping it into a trash bag. It doesn't take him long to understand why. *The soil is dead.* He hears its dry crumbling all the way from his room. The dehydrated particles have no nutrients. The dirt breaks apart in his mother's hands, which she uses as a shovel.

Kota decides to go help. He dashes down to her in less than a second. "Oh, my!" Odina shudders in fear.

"Sorry...you guys aren't used to that yet," he says, apologetically clenching his teeth.

"Maybe give a signal first."

"I'll whistle next time." Kota bends to help her dig out the ruined soil. "What are we planting?"

"Vegetables and fruits. I all but puked from the ones in the house. I can't believe your Grandad is eating poison. I taste all of the horrid chemicals."

"Wow..."

"So, a garden is ideal."

"It is." Kota sinks his palms deeper than his mother's, going a few feet in depth. "That sounds fun... I'll help."

"It'll be a family project." Odina rests her hands on her lap. "The problem is finding pure dirt. I'll look into purchasing imported soil."

"Or I could sniff it out for you... free of cost."

She raises her brows. "You can do that?"

Kota lets the coarse dirt splatter from his palms to the ground. "I hear the damage...plus, the smell is tough."

"What does it smell like?"

Kota sniffs, cyphering a gassy scent from the atmosphere. "Like...nitrogen."

Odina tries to whiff the air to distinguish the scent as he does; but fails. "That's remarkable."

"Yeah...there are cool perks to this curse."

"True... but killing isn't one." His mother lectures. "I know you all too well, *walela* (hummingbird)." She shakes her head. "Your appetite to slaughter is unneeded. I agree with you about getting justice...I wish to make that demon suffer for what it did. But you want to avenge your friends' deaths... and yours."

"Shouldn't I?"

Odina takes hold of his forearm. "No... sometimes we must forget in order to move on."

"I can't do that," he scowls.

"You must... don't destroy your soul."

Flashbacks to the bloody night plagues him. The party in the forest with his deceased friends. Carelessly gorging on pizza and beer. Embodying the rock song as if on stage. Their companionship is haunting. The burden on Kota's soul when he couldn't save them. The survivor's guilt. He stands fast. "I'll track down the soil."

KAYLA

I want to call Darius. Kayla surveys the hallway, inspecting it for her father since he hasn't ended the restriction. *I wonder how long this will last! It's so annoying! I did one bad thing out of all of my life and got the worst punishment ever?? I miss Darius. I needed him there at my show. My dad could have at least allowed him to attend. We've never been apart for this long. He even drives me to school, so I can't walk with my boyfriend anymore. This is getting ridiculous. Why is my mom going along with it??? Why are they controlling my life??!!*

Kay dials in his number. It's 5PM—he should be home working on music. The line doesn't take long to cease its trilling. It only rings twice. "I miss you," she murmurs.

"Hi, superstar."

"Hiii!! I miss you so much," she mutters softly so her father doesn't hear.

"Is your dad still mad at me?"

"Yes."

"Wow..."

"I know... it's so unfair."

"Do you know how long you're grounded for?"

"No clue..."

"I gave Jia a mixtape to give you."

"You made a new one?"

"Yeah, I'm entering a contest, so I'm making a bunch."

"I didn't know you were submitting it! That's great!" "It is...and could get me into art school, which is—" "Your dream," they say in unison.

"I'll wish you all the luck. If you were here, I'd hug and kiss you," she beams, curling the braided telephone cord around her fingers.

"If you were here, we'd be cuddling in my bed."

Kayla gasps. "Darius...!" Her cheeks flush a fiery shade, and her heart backflips.

"KAYLA!!" The phone drops from her hand; swinging. She whips around fast. James glowers at her. "Hang up the phone this instant!" She obeys him in blinding speed. "I haven't given you permission to speak to him!"

"How long before I can??"

"We'll let you know."

"That's so unfair!!"

"Don't raise your voice at me! You just extended your grounding." Kayla grunts in annoyance. "Do you want to go for a full year??"

"No!"

"Then correct your tone."

She peers to the side, full of resentment. "I'm sorry," she mumbles.

"Go to your room."

She slouches away, her posture as bleak as her blue heart. *All I want to do is talk on the phone. Dad is overreacting and attacking me for no reason! How many times do I have to apologize??? I HATE HIM!!* She slams her door so hard to the frame that it jiggles the wood casing. Then she locks it…caging herself away. Kay picks up wired headphones. Her frazzled fingers plug the aux jack into a Walkman cassette player.

She flings herself onto her princess bed and plays the mixtape. A romantic and stunning instrumental streams the air: piano, harp, flute, ocean. The music sends sedative shivers through her body. Kayla daydreams the inside a seashell, imagining the lovely tune as the ocean's acoustics. A chime within a shell. Her mind envisions a lone seashell on a beach at night, trapped in a cold void… all by itself. Just like her.

Doesn't Mom and Dad understand that I love him? Do they even know?? Maybe if I told them this, they'd lessen my punishment. Kay sheds tears…enough droplets to flush her face with squiggly lines.

When James visits her room to call her to dinner, she protests. "I'm not hungry."

"Don't be ridiculous, you have to eat."

"Just leave me alone!!" She sniffles into her pillow and wipe the waterworks from her chin.

"I'll handle this," Mary shoos her husband away to be the middleman. Her mom sits beside her, rubbing her back. "I know you think we're being bullies… but you have no idea how bad that night was. We thought you were lost. Hurt. Kidnapped. That's why we called the police. You didn't ask our permission. I was your age once. I know how your mind tricks you—like you're trapped. Like you're not in control. I'll never wish that on you." Mary kisses the top of Kay's head.

"But you do!" she sniffles. "You're just like Dad."

Mary exhales. "Parents are overprotective. We fear the worst. To us, there are boogeymen around every corner. There are monsters walking this planet. We view the world as a danger zone. Your dad and I just want to protect you."

Why did she say monsters?? Out of all the words to use…she uses monsters? Does she mean evil humans?? Or does my mother know about the paranormal? "Monsters?" Kay queries, trying to quench her curiosity.

"Some humans are living demons. But I guess we can't have such a stronghold on your life because of paranoia. I'll consider easing up. I'll have a chat with your dad."

Kayla hoists herself onto her elbows. "Really? You'll loosen the leash?"

Mary nods. "Just a little."

Kay cuddles her mother tightly, expressing inexplicable happiness. "Thank you."

"But you'll have to wait until you're un-grounded."

"Okay... I can do that."

Mary takes her daughter by the hand to bring her along. "Now let's eat. I'll tell your dad to take a chill pill."

"Eww... Mom, don't ever say that again." Kayla snorts.

"What? I'm hip and bad to the bone." She imitates Michael Jackson's glove dance. The hip thrusts and head jerks tickle Kay's funny bone.

"MOM! STOP!" she snorts aloud same as a donkey.

"James! Come quick!"

"No, Mom, don't!"

"Your princess is a donkey in disguise!" Mary cackles, buckling over. Kayla lets out an amusing donkey sound; helpless to stop herself.

KOTA

I travel far for clean soil. But I don't mind the detour. I needed to escape that conversation before guilt set in. I can't forget and move on as if I didn't witness Liz, Jimmy, and Mike slaughtered before my eyes. Right in front of me! I was useless! My parents will never understand the depth of failing the people you love. *Maybe if they lost me or Dyani to death, then they'll know how crippling and worthless the world becomes.* They've never had loved ones killed while they watched. *NEVER!*

Kota isn't sure where he is. Somewhere north, near the rim of Lake Michigan. There's more beach and concrete and less human interference. The soil is nice and damp, free of toxic fumes. He scoops it up. It's fine and soft in his hands, warm and moist. *That's perfect. I should have thought this through. I don't have anything to transport the soil. Maybe sand buckets would be ideal... there has to be some around.*

His speedy feet lead him to the sandy shore. His bright eyes shimmer through the curtain of night, inspecting the grainy surface. He's surrounded by grass and trees. The area is completely isolated from the city. A hidden paradise. If not for the urban, ambience, one would think they weren't in a city. This place is peaceful. So tucked away from the rest of the world.

Kota has no luck locating sand buckets, so he doubles back around to try the other direction. His footsteps possess an echo. *Huh? That's strange.* He figures it's a trick of his mind. Or that it's the pebbled surface below causing the illusion of two pairs of feet. He continues on, ignoring it. Once he passes the tree line, his nose detect a venomous odor.

Cherry colored eyes watch him from the tree line. Kota isn't aware of being studied. He's too busy registering the awful scent. His nose flares back in disgust. The scent is similar to a skating rink; a bitter, cold aroma. Accompanied by a repulsive, peroxideesque fragrance. If he were human, he would throw up, but Kota's stomach is made of steel.

Just before he can rotate in the direction, the burgundy irises disappear in the dark. Kota observes the edge of the tree line. There's a sidewalk cutting through the pathway… nothing more. *But what is that smell?? It isn't the soil…it's too rancid to be from the ground.*

Kota nears the source of the stink, hoping to unveil it. The tree line is clear. *There are rodents here. Maybe a skunk sprayed. Maybe…?* He concludes, still oblivious of the evil one stalking him from the tree line, hunched and hidden from sight. The inflamed eyes trace Kota's every motion.

He steps along the shoreline, which leads to the main beach. He can't help but rake his mind for an explanation. *What was that subzero fragrance? As if Arctic ice had somehow visited the city??? And the hydrogen peroxide fume?? That's strange…*

Halfway down the sandy ground, Kota is urged by his instincts to turn around. He does so…eyeing the top of the trees. Where the vampire just was. Kota peers. *It has to be a rodent hiding on a high branch.* He convinces himself, unaware of it being an immortal being. The main beach has what he's looking for. Many buckets litter the sand. A few are swept away into the black, rippling water. Kota chooses two large ones that were previously used for a sandcastle, which was trampled by the receding lake. The remains of the structure are diminished to soggy, wet mush.

As he shakes out the wet sand, a sixth sense forces him to view the murky water. This time, he almost spots the hell fire eyes. Almost. The sinister, blonde vampire dips below without a sound. Without causing a disturbance in the tide…not even a ripple. Kota sets down the buckets to analyze the spot. *Okay… now this is weirding me out. I'm tempted to swim to see. But I'll likely waste my time over jumping fish. What else could it be?*

My amplified senses are overcomplicating simple occurrences. That's all. Now… I have to get back home. I know Mom is worrying. I'll apologize for running off like that.

He retrieves the buckets, cleaning them in the ocean before packing handfuls of soil into each. He doesn't stop until each one is filled to the brim. Then he sprints off.

Kota zooms so rapidly that the buckets have no time to react to the velocity. His feet never touch the ground. His arms work too fast to register their next swing. He's unseen by the naked eye. The humans notice no change in the wind. No sound of supernatural footsteps. No presence of a vampire racing the streets.

When he comes to a stop in the backyard, the buckets finally respond to the insane momentum. Both of them swing forward, looping his wrist. Not a drop of dirt falls out…not a single grain. The delayed reaction astounds him. *Whoa!! Narly! I was moving that fast??? Was I shifting through space and time? Blurring the lines in another dimension?? I just defied gravity!*

"Whoa, baby bro!" Dy cheers from the back porch. "You better hope that little trick of yours helps Mom to forgive you."

"What do you mean??" He sets down the buckets.

"You disappeared… and reminded them of that…night. I'm pretty sure she's experiencing PTSD. You know that crap from Vietnam?"

"Oh, no…" He leaps up the steps and into the kitchen. His mother isn't there. He uses his nose to locate her. Odina's natural aroma is just the same as he remembered. A delightful perfume. As if she rolls sweet dough on a daily basis. This rids his nose of the horrid odor from the beach. He's lured to the front porch, where his mother is sitting.

She's in a swinging chair, rocking in it to tame her building tension. Kota does a light whistle to alert her. Odina responds better this time yet is still startled; there's a slight jerk of her back. "Kota!" She leaves the chair. "Where did you go??!"

"Sorry, Mom… I needed to think."

"About what??"

"If I don't avenge them… then their deaths will always be in vain. I can't forget. My mind won't let me. Time won't let me."

"Dear…" She cups his face in her palms. "Please… don't ruin your soul. Say your farewells. Visit their graves…find closure."

CHAPTER 23: UNITE

KAYLA

My granny is on her way here. Mom went to get her. I wish I could've gone, but I'm on house arrest. I guess I should be on good behavior to end it faster. Mom talked it out with Dad, and I apologized once again. I hope he releases me from this jail. Although he isn't budging on Darius. He really does think he's a bad influence.

Of course, I shut my trap and didn't bicker... but that sunk my gut to the depths of my stomach. This can't be forever, can it? Is this a permanent arrangement? Will I ever see my boyfriend again?? I can't imagine this being forever. I don't even think I could love again.

Kayla's mind blooms with the image of Kota. His alluring essence, silky dark hair. His ivory irises. The softness of him.. *I sensed no danger...or evil in him. He must be a good type of vampire. One with a heart. His graceful eyes grabbed my attention... regardless of there being hundreds of others in the crowd. He stole my attention...and I liked it.*

She wags her head like a puppy to clean it of the thought. No... *what am I thinking??! I'm with Darius! Our separation is temporary. I can't give up on him. Kota will be a friend... and nothing more.*

Kay sits on a bench built into the windowpane, with a blanket wrapped around her shoulders. She peeps at the morning sun as it reflects the shiny sky rise towers. The slow rise over the mad city...is so pensive. The elevator dings open. Kay dashes from the bench to greet her granny. Her grandmother has her salt-andpepper hair in a high bun. This highlights her cheekbones and bluegray eyes. Kayla embraces her gran, loving the perfume she wears; one that reminds her of a gingerbread house. Of the many childhood Christmases when they crafted the dessert together.

Her mind time-travels; vividly revisiting her and Gran, squeezing the white cream along the beige edges and creating the buttons for the doors. This time her freaky time-traveling skill isn't alarming… she's thankful for the crisp memory playing in her mind.

"Hello, my firefly." Gloria's voice is full of spunk.

"Hi, Gran-Gran."

"How are you holding up?"

Mary, who departs the elevator, is taken aback. "What do you mean by, how is she holding up??"

Kayla beats her Granny to the punch before she can expose the big secret. "She means about the grounding…" Granny gives a stunned expression. A dazed response, which translates to: *You haven't told her!*

"Oh." Mary shrugs. "I mean...you grounded me hundreds of times; this is her first."

"Yes... that comes with the parent role. Although you were unruly. Your mother rode motorcycles. Got tattoos...and totaled my car. Just to name a few." Gran puts her hand on her hips. "And she has the nerve to ground you?? What did you do?"

"I went to a Halloween party."

"HA!" Gran laughs roughly. "I wished she only went to parties. That would have been less of a headache!"

"Mom...enough." Mary stops the mechanical doors from closing. "Kay, come get the suitcases."

"Don't get embarrassed now, dear." Gran slaps her daughter's shoulder. Mary throws her mother a chiding stare.

"Uh oh..." Kayla cringes while rolling two suitcases from the metal lift.

"I'm not afraid of that look... you learned it from me." James's dress shoes tap from down the hall. "Ah, son-in-law! It's been a spell, hasn't it?"

"Yes... five years. We missed you." He goes in for a hug.

"How's the patent business? Any crazy inventions?"

"Well... there's this idea for a video disk that could replace the VCR tape."

"Oh! That would be lovely! The hassle of unjamming the film on those darn things are a pain in the as—" Granny rephrases her curse word since her granddaughter is present. "Pain in the tush." She uses the clean version.

"Yes...that would be something."

"Thank the patent holder on my behalf." "I'll
place it on my to-do list." James pokes.

"Is there a sketch?" Kayla requests, her artist side is intrigued.

"Sure is... it's on my desk, if you want to take a peek." "Put
away the luggage first." Mary demands of her.

"Okay." Kay quickens her stride, going to the guest bedroom, which is a carbon copy of the rest of the house.

The paneled walls outlined in gold, the plush carpet. The only difference is the jumbo bed, a floral pattern along the sheets and frame. She rolls the suitcases to the side of the bed and parks them, then hurries to her dad's office. His desk is cluttered with folders that stack higher than the chair.

She circles around the towers of documents to locate the sketch. *I haven't drawn in a while... that's why I'm eager to see it. I don't know many other artistic people. This is the only graphic I've seen drawn by someone else.* The flat disk drawing resembles a dinner plate. A saucer. *It's so futuristic... so compact. How will that play a video?? It must have some type of device inside it. But where?? It's so...flat.*

Granny posts beside her. The elderly woman checks if the coast is clear... her daughter and son-in-law didn't follow her in. "Why haven't you told your mother?" she mutters lowly.

"I don't know how to... I was hoping you could."

"You have to tell her the truth. You can't have me do it."

"Mom will think this is a prank, like she thought with you."

"Then you'll have to show her by casting."

"She'll have a heart attack!"

"Dear... you have to be brave. Don't let the truth stay hidden. Your mom and dad will ask about the meeting."

"Not if we do it in secret."

Gran-Gran gives a harsh scoff. "Where exactly? You're on punishment and can't leave the house."

"We have to leave, anyway. We're not meeting with the Ahokas here. It's too risky! Maybe if you break my grounding, they won't be mad. You could say we're making up for missed years. We haven't seen each other in forever. They'll buy that excuse."

Granny's forehead wrinkles: her eyes go beady. "I suppose I can't get into any trouble over it. But when will we leave?"

"Mom is out at 7:30. Dad at 8:00. We're meeting at their place; I just have to give them the time."

Her grandmother pinches her lips together. "And you said their son isn't dangerous?"

"I don't think he is."

"I'll train you on how to read auras. Some people can trick you into believing they're safe. Seeing the energy they emit eliminates that threat."

"Wow... seeing energy??"

"Yes...imagine the bedroom encounter, but triple-fold."

"I can't wait!" Kay exclaims.

"Can't wait for what?" James wanders into the room, going to his desk to take a seat.

Gran thinks of a quick cover-up. "To open the crystals, I bought. I felt bad being away from my grandbaby for so long, so I may have done some spoiling." She scoops Kay into a deep hug. "We have so much catching up to do!"

KOTA

Mom and Dad are laying soil in the garden in the backyard. Dyani is out with Grandad buying seeds to plant. I'm alone in the house, scowling at the picture I drew of my enemy. My mind thinks back to the beach… to when I felt I was being watched.

Was it a rodent? Was it a fish? Did I encounter something more? I'll have to go back and investigate. I know the difference between nature's pets. In Oklahoma, so many animals visited us for food. So many deer, horses, raccoons, and dogs stalked our house…with good intentions. Whatever was watching me last night didn't have good intentions. It felt too…eerie.

The phone is about to ring…he's glad it hasn't yet. Another perk of vampirism is knowing a sound is coming before it does. A delayed action in real time…the ring has a 5 second buffer window. The electrical wires fizz off before the chime does. Kota rips his eyes away from the picture and zips downstairs to the wall receiver just in time. Answering it before it can even warble.

"Hello? Mr. and Mrs. Ahoka?"

His heart squeezes. Just from hearing her speak, the dead organ livens up, imitating a beating heart. The empty chambers gush with blood, palpitating an intense rhythm. *How is this possible??!! I'm dead!! How am I able to feel this??*

"Hello… is anyone there??"

"Yes…I'm sorry about that." He responds in a distracted tone.

"Oh… should I call back later?" Kay assumes this isn't a good time.

"No, now is fine. You can tell me whatever it is." His chest thumps up a storm. Kota holds a hand to his heart. *Blood clashes it. Can vampires have heart attacks??!*

"My grandmother is here. We're able to meet at 10:00." Kota checks the time on the kitchen clock. It's 7:35. "Is that time okay?"

"It should be. I'll let everyone know."

"Thank you. See you soon, Kota." She says his name so easily…as if they are good friends already.

"See you soon, Kayla." He states her name as effortlessly as she says his.

A fluttering sensation attacks his gut. Kota hangs up. *What is this?? I'm dead! How is she arousing my heart and stomach into a frenzy?? The stream of oxygen in my veins is bizarre. An adrenaline rush. A thirst. The*

Kota updates his fam about the meeting time. Of course, his mother and sister tidy up, although the house is spotless. Grandad goes to whip up an egg, bacon, and oatmeal casserole while Mato has a chat with his son. "Your attendance is needed at this meeting. There's no need to be as cautious, especially since she's aware of you."

"How do you kno—"

"My father told me of her visions. She's seen you and the other one—the one you believe is the reason for your curse." "I'm certain of it," he declares with undeniable confidence. "If this is so…you won't take matters into your own hands. Your mother and I will cage the monster away. That's final." He ends the discussion by walking off.

I don't understand why he and Mom are against real justice!! Caging him away doesn't fit the crime. It lets him off easy. It allows the wicked man to live! Why should he live when he's killed? That's not justice… that's mercy! Kota ramps up angrily. *Mom isn't even asking what's wrong with me. Dad must have confided in her… and took control of the issue.*

I'm sick of being treated as if I'm wrong. I don't care what my parents say! I'm not forgetting and moving on! I'm not letting my father take charge of something he doesn't even understand!!

He would've carried his temper into the conference if it weren't for Kayla's effect on him. The tune of her essence alleviates his anger. Her light source has a formidable refrain. He can only compare it to a stringed orchestra; a melody of bliss that radiates from within. *I wish it were louder… it's faint.*

A volcano ignites his heart. His lungs fill up. Aching spikes from his arms to his forehead. Kota's entire body thrives. He flames all over. The icy temperature of death no longer riddles him. *I don't understand… how is she doing this to me?*

There's a knock at the door. Odina goes to it. Kota focuses on the current situation, knowing he has to get ahold of himself. *I have to relax. I can't overwhelm her with…whatever this is.* He wills his body to meditate through breathing, to lessen the abnormal reaction and tame this oddity. When the door opens, her brightness impairs him.

"Good morning," his mother greets the guests.

"And a lovely morning it is, thank you."

That must be her grandmother. My sight is hazy…I hope it clears up soon. I need to see Kayla.

"I'm Gloria Cooke. Nice to meet you."

"Likewise. Please come in and have a seat." Odina leads the guests to the dining table.

"Welcome," Grandad begins. "Help yourselves to breakfast casserole." He passes down bowls of the meal in a supply chain line until everybody has one.

"Thank you." Kayla sits down.

Kota enjoys the sound of her voice. *I have to see her.* He compels his brain to enforce better imaging. A normal boy would've popped a head vessel doing so. Kota restores his eyes. Kayla is…staring at him. *I know that she's magical… but her appearance indicates she may not be mortal. Is she human?? The radiance she has. The divine beauty. The blazing glare of her skin. She's an enchantress.*

KAYLA

His ivory eyes should freak me out… instead, they're fascinating. I could get lost in them. I should focus elsewhere, but that's impossible to do. I've never been so fascinated in my entire life. He's the prettiest boy I've ever seen! He should be sculpted! Kota already has marble skin…he just has to be placed on display for the world to see.

"Uh…ummm." Granny clears her throat. Kay snaps back to reality. *Oh, no… was I just slobbering over him?? Did everyone see?? I hope not. I can't help it. His irises are an X-ray.* "Shall we begin?"

Kayla peers down at her hands. "Yes."

"Introductions should be revisited, for your grandmother's sake," Mr. Ahoka proposes.

"That'd be great." Gloria simpers politely.

"Mato."

"Odina."

"Elu," grandad offers his real name.

"Dyani, the big sis." She jabs a finger at her little brother. "It's obvious who he is."

He needs no introduction, yet he still gives one to be respectful. "Hi…I'm Kota." He zeroes in on Gloria instead of Kayla, so he doesn't get lost in her.

"It's nice to meet you. My granddaughter has told me everything. I'm so sorry that this has happened to you." She shares a pitiful frown. "I'm sure the three of us can work out a plan."

"Five," Odina clarifies. "My husband and I can offer magic."

"You're also Spell Benders??"

"No…I'm a second-grade caster…the gene isn't with me."

"And you?" Gloria looks to Mato.

"The gene has passed me, but I still activated the right to cast through initiation. So…I'm practically a second-grade too."

Gloria eyes Dyani and Kota. "What about your children?"

"Dyani can initiate as a second-grade speller once she's of age."

"What about him?"

"He's unable to cast."

Kota gives a tangled look to his father. He recalls releasing himself from the locking spell Mato had set upon him. "I used a freedom charm to break myself from your magic. How… when I'm not of age?"

His father mumbles in agreement, "That's true… he did."

"That was the bloodline's final attempt to guide him to the light." Grandfather gives an answer to this.

"I believe so," Gloria agrees with Elu. "The ability revealed itself for the first and last time. Vampires cannot cast."

Kayla explores her mind, speculating how she was allowed to call upon the wind when she didn't initiate. *Even Jia wondered how I performed witchcraft without instigation.* "I didn't initiate either for my first time. But I was able to summon. How?"

"Because you have the birth gene… you can cast freely since you're not second grade. As Benders, we do not need to activate our power," Elu provides the reasoning behind this puzzle.

"Oh…" Kay mumbles while avoiding Kota's electric eyes, although his are on hers. She finds breathing difficult, experiencing what she believes is claustrophobia. He has the ability to hack her system…to rapidify her heartbeat. She reaches for a glass of water, pretending it isn't essential to control her vitals. Kayla sips slowly, when she wants to gulp it down as if dying of thirst.

"When will the remedy be uncovered?" Kota enquires, addressing her one on one.

Kayla adores his tender voice. *It's better than I imagined.* "I have to be trained first. My gran says her strength isn't what it was before. Meaning I'd be the main speller for the cure."

"We'll be your anchors, Kayla. Elu and I will work as links for Odina and Mato. Think of a car needing a jumping cable. With the five of us, we'll have enough range to discover a healing method," Gloria says, without a doubt.

"When will the training begin?" Kota wonders.

Kay gazes at her grandmother. "When will we start?"

"Tonight…when your parents are asleep. You still have to tell them."

"I know…I'll tell them tomorrow."

"I apologize for not having an exact date… but I'll work as quickly as I can to hone her skills," Gloria stresses to the group. "Any other questions?"

"Yes." Kota decides to ask the big one. One that'll give closure. One that will begin the quest to execute his foe. He unravels the drawing. "Kayla…" His tone of endearment is slightly revealed, but he doesn't care. "I drew the vampire." He slides the artwork her way.

Her artistic mind is seized by his craftsmanship. *Is he an artist like me?? I doubt a rookie could sketch this well. Or does his immortality gift him with perfect skill? If so, that's impressive. I want to ask, but now isn't the time. I should stay on task.* One glance at the art tells her what she already knew.

That's the same guy from the campfire. I knew it. I should say yes. That it is, without a doubt, the same devil man. Although I don't want to begin a blood bath. Should I lie to prevent Kota from the truth?? But lying isn't a strong suit of mine. He'll know. Everyone will. Then I'll have to explain myself. That'll be… awkward. I'll just give Kota what he wants.

Kayla locks eyes with him and says, "Yes… that's the man I saw in the vision."

CHAPTER 24: VILLAIN

KOTA

He zones out of reality. The word "yes" is all he registers. The rest of her sentence is inaudible. *I KNEW IT! NOW I MUST DESTROY HIM!!* "Where…?" He speaks in a lethal calmness. "Where did you see him? Tell me…"

"He doesn't need to know…" Mato's eyes dart to Kayla, cautioning her not to answer. "You can tell me in private. My wife and I will handle the predator."

"NO!!" Kota shouts maliciously, knocking the chair back hard enough that it shatters into pieces.

"CALM YOURSELF!" Mato bellows.

"YOU'RE NOT TAKING THIS AWAY FROM ME!! HE LIKED KILLING MY FRIENDS!! YOU DIDN'T SEE WHAT I SAW!!"

Odina stands to stretch her arms between them, fearing a fight. Her son is unstable. Addicted to revenge. Out for blood. "Please, let us handle this, son!"

"BY LETTING HIM LIVE??!!" His voice distorts. The old fiend influences him yet again. The evil ego leaches out. Kota is no longer his sweet self. He's possessed. Dyani freezes in place. Gloria gets up fast to shield Kayla behind her. Scared.

"This meeting is over… I'm sorry for the inconvenience." Mato addresses Kay and her gran without taking his eyes off his son. "Until next time."

"I completely agree." Gloria directs her granddaughter to the door in hasty terror. "Time to go." Odina doesn't walk them out; she's too weary to lower her arms that are acting as protector barriers. So, the two show themselves the exit.

"Settle down," Mato disciplines him.

Elu pouts at the sinful wrath of his grandson. "Don't lose yourself to this madness…"

If steam could leave Kota's body, it would fog the room. All he sees is retaliation. His face creases: his mouth snarls. His eyes flicker white and black, slowly inviting the dark one in. He mugs down his father. "I'LL KILL HIM… THERE'S NOTHING YOU CAN DO TO STOP ME!!" His light voice is demented, glitchy. "THAT'S FINAL!"

His old fiend resurfaces. **KILL! KILL!** It cheers him on, desperate for chaos. **KILL OUR VILLAIN!!** Black fluid overtakes his eyes.

Mato signs a hand symbol; the air outlines white, prepping for the casting. But Kota disappears in a flash. Elu wobbles up from the chair in great dismay. Odina gasps.

"Oh, no…" Dyani huffs out tragically.

Miles away, Kota and his dark side thrives. **DEATH TO HIM! DEATH! REMEMBER WHAT WAS DONE TO YOUR FRIENDS. YOUR SWEET FRIENDS…**

"Yes… what was done to them."

The flashbacks of long talons slicing Mike and Jimmy's necks wide open. Squirts of splattering crimson. Liz's bone crushing screaming. The creature chewing her neck. The grotesque crunch of her bones. The fleshy pieces of Liz's neck ripped away. The raining blood. The animal's swallowing…feasting. Liz's body dropping unresponsive due to the shock. The groans of throaty pleasure.

"HE WILL DIE!!!" His blurry feet shatter down the streets as fast as lightning.

All this reminiscing grants him a new detail. The past speaks to him. The wind from the horrid night carries a cruel aroma. The same one he encountered on the beach. Only his nose was oblivious of the meaning. *Nothing on this earth has that revolting smell. Something that belongs in hell. That was him! I should've followed my gut. That was no squirrel, no skunk, no fish. That was him!*

"I CAN TRACK HIM!" His nose singles out the icy, chemical scent.

Trees haze as he sweeps the west side of Chicago. Kota bolts forward. Passing residential homes in milliseconds. Rocketing past train tracks, boarded-up houses, and gas stations. He accelerates beyond the eye can see. His legs whip past fields of wheat and corn, passing barns and farmhouses. His nose flares, searching for the fragrance. From miles away, he whiffs out the flavors of gas, money, alcohol, cigarettes, and asphalt.

DAMN IT! IT'S NOT THERE!! Kota pushes ahead, willing his nose radar to span further. But it only singles out planted foods, fruits, and vegetables. He streaks the border of Indianapolis, searching for the fume. Spanning the entire state. Every fiber of plant life, every inch of human skin, every repulsive odor. Finding nothing out of the ordinary.

Nashville is next. The cologne of his foe is nowhere within the state. Alabama is a giant state, so he has to curve in a U-shape along its lower region to access every living fiber.

"COME ON!!! WHERE ARE YOU!!!" He combs through Tallahassee before venturing to Georgia, another massive state he spends a lengthy time hunting in. *How is there nothing?? I have to find him! I have his scent… how is there nothing???*

Florida and the Carolinas present the same failure. Kota travels up the coast states. Washington. New Jersey. Rhode Island. Boston. Portland. Maine. New Brunswick. Quebec. Canada. The Arctic atmosphere hides all of the stenches in the country. The microorganisms are less dynamic in subzero…meaning aromas are cloaked.

"DAMN IT!!!" His legs sweep Lake Michigan, inhaling for one last investigation. *The asshole isn't here. I need his location!!* Kota slows to a jog, realizing how exhausted he is. His energy is reduced. So much that his black eyes vanish due to fatigue. He covered thousands of miles. The sun is dimming. Nighttime creeps in…so does depletion.

I'll try again tomorrow. I need to rest. Maybe I could get his whereabouts from Kayla. I have to get the piece of shit before my parents do. I will have him in my clutches. He'll suffer… nice and slow. He visualizes the torment he'll unleash on his rival:

Tearing the skeleton from his skin inch by inch. Day by day. Dragging out a sentence worse than jail…worse than hell. All while I leer triumphantly over his pouring blood. He'll beg… cry…and hurt, just as my friends did! I'll detach his heart from its chest… vein by vein!! Only then, he'll know mercy.

By the break of day, he climbs through his bedroom window, so his parents don't grill him. *I don't want to hear their mouths… or their nagging. I'm doing the right thing. They're wrong. No one understands what I'm going through. No one cares that Liz, Mike, and Jimmy's deaths are a living nightmare. I have to do this on my own.*

KAYLA

Kayla dials the Ahokas' number for the fifth time, wanting to check in on him, since this is her fault. *I should've lied. Even if I'm bad at it. Why did I tell the truth?? Now Kota's out there being reckless. Because of me.*

Odina answers. "Hello?"

"I'm sorry that I keep calling, but is he back?"

"Yes… he's resting in his room."

"Good." She huffs, relieved. "I'm sorry…I was going to lie…"

"No, we're glad you didn't. Kota needs to let off all of that steam… it's been bottled up for too long. Don't be sorry."

"It's hard not to be…"

"You gave him closure."

"What if he killed the thing??"

"There's no smell of the beast on him. Mato and I gathered its fragrance from the woods. Kota didn't find him." "Good… good." She exhales in relief.

"We'll need the location soon to handle the beast. But it can't be said aloud. My son will hear."

Kayla thinks of writing it down and giving it to her granny to deliver. "I know a way… you'll have the location by tomorrow."

"Perfect. Goodnight, dear."

"Goodnight."

Gloria watches her hang up the wall phone. "Don't stress over it. Kota has to work out this drama on his own."

"You're right…"

"If he kills anyone, that's not your fault. You only wanted to help." Her gran tugs her closely. *She's right…both of them are. He needed a target to release his guilt on.* "Now," Gloria ends the hug. "Your training will be at midnight. Where is the best place?"

"The balcony…we can close the doors, so we're not heard."

"That sounds like a plan.."

DING. The elevator doors slide open with a soft mechanical hiss. Then heavy footsteps come. Her father is pissed; the click of his dress shoes pounds, even though there's carpet. But it's her mother who truly sends a chill to her backside.

Mary barrels her way over to her daughter, eyes blazing, her heels striking like soft gunfire. "I got a voicemail from the receptionist. You left the house???!! Explain yourself!"

"We're waiting!"

Kay scratches the back of her head, seeking to arrange a good enough excuse. But her grandma saves her. "It's my fault. I took her out."

"Why would you do that, Mom!!"

"Yes, why would you?" James interrogates his in-law.

"You two need to go easy on her. She's miserable. Missing out on life… and fun. Blame me for this, not her."

Mary massages her forehead. "Mom… you're way out of line here. You're interfering. Kayla is my child! I choose if I want to go easy on her! Not you. She's still grounded!"

Gloria puts on a crying show, one that silences her daughter. She sobs hard, holding her chest and fanning herself. "I just wanted to make up for all the years I missed. That's all! I just wanted to make up the time!" Granny sniffles and covers her tearriddled face.

"Aww…I'm sorry. I'm not mad at you. It's okay." Mary hugs her weeping mother. For the rest of the night, she caters to Gloria, even giving her extra chocolate cake to make amends.

I can't believe Granny went for the full show! She cried on point as if a professional actress. Her plan worked masterfully. Those acting chops belong on the big stage. Mom and Dad haven't mentioned me sneaking out again. Maybe they'll let it slide. Maybe now they'll rethink my punishment.

At midnight, she and Gloria ascend the glass staircase to the art studio. Her granny appraises her artwork. "Wow! You've gotten better!"

"I took classes."

"They paid off well."

"So did your acting class."

"Once a drama major, always a drama major."

"I must get my creative side from you."

"Damn straight, you do."

"Gran, you just cursed!"

"Actresses are deceiving…so are witches; we go hand in hand."

"Brava." Kay claps.

"Thank you." Gloria bows.

Kayla leads her to the balcony and closes the door. "Now, where do we start?"

Gloria takes in the Windy City, inhaling a huge whiff of the cool breeze. "Breathing techniques."

"Aw man… breathing?!! I already know how to do that!"

"Shhhh…"

"Oh… right….sorry." Kay realizes it's the middle of the night. She reduces her voice to a mutter.

"Not that type of breathing. I'm referring to the one that attach you to the earth. The planet intakes air… same as we do. Yet we never feel it inhale or exhale. You must master the skill of shadow breathing before advancing to sight and hearing."

"I thought I knew sight already."

"No… just because you have eyes doesn't mean you see."

"Huh???"

"Exactly," Gloria states matter-of-factly. "Align your spine with your neck and shoulders." Kayla follows the instructions. "Breathe far into your diaphragm…use the full capacity of your lungs. Long, deep… in and out." She demonstrates the proper way to do it so Kay can understand. "Hold for five seconds. 1.2.3.4.5. Release. 1.2.3.4.5. Feel your abdomen expand. Push your ribs and chest forward. Exhale." Kayla learns the posture easily, since ballet is all about proper stances. "Exhale for 10 seconds."

Kay finds this difficult and buckles at the 6-second mark. "I can't…"

"Practice makes perfect. Don't rush it. Try again. Hold your stomach to engage your chest. Let's try for 5 seconds…then try out 10 again. In and out."

Kayla inhales for 5 seconds for both rounds, then attempts to exhale for ten. Once again, she strains at 6. She bullies her lungs to stretch the oxygen further.

"Don't force it… let it glide out seamlessly." Gloria shows off her skill of exhaling for ten seconds. She doesn't command her lungs to push; she effortlessly lets the sustained air escape.

"How did you do that?"

"Pay attention. Go again."

The two continue with the technique training until 1 a.m. Kayla is bummed out. She only reached five seconds. *This is impossible! Can't she give me the cheat code?? I want to get to the fun stuff already! These breathing practices are boring! When will the cool stuff start?*

After homeroom, Kayla, Jia, and Mya meet at their lockers. "How have you two been?"

"Oh, just a nightmare about bloody teeth, I'm doing super!" Mya is sour. Under that sourness is trepidation. The bombshell of vampires existing in the real world isn't sitting well at all.

Jia tries to act normal, but she's just as apprehensive. "Cool…I've been cool…so cool." She doesn't believe her own words.

"Be honest." Kay glances between the two. "How are you really feeling?"

"Petrified!"

"I'm in the twilight zone," Mya confesses. "So…can you do me a favor and don't involve me in this?"

Is she serious??? "Mya… I can't do this by myself!"

"This is too much!!"

"So, you don't want to be friends anymore??"

"I didn't say that!" Mya bellows. "Just don't involve me in this shit anymore. I'm losing sleep over it!"

"You don't think this is overwhelming for me??!! I'm the one going through it! NOT YOU!!" Their screaming battle catches the attention of students hanging in the hall. All eyes are on them now.

"Chill out… let's not make a scene…guys." Jia acts as the peacemaker.

"Too late! She already made this all about her!" Mya groans and steps off in a pissy mood, removing herself from the argument. "You know it's true. That's why you're leaving! Don't talk to me ever again!!"

Jia shushes her. "Kay, don't talk like that… be nice."

"She's ridiculous! Totally unbelievable!!!" she expresses through gritted teeth.

"Let's calm down, please."

"She ruined my day!" Kayla scrolls in the combination for her locker with harshness. "Knowing her, she's happy causing all this drama!"

"Darius gave me a mixtape." Jia lures her friend away from the toxic animosity, defusing the situation. "He told me to give it to you… something about a contest." This does the trick…and divert her mind from the argument.

CHAPTER 25: CAUGHT

KOTA

I slept for a day. I expelled my natural resources. I traveled sixteen states… I've never done that sort of exertion…ever. I need to recoup. I guess my kind needs to slumber despite being immortal. If I think about it… old stories of vampires always refer to them hibernating in the morning, then waking at night. Is that side of pop culture true after all?

It's the next day. 10 a.m. Kota is amazed by the time. *I never woke up this late before…I'm an early bird.* He leaves bed, preparing to exit the window to continue his hunt. Kota should be accustomed to meeting a hidden barrier, given this is the third time he's smacked into one. Yet he's still flabbergasted. *Did my parents confine me to the house??? HOW DARE THEY??!!*

"You're not   leaving   until   you   accept   the   new arrangement," Mato lectures from the doorway.

"LET ME OUT!!"

"No…you're grounded until you learn to let go of this rivalry."

"LET GO??!!!" Kota spins around. "No, I'm done listening to you!"

"We're telling you to listen, or you'll never leave this house again." His mom is harsh, same as his dad.

"If you keep behaving this way, we'll limit you to this room."

"So, you're jailing me??!!"

"We don't want to," his mother discloses. "But you're forcing us."

"None of you understand what I'm going through!"

"We do… trust us," his father is tender. "We know this life is a nightmare."

"That night is on a loop! Their deaths stalk me, and you don't care!!"

"I offered the perfect solution… visiting their graves is the best—"

"MOM, THAT'S BULLSHIT!! HOW CAN YOU TELL ME TO DO NOTHING!!"

"Because you're too young to have murder on your mind."

"We're enrolling you in school. That way you can get back to a normal life."

"I'm not going back to school, Dad!! Are you serious??! I'm not normal. I don't belong there." "It will help you cope, son."

"We know what's right for you…" Odina nods.

"YOU KNOW NOTHING, BOTH OF YOU ARE IDIOTS!!!"

Mato reprimands his son by closing the gap between them. His aura is intimidating and sharp. "No… don't!" his wife petitions.

"He's lost respect…"

"We can talk it out, please don't!"

"No…I tried it your way…this is going my way now." Kota is too dumbfounded to lash out. *What is he going to do??* His dad draws a simmering symbol mid-air. An illustration of sound waves. The mystical ripples float to Kota's lips, shivering the skin there.

"**ᎣᏁᎤᏇᏴᎤ** (VOICE)," he speaks in Cherokee.

His son clutches at his throat; there's detachment within. All motion terminates. He can't form words… nothing escapes when he tries. Not even a peep leaves his mouth. *WHAT???!!* Kota expresses devastation through dramatic facial cues. Knitted brows, wrinkled forehead…mouth ajar.

"Nooo!" Odina wails.

"Stop babying him…he deserves it!" He rebukes his wife, then frowns at his son. "You'll regain the right to speak once you regain respect. You will no longer shame our family. Adjust yourself… and comply. You're returning to school! END OF DISCUSSION!" Mato emphasizes dominance through every vein in his body. Kota cowers away, slinking his head down. "NOD TO AGREE!"

He nods, knowing this is beyond unfair. *I hate him… and her!! Now I see why kids run away from home. Only I can't…I'm bound to the house. If I could, I would take off and never come back. That'll be the only way to show them how wrong they are. Just because they hold the parent role doesn't mean they know everything.*

KAYLA

Kay goes to the school's roof to get away from the world. She's supposed to be at lunch…but isn't hungry. Heartbreak is on her mind. *I should listen to the mixtape, so I'm closer to Darius. I don't think I'm in the clear to see him yet. Mom may be open to the idea, but Dad is driving a hard bargain. He has a strong dislike for Darius. One I don't think is going away anytime soon… or at all.*

He's such a brute about keeping me away. I wish he would just listen to me…instead of thinking he knows what's right. He doesn't know what's best. He's dead wrong for splitting me from my boyfriend!!

She inserts headphones into the cassette player and presses play. A drafty soundscape whooshes from the earpieces, as if the recording was taken while skydiving. The high-pitched guitar sweeps her body. The harp reminds her of crystals; if diamonds had a sound, it'd be this glistening noise.

A sky-high, beyond falsetto melody. The string instruments portray an antigravity impression. The harp and guitar are electrically spirited. The musical chords invoke her imagination, causing her to stare into the sky at fluffy clouds. The buoyant song is light as a feather…free as a bird.

I wish I could fly. I'd fly to Darius and never leave. I'd run away and never return. Only then my parents will know how wrong they are. They don't know everything just because they have a kid. Parents can make mistakes. They aren't flawless. Kay shuts her eyes to savor the gorgeous music… wondering what was on Darius's mind when he composed it.

When the song sums to a conclusion, she rewinds the tape. The same weightlessness consumes her. *I want to listen to it with him. I should call when Mom and Dad are sleep. I miss his voice. His essence…the passion radiating in him. I love him.* Kay uses her diamond-designed pager to send him a row of hearts. *I love him with all my life…all my body…and all my soul.*

When lunch is over, she returns to mingle with Jones Prep High. The endless sea of heads spread from the front to the back of the hall. Just as she makes it to a door, she spies the principal exchanging words with her teacher. "Ah… there she is! Please excuse her for a few minutes," the bald, tall man requests. The model-esque man moves her way. "Come with me, Miss Harris."

Oh, no… why am I going with the principal? Am I in trouble??? If so…for what? I have the cleanest record and highest grades. What is going on??? "Mr. Hamilton, what is it?"

He escorts her to his office; opening the door to invite her in. The office is all wood, much like a den. The desk, walls, and floor are the deepest brown she's ever seen. She halts in place at the threshold…worrisome about going into the office. *Am I in trouble?*

"Don't worry, you're not in any trouble. Your grandmother called… and said it's important."

"Oh…" Kayla relaxes with a long exhalation.

"Do you think the valedictorian is on my bad list?" He laughs. She titters at the silly thought along with him. "She's on the line… I'll give you some privacy." The principal shuts the door on his way out.

There's a rotary phone on his desk. She picks up the receiver. "Hi, Gran-Gran."

"You never had the talk with your mom and dad, did you?"

"I totally forgot…I'll tell them tonight."

"You keep putting it off… you can't continue this. The truth will come out whether you want it to or not. Parents always find out…it's best you avoid that dilemma."

"I'm not ready…"

"No one ever is…"

Kayla bites the inside of her jaw. "I'll need help."

"You'll have me at your side for support."

"Okay…tonight it is."

"Good…as for the note, I delivered it to Odina. I hope they capture this devil soon."

"Me too."

"Although Belgian, Zonnebeke is quite far."

"It is…maybe his parents won't have to travel so far. Can't they capture him from here?"

"Not without your help. As Elu said, they're all secondgrade casters. You're first grade…having the Bender gene. You're our ultimate weapon."

"Right…"

"I won't keep you any longer. Return to your studies. I'll pick you up after school."

Wait…Granny is picking me up from school now?? What happened to dad doing that? "Oh…did dad get busy…or something?"

"No…but it would be nice to cut him some slack. I don't mind being your ride from now on."

"Okay…cool. See you after class."

"Bye, firefly."

"Bye, Gran-Gran." Kayla hangs up and goes to history class.

The assignment is fictitious. It prompts the students to write a paper visualizing what's inside the WWI dugout. *If I was honest about what's below, I'd be wheeled off to a psych ward, placed in a straitjacket… and locked in a padded room. I should write a rational paper…a mundane prediction is the best way to go.* She titles the essay with her name, date, and class period:

I believe the remains of dead soldiers are within the dugout, along with rusted weapons, battalion stations, and old food rations.

As soon as she circles the dot at the end of the sentence, a premonition assaults her third eye. Kota's enemy…lurking in the treetops in the night. Menacingly scrutinizing the beach. Its scarlet irises obscured by nature.

That looks like Chicago Beach!! Is the villain here?? In the city??? But… I was shown that he's in Zonnebeke! Was the Ouija board incorrect? I'll have to give Gran another note to deliver. Calling Mrs. Ahoka isn't a choice; Kota will hear that his opponent is close by. So, I have to do another letter….not a phone chat.

Before dinner, she slyly trades the note with her grandmother to deliver in the morning. She doesn't have to say anything; her gran knows the deal.

Homemade veggie pizza is the meal of the night, topped with bell peppers, onions, spinach, and kale. Mary perfected the crust by coating it with butter and garlic. She whipped up two pizza pans' worth, which she delivers to the dining table like a fine chef.
"Hon, grab the cucumber juice."

"Sure!" James hustles to get the jug.

"My, my, my…" Gloria is proud. "Look at my girl being a chef."

"I wasn't always this good." Mary humbles her mad skills despite the pizza five-star appearance. "Cooking cable is my savior…if not for that, we'd have takeout every night."

"Don't sell yourself short…you get the golden touch from me."

"I wish! I have tried and tried to recreate your peach cobbler!" she voices hardship while loading plates with slices and steak fries.

"I'll give you a lesson on it." Gloria gives a transparent gaze to her granddaughter. One that preps her to confess her secret. "Kayla has something important to say."

NO! Why would she spotlight me like that??! I'm not ready yet! Maybe after dessert I'll be ready! Kayla chomps on the pizza to buy herself more time to stall.

Mary shifts her attention to Kay. "What is it?"

James returns with four glasses of ice and a jug of juice. "If it's an ultimatum to see Darius, the answer is no." He passes glasses around to everyone.

"Baby, I think it's been long enough. We can't keep her away. You know how special teen love is."

"She's too young to know what love is…"

"NO, I'M NOT!"

"Let's stay on track, firefly. Tell them what's important." Her grandmother aims to navigate her in the right direction, but Kayla is livid.

"No! He can't tell me what I feel! I do love Darius! Why can't you agree with Mom?? SHE'S RIGHT AND YOU'RE WRONG!!" Kayla bangs her hands atop the table.

"You've just extended your punishment!"

"I don't have to listen to you! Mom is on my side, and what she says goes in this house!"

James threateningly leans forward. "You're not stepping foot outside for the rest of the year. To school and back, that's it!! I'm calling Isabell in the morning to end your ballet! You better learn to show me some respect!"

"I HATE YOU!!!" Kayla flees to her bedroom, shedding tears of pure misery.

"We should talk this over…" Mary says from down the hall.

"No… I've decided. She lost her damn mind thinking she can speak however she wants!"

Kay hammers the door hard into the frame; the slam echoes the entire penthouse. She locks it and runs to her bed to weep. *I really should run away! That'll show him! I used to love my dad… used to be Daddy's little girl. But that's over. He only cares about what he wants! How can Mom be with him??? He's so difficult!!* She whimpers in agony. Her throat clogs with dryness. Her stomach aches up hell, sinking, drowning her gut into oblivion. *I wish I could go away. I'm in prison in my own home. Caught and held captive…a damsel in distress.*

When all is quiet, Kay sneaks from her room. Her parents are sleeping. The time is 11 p.m.… they have to be up for work by 7 a.m. So, she won't get caught by her dad, yet she still tiptoes to not draw attention. The floorboards are creaky at these late hours. The lack of moisture has the boards squeaking like crazy. She has to tiptoe lighter than she already is.

She goes to the kitchen phone and dials Darius. The looping cord on the receiver is long enough to drag away from the kitchen. She stretches it far to a closet to eliminate being found out. Kayla even closes the door for extra protection from her father. Her fingers un-jam the curly cord that's caught under the frame.

He accepts her call on the second ring. "Hello?"

"It's me."

"I was just thinking about you."

"Aww… you were??"

"Yeah, every time I mix a track, I think about you."

She swoons. "I love you."

"I love you more."

"Times infinity."

"Times infinity squared." He pokes seductively.

"Times three thousand squared."

"Wow…that much??" His serene, deep voice has her heart floating from her ribs.

"Yes, that much… just as much as I love the music."

"You liked it?"

"Yeah… it's incredible. You should definitely enter it."

"But you haven't heard the new one."

"True…but this one is my favorite…I swear I was skydiving."

"That's how I feel when I kiss you."

Kayla's heart melts to mush. "If only you could be here. But…I already got you in too much trouble."

"Me too…but I want to see you in your creator zone," she complains. "It's unfair, you see me in mine all the time."

"Maybe next week your dad will chill out."

"No, not happening…he extended my grounding… it's so bogus. I did one bad thing and now I'm caged in."

"Wow…why is he being so mean??"

"I don't know…" she grunts. "But screw him! Let's ditch school."

"You most certainly will not!" The closet door pulls open.

"Gran!"

Gloria takes the phone away from her. "Kayla has to go. Don't think about skipping school or I will tell her father… and yours." She treks to the phone holder to hang it up.

Kay flashes from the closet. "Please don't tell Dad!"

"I won't if you agree to not ditch school."

"I won't!"

"I understand what you're going through. He's your high school sweetheart…we've all been there. I get it…but you have to obey your father. Promise you will, or I'll tell him about this!"

"I will… please, don't! He'll ground me for life!"

"Hush now…and let me think." Kay shuts her trap, knowing this outcome will damage her life more than it already is.

"I'll forget this… but the next time you're reckless, I'll inform your dad. Agreed?"

"Agreed."

"Now… come, it's time to train."

Kay stays mute to avoid any further drama. She complies with breathing practice as obediently as a foot soldier. The standard 6 seconds is still her best measure, but she doesn't care to improve on it. She just wants it over with so she can pine in bed. Magic is the last thing she's interested in right now. It fails to excite her.

Her posture slumps, her breaths weaken with each attempt. Inhales come shallow; exhales break too early. Her lungs are stiff, and her focus is fractured.

CHAPTER 26: TIME

KOTA

Since Kota doesn't have his voice, he lives in his mind. Thinking back to when he and his friends watched Friday the 13th in a drive-in theater. When life was normal. When he was in the good days. Huddling in the grass with Liz, Jimmy, and Mike, devouring popcorn and milkshakes. The large projector screen and the mysterious scene of the old man. "You're doomed...you're all doomed!" He warned the teens.

"They should listen to the man...he knows something is off." Liz inputs wisely.

"Oh, like you'd believe some lunatic right off the bat. Be serious." Jim scoffs.

"I would."

"So....you'd run??"

"No...I'd simply pack my things and go." "That's the same thing." He disputes.

"True..." Kota sides with him.

"Have we unlocked your fear?? Scary killer men!" Mike imitates a haunting, ghost voice.

"You guys would jet off as fast as possible." "Would not!" The boys rebuke in unison.

"I'd fight him; all he has is a knife." Jim swaggers.

"He's supernatural...you silly lames will lose. Sorry."

"Uh uh." Mike is offended. "I take karate classes; I'd put my skills to the test."

"Knowing how to break a board with your face isn't selfdefense."

"Jealous queen."

"Thank you for the crown." She throws popcorn at Mike.

"You honestly think we'd stand there and let him kill us??!" Jim is annoyed by this. "You underestimate our courage." "I'll grab a bat." Kota sips on a chocolate shake.

"A bat...really, Kota? These are your bats." Jim balls his fist and kisses each of his knuckles."

"Be serious...in the face of death, you wimps will pee yourselves." Liz trolls them.

"I call bull! You're projecting yourself onto us, sissy missy." Jim steals some of her popcorn.

"We would fight." Mike agrees.

"Yeah, as long as we have weapons." Kota remarks.

"You're making us look bad, man." Jim face palms. "We have natural weapons..."

"Muscles!!" Mike sings.

"I'd leave you all for dead..."

"Meaning you'd run like a little girl." Mike pinches her cheeks. "Don't worry, we'll save you."

"Whatever...shut up." She chews on popcorn, focusing all her attention on the movie.

At the time, I thought she was fed up with the assumptions. Now...with this vivid mind of mine, I perceive things differently. Liz was hiding behind her attitude. She was terrified of Jason and how he preyed after his victims. Liz was all talk...her hardness was a defense mechanism to not seem weak. She didn't want to seem like the average girl...when deep inside; she was. How she held her breath and gulped when Jason slaughtered with his machete. The squirts of blood. The gore...the violence. It was all too much for her to bear...yet she bottled her grim triggers.

Us guys were just as ballsy. We said what we thought would be true. None of us protected Liz. We didn't save her with our mightiness and slay the killer. We physically shut down. Our minds couldn't process what we saw. Fighting didn't come as naturally as we thought it would. At the end of the day, Jim, Mike, and I were little boys controlled by the boogeyman.

Liz had enough strength to flee....so I guess she stayed true to her word. She did attempt to run. Tried to save herself. The sight of her flimsy body thudding to the ground tears his gut apart.

Once again, Kota doesn't understand why he's able to cry. He wipes his eyes clear of droplets...lying in bed, staring at the ceiling. *I need to think of something else...because I can't avenge them. No matter how much I want to.* Kota treks to the window. There's no way out; his fingers can't pass the barrier. The obstacle is well secured.

A bassy rumbling sounds from it when his hand meets it. His demon eyes perceive a misty energy. *It's similar to the wind particles I saw...only heightened. It's impossible to overlook the dusty matter.*

His short boots tread the creaky floor. The time is 1am. He doesn't care to be polite and remove his shoes to stop the loudness of his steps. His old self would have done so. *I can care less if I wake them...I'm pissed! Why should I be considerate?? My parents aren't. Dyani isn't...she let me; her little brother, face the wrath of our father! Where was she when I needed her?? She heard the yelling....dad has it out for me. Yet...she didn't come to my rescue? What kind of big sister is she??*

And grandad...this is his house, and he let me get grounded??! Not a single word was said to combat dad's actions!! Everyone is against me. That's why I have to go. If only I could use a symbol like I did the first time. I'd hunt for the devil. But I'd be without a voice. How can I scare my enemy if I can't speak violence his way?? I wouldn't be intimidating.

He press his fingertips on the magical dust; his digits cannot break in. He lays his head against the barrier, letting the chill seep into his skin. The magic pulses faintly, a second heartbeat; one that isn't his.

"Kota..." Odina taps on the closed door. *Why is Mom up?? She's never up this late.* He goes to pull it open. "Oh, honey, I'm sorry." She clinches him close. "When your father gets that way, there's no stopping him. This is all too much. I never agreed to this..." She examines his snowy eyes, recognizing brokenness. "I know you're hurt...I know. But please get back to life. School. Friends. You could be close to Kayla. Find a new normal...." Odina combs her fingers through his dark hair. "Atuyasdodi avy, walela (Promise me, hummingbird)."

His hopeless eyes fall from hers. *Could I drop this? Could I start fresh? I know what she wants me to do. Mom is hoping I say my peace at their graves. Hope I say goodbye to my past friendships and start a new one. Could I befriend Kayla? Is it possible to have a new beginning? Or should I go on chasing down my opponent?*

Kota hops between the two choices. He can't promise his mother he'd let the chaos rest. Yet he knows that's the only way to regain his voice.

"I'll undo the spell once you agree to leave this all in the past."

I've never lied to my mother before. I'm always truthful...not just in my eyes, but in my heart. But I may have to lie. I may have to agree to school. I would do it grudgingly. But I would like to be closer with Kayla. We could be companions...or more. Not many girls have the ability to daze a vampire. I'm not sure most girls act as a cure. When I'm around her, I'm everything I thought I lost. I'm everything I was...everything I took for granted.

"She's very beautiful." His mother reads his mind. *That she is. The world's most captivating girl...more than Macy Hart. I thought no one could top her looks...I was wrong.* "You could attend her school, so you'll have someone who's inhuman...like yourself."

I want nothing more than to be around her again...this is very tempting. But my instincts are pulling me away. My villain is out there, but...in order to start my mission...I'll need my voice back. I'll have to leave this house to begin the quest. I'll agree. I'll act as if I'm over this vigilante phase.

I'll lead my family on with this lie until I have a trace on the vampire. I'll play the role of an average teen boy. Kota nods, mouthing the words "I *promise"*, knowing it's half true. *I'm only promising to be with Kayla...not to end my vengeance. I gave her the words she needed. Not the ones she deserved.*

Odina kisses his cheek, "Wado, (thank you)." His mother poses her hands to conduct the spell. She draws the same mark Mato did, only it's in reverse motion.

The bright sound waves flow backwards. The ripples revert from his mouth, performing the shakiness from before in a rewind. Her son clutch his throat, which attaches back to his body. All of the inner workings are repaired; Kota's throat is operational once again. "Wado, Unitsi, (Thank you, mother)."

"Give me a few days to work this over with your father. Remain silent; don't let him know you have your voice. There can't be another blowup."

"Okay, I will."

"I'm so proud of you!" She cocoons him in her arms. "Choosing peace will bring a better future, trust me." She doesn't spot his deceit...or the predatory glint of his cold irises.

KAYLA

In photography class, Jia and Kayla work on their 298th image. Ms. Ruby writes the words **SILENT BEAUTY**, on the chalkboard. She gets into this theme, so much that she doesn't make a peep. The teacher then writes: **SILENT ART**.

Huh? What is silent art? That makes no sense. Art has no sound to begin with. Kay raises her hand. Ms. Ruby mimics a pen and paper motion, indicating that she wants Kayla to write it down.

"I'm lost…" The skater boy begins.

Ms. Ruby place her finger to her lips and writes on the board:

HEAR THE HIDDEN BEAUTY OF LIFE. TAKE A PHOTO OF UNAPPRECIATED ART. ALSO KNOWN AS SILENT ART. THINGS THAT ARE OVERLOOKED YET PROVIDE ARTISTIC IMPACT.

I'm with Jasper, I'm lost too. Kay and Jia share a befuddled glance.

The teacher writes again: **HINT: THE ORIGINAL ART**.

Kayla jots down a question in her notepad, then holds it up: **Can we find it inside the school?**

Ms. Ruby nods, then shoos them away to the hall, egging them to begin their venturing. Kayla is happy to leave the room and speak like a normal human being. Once in the hall, she tries to start a chat, but Jia shushes her. *Wow…is she actually going to follow the quiet demand? I need to fill her in about what happened last night.*

Jia takes Kay's notebook and writes: **We have to be quiet to hear the art.**

Kay rolls her eyes, taking the pen to scribble: **But it's important. It's about me and Darius.**

Her bestie sighs, then writes: **The faster we find the art, the quicker we can talk.**

Kayla takes her by the hand, leading her to a garden enclosed at the center of the hall. A greenhouse, complete with fountains, and birds that swoop in from the open roof. She pushes in the see-through door and points at the fountains.

The original art is most likely what the earth has made. I was thinking actual noise at first…now I see it's of earthy ambiance. *Jia and I may be the first ones done. This assignment wasn't as hard to crack as I thought. Our teacher needs to up her game.*

Jia, who has the Canon camera around her neck, takes the photo. The mechanical shutter from the lens prompts Kay to speak. "Now…"

"How did you figure it out so fast?"

"Nature is overlooked every day. It has a song of purity and calmness, meaning it's the first art form. Untouched by human influence. AKA silent art."

"Wow! Let me write that down!" Jia transcribes what her friend just says.

"Now…can we talk. I need to tell someone."

"Sure. What is it?"

"I don't think I'll ever see Darius again…" Her chocolate doe eyes well up. "I'm on home arrest for the whole year."

"Seriously???"

"My dad is impossible…he's a ramped-up bull. Just the mention of Darius gets him heated."

"He really didn't like you going to that party…huh?" Jia coddles Kayla into her arms. "I knew it was a bad idea."

"Me too…I should've followed my gut and said no."

"Yeah…then you wouldn't be in this mess."

"I can't even call him."

"Your dad is way too harsh!"

"I don't understand why!" She bawls her eyes out, wailing into Jia's shoulder.

"Aww…I'm so sorry. I wished there was something I could do."

"It won't matter…my dad will just ban me from speaking to you too!"

"Do you think he'll take it easy on you if you tell him the truth? You know, with the magic world? Maybe he'll cut you some slack."

"He doesn't know…I haven't told him… or my mom."

Jia pulls from the cuddle. "Wait…you told me and Mya…but not your parents???"

"It was easier with you two…my parents will think I want attention or that I'm trying to distract them from my jail sentence."

"But your mom collects the books."

"She isn't a believer."

"Well…you made us believers by showing us."

"True…but they'll probably need an ambulance if I showed them. You two are my girls…it's not as hard to tell y'all my secret."

"I guess…" Jia shrugs, then gives a light smirk. "You said we're your girls…meaning you want to make up with Mya??"
"Jia…don't." Kay exits the greenhouse.

"I'm just saying…you two need to apologize, that's all."

"Mya was out of line, not me!"

"Can we sit together at lunch and work it out?"

"No…you can sit with her. I'll be elsewhere."

Jia is mute as a church mouse all the way back to the classroom. As expected, they're the first ones done.

Ms. Ruby grades the picture they took for the assignment. She claps, indicating that the silence has been broken. "BRAVA! THAT'S AN A+!!"

"Thanks." Kay says lifelessly on the way to her desk.

"It was all her; I just snapped the pic."

"Teamwork makes the dream work! You're both getting the same grade."

"Wow, so cool! You're the best!" Jia claps for Ruby, who goofily bows.

Kayla lays her head on the desk, hiding behind her arms. *I'm not even excited about the grade. I can care less about acing the assignment. I want my boyfriend! I want to lay in his bed and listen to his music. I want to see him thinking of me as he creates art. I don't want to be here…or at home. I don't want to be anywhere. I want to disappear…forever. Like my heart. It's gone…without my other half.*

"What if I told you I cooked up a plan to get you and Darius back talking?"

"What is it?" Kay grumbles through her folded arms.

"I could catch Darius after school, when your grandma picks you up."

"How is meeting him after school going to do anything??" She tightens her arms around her head like a nest.

"Well…I was thinking maybe I'll give him my walkie talkie so you two can talk in secret. No phone needed."

Kayla springs out of her arm cocoon and gapes at Jia. "OH MY GOSH, YOU'RE A GENIUS!"

"But there's a catch…"

"I don't care; I'll do anything!"

"Even if it means promoting your ex-bestie to her former title?"

Kay no longer cares about the beef with Mya. She just wants to hear him. "Deal…please give him the radio!"

In law class, Kayla groups with Fred, Chester, and Izzy to draw up a courtroom illustration. Mr. Smith examines the posters, which follow a prompt written on the board. Distraught mother, plaintiff, and a crazed defendant. Kayla is the only drawer in the group, so she tackles the character designs with her pencil. Fred, Izzy, and Chester write down details for appearance of the jury….listing hair colors, face features, and outfits to add personality.

"Are you still grounded?" Fred mutters, keeping his eye on Mr. Smith in case he's caught speaking.

"I'm chained up for the year…"

"Aw man, that reeks! I'm throwing a bonfire.".

"A bonfire?"

"Yep…on the beach. Maybe by your birthday I can have another one."

"I hope so….have extra fun for me."

"Sure, I'll do ballet on your behalf." "I can't stand you." Kay sniggers ecstatically.

"I know …" He sneers.

In gym, Marla, Fred, and the new kid, Luke, shoot baskets. Fred spins the ball on his finger, then tosses it high. They all dive for it, ending up with their arms in a tangled mix.

"I got it first."

"No, I did, Fred." Marla argues. "What happened to ladies first?"

Fred clears his throat. "How dare you not acknowledge me?!" He speaks in a shrill voice. Very cartoonish. "I should report you to the authorities for that rude comment!" Once again, he has Kayla buckling over in laughs, especially when he swishes his hips.

The lunch meal of the day is nachos and burgers, complete with fudge brownies and chocolate pudding. Jia and Kayla stand in food line, choosing the healthiest option. Pasta and veggie casserole with turkey. Mya is already at the table, waiting for them.

Jia is the first to break the ice. "So…" she says while sitting. "I found a fix that'll make everything better. But apologies are needed first." She eyes Kay, who gives in by being the bigger person.

"I'm sorry for calling you selfish."

"Good. Apology accepted." May gives attitude.

"You have to apologize too!"

"For what?? You attacked me for being honest. I'm not in the wrong here!"

"Why can't you just say it back so we can move on??!" Jia groans, tilting her head backward in annoyance.

"Because she did this, not me!" She spits.

"No, I Didn't!"

"You made it all about yourself! You're the selfish one!"

"Just say sorry, Mya!" Jia begs her.

"NO!!" She collects her food tray and marches from the table, straight out of the lunchroom.

Kayla glares after her like an aggravated snake. "She's being difficult! I said sorry! I kept up my end…so that means you have to give Darius the radio."

"Sure…I'll find another way to fix this."

After school, Kay shoves through the cramped sidewalk to a Volkswagen Beetle where her grandmother is awaiting her. She spies Jia at the crosswalk chatting with Darius. *Why am I jealous?? She's just handing him the walkie talkie. That all. It doesn't matter how close her body is to his…or that I wished I was in her place. Just to be by him.*

Her eyes clasp on her boyfriend. His gorgeous, dark skin, his chestnut eyes. The charming way he blinks. The fluid way his addictive mouth forms words as she speaks. Her legs stop working, floored in place right to the spot.

The car window rolls down; Gloria leans over to the passenger seat. "Kayla…"

She snaps out of the deep daze, peddling her legs to the door. "I'm sorry, I just haven't seen him in forever…" She mumbles.

"Go." Gloria grins.

"What??!"

"Go…I'll give you a few minutes."

Kayla doesn't waste time; she sprints with a smile from ear to ear. *Wow! I can talk to him?? This is the best day of my life! I love my granny. She' so superb for doing this!*

Darius registers her darting his way. He jogs over with a celebratory grin. "KAYLA!" Her boyfriend spins her around in his arms, intensely dancing his mouth upon hers. "I love you! I missed you so much!"

Darius wipes away her tears. "I love you more…and miss you more."

Kay sniffles, diving back in with a roasting kiss. His lips are addictively sweet…warm caramel, melted on her skin. Her mouth falls deeper, desperate. Her fingers slide into his hair as their lips crush and part. She drinks his flavor, rejoicing in a soft moan. *God, I need more. All of him. EVERY SINGLE DROP!*

Jia clears her throat. "Umm…Kayla…your granny."

Kay drops her mouth from his, loathing that she has to end the tango. Gloria is outside her car, concerned about the sensual PDA. "I gotta go."

"We should runaway."

"Don't tempt me." She chortles nervously. "We'll talk later." She and Darius stare down at the radio.

"Kayla!" Her granny summons her back over.

"Bye."

"Bye, baby."

Kay begrudgingly part ways, power walking back to the car. Her grandma is put off by the inappropriateness. "You can't behave that way in public!"

"We were just kissing."

"That was more than kissing…and implies that something more is going on."

"It doesn't imply that…." She rolls her eyes.

"I hope you're being safe."

"It's not like that...yet."

"How long have you two been dating?"

"This makes month 5."

"Hmmm…I'm impressed." Gloria gets into the car; Kayla opens her door and slides in. "Maybe Darius isn't as bad as your dad thinks."

"He isn't." Kayla straps on the seatbelt. "He doesn't pressure me into anything I don't want to do."

"It looks like James is against the wrong one…wait until he finds out about the vampire boy."

The same premonition from before blooms in her third eye. The crimson eyed vampire prowling in the treetops. Kay grips the seatbelt hard.

"Is that sighting still bothering you?"

"Yeah."

"Don't worry, as soon as the culprit is caught, those will end."

"Has Odina and Mato found him yet?"

"No…but give them time…they will."

How is she so certain? It seems this one is elusive. Frist he was in Zonnebeke, underground, now he's here in Chicago? And has yet to be found? How is the evil thing hiding so well…hiding from magic??

CHAPTER 27: STRINGS

At midnight, Gloria and Kay begin to practice. This time she's able to breathe in and out for 10 seconds. She bounces up and down like a wild bunny. "I DID IT!"

"Shh…" Gloria observes the door of the art studio. "But yes, you did it!" she exclaims in a lower shout.

"What's next?"

"We're still on shadow breathing, dear. You haven't accomplished anything until you breathe in and out for a full hour. When you master that, you can stop breathing for years."

"How am I supposed to stop breathing for an hour?"

"Close your eyes." Kay does as she's told. "You have to learn to ignore the urge to breathe by finding an anchor through nature. This will extend your lifespan."

"What does that mean??"

"The less you breathe, the longer you live…and the slower you age."

"This can slow down aging??"

"Yes…by borrowing from the earth."

"How long could I live for?"

"My mother is 210 years old. Of course, she had to fake her death and disappear to not reveal this secret."

"Whoa…wait! My great granny is alive?? 210 years old???"

"And she doesn't look a year over 50."

"TEACH ME HOW TO DO THAT!!"

"Calm your voice…you'll learn in time. It's best we take small steps. Now…be silent. Let's try for breaths in and out for 15 seconds."

How does she expect me to be silent after that bombshell?! I can live to be extremely old?? I wonder what's the highest age limit is. Can Spell Benders die? Are we immortal like vampires??

"We'll begin with pursed lip breathing; this will reduce your lungs to work less by keeping your airways open. The key is to decrease lung activity. Inhale slowly through your nostrils. Pout your lips as if you're blowing outward. Breathe out as slowly as possible through your mouth. 15 seconds out. Then hold."

Kayla does the technique with ease; to her, it's simple enough. Even when her granny has her repeat it. She does so naturally. While meditating, she gets lost in a world where she could be immortal.

Could I live longer than Kota? Given vampires that have endless life…could I also have that? But I wouldn't want to outlive Darius. That'll be the worst! Unless…I can slow his aging too? I have so many questions to ask Granny.

Kay is captivated by her chest, which moves less than before. Its motion isn't as long in duration. It should be working every millisecond…now it moves every 10 seconds. "I can't believe this…" *It works on its own to pump up and down. My respiratory system is laxed. My airwaves are full enough without me struggling!* "It's like it's on autopilot!!!"

"Shh…!"

"Sorry…but this is so cool!" She whispers.

"In our next lesson, you'll be breathing with the wind. So, practice this every morning."

"Yes, ma'am."

"Don't stay up all night with that boy. You need rest."

"How did you…?"

"I have eyes…I don't have to access my third one to catch a clue."

"Oh."

"Darius has a bright aura… he's good for you."

Kayla blushes. "I know…he was shining."

"Yes, love is a marvelous thing. Your dad will see this soon enough."

"I hope so.." Kay pinches her mouth to one side.

"Goodnight." Gloria steps from the balcony.

"Night." She tiptoes to her room and slips into bed, retrieving the radio from under her pillow. Turning the volume up only by a notch, so the feedback isn't loud. She holds down and says, "Darius, come in. Do you copy?"

A low hum of static buzzes from the speaker. "I copy, superstar."

"What are you doing?"

"Thinking about you."

"What exactly are you thinking about?"

"Our make-out…it got me all excited." His buttery voice sends shivers down her spine. "Maybe we can do that again tomorrow."

"How? I can't see you, remember?"

"After school. I can meet you at your locker."

"But my gran waits on me after school…"

"Just say you forgot something."

"I could…" Kayla quickly muses over a plan, deciding on something simple. "I could say I left my pager in my locker."

"That's not bad."

"But…then it won't be long enough; we'll have to rush."

"That's fine…as long as I can touch you."

"Aww." Kay snuggles into the pillow, swooning. "I missed touching you too."

KOTA

This is day three of being trapped inside my room. I'm going insane due to lack of space. To the bed and window is only ten steps. I'm doing dozens of laps…since I don't need sleep, I do this. I want to go out and search until I have the disgusting smell of him in my system. Mom said to give her a few days. Has she told Dad yet? Will he fall for my lie as she did? I hope so. I have to get out of this place. I have to speak with Kayla alone…she has to know where the scum is.

Her grandmother has visited twice to hand over papers. My parents are silent when opening the door. Usually, they greet visitors, not inaudibly accept a paper as if dealing drugs. I think they're all communicating through writing, so I can't know what's up. If I ask Kayla, she'll tell me. She told me the truth before…I think she'll be honest again. She wants to help me…unlike my family. They just want to silence me and make me fake as if I'm normal. I'm not.

He hears the chairs of the dining table scrape backwards on the floor. It's suppertime. Ravioli, avocado sauce, and steak are the main meal. His nose registers each pinch of seasoning, each baking ingredient as if tasting it as a mortal.

"Dear…we shouldn't have Kota in his room all day."

"He leaves when I say so."

"This is bad for his well-being. He has to go back to school."

"Mom's right…" Dyani declares, as meek as a mouse. "Kota's not leaving that room until I see fit!" Mato blows out like a rhino. "Now…let's eat!"

The scraping of silverware on plates overtake the room. *No one is willing to protest Dad when he's like this. It's hopeless. I'm stuck here for all eternity. The thought of school is appealing as of right now. At least I can be on my own. Away from them all.*

Elu clears his throat. "Gloria phoned about Kayla. She will be well prepped to detect a cure in no time. I would say by the end of the month."

"That's great!" Dy scoots back in the chair with much enthusiasm. "I'll tell Kota."

"NO!"

"BUT DAD?!"

"I SAID NO!"

"Son, this is something we should celebrate as a family." Elu's states as soft as a feather. "Please…"

"Kota can hear fine enough. Now. Eat."

Dad is a bully. He reminds me of Macy's boyfriend. The jock. He thinks everyone has to obey him. What's his problem? I wasn't as disrespectful as he's making it seem. I yelled and said one curse word. Only one!

I wasn't in control of myself. They all saw my eyes change…they all saw me being possessed. I hope Mom is explaining this to him. But I think she was right…there's no stopping him when he's like this. She knows him better than I do. I'll have to wait until he settles down. Until he's my father again…not this dictator.

At midnight, there are footsteps outside his door. He thinks it's his mother again; but is wrong. "Kota…" Dyani uses a hushed tone. He goes to open the door. His big sister has a bowl of chocolate pudding. She offers it to him. "I know you don't eat…but it's your fav." His sister simpers. "Mom told me what she did. Dad went too far." She slips into the room. "He's being a pain in the ass. I don't get why he's treating you this bad. But you running off like that was scary…and you did shout and curse. But…"

"The crime doesn't fit the punishment. Rebellious teens aren't permanently glued to the house."

"He doesn't know the trauma you went through. Anyone would want to kill a murderer."

"So…you're on my side?"

"Yes, I'm with you on this…they all think your violence is uncalled for."

"It's not…"

"I know…you feel like their lives were wasted."

"No…I should've died instead of them."

Dy's brows curl to her hairline, pained. "Why would you say that?!"

"Because I shouldn't be alive…I don't understand why I am." Kota's dull pupils mirror the bleak words. "I just stood there and did nothing…I let them die. So why should I care about dying?"

"Stop speaking like this!" Her eyes moist up.

"That's how I feel…"

"I thought you just wanted to off the guy…!"

"The one thing I need is off limits. They won't let me kill so I can heal. My life is pointless."

"Mom told me you like Kayla…you can start over." He doesn't have a comeback for this. *I considered us being friends…but could we be more? My affections aren't one sided. I saw the look of desire. The way she limited eye contact with me. As always, this is a tempting outcome.*

"How? When I can't even leave the house to try?"

"Give the old man time…mom is hatching up a plan."

"He's a bull…I'm never leaving this house again."

"This isn't forever….just let him cool off." Dyani hugs her little brother, tussling his hair atop his head. "Don't scare me like that. I don't want to hear you talk about dying ever again. You hear me??"

I can't promise that'll be the last time I'm morbid. If I stay in this room, I'll relive the past and fall back into deadly thoughts. If I were out…it would be easier to ignore the urge. The survivor's guilt would be tolerable.

When his sis is gone to bed, Kota decides to draw. He has nothing else to do and doesn't want to keep strolling the tiny room. He sits on the ledge of the bed with a pencil and paper, staring at it. Browsing his mind. Nothing positive comes along…because of his glum mood. So, he resorts to illustrating the evil vampire.

I hate that I know every curve of his face…every hue of his hair…every pattern in his eyes. The infuriating curve of his mouth. But I have to release my torment somehow. The burgundy irises he sketches are empty as a pit. The sharp teeth, and pointy nails. His claws are the signature of Satan. The blond hair is as multicolored as stacks of hay. Kota tears the paper up in rage, ripping it into long shreds. *No…I need to focus on something happy.*

He starts on a new sheet of paper. Kayla's face appears as a choice. He doesn't question why…Kota just follows the urge. His fingers conduct the pencil to etch the ends of Kayla's curly, bushy hair. He selects a shade of brown to fill in the color.

Her hair is the same hue of her eyes. Her skin is rich as soil. Kayla's hairline is as well molded as her heart shaped face. Button nose. Doe eyes. Cupid's bow…and lush lips. The pencil streaks fast to define the lines of her. To color in every inch. The last part he fills in is her velvety mouth. A perfect darkness.

I wonder how sweet she tastes. Is her mouth as soft as it looks? As magnetic as her voice? As electric as her presence? Will a kiss from her liven me…just as she reanimated my body?

Kota inspects the portrait he's just crafted. Calmed by her penetrating gaze; reminiscing their fleeting eye contact. A tidal wave of hope lightens his despair. His hand rush to grab another sheet of paper. *I have to see her…not just for selfish reasons. Not just to smuggle information out of her…but to be bathed in her sunlight. I want to be with Kayla. I need joy in my life.*

On the paper, he writes a letter to his dad:

Father,

I was out of line. I'll apologize for years if I have to. I was blinded by fury. The voice in my head made me behave irrationally. The possessive entity persuaded me to disrespect you. I lost control. I'm sorry. My old self would've never spoken to you and Mom that way. But I'm not my old self anymore. I'm trying to be, but I can't help that my soul is damned. I wish it wasn't. I wished I was normal again. Kota glances at the drawing of Kayla; then back down at the paper:

I don't know if Mom has told you, but I'm willing to attend school with Kayla. I'm better when I'm around her…and think we could be great friends. I'd like to enroll at her school, so I'll know someone who's inhuman, like me. I'll stop trying to kill and let you and Mom handle the vampire. I'll let my violence rest, just like you want. Please forgive me for challenging you. I just want our relationship back. I need my father back.

Kota rolls up the paper and walks to slide it under the door. *I should keep working to occupy my mind. I could make something else for Kayla.* He inspects the nightstand, then goes to open the bottom drawer made of striped, white wood. Kota gets an idea. *I do miss wood shop. missed working with my hands. I could easily remove the wood.* He does so by unhooking the front of the drawer to slide the bottom out. Instead of a saw or a stencil tool, he uses his sharp nails.

His talons carve the wood, carefully creating a chain-link for the first thing that pops into his mind. A necklace. *Should the center be a heart? Or would that be too desperate of me? Should I hold back my confession of my crush on her? What if the shape is too much?*

Further down the chain-link, he decides to carve the center as a sun with squiggly lines going outward to represent sunrays. This is a better choice…since Kayla has such a remarkable glimmer.

By sunrise, he's done detailing the patterned wood. He blows the dust from the necklace and holds it up to take in his craftsmanship. Odina is stepping up the stairs; this attracts his attention. Kota lays the pendant down and zooms over to the door.

His mom stops; her shadow spreads larger as she bends to pick up the paper. "Walela (hummingbird)." She mutters. "What is this?"

"Please give that to Dad for me."

His mom retreats down the stairs. *Everyone is in the backyard planting seeds. Dad is there; I hear his rough breathing from the shoveling.* His mom exits the back door. "Mato...come here, please." "What is it?" He pushes the shovel deep into the soil.

"Your son wrote you." She waves the paper in her hand.

"He did what??" His father doesn't sound severe...just confounded.

"Read it." Odina hands over the note. Mato unfolds it.

Kota steps to the window to perceive his father's expression. *I hope he finds it acceptable. I hope he lets me go.* His dad reads the sentences, moved by the delicate words. His breathing slows...his shoulders loosen. Mato's demeanor switches from critical to sincere. He's influenced by the letter. The ending has him tugging his mouth into a light smile.

"What does it say?"

He shows his wife the note. "I don't know if I should believe him." Mato is crossed between emotion and authority. "Does he like this Kayla girl? Or is he fooling me?"

"You didn't see how he looked at her...but you're a man, I can't hold that against you."

"How did he look at her?"

"As if she was the only girl in the world...she gave him the look too."

"She did??"

"Sweetie, learn to use your eyes. Why wouldn't he like her? She's radiant...powerful...and a ballerina. That's what some call a triple threat."

"Hmmm..." Her husband grumbles. "He did ask to register at her school."

"The fact that they're both supernatural will help...they'll be fast friends."

"Hmmm." He mumbles pensively.

"I could drive him today. I'll call Kayla for the address. I think it's companionship he's missing; that's why he lashed out. He has nothing else to target but retaliation. This will correct that. I know it will."

"Maybe you're right." Mato sighs hard. "I was a little too hard on him. Wasn't I?"

"A little."

"I'm sorry."

"I know."

"I'll make things right."

Odina kisses him softly. "Thank you, my love."

It worked?? Did I just free myself?? Kota backs away from the window, impressed that his plan was successful. A wide smile spreads his mouth. The same animated delight of a child consumes him. *I can't believe it!*

Mato visits his room. Kota tries to hide his satisfaction but can't; his jubilant eyes are a giveaway. "You must have heard..." His father chuckles. "I didn't mean to be this man you don't recognize. I just wanted to protect you from the darkness. I hope you don't hate me." Kota attempts to speak but remembers that his father doesn't know that the spell was lifted. So, he just nods. "I'll return your voice...and I accept your apology." Mato performs the same reversal spell Odina did. The same mystical airwaves. The same symbols and vibrations.

Oh, no...will it work? Or will he find out that Mom has already saved me? This may enrage him. I should say something. Right??? The pressure on his mouth and throat convince him that the casting is working. The airwaves fade. Kota acts as if this is the first time this has happened. He holds his throat, clearing it loudly. "Wado, Adadoda, (Thank you, Father)."

"Gvlielitseha, (You're welcome)." He hugs his son. "Although your mother already undid my charm."

"Oops..."

"Don't worry...it's fine. Let's put the rage behind us."

"It's good to have you back, dad."

"It's good to have you back, son." Mato passes to the hall to remove herbs from above the door. His fingers summon them to fall. Before the leaves can brush the floor, each one burns away. White Flames....to ashes. Then nothing. "The window seal will stay active until I'm certain I can fully trust you."

"That...seems...fair."

"Your mother will drive you to school. Until then...come help us plant in the garden." He invites his son from his room. Kota picks up a quick stride, loving that his feet can reach past the door.

KAYLA

Before she can board the elevator for school, the house phone rings. Kay slips from the lift and jogs to answer. "Hello?"

"Good morning, Kayla. I'm calling to ask for your school's address. Kota has agreed to return to a normal life and would prefer to go with someone like himself. Although you're not a vampire…you're both supernatural."

"Oh…" She's staggered. "That's a great idea. I assume he's doing better?'

"Much better now that the rage is gone."

"That's great! I'll get the address." She goes to the mail table by the elevator, dragging the corded phone with her. Atop it is an address book. Her mom always jots down locations here, so she doesn't forget them. Everything is in alphabetical order. Kay flips to the J section and unclips it from the binder. She recites the address. "700 South State Street."

"Lovely."

"How soon will Kota start?"

"Hopefully tomorrow."

"I can't wait!" Kay reveals her raw desperation *Oh, no…I should tame my joy…I'm still with Darius.*

"Neither can he." Odina giggles. "Thank you, dear. Have a glorious day."

"You too, bye." She hangs up fast…hating herself for being so excited. "Why did I say that out loud…?" Kay face palms and groans. "I have a boyfriend, remember?" She advises herself. Kay returns to the elevator, calling it up. "So…Kota is excited too? His mom said he can't wait either?? Hmmm."

Gloria is down in the Volkswagen, waiting for her. "You're going to be late."

"Mrs. Ahoka called." Kay straps into the compact car.

"About what?"

"Kota will be at Jones Prep soon."

"Oh, really??"

"Yep."

"I bet you can't wait for that."

"What do you mean?"

"You have a crush…your little moment at the meeting spilled that truth."

"I have a boyfriend!"

"It's normal to like more than one boy. I had a list at your age. You'll have one too."

"Gran…no, I won't. I'm with Darius." "For now…" Her granny chuckles.

Kayla looks away to avoid the conversation. *Could I fall for him? Where would that leave my boyfriend? He'll be hurt. I'll feel terrible. I can't break Darius's heart. I can't! Kota will be my friend. I'll put aside this crush I have…and draw a fine line.*

His static irises interrupt her thoughts…swaying her against the plan. *But…I do want to get lost in his eyes. Ease his pain with a hug….and a kiss. I want to hold his hand through the storm that disrupted his life. This can't be easy for him. He lost friends…and his soul. He's wrongfully doomed by death. I can tell that he's super sweet. Kota looks like he wouldn't harm a fly…yet he was given this faith? It's so surreal how the world works.*

Jia awaits her at the lockers. "Hey, we missed you at practice. Don't tell me dancing is forbidden too?"

"It is…my dad stopped my trainings."

"That's too far!! Why would he think that's justified??! You won the stage…your dad can't hide you away! What if an agent stopped by the studio for you?!"

"It's best I don't know." Kay grimaces. "Anyway." She changes the topic to tame the heavy weight in her gut. "I got something to tell you. Well…actually two things to tell you." Kayla beckons Jia closer using her hand. The two huddle up. "The vampire boy…the one from the call. He's coming to Jones Prep."

"WHAT?! WHY! That's not a good idea…we wouldn't be safe. None of the students will be safe!"

"It's fine…I got a good read on him."

"With your magic?"

"No…gran hasn't taught me to read auras yet. But…my intuition tells me that he's safe."

"He's a vampire!" Jia stutters lowly. "According to the lore, they're all bad."

"You can't use pop culture as a guidebook."

"What else can I use??"

"You can trust my word."

"I don't know…" Jia anxiously backs away. "Even if I trust what you say, what if he hurts someone? Being around blood is an issue…right?"

"I'm assuming not if his mom is registering him. This was her plan…so Kota must have a grip on it."

"How?"

"I have no clue."

Jia crosses her arms, disturbed by the thought of an inhuman boy walking the halls. "So…what's the other thing you have to share?"

"Please don't think it's…strange."

"Why would I think that?"

Kay scrolls in her locker combination, keeping her eyes straight. *I can't make eye contact with her when I say this. I dread her reaction.* She opens the locker and pretends to search inside to hide her face. "I…might have a….small…crush…on him." She glances at the metal door, knowing the exact dramatic reaction Jia is giving without having to see her face.

"YOU WHAT??!!"

"It's just a tiny thing."

"Kayla, that's dangerous! You know what he is, how could you?! And…and…you're with Darius!"

"I know…I know…but…I can't help it." Kay pushes back the locker door to meet Jia's appalled eyes. "Isn't he scary?"

"No…I mean…I would say unique looking…if anything. Although he did have a scary...but that was justified."

"How is being scary justified??"

"He and his friends were attacked by a bad vampire…his friends died…." Kayla reports, sullenly peering down at the floor. " He got mad over this….which is normal. He wants payback on…"

"Killed?" Jia eyes pop wide. "Did you just say killed."

"Yes."

Her face goes pale. "You mean as in…dead?"

Kay frowns. "Yes…dead."

"Oh…wow…that's so sad." Jia's hostile disposition is now broken. "No one should have to go through that…."

"Exactly…that's why I'm glad he's coming here…to make new friends."

"I still think he'll be hazardous."

"You have to give him a chance before you write him off. At the end of the day…he's a victim…he didn't ask for this."

"True…" Jia mumbles. "I'll try to be accepting."

"Thanks."

Her bestie beams big. "So…how cute is he?"

"I don't even know where to start." The two squeal enthusiastically. "All I will say is he should be sculpted in marble."

Jia claps fast. "Tell me more!"

KOTA

Kota and his mom sit in the principal's office. Mr. Hamilton looks over the registering form...seeming to have an issue with the information. The bald man strokes his chin and exhales roughly. "There's a problem here..."

"I'll try to get his transcripts mailed as soon as possible." Odina vows.

"That's only one of the issues...the other is that the school isn't within the district of your home. I could recommend the ones that are. I'll print a list out for you."

Oh, no...so I can't go here? I have to...Kayla has to be in my life. I'll be an outsider without her. If I go to another school...no one will talk to me. My appearance is a human repellent.

"Mr. Hamilton...please, Jones Prep is very elite. A school any parent would want for their child. Is there a way to pay the tuition out of pocket?"

"I'm sorry...that would be illegal. This is strictly a geological hiccup. Each school has an assigned code...I can't break state regulations. I'm sorry, Mrs. Ahoka."

NO...NOO! This won't happen. I won't let it! He will change his mind. MR. HAMILTON, CHANGE YOUR MIND! Kota's crystal eyes flicker black. The principal is stupefied...he halts in place as the planet still spins the room. There's no gravitational sway impacting his body...no rotation. Mr. Hamilton appears as someone trapped in a photograph...the moment of motionlessness after the flash.

WHAT DID I JUST DO?!

"SON...WHAT DID YOU DO?!" His mom shoots up from the chair.

"I don't know! I was just thinking!"

"About what?!"

"Him changing his mind...so I can attend."

Mr. Hamilton winds down from the frozen state, much like a battery-operated toy powering down. The odd motion resembles a puppet whose master set it in a seat. Only thing is...the principal isn't a stringed dummy. He's made of flesh and bone. The way his arms and legs swing, the way his head bobs up and down. Blank and soulless.

"Yes...Mr. Ahoka...you will attend Jones Prep...everything on the form is up to par." He speaks as a ventriloquist doll would. Reciting hollow words...controlled by the conviction of Kota's mind. "I'll have my secretary arrange your schedule. Welcome to Jones Prep."

CHAPTER 28: CHANCE

I can't believe I just used mind control! Just from thinking? I didn't know I could do this! Grandad did mention it before. Vampires have compulsion and can control...as if a puppet master. Those were his exact words...and that's exactly what happened! That was Darth Vader level of cool! Can vampires do more? Or is compulsion the only power we have??

Odina lowers back into her seat, dumbfounded. "When can he begin classes?" Mr. Hamilton doesn't react to her words; he's zeroed in on Kota as if he's the only one in the room. "Ask him."

"When do I start class? Can it be today?"

"Today...yes." The principal obeys Kota a command.

"But I have no supplies..."

"No need to worry, our student store has backpacks and class supplies available. I'll have a word with my secretary about a wavier for the fees, and to print your program." He stands from the desk. His legs go forward with too much emphasis; deliberately walking on instruction.

When he's out the door, Odina gawks at her son. "I didn't know you could do that?!"

"Me either!"

"Although that was wrong...but due to certain circumstances, I will let it slide."

"That's so modern of you, Mom." Kota grins.

"I can be cool sometimes...or radical." Odina winks. "I know the new slang."

"Very radical."

Odina leans in closer to him. "So...when will you ask her out?"

"Ummm...I don't know."

"Act fast, that's my advice."

"What if I ask too soon?"

"Hmm...maybe you're right. These new age girls are more innovative than I was."

"If I were you, I'd I'll play it safe and wait."

"That's a good strategy."

The office door opens; it's not the principal, it's his secretary. "Come, Mr. Ahoka, I'll assist you with admission."

He's used to bewildered looks from humans, so hers doesn't bother him. Kota sticks out like a sore thumb. He's used to the peculiar glances. On the way through the main office, the workers nearly break their necks to get a good look at his unusual appearance. *This isn't the worst part…wait until I mingle with the students.*

"Don't use the brain trick on her." Odina mummers.

"I won't."

They're taken to a lab full of humpback computers. "Have a seat." Kota does so. "The classes on the screen are the ones available. You're in need of 1 of each." The lady points to the category sections. "English. Art. Language. Science. History. Tech. Math. Please take your time. You must be close friends with the principal. I wouldn't want to rush such a special acquaintance."

Her snide remark isn't missed. The bitterness isn't hidden. *I guess she thinks I'm part of some nepotism. Or that my mom and the principal are a thing. If only I could read minds to know which one it is.*

"Thank you, Miss Secretary." Odina shuts her down with politeness, killing her with kindness. The woman taps away in annoyance. "Such great hospitality."

"I think she's onto us."

"I'll allow you to play with her mind." "Mom?!"

He gasps.

"I don't care for ugliness."

Her son reads the computer screen. "Yes! Wood shop!" Kota's nerdy pleasure shows.

"Perfect!" Odina celebrates with a high five.

After enrolling, he and his mother are taken to the printer station to collect the schedule. "You may start class by the next bell. That'll be biology with Mr. Knox. The waiver was accepted for your bag, notebooks, textbooks, and pencils. You're all set." The lady is still aggravated. "Usually, onboarding takes a week to process. You're lucky to be so important. Have a nice day."

"Many great blessings and good fortunes to you." Odina destroys her with humanity once again.

"Many great blessings and good fortunes to you." Kota repeats it as well, to provoke the woman, who spins on her heels to stomp away.

He and his mom share a comical gaze, cracking up. "Have a great day at school…take it easy. You're okay." Odina cuddles him. "You can do this." *I can…she's right. The idea of blood has popped into my mind. But that's an unneeded phobia. The necklace works well at ending all of my hunter tendencies.*

By the next bell, Kota is in the hall, studying the schedule like the newbie he is. The eyes of every teenager, boy and girl, are on him. Taking in his supernatural features, they aren't quite certain what's wrong about him. The thought of Kota being a vampire is an unachievable conclusion. Most believe he has eye contacts. Others believe he's gothic, due to his jet-black hair and oddly pale skin.

The teachers get a good look too, debating if he'll be a problem…mistaking his bizarreness as danger. A biker kid…a druggy. Of course, Kota can't read their thoughts, but their responses are transparent enough to know what they're thinking.

The way into the classroom is a walk of shame. Everyone whispers while eyeing him down. Kota keeps his sight on the paper to avoid scaring the classroom. Someone taps him on the shoulder. He turns to find a girl in a pink dress.

She has a superior vibe, as if she rules the school. Very queen bee and superficial. "Hi, you, the name is Vanessa." She flirts. "I'm guessing you're new. I love the gothic take. Where did you buy your contacts?"

Before he can make up a good lie as to where he get his eyes from, the teacher whistles. "EYES UP FRONT! Miss Skye, no chatting!"

The popular girl bats her lashes at Kota. "We'll talk later."

Umm…what? Why is she speaking to me as if I'm not a freak in the crowd? She has some odd bravery to address me when everyone else wouldn't dare to. I wonder why. I'm sure my skin is still dead…and that my eyes are the wrong shade. Nothing has changed. Kota explores his brain for an answer. *Her behavior reminds me of the girls at my old school. Who were all flies drawn to a light bulb.*

Did my irresistible ways transfer to my vampirism? Has it multiplied? Kayla had the same stare when she saw me. The same incarcerated hold was on her too. I'm guessing I'm still a chick magnet.

"Homeostasis." The biology teacher lectures "A state of chemical balance which reproduce and evolves over generations. You'll find the chapter lesson on page 294." Every student, including Kota, flip open the textbook. "NASA use this very term in their space investigation. Are there other life forms out there?"

That's easy to answer. Yes. Other life forms exist. Although I'm not sure about aliens. That would be insane. I wonder if they're real? Anyway, I need to do my classwork. Kota reads the chapter of Homeostasis, yet his mind ventures off. *I wonder if Kayla is as hooked on me as this Skye girl is? I can't tell for sure.*

Next period is French. The teacher instructs everyone to translate what she's saying onto the board. Most have no clue and skim the textbook for help. The woman has an insanely thick accent, which isn't easy to decipher. Kota is just as ignorant as the rest.

I've never taken French. Back home, we only learned English since America favors that tongue. I'm just as dumb as the rest of the class. Who all frantically write guesses on the board to beat the timer, which ticks down from 2 minutes. Kota hides at the back of the room. A misfit. A wallflower. A missing link.

KAYLA

Kay enters the gym room, wondering what everyone is chatting about. She steps up the bleachers in a tank top and joggers, making her way up top. Marla, Fred, and Luke are there. She hears one of the conversations as she climbs. A group of girls are loud enough for her to overhear.

'I got the creeps when I saw him." One judders.

"Something's really wrong…I don't want to talk about it anymore." One groans nauseously.

"I think he's hot."

"Eww…more like not!"

"No dice…uh…not at all."

Her group has the same chat when she reaches them.

"Those gotta be Halloween contacts or something." Fred says.

"I'm getting biker vibes." Marla inputs.

"I haven't seen him yet to know…" Luke shrugs. "What's the gossip?" Kay plops beside Luke.

"The new boy…I hear he looks a little….off."

Kota is here already??! Her mouth hangs. "New boy?"

"Yeah." Marla answers. "And Vanessa was the first one to greet him."

"Vanessa?" *Aww….I wanted to be the one to welcome him! Screw Vanessa. The bully. I'll tell Kota all about how she terrorizes girls by bulldozing them out of her way. Her and her girlfriends in pink! He won't like her bitch side. Or…will he? Some guys are into rotten girls. I hope he isn't.*

The gym teacher claps his hands to get everyone's attention. "Track applications are open…as well as swim team tryouts. Sign up if you're interested; the forms are on the table." The muscular guy points at a table pushed against the back wall. "Alright, everyone, front and center. Soccer is the game of the day, choose your team!"

Kayla mindlessly marches down the bleachers with her peeps, still annoyed that the ice queen spoke to Kota. *How dare she?! Just because he's new, she wants to stick her claws in! I hope he doesn't like her. I know I shouldn't want him for myself…since I have a boyfriend. But I knew him first! I know something she'll never know. I know his secret. I hate her! I hope Kota has class with me, so I can claim him for myself.*

After class, she nears the cafeteria; the same, familiar buzzing frequency fills her ears. This time it isn't as much of a headache. It's restrained. This assures her that Kota is close…just as it did the night of her show. Kay stops to scan the faces of passing students, urgently searching for his gemstone irises. When she finds them, her heart dies. The beating within disappears.

I forgot how stunning he is. Kayla gives him a tender smile. She waits for the crowd to thin so she can go to him. The seconds drag on. The distance is devastating. The mob of teenagers filling the hall never comes to an end. *Come on, get out of the way already!* Kota picks up on her irritation from the way her eyes shout annoyance. *Oh, no…I need to play it cool. He can't know that I'm stressing out.*

She poises herself by using breathing techniques. In for 10 seconds. Out for 10 seconds. Kay repeats this until her heart is stable. The vast sea of students finally disperse, leaving them alone in the hall. Both she and Kota step forward. Both secretly craving to clear the distance by running, but they compose themselves.

"Hi…again."

"Hi." His silky light voice turns the single word into a melody.

"I didn't think you'd start today."

Kota adjusts the strap of his bookbag, which he wears on one shoulder. "I kind of…accidentally…used mind control on the principal." He scratches his head nervously.

"You what?!" Kayla titters.

"Yeah…I have to be careful. I don't know how to fit in."

"Just act human."

"Says the sorceress?" He jabs playfully.

"Yeah…good point." She shyly stares down at her feet. "I heard Vanessa spoke to you."

"I forgot how fast gossip spreads in school."

"What did she say?" Kay glances up in a way that causes his veins to implode.

"She wanted to know where I got my eyes from." Kota skips over the part where she hit on him. "I should've told the truth to fend her off."

"Yeah, you should've…she's rotten to the core. She and her Plastic Pinks are bullies. Rich and spoiled."

"At least I know one that isn't so bad."

"I'm not spoiled!"

"I bet your room belongs to a princess."

She can't find a retort, knowing that this is true, the glittery canopy bed, the dollhouse aesthetic. "Whatever…let's eat."

"Yay, step one of being a human, fake eating!" He cheers sarcastically.

"Oh, right…" She clamps her teeth together. "I'm sorry."

"It's fine."

The two head into the lunchroom. Of course, everyone inside scopes them out, assuming that they're dating. *Here come the rumors. By the end of the day, we'll be labeled a couple. Which we're not.* The two receive looks of judgment in the food line. Vanessa eyes Kayla down, full of jealousy. It doesn't end there…many girls are bitter with envy too.

I guess I'm not the only girl who wants to be with him. Does the vampire appeal increase the effect he has on girls?? She chooses white chicken chili, blueberry bread, and watermelon juice. Kota is a copycat; he selects the same meal. "Poser!" She scoffs sarcastically.

"Well…considering what I am…that's a given." Kay nudges him with her elbow.

The resentful gazes stalk them all the way to the back of the cafeteria. Mya and Jia are utterly confounded from their lunch table. They're unable to blink. Kay picks another table since she and Mya are still enemies…and because she feels Jia can't handle a vampire. *She said she'd try to be accepting….but Kota is too alarming. Maybe next time I'll invite him to our table. Today may be too fast for them.*

"Is here okay?"

"Yeah, no matter where I sit, I'll be a circus."

"You're not…at least not to me."

"I'm glad." He waits for her to sit before he does.

"So…where's your schedule." Kota brandishes the paper from the side pouch of his bag to compare it to hers. *Oh, no…* She frowns. *We only have lunch and common room.* The internal disappointment is demolishing. *That's so annoying! I won't see him much at all.* Her lovely doe eyes scale down, intrigued that wood shop is on the list. "You chose wood shop?"

"Yeah…my dad taught me."

"Interesting…" Kay observes his crystal eyes. "Do you draw?"

"A little."

"I assumed you did."

"Really…how?" His electric irises prickle her skin.

She drops her gaze to divert her eyes from becoming vulnerable. Kay munches on the chili to hide her yearning for him. "Yeah…the picture from the meeting was impressive. I'm a sketcher…I detected that you were too."

"That must be a magic thing?"

"No…you just seem very artsy."

"I wish I had that radar. I would've never labeled you a ballerina. That was surprising."

"I thought it was obvious…ballet is my life…every part of my soul is in it."

"It definitely is…"

"Although…I'm banned from it." She pouts.

"Why? What happened?"

"I snuck to a Halloween party…and got grounded. Now I can't go to rehearsals."

"That's not fair."

"Tell me about it."

"Parents can be melodramatic, but you can make them forgive you."

"My dad won't budge, no matter how much I apologize."

"I may have the secret for getting un-grounded." He boasts.

"Tell me!" Kay reaches to touch his hand.

The flesh of his hand splits into cracks, ripping apart. Dividing his skin. Underneath is pure shine. The lifeless veins of his spark as lightning does across a stormy sky. Jagged. Wild. Bright. Kayla withdraws her hand, wide eyed and staggered. Kota's shredded skin heals, sealing back to its previous state.

KOTA

It's already difficult being around her. Now this? I have to endure the halo edging her body. Her magnetic pull on my dead soul. The sound of her destabilizing voice. Kayla reanimates me without knowing she does. The organ in my chest is knotted… rigid with compression. My imitation heart throbs; palpitating at her control. I thought the fever she spelled me with was impossible to handle. The inner tornado is no longer the only curse she's given me. Now…Kayla is capable of altering my skin with a touch.

"I'm sorry."

Kota shakes his head. "Don't be."

"I'm still learning." She worriedly peers to the side.

"My grandad says you're learning fast."

"I guess so…my shadow breathing is advancing."

"What's shadow breathing."

"I can't share that…it's top secret."

"I could use my mind trick on you."

"That'll lead to a war."

"How could I ever defend myself from your breathing?"

"Just you wait…I'll magic you into another dimension."

His white irises shuffle side to side, impressed. "You can do that?"

"Sure can." Kay boasts like a boss, tilting her chin up.

"I'll stay on your good side then…" He holds his hands up as if surrendering to a police officer.

"You better."

Kota scoops up some of the chili. *Hmmm…it smells delicious…but will it taste the same?* He cautiously inserts the spoon into his mouth and chews. The flavors are absent…it's blander than bland. Flavorless as water. His tongue has no active receptors. But the scent is enough to fool him as if he has tastebuds.

"What does it taste like?" Kayla mutters lowly.

"Nothing." He mimics her whispering. "But it smells incredible."

"So strange!"

"Yes…this is strange." Vanessa approaches their table. "I don't understand why the new boy is so smitten." Her pink squad stands behind her. They each sport leather jumpsuits, handbags, and sunglasses. "I have status…she doesn't…so rethink this little alliance." She sits on the ledge of the table facing Kota. "How about we go to the Golden Leaf dance?" The ice queen crosses her legs to demonstrate dominance.

I don't like her at all. Kayla was right…she's rotten. Vanessa insults, then tries to get her way. And she's blocking my view of the true queen bee. "No, thank you…I don't care for ugliness." He quotes his mother.

"Ugh!" Vanessa heckles, wrinkling her forehead like an angry feline. "Do you know how many guys want to go with me?!"

"I honestly don't care."

She stomps from the table. "Have fun being tagged a loser!"

Kota shakes his head. "Ignore her. She's jealous of you …you have the new school toy at your disposal."

Kay stabs at the beans. "Yeah….I guess."

Aww, she's scarred by the queen's words. "Hey." He leans forward. "You're the one who ruled the stage, not her. That's true status...not silly popularity."

"You didn't want to be popular at your old school?" She keeps her eyes on the plate to hide her bashfulness.

"No...never."

She peeks at him with a light simper. "Thanks for cheering me up."

"Anytime, princess."

"I'm not!"

"You live in a glass castle."

"It's more like a tower."

The bell chimes. Her eyes drain of all of the previous delight. *Why is she sad?* "What's wrong?"

"Lunch flew by..."

"We have tomorrow." Kota looks on the bright side, although he doesn't want to leave either.

"True..." Kay shrugs. "I'll see you then." She hesitantly gets up from the table.

"See you then." He grins, lingering to the musical note from the core of her soul. The memorable tune of strings of an orchestra. Kota hates when it fades away. Hates when she's swallowed by the crowd. *I want to ask her if she knows this. Does she know her spirit has music? Does she know that her body generates the theme of paradise?*

KAYLA

Every time I blink...I see his face. The blackness of my eyelids hold his image. They're stained. It's unbelievable that such a luminous boy can belong to hell. Kota belongs to the sky...he deserves wings...not fangs. He's very ordinary for a vampire. Not once did I spot him struggling with being part of a human herd. I'll have to ask him how that's possible.

History is still stuck on the same subject...only this time, the class has to draw what they think is in the vampire dugout. An illustration is needed for the last assignment, which was to write a prediction essay. The students are ordered to remain silent for the duration of the period.

Kayla isn't for this choice; all the quietness does is give her an excuse to think about him. *So...he doesn't like mean girls? That's good to know. I was worried. I liked how he stuck up for me...and how he refused her invite. But that won't be the last girl to ask him out. He traps them in as the Pied Piper does pests. He does the same to me.*

After school, Kayla is given more proof to her conclusion. Kota is at his locker, while dozens of girls check him out from head to toe. She overhears one say, "No, actually I think he's hot…forget what I said."

"Amber, you can't switch sides!" Her friend quarrels.

"Yes, I can…especially now that he rejected the queen. I should ask him out."

Wow…even the ones who were creeped out, are now fantasize about him. The girls who were turned off are now full of thirst. Kayla studies Kota…speculating what it is that has once disgusted girls, suddenly attracted to him. *It has to be the curse….the allure of death is attractive.*

"Kayla!" Darius calls her. *Oh, right…we agreed to make out after school. I forgot!*

She shifts around. "Darius!"

He hungrily smooches her as if starving. Kay can't help but fall to pieces under the touch of his lips. After all, she does love him…but she hates that he didn't wait. *We planned to do this in private…not right in front of people! What is he thinking?? Why would he do this? Everyone sees us…Kota sees us.*

"Let's go!" His horniness cuts clear through his deep tone.

Kayla doesn't dare look back….because she knows what she'll find. Kota is crushed. Shattered to fragments because of the truth. He doesn't have a chance. *I'm evil. I should have told him I'm not single. I led him on. I don't want Kota to know I'm taken. Vanessa was right about him being smitten. I'm into him the same way he's into me. Gran was right…I have a crush. But I can't choose because it'll hurt both of them. She was also right when she said, it's normal to like more than one boy. Those words couldn't be any truer.*

Darius rounds multiple corners, scoping out the perfect spot for their mouth feast. He goes a good distance, so they're not interrupted. The chattering hall is now miles away from them. The back of the school is secluded. "Okay…here is fine."

"I wasn't able to tell my grandma the lie. She'll come looking for me."

"We should make it quick then…" He grabs her hips. Tugging her into a swooping peck. Her arms hang from his neck. He props her against the wall, deepening his mouth.

Kay hopes for the same passion to engulf her. But his effect on her body is absent. *I usually enjoy kissing him…but for some reason, I'm stressed…and distracted by Kota.* Her mouth's embrace isn't as ferocious as his.

Darius is caught off guard by her limp lips. He stops to assess her face. "What's wrong?"

"Nothing…"

"No…it's something…tell me."

"There's just a lot going on. I'm stressed out. Sorry…I should've told you."

"What has you stressed out?"

I wasn't expecting him to ask this. Quick! I need to give an excuse! Any excuse besides Kota…the other boy. "I'm not in ballet anymore…my dad terminated the program."

"Oh, no…but ballet is your everything!"

"It is…" She agrees….thankful that he believed her lie. "I'm sorry about today…we can try again tomorrow."

"Anything you want."

"So, you're…cool with stopping? I mean, don't guys stay…" She tries hinting at aroused in a friendly manner. "Ready for it?"

"I'll be okay." He snorts.

"Are you sure?"

"You can make it up to me over the radio."

"Okay…that's fair." She tiptoes to clasp her lips to his. She's sure to give a long kiss, hoping it voices how sorry she is. *I really don't want to harm him…or Kota. I want to protect both of them. Does that make me horrible? Am I being a bad girlfriend? Or a good pal to Kota? He has feelings for me…I just want to protect his heart.*

Once in the car, she is non-verbal over this new dilemma. She's thankful that the radio is on the news station; it gives her a few seconds to think. Her granny is unaware of her silence. Gloria drives the city streets, listening in on the radio news.

"5 beach goers were killed last night in what is assumed to be a cougar attack. Although they rarely populate cities and are mostly drawn to rural areas. Still…be alert people, stay safe."

Her gran tugs her mouth downward. "Have you seen any other sightings of that vampire?" Kayla stays mute, too engulfed in teenage drama. Gloria peeks over at her. "Is something the matter?"

"I don't want to talk about it…"

"Why not?"

Kay mopes, then leans her forehead on the cool glass of the window. "I just don't, gran."

Gloria looks behind her before changing lanes. "I'll call the Ahoka's for an update…something else is going on here."

Kayla doesn't even want to hear any updates. She's colored blue. For the remainder of the ride, she scopes out the glass, city towers to take her mind away. Her sour mood has her wishing she'd never been friendly. *He made me forget I had a boyfriend. How is that possible? For the first time…Darius didn't exist.*

At home, she goes straight to her room. Her parents aren't in yet, which she appreciates. *Good…no one else will ask me what my deal is.* Kay buries her face in her pillow…screaming out frustration into the cushion until her throat hurts. She eats little at dinner, which is warmed up leftovers. Homemade pizza. Her parents are working late.

Gloria studies her granddaughter. "It can't be that bad." "It is…"

"Let it out…keeping it bottled up only makes it worse."

Kay spears her veggies with a fork. "I was dumb today."

"How?"

"I can't like them both…it's wrong."

"No…what's wrong is thinking you have to choose right away. Affections are complicated…"

"It feels like I have no time."

"Don't worry about it…just put your attention on practice."

Kayla sadly eats the greens. *Is she right? Will distracting myself help? But how does ignoring a problem fix it? I don't know…*She stops pondering because it's causing a headache.

After dinner, they go to the balcony. Gloria doesn't participate in the training; she just stands there. "Try it by yourself this time. Channel your attention to the night wind."

Kayla closes her eyes to listen. The rippling winds slash through leaves. Her mind visualizes the flow, picturing the air as clear…it's a mist. A grainy texture frames the vapor. The wind particles bustle. *Channel my attention…to the wind….be the wind. In and out for 15 seconds.* Her chest fills with the traveling wind…which swells from the sky…to pump through her. "I did it!"

"You're getting better…try again!"

Kayla waits for the next gush. Her airways don't fill…her lungs are flat…until the next rush. She's serene enough to get lost in her mind. *Who was the first Spell Bender? How did they know we were connected to the elements? Is the first one still alive? I would love to meet my ancestors.*

The next gush of air lasts for 15 seconds yet again. Kayla doesn't struggle…the earth breathes for her…through her…with

her. The cold force explores her lungs, thrusting inward. The air god
works her body...flooding her vessels with an enraptured surge.

CHAPTER 29: CRUSHED

KOTA
FLASHBACK

I didn't know Kayla had a boyfriend….I assumed she was single. But a girl like her is bound to be taken. She's too magnetic. I should've known better. I can't say it doesn't hurt. I'm connected to her…even more than I thought. I still don't understand what went on with my hand. I'll have to ask my mom for answers about this when I get home. He shuts his locker and swings his bookbag around his shoulder. The girl who called him strange, blocks his path before he can even walk. "Your name is Kota, right?"

"Yes." *Oh no….my effect is present…just like back home. I wonder if I'm really a Casanova now. This was an over exaggeration before…now…I don't think so it is.*

"Do you have a date to the dance?"

"I won't be going." He admits. *Why would I go if I can't have Kayla at my side?*

"Oh…bummer…well, let me know if you change your mind."

"Sure." Kota says politely.

Outside, the curbs are full of yellow buses. He doesn't know which one to take home. *I should go back in and ask for a map…but I'll probably be bomb rushed by another chick.* Even now, he's being sized up as eye candy. A few girls almost break their necks to get a longer look at him. Their feisty eyes reveal their heavy thirst for him. They drink him up. Per usual, the guys throw nasty glowers his way, jealous of him. Jealous of the ultimate dreamboat effect he has. Some climb onto the bus, others mug him down. *Yeah…my old school life is definitely on repeat.* He stands by the bus stop, debating what to do. *I could go back in…but the staff will eye me the same way everyone else is. As if I'm a relic. I'm bizarre…my skin, my eyes. If only I could hide them.*

Kota leans against the bus stop sign, which garners even more attention from the girls. They assume he's a loner…too cool to ride the bus. The simple lean is romanticized by them. The chicks drool over his mysteriousness, their eyelids hooded by lust.

Vanessa and her pink squad are possessed too. Blonde hair and designer handbags hook from their elevated snooty, palms. The copy and paste group fond over him, his hair, eyes, lips, height.

The bus drivers honk their horns at the teens, whose feet are rooted to the pavement, enjoying the show. This loud noise kills the daze; reality beckons them back enough to continue to the buses. While driving off, hundreds of students peep at him through the windows. No different than a safari tour of the wild ….no different than exotic fish in a tank.

When all are gone, Kota checks to see if anyone else is around, inspecting the doors and windows of the school. The area is vacant. *I'll just run home…I would've got on the bus with Kayla…but I don't think she takes it.* His feet trace the ground as slick as rain and booms through 23 blocks in a span of one minute.

The gushing pressure on his flesh frosts over due to the autumn season. He slows down when he's closer to home. None of the humans pick up on his speediness. He flows between space and time, coming to a stop once on the porch.

"Why would it be here?" Odina is heard from behind the door.

"I'm not sure…last we checked; it was gone from the surface." Mato says.

"Could it be living underground?"

"That's possible."

"We'll need another meeting to work this out."

Kota doesn't move a muscle…he's stiff as a mannequin. *My foe is back in the city?? Kayla must have had another vision. I have to get answers from her. He was at the beach…surveying me. My instincts weren't wrong.*

The front door pushes inward. "KOTA!" Odina holds her chest. "You can't keep scaring me like this!"

"I…I…I forgot to whistle."

Dyani is behind her; the two are in jackets, ready to leave. "He can't help being a creep."

"Don't call your brother that!" She scolds her daughter. "You look flushed. Is something bothering you?" Her maternal care peeks out.

"Yeah, how was school? Did you hang out with Kayla?"

"I'm fine. It's just the weather…I ran home." He fibs. "School was fun; we had lunch together."

"Aww, that's perfect, son! I'm glad you had a great day."

"Me too." He steps to the side to let them pass. "I have to talk to you later, Mom…when you get back."

"Sure, we won't be gone long."

"Later, kiddo."

"You're a kiddo, too." He smirks.

"Whatever…" Dy sticks out her tongue like a toddler. Kota sticks his out too then goes to the living room.

Mato is in an armchair reading a newspaper. "What do you have to talk to your mom about?"

Can I tell him about the ordeal with Kayla? I don't know if I could talk about girls with Dad. It might be awkward. Mato lowers the newspaper.

"Is it about Kayla?" He notes his son's uncomfortableness; Kota scratches the back of his head as a nervous tick. "You can talk to me about girls. I was your age before."

That's true…he was my age once. I can chat with him. "Something happened…"

"I'm sure it did."

Oh, great…he's assuming something else. "No…not that…she has a boyfriend."

"The good ones always do."

"I know…"

"That doesn't mean you give up." Mato gestures to the sofa.

Kota sits. "But she's taken…wouldn't that be rude?"

"Your mother wasn't single when I met her."

"Really??"

"Yes…." Mato folds up the black and white news paper, laying it on his lap. "I waited… to become her friend first. Once her boyfriend did the wrong thing. My time arrived. We've been together ever since." He grins, fondly thinking back. "Girls appreciate a patient guy. That's all it takes."

"I never thought of it that way. Kind of like the slow turtle wins the race?"

"Exactly….it's considered romantic when us guys do that. Nice guys win the race."

Hmm…can I win? Kayla is so involved with him. I can't label Darius a bad guy just because he's with her. "What if her boyfriend is nice too?"

"Only time will tell. If you're meant to be, then it will happen."

She marked my hand with light. Does that symbolize that we're meant to be? It has to. "Something happened when she touched me."

"Ahh…the first touch….the tingling." His dad reminisces fondly.

"No…it wasn't that." He stresses, hoping he won't sound manic for saying the next part. "My skin changed…."

Mato leans forward, heavily invested. "What do you mean?"

Kota tries explaining the impossible, raking his mind for the right words, "When she touched me…my skin split in half." He ups his hand, hoping to somehow demonstrate this by trailing his nail across the flesh. "My hand cracked open…."

"I don't understand." His dad strains his eyes to look closer.

"Ummm…I don't know how else to say it. My skin cracked open…." His dad stares to the side, bewildered by the explanation. *If Dad doesn't have an answer, why would Mom?*

KAYLA FLASHBACK

After magic practice, Kay goes to bed. Although she doesn't sleep. She cuddles under a fluffy blanket and switches on the walkie talkie. "Are you awake?"

"Yes, baby."

She loves how he calls her that. "I'm sorry about earlier."

"Don't be."

"I won't do it again…"

"I forgive you."

Would he say that if he knew I liked another boy? I don't even know how to tell him. It'll only start a fight. I like that we're a drama free couple….and want to keep it that way. I'll safeguard our harmony...by hiding the truth. "So…about making it up to you. Shall we play a game?" Her light voice sizzles.

"What do you have in mind?"

"What if…we went to the beach. What would you want me to wear?" She nibbles her lip

"Definitely a two piece."

"Bra and underwear only?"

"Yes."

"What color?"

"Pink."

"*SO* typical." She giggles.

"You look hot in pink."

"I'm thinking Victoria Secret."

"You'll look great in anything,"

"What would you wear?"

"Shorts." H answers fast,

"Just shorts…nothing else?"

"Yes, just that…."

I've never seen him in just shorts. Never seen his chest. I don't even know how to picture him half naked. "You'd be so hot without a shirt…" Kay teases. *We've been so blocked because of my parents. We never go out alone….never hang out at his place. Honestly, I told Mya I'm fine with us taking it slow, because we can't go fast. My parents are always around.* "Have you ever wanted to see me in my bra?"

"So many times…"

She dotes on his husky voice. "Why didn't you ask to see?"

"It's kinda hard to with your dad patrolling."

"Yeah…true. But…I could sneak you in."

"Really?" Darius stutters.

"Yes…"

"What would we do?"

She shyly covers her eyes. "I've thought about our bodies touching. Have you?"

"Yes…"

"What else?"

"Tongue kissing."

"We can try that."

"What do you want to try?" Kay bites her nails.

"I want to make love to you…."

Did he just say make love??? Aww, he's too delicious! He didn't refer to it as the F or S-word. I love that! I know he's a nice guy…but it's a relief knowing he actually cares for me. I'm not a game. Most boys at school hook up and move on. My baby is set on me.

"I would play this song." He sets the radio down and hit the play button on his digital recorder. A robust saxophone generates long notes. The suggestive melody and the vaporwave collide into a stimulating heat. Kayla rests her hand on her chest, taken aback by how it's so different from the rest of his work.

This sounds…adult. There's an ecstasy appeal. A trance of a natural high….without drugs. Kay imagines a nightclub where there'd be no kids allowed due to vulgar dancing. The tempo is slow and buttery…wild and erotic. The saxophone burst her body's sensory beyond its limit. Her narcotic thirst for him is rough on her abdomen. *He activated my drive…just with the song?!! Do I tell him I want love making sooner? Or am I being irrational? Now isn't the time. I can't rush something so important because I'm feeling the moment. I have to be careful.*

The next day, in a noisy homeroom, Kayla counts the seconds until Kota blesses her eyes. She knows it's wrong to do this…especially after last night with Darius, but Kota is a drug. A heavier drug. *Darius is a small taste of a sedative…Kota is the full dose. I swear when our hands touched. That static shock…it felt right…and I don't know why it felt so right.*

Does he feel the same? No…no…no. I need to stop thinking this way! Kota is a friend. We're buddies. I can't. I belong to Darius.

That statement falls apart as soon as Kota piles into the classroom. Her mind turns to slush. Her firm disposition is now extinct. Her babydoll eyes slow their blinking. Her chest collapses in on itself. Kay forgets she has a boyfriend yet again. She slightly waves at him, trying to compose her zeal…but her enthusiasm is hard to conquer.

Kota smiles and makes his way to sit beside her. "Good morning."

"Good morning!"

He sniggers at how hyped she is. "It must be a good day?"

*Now it is…*she wants to say but doesn't. "I'm looking on the bright side."

"I'll do the same." She sizes up his hand, wondering if she can brush her fingers over it again. Kay hurriedly looks away, rubbing the back of her neck. "So…" Kota observes her hand too. "My mom thinks the hand thing was a chain reaction from your training. It's called triboelectric effect…I looked it up in the dictionary. I think it's that…"

"I never heard of it."

"You ever zap someone after touching metal…or getting clothes out of the dryer."

"Oh.…so that's what it's called!"

"Yeah…triboelectric effect. That's the logical explanation." He looks away to the board.

She suspects he's thinking about the after-school scenario. She has nervous ticks too. *It seems Kota scratches his head, and I rub my neck when feeling discomforted.* "I'm sorry about not telling you I had a boyfriend. The topic didn't come up." "I understand…no worries."

The teacher stands at the board. "Alright.…volunteers for the golden leaf dance are still needed. The gym room requires decorators, servers, and a DJ. Any student can apply, just allow the principal to preview the playlist. Clean music only. Now for head count. Raise your hand when you hear your name." The woman calls out each of them. All 55 teenagers. One by one, they fling their arms up to be marked as present for the day.

After homeroom, they have five minutes to collect their assigned textbooks from the lockers. Kayla's is nowhere near his; hers is down the hall at the very end. "I'll see you at lunch. I need to know how to free myself from being grounded."

"Can't wait to share the greatest plan ever. Guaranteed to bail you out." He beams like the growing sun.

Kay smiles big. "See ya." She goes down the hall to her locker for a notebook and pen. From her peripheral view, she spots him opening his. Dozens of handwritten notes tumble from the bottom of it.

KOTA

I can't say I expected date mail in my locker. That's new. These chicks must have stuck the letters through the vent. There's so many! How do they expect me to take them all to the dance? There's a hill of handwritten letters at his feet...and he doesn't know what to do about it. The bell hasn't rung, meaning he and his fangirl mail is spotlighted for everyone to see. The halls are full, and all eyes are on him and what he'll do next. Everyone is watching...and ready to spread the gossip. He removes the textbook for wood shop from his locker, then observes the bottom. *I can't even close it...the door is blocked.*

Kota bends to scoop the tiny papers up. *Should I throw them away? There's a garbage can right there. Or would I be deemed heartless? I don't want to be that.* He cogitates on what to do with the heap of letters. *I'll be the worst guy in school if I toss them out. I'll stay after hours, so no one sees me doing it.* Kota shovels the papers into the bottom of the locker; it takes five dumps to finally clear the floor.

In wood shop, his classmates finds it hard to pay attention to slicing planks in half. *I figure they only heard about me being odd. Now that these students finally see me, it's a different experience.* Kota splits the wood in half, trying to escape into a creative hub. But the extra attention is obscuring him from mellowing out. Even the teacher is preoccupied with him. The old man attempts to grade papers at his desk but glances up more times than Kota can count. So much wonder in his eyes.

On the board is today's assignment:

CREATE A MINIATURE BOOKCASE.

That's easy enough...however, I can't move rapidly; I'll have to work at a human tempo...not a vampire one. He divides the wood into eight slabs. He sands down the middle on both sides and files the corners to a smooth finish. He's still speedy with it…but not enough to cause a scene. While he props the shelves together for the base, he thinks, *I hope that locker thing didn't upset Kayla.*

I know she likes me. Maybe she wants to go to the dance as friends. I wouldn't mind that. I want to do more things with her. Homeroom and lunch aren't enough. Maybe after I help her free herself from house arrest…we could hang out. Alone…

Kota glues the outer shelves together with ease; he doesn't struggle to hold all four walls of the bookcase at once. *This isn't cheating…even as a human, I had pretty steady hands. None of my vamp perks are being used.* Next, he lines the inner shelves with glue and insert each one by one. He's done with the project within 10 minutes.

All the other students are still working on the outer wood of the case. *This is déjà vu. Just like back home….I had free time in my last shop class. Now that's happening yet again. I'll work on something else. I always wanted to make a flute…but I don't know if it'll be operational. It could be decorative for grandad's place.* Kota sets aside the finished bookcase.

The gazes from annoyed students don't bother him, nor do their comments. "How did he finish already?" "He had to take this class before." A girl replies.

"Show off." A spiteful boy grumbles.

Kota directs his hands to tie a string around a cylindershaped piece. This prevents the wood from splitting when drilling. He loops the rope five times before pulling it firmly. A handheld drill, one that's long and sharp, is what he uses. He cranes the circular wood onto a stand, which mounts it high enough to drill through. Like a pencil sharpener, the drill spins into the piece, releasing shreds of fine wood. The deeper it goes, the easier the winding is. This lures the teacher's attention. The elderly man sits down the stack of papers and remove his reading glasses.

When the drill is cleaned through, Kota shaves it with a sharp blade. He slices away access to decrease the width and length. He's fluid with the sculpting; his hands work as an industrial machine; trimming evenly. There's no break in the motion of the blade from the front to the back or side to side. Kota even spins it around while keeping the same workflow. The last thing he does is chisel finger holes on each side, shut off one end, and clear out the dusty debris.

"I see you're going to be my favorite student." The teacher walks over to review both the flute and bookcase. "Two projects in one period…I've never seen that before. And both are antique worthy!"

"Thank you, sir."

"I take it that this is a hobby of yours."

"It is…my dad taught me."

"It shows. If you're interested in entering any shop contests, let me know. I'll help you apply."

"Oh, wow, that would be cool! I'll have to work on a new project. I'll let you know…thanks." The old man, who could fit in well as a fine arts critic, grins.

I never thought about contests. That would be something new to try. On his way to his locker, Kota tests out if the flute will make music. He places the instrument to his lips and position his fingers before blowing. The calming, harmonic note that escapes brings on great accomplishment.

"YES, IT WORKS!" He's beyond chipper all the way to his locker. Until the same outpour platters from it. This time the mail pile is bigger. *Right…I forgot about that. I think more has been added.* Once again, he tackles the papers back into the locker using his hands as a garbage trunk dumper.

In biology, Vanessa frostily peers at him as he goes to his seat. *I feel bad for the girls who asked me out…bad because I turned them down. However, I don't have any sympathy for the ice queen. She doesn't have a soul. She can eye me down all she wants. My mind is made up.* "I heard you're a shop nerd…" She ridicules him.

"I am." Kota looks straight ahead at the board.

"You won't go far in this school; you just ruined your reputation."

"If that's true…then why are you talking to me?" Kota slightly turns his head, waiting for an answer.

"Whatever." She slams against the back of her chair with a salty expression.

He leers at her lack of a retort. *I doubt that the only vampire in school will lose any sort of reputation. She's so sour about me rejecting her and even hopes it ruins my status here.*

In French, the teacher has the class reading a full article in the language as if they understand it fully. "Can we use a translation dictionary?!" One peer pleads.

"No!!" The woman responds in a thick accent with much austerity.

I think I made a mistake choosing this subject. The teacher is too stringent. I might fail this class…that'll be a first time for me. Kota reads the foreign article, not understanding it at all. *This looks like alien text. I'll need a tutor. I wonder if Kayla knows French. I could ask at lunch. I can't bring a bad grade home. I'll be lectured for not performing my best.*

Kayla isn't in the food line as he expects. *Hmmm…where is she?* He hurriedly grabs a cup of chopped green apples and a carton of white milk. Kota singles out their table; it's empty….*Kay isn't there.* He listens for her body's harmony, picking her out from the mass crowd in less than a second.

She's talking to her girls, who are opposed to what she's asking. "I don't care if she doesn't want to, but Jia, you gave your word that you'd try to be accepting. Come sit with us."

"I know…I did…but that was before I saw him."

"He's not going to attack you! You're being ridiculous!"

Jia cautiously zooms her caramel eyes to the side. "I'll try some other time…I promise. It all just…happened too…fast. I wasn't expecting to meet him this soon. I need more time."

"I can't believe you…you're starting to sound like her!" Kay points at Mya.

Who laughs bitterly. "Maybe because we're behaving like normal people…and you're not. I'm not alone in this. We're not being mean…we're being truthful."

"Unbelievable! I can't believe you two!" Kayla trudges off with her plate of fruit. The berry platter jiggles, dropping a few of the sweet snacks to the floor.

Oh, no…I caused this. I don't want to distance her from her girls. They seem nice…I understand how hard it is to adapt to me. I'm not a normal human. The girls know what I am, so they don't fall for my lure. They're not under my hypnosis, like the rest of the school. When they see me…they know my true colors.

Kota waits a few moments for Kayla to cool down. She picks up grapes and chews them angrily. Her beady eyes all enrage *I should give her the necklace…at least that would cheer her up. But then again, it implies more than friendship. I want her as mine when I hand it over. She can't be his when I do it. I have to wait Darius out…like Dad said.*

Kota deems it safe enough to join her at the lunch table when she stops chewing so roughly. "Hey. What's up?"

"Do you want to decorate the gym for the dance? We can volunteer. I was going to ask my…friends, but they're preoccupied."

"Sure, that sounds fun." *Yes, anything…I'd do anything she wants as long as I'm near her.*

"I'll sign us up."

"Are you going to the dance?"

"No…I'm grounded, remember? I need your cheat code."

Kota opens the fruit cup and snacks on a few pieces. "Well, since you're my friend, I can share it with you free of charge."

"You better or I'll disown you."

Kota holds his chest to act wounded. "Wow, princess, you crushed my heart."

"Hmm…I thought it didn't work?"

Do I admit that it works for her…only for her? Or is it too soon to tell her this? "It's complicated."

"Does it have to do with the necklace?"

HOW DOES SHE KNOW ABOUT THAT? CAN SHE READ MY MIND??! "What necklace??" Kay points to his chest. This ends his panicking. *I thought she was referring to the one I made her.* "Oh...right. Yeah…it does.'"

"How is that possible..." She looks over the arrows attached to the chain.

"My grandad made it for me to help with obstacles."

"Is that why you can be around humans and not…" She leans onto the table to say the next words privately. "Drink from them?"

"Yes…it also allows me to be in the sun too. It's spelled."

"Oh…"

They both look to the side, detecting that they have an audience. Dozens of students oversee their close interaction, speculating that they're a couple. Their peers whisper, leaning over their lunches to get a better view. Every table views them like a cinema show….purely entertainment. Even the lunch aides pause their catering routine in the food line, eyeing the two. At the staff table, the teachers share perceptive glances, just as involved as the teens in the chatter. Principal Hamilton, seated near the back with a clipboard in hand, briefly looks up, taking note of the quiet wave in the room.

"Wait until the rumors start." She rolls her eyes.

"Yeah….everyone will think we're dating."

CHAPTER 30: BREAKAGE

KAYLA

Why would he say that? Unless…dating is on his mind? Does Kota want me? Or is he too overwhelmed by all the other girls racing after him? "You don't have a girlfriend?"

"No."

"How come? I mean, you have them lining up."

"You'd think that would help…asking is harder than it seems."

Really? He finds it hard to ask someone out? Why? He's a model amongst all the boys here…all the boys everywhere. "You're telling me you're shy?"

"Believe it or not…some boys are."

"But…. you're…."

"I'm what?" Kota curiously squints at her.

"Don't make me say it…"

"I want to hear you say it."

I need to get out of this! I said too much! I could go back in line and grab something to drink. I forgot to take a beverage. She stands. "I need to grab a drink; I'll be back."

This is the perfect excuse to flee! I can't believe I said that! I also can't believe Kota wants me to call him hot. He must know that he is. All the special attention he's getting is enough proof. Does he want his ego stroked? Or is he actually unaware??

Kayla selects cucumber lemonade and hustles back to the table. "Okay…I'm back."

"That's a good cover story…10 out of 10 for creativity." He claps.

Kayla flings a strawberry his way as a means of retaliation. Kota swiftly hooks it in his hand and eats it. "You can't cheat by using superpowers."

"Fine, I'll cheat by showing you this." He says between munches while reaching for something in his back pocket. The letter he wrote for his dad. "Behold…the ticket to your freedom."

Kay yanks it from him. "Yes, finally!"

"You're welcome."

"Thanks."

"No sweat."

"How fast did it work for you?"

"Within seconds…that there is a bona fide release form for any warden on this planet."

"You're a lifesaver!" Kayla reaches past the table to hug him. Her simple embrace creates volts of lightning through his whole body. From his toes to the top of his head. His splitting skin feels greater than before. Heavenly. Addictive. Rejuvenating.

His heart clusters into twisting ties. Heavy. Pounding for her touch. A hurricane of pressure. Kota gasps for oxygen…forced to draw in air as if he's a mortal being. The veins on his skin spark.

"Oh no! Sorry, I did it again!" She retreats from the hug. "Sorry…I'm a hugger."

Kota chest heaves up and down…when it shouldn't. Kayla is suspicious of this just as much as he is. "I'm okay." He says honestly. His entire body is alive…cured. But only for a few seconds.

"How does it feel?" Kay twiddles her thumbs, observing his unraveling skin seal back together as one. "Does it hurt?"

"No…it doesn't." Kota slowly squeezes his hands together, feeling empowered. "It feels…normal."

"I don't think I should keep doing it." She croaks out in panic.

"No…you should…it's nice."

"Anyway…um…I'll utilize your letter tonight. Wish me luck." She chomps on the fruit platter and hunts for something else to talk about to steer away from the hug. "So, yeah…we should decorate the gym."

"We could." He nods. "Umm…there's something I want to ask."

"What is it?"

Kota enjoys how her fingers curl fruits from the plate and between her juicy lips. This distracts him. "Ummm." He shifts his sight to the windows to combat fantasizing about kissing her. "My parents have a new lead on the vampire…one that's…pretty strange."

"Why is it strange?"

"Because I had an encounter with him on the beach …."

"You did?! That's insane! I saw it there too! It looked like it was stalking someone!"

This confirmation promotes his vigilante mode. "How about in the lake? Did you see it there??" He angles his elbows completely onto the table, fully engaged in recovering more information.

"No…I only saw the devil eyes in the trees."

"I felt him in the water."

The bell rattles a high ring. Many kids moan in annoyance as they get up to leave. A few teens loiter behind, not afraid of catching a late bell. Kota and her are a part of this late crew too.

"Is that the only finding you've had?"

Kayla is smart enough to shake her head side to side. *He can't know about the dugout. That may be where the thing lives. Kota has moved on…I shouldn't help him regress to a hunter again.* "I should go." Kay gets up from the bench table.

"I have more questions; can we talk after school?"

"Sure, we can."

"See you then." Kota remains seated and is in no rush to go to the next period.

There must be a lot on his mind. I just revealed that his enemy is in the city. I hope I didn't cause another problem. Since we're friends now, I have the right to shield him. I didn't like how he changed into a beast. He lost himself. I don't like him when he's that way. I hope I didn't wake up a brutal appetite.

As soon as she walks into gym class, Fred says, "You're sitting with the new guy now?" He coolly leans against the brick wall.

"I am…are you jealous?"

"Maybe…" His green eyes dart to the side.

"Don't worry, you're forever my basketball crush."

"And you're my baller…rina." Fred coins cleverly while mock shooting an air ball.

Kay snorts cutely. "That's a good one!"

"I know…I hate that it took me so long to come up with it!"

"You're still a joke master, don't sweat it." She joins him, leaning on the wall.

"So…it's nice of you to welcome him to prep high." "Yeah…no one should start school sitting by themselves. I mean…look at Luke." She waves to him as he converses with Maila on the bleachers.

"Your work is impressive…maybe he'll get another friend soon."

Oh, no…is he suggesting that Kota needs to stop talking to me. Fred sounds…protective. Does he have an inkling about Kota's dark side? Can he see past the supernatural pull that blinds everyone else?

"We'll most likely stay friends like I am with Luke."

"There's a rumor that you two are a packaged deal."

"I expected that." She giggles. "We're not."

"You two looked pretty comfy at lunch."

Is Fred into me?? If so…when did it happen?? We're just buddies….he's never shown interest like this. Like a scorned guy who didn't get the girl. "Fred…every guy and girl doesn't have to date. There are platonic relationships in this world, you know?"

"That'll be surprising if you can resist joining the frenzy the other girls are in. Did you see how many letters are in his locker?"

"I did…those broads are silly…I'm not."

"The gossip is that you two are going to the dance together."

"Freddy…don't believe the rumors."

KOTA

They're for sure dating; it's so obvious."

"No…Kayla has a boyfriend, remember?"

"Then she's cheating on him."

The girls sitting in the row before Kota aren't even trying to keep their gossip down. *Or are they? I have amplified hearing after all.* He's in lab. The class is tasked with answering trivia questions on the industrial computers. Kota works on the quiz, looking over the A to D answer options:

Who invented the floppy disk?

A) Alan Alcorn

B) Ray Tomlinson

C) Jade Cooper

D) Steve Wozniak

Who invented the cell phone?

A) SONY

B) U.S. NAVY

C) MITS

D) Martin Cooper

What year was the Apple Computer invented?

A) 1969

B) 1980

C) 1976

D) 1955

I know none of these answers. Some of the inventions I've never even heard of. They all sound so futuristic. I need to read up on Tech advances if I want to get a passing grade for this period. Oh, that reminds me…I forgot to ask Kay if she knows French. I have a feeling she does. Most people who are deep into the arts, such as ballet, know foreign languages. Especially ballet, which is renowned in Paris.

"I bet ten dollars they go to the dance together."

"Hmm…I doubt it, but you're on." Two girls curl their pinkies to form a sacred swear.

I can't even get mad about the gossip. I secretly want to go with her. I've thought about being more than buddies. But Dad is right….I have to wait for my time. It's torture. I sting for her explosive touch. Yearning for another hug…another interaction.

Between 6th and 7th period, he spots a posse of girls sliding notes into his locker. Kota dips into the bathroom, so he isn't seen. *Will it ever stop? Will I have to stay after school every day to trash their notes?* He huffs and throws his head back. *I'll have to say I'm not looking…maybe I should tell one of the gossipers this so the word can spread.*

Kota wash his hands, although he has no need to kill germs off his skin as humans do. He feels this will make him seem normal to his peers. As he washes, he runs over a plan he set in place a while ago. *I also need to get the location from Kayla. She's giving my parents leads on my foe…I want the same information. I need it.*

Calculus is his 7th period. The teacher writes 20 equations on the board for them to copy down in their notebooks. He numbers his paper and then works on an equation:

1: F A D S = ?

"You should ask him out in person…they're all slipping him letters. Asking face to face will make you stand out from the crowd."

"Should I?"

"Yes." Two girls chat in what they think is stealth mode.

"But…he's out of my league."

"Says who?"

"Well…look at him."

He senses their attention on him but acts as if he's invested in work. Which Kota wishes was an attainable excuse. *I can't even ignore what's being said about me. My ears should have an off button…a mute accessory. I wonder if there is a symbol to dull my hyper senses…then again, I need it. The night at the beach confirms that my sixth sense is a necessity. If not for it…I would have never known I was being followed.*

After school isn't the blessing in disguise he wants. Kota hangs out down the hall at Kayla's locker, away from his. Dozens of girls broadcast their courage to ask him out, slamming notes through his vent. He turns away so that his face isn't seen.

"You're better off running." Kay pokes.

"I don't run like a normal guy."

"How fast are you?"

"Faster than the wind." He swaggers. "23 blocks in the span of one minute."

"One minute!!" She holds her face and drops her mouth.

"Yep."

"That sounds fun…but horrifying!"

"It's not…it's better than a rollercoaster."

Kayla unlocks her unit and loads her books inside. "I love rollercoasters; I feel like I'm flying."

"Hmm…I haven't tested out flying yet."

Kay scans the area before saying, "You can fly? Like Dracula?"

"I have no clue."

"Let me know when you find out." She puts away an Italian language textbook.

"I've been meaning to ask if you know French. I'm not doing so hot in class."

Kay shuts her locker and proudly flicks her hair back. "Tu paries! Je le connais depuis l'âge de 8 ans." (You bet! I've known it since I was 8 years old)."

"You're a lifesaver! Please, I need help."

"Puisque tu as dit le mot magique, je vais t'assister." (Since you said the magic word, I'll help you)."

"Huh??"

"Ugh… amateur." She mocks. "I said I learned it at 8 years old…and yes, I'll help you."

"8 years old?!" He's rocked by this.

"I could live in Paris without an issue."

"I had a feeling you'd know it because of ballet."

"France and Italy…although Italy created the dance form. That's why I'm taking the language." She flings her bag across one shoulder, copying Kota. He admires this. *She's wearing her bookbag like me now.* "We can walk and talk. Do you need anything from your locker?" Her words seethe with comedic irony.

"Ha, ha very funny…"

The two walk around the corner, away from the rush of the end of the day mob. "So…what else do you want to talk about?"

Kota tries to reword what he's about to say. *Should I be blunt and say, I know about her gran dropping notes about my foe?* Before he can decide, a piece of pencil shaving bugs him. It's caught in Kayla's hair…tangled in her coils. Kota reaches a hand to remove it from her bushy mane. His motion is slow…cautious. He doesn't want to alarm her with his vamp speed.

Her breathing slackens; her eyes intoxicate. Her pupils dilate. Kay physically weakens for his touch, going dizzy with infatuation. His fingers slide along her pointed chin. She allows this cute gesture without backing away. Not afraid of the arctic temperature of his palms. *I like how he's touching me…how he feels…on me.*

"KAYLA….??"

She drops her hand fast, breaking out of the dreamy stupor. Her eyes increase two times their size. "Oh…no!" She gulps.

Kota is quicker than her; her mortal pace is slower than his. But she knows the voice well…he doesn't. He has to look to witness who it is. Darius. *It's her boyfriend. He saw…us.* His eyes are smashed beyond repair. His lip quivers. His soul drops to the bottom of his gut. Crashing. Twisted anguish corrupts his brows…his forehead.

"DARIUS…I CAN EXPLAIN!" He gives her an enraged glare, his dark eyes all glossy, ready to leak. "PLEASE…" Her boyfriend marches off, pounding his shoes on the floor. "WAIT!" Kayla chases after him, leaving Kota by himself.

KAYLA

Her knees grow weak and shake. Her hands vibrate. Her palms sweat. A lump in her throat builds bigger by the second. She chokes on sobs. The waterworks drench her pupils. As she runs after Darius, her mind replays their precious moments. *His lips brushing her forehead. "I love you." Darius caressing her hair. How afraid she was to say the three words back to him. How she mouthed the words, "I love you," when turned away. How she used a different language to confess her love. "Je vous aime, (I live you.)"*

"Huh?" Darius is clueless. She kisses him swiftly.

On Halloween night when she and him were given alone. When she peered up at her darling with eyes of burning desire. "I love you."

"And I love you…"

The way they cuddling on the couch watching movies. Kayla's arms around his waist. Darius slowly kissing her. How she got lost in his mixtape on the rooftop. When she cried in bed from being apart from him for too long.

Kay's eyes are red, full of regret and ache. The whirlpool of the past blinds her…along with her falling tears. She blinks it all away, running after Darius, who's a blurry blob in the distance. "DARIUS, PLEASE!" Kayla shouts woundedly, all the desperation, all the turmoil of the heart consumes her.

Her boyfriend is by the exit, holding the handle, paused in place. "How could you do this to me!" Darius spins around and yells. "You said you loved me!"

"I DO!!! Please, let me explain!"

"I don't need your excuses! I know what I saw!"

"It's not what you think. We're just friends."

"Don't give me that line!" Darius tramps over to her. "You're cheating on me!" He jabs a finger her way.

"I'm not! I love you…you know this!"

"I don't have time for lies!"

Kayla puts both hands on her forehead, hyperventilating. "I'm not lying!"

Darius stares off, allowing a few tears to fall. "Only I can look at you like that…I wouldn't be so pissed if you denied it. But you didn't…that makes you a BITCH!" His eyes are violent, scorned, and full of hell. Her boyfriend storms off to the exit door, whamming it opens so hard that it bangs against the outside wall.

Kayla loses her balance; her knees buckle. *He just called me a bitch! How could he say that to me? How could he speak to me that way? Darius never treats me this way. I thought we had a picture-perfect relationship. There was never any arguing or name calling. Not until now. I guess we are like Scarlet and Rhett after all. Our love is gone with the wind. He hates me. Despises me. He cursed at me…called me something I'm not! Why didn't he listen to what I said??!*

Kota is a friend. Is he, though…? The little voice in her head opposes. *I looked at him with the same imprisoned soul…the same spiritual worshiping. A tango of passion. A dance of tenderness.*

Kay sits down on the floor, against a locker, her body sliding all the way down. Defeated. Slowly and sullenly. She covers her eyes and wails. *Do I want Kota? Do I long for him because of his vampiric appeal? Would I want him if not for that? I want more. I need his heavenly escape. Kota feels…right. Faith had to send him to me. Darius was right…I am cheating…not physically, but mentally. I should know better! WHAT'S WRONG WITH ME??!! I'M SO STUPID!!*

I just ruined a perfect relationship. Darius and I are epic. He encouraged me…waited for me…gave his love to me. Hopefully, I can fight this…hopefully this isn't a breakup. It can't be. I love him…I can't lose him…nor can I lose Kota. I'm being cold…maybe I'm a bitch for being so selfish…for wanting them both.

There's faint walking from down the hall; the building is abandoned. Everyone has gone home. It's just her and whoever's walking her way. Kay doesn't care to lower her hands to see who. *If it's Kota…I honestly don't want to talk. I hope it isn't him…I need to be alone.*

"Firefly…" Gloria stoops beside her. "Are you okay?"

"No…"

"Tell me what it is."

"I just want to go home!" She cries.

"Okay…okay…let's get you off this floor and go." Granny helps her stand. Kayla lies against her as limp as a rag doll.

At least it's the weekend.…I can escape this for a few days. I need to forget. Maybe that'll make this better. At home, as soon as she exits the elevator, she slinks to her room.

Before she can close the door, Gloria holds a firm hand to it. "Don't let this pain define you…use it…focus it. Emotion is raw energy…which you can transform it to power."

"I don't think I can!" Kay sniffles, crossing her arms into a despondent body hug.

"You can.…it'll help you forget…like last time. Trust me."

I would like to forget again. Last time was nice. Although the last time I used magic to distract myself, it wasn't as serious as this. My stomach is stabbing itself. The sharpness is raw and deep. Crippling and constant. If I don't stop it…I may bleed from the gut. I might die.

"What are we practicing?" Kay collects herself, trying to be brave through the heartache.

"Go to the window." Kay and her grandma close in on the elongated window. Gloria unclips the bottom; her granddaughter aids her with lifting the flat glass up. It's now mounted above their heads, allowing glacial weather to whoosh in. "Watch the clouds and their motion; concentrate on their stream. Tell me what you find there."

She does so silently. The fluffy mist sways in dense streaks, fading with each breeze. *It's almost like a river…but slower moving. The motion is somewhat self-conscious. The clouds move inch by inch with tolerance, while the trees and grass are exasperated. The clouds have their own stream…separate from the rest of nature.*

"The motion is measured." Kay says, studying how a cloud puffs out in skillful formation, same as a chest rises up. "It breathes like a spell bender."

"Yes…and sees as we do. Close your eyes…and let it connect to you. Speak the words Wina coum five times." Gloria recites ancient Amharic, an Ethiopian language.

Kayla shut her lids to see all darkness. She repeats the word. "Wina coum." The first time nothing happens, there's nothing out of the ordinary, just blackness. "Wina coum." Little by little, the ruckus of the city noise decrease….yet her imaging is still dormant. "Wina coum." The soundtrack of the city disappears completely. "Wina coum." The thud of what is believed to be a tornado crashes all around her. Kayla doesn't jump; this has happened before. She's not afraid. "Wina coum." Her dark eyelids blaze white.

A rolling tidal wave maps out the city. Chicago looks the same, only the color is off., inverted neon white and black. The clouds are dark as space, same as the buildings. The thrashing wave of white rages her way. The humming song from her dream is easily understood now, unlike before. It states, "wina coum" in a distorted voice. Kay is a little shaken by the demented tone but doesn't have time to express concern.

Immediately, the wave engulfs her. Its touch is chilled and refreshing, and light as it wraps around her body. The air god gifts her its sight of the vast world. She views it from an angle that God would…far past the ozone.

The countries of the earth are laid out below her in black and white neon. All nature and oceans beam bright. Her astro-self hovers above the planet without a body. One with the essence of life. A variant of Mother Earth.

KOTA - FLASHBACK

I should go after her…but I'll only make it worse. His shoes hop between going after Kayla or staying put. He does an awkward leg dance, struggling to find a solution. *I already caused enough trouble. I should leave her alone. I didn't mean for Darius to see us. I should have been vigilant…I should've been careful. But when I touched her, I got numb of all my senses. I lost my power. I couldn't hear Darius…not his breathing…or his steps. I should've but…but Kay renders me useless.*

That's a good and bad thing. *I can't lose my alertness…but I loved that I felt mortal. Being human was reduced compared to a vampire. The sensations I felt as a mortal were so shallow…so suppressed. I enjoyed feeling normal again.*

Kota looks intently at the end of the hall…empty space, but he hears Kayla's screams. Hears her terror…her sorrow. He decides to occupy his time by collecting the fan mail from his locker, trying his best to block out the couple's heated argument. But his ears irritatingly transport him to their private spat.

"How could you do this to me! You said you loved me!"

"I DO!!! Please, let me explain!"

"I don't need your excuses! I know what I saw!"

"It's not what you think. We're just friends."

"Don't give me that line! You're cheating on me!"

"I'm not! I love you…you know this!"

"I don't have time for lies!"

He collects the heaps of paper swiftly, stuffing them into his bag so he can give them privacy. *I hate that I can't turn off voices. I hate hearing her hurt like this.* Kota uses his vampiric speed to quickly load up the notes and blasts away. In one minute, he's at a dumpster, which he smelt his way to. The rotten, dead rodent, sewer scent makes him queasy. He pours the letters in, then zooms off home.

His family is in the back garden, which is plowed neatly into dirt hills full of raked lines. Elu gently pats the soil to saturate it. Mato uses watering jugs, walking alongside the tiny, plowed field. His sis sets up solar panel screens to retract the sun to the plant life. She stabs the mount beams into the grass and tilts the screens to angle the light.

Kota assists her with this. "How was school?"

"It was okay…"

"Just, okay?" Dy is skeptical.

"What happened?"

"I don't want to talk about it."

"Come on…is it about Kayla?"

"Dyani, let your brother be!" Their mother intervenes. "He doesn't want to talk about it."

"Fine. I'll change the subject. So…mom and Dad want another meeting."

Kota already knows this from his eavesdropping, but he plays dumb. "Oh, really…when?"

"We'll have to wait for Gloria; she's tied up training Kayla. Possibly Monday morning…." Mato rationalizes.

"Did something happen?" He goes on playing clueless. His mother and father share a hasty glance. "We think we can tell you the truth." Odina frowns. "But we don't want you going wicked again."

"I won't…I promised to let it go. I mean it." He convinces them with a gentle tone.

His mother believes his lie…so does his father. "Very well." She directs her eyes on him very guardedly. "The vampire is here in the city." His dad explains.

"According to Gloria, his movements are erratic; that's why she's increasing Kayla's training. The attack on the beach goers wasn't a cougar; it was him. We need to deal with this before more innocents die."

Since they're being transparent, he chooses to share what he learned today at school. "Kayla had a sighting too. I think he's here for me…she saw it stalking me on the beach."

Dyani almost trips over the solar screen but clutches the poles for balance. "Wait…what?"

"It was in the trees tracking me."

"Why?" Odina stifles her breathing.

"I'm not sure…"

Mato's forehead prunes up. "Did she tell you anything else?"

"No…that's all she knew."

"Why is it bothering you?" Dyani is weary.

"Maybe it thought I died with my friends."

His sister shivers at the thought of him dying. Odina is queasy from just the mention of her baby boy as dead.

Grandad stops patting the damp soil, looking up from his seated position. "Or it may sense your spell bender lineage. You must mystify the creature. You may still have a slither of magic in you. That's what the evil one feeds off of."

"Hold on…." Kota eyes buck protectively. "If he can detect me, that means he knows where Kayla is!"

Elu shakes his head in disagreement. "He would be a fool to confront a young bender; Kayla is in her prime and has Gloria protecting her from corruption. Her Grandmother is aware of the prowling vampire."

"What do you mean she's aware??" Kota is distressed by the news. "You said prowling…meaning it's been near Kayla!"

"Yes…only briefly, and not in close quarters."

"When??! Why didn't you tell me!"

"Kota…all is fine, trust us. Gloria and I have dealt with this Greyson Mcintyre before."

That's his name?? Great, now I have a name to hate just as much as a face. "What does it want?"

"I wish we knew his motive…all we know is that he corrupts our kind and takes them away to never be seen again."

"You mean like kidnapping?"

"Yes…but far worse…more so like prisoners doing his bidding."

"Doing his bidding??" Kota is baffled. "Doing it where?"

"Somewhere hidden."

"Like that dugout in Zon-"

"DYANI, HUSH!" Her mothers silence her with a hiss. *Huh? A dugout. What dugout??* "What is she talking about?" Kota squints.

"Son...we would love to drive you back to Oklahoma to your friends' gravesites." His father attempts to maneuver away from Dy's slip up.

"No...tell me what she meant." Kota isn't falling for the trap. "What dugout?"

"Just a dead end...a useless lead." Elu fables briefly.

"Then...why did Mom shush Dy?"

"Drop it, son." Mato places down the watering jug. "Now, about Oklahoma."

Kota backs away with a suspicious gleam. "There's something you aren't telling me! I know about Gloria dropping hints on his whereabouts. I'm not stupid....you guys talk in code when discussing it. TELL ME NOW!!"

"No...now leave it be, son."

His mother extends her hand to stroke his face. "We want to talk about you going back home to visit your friends..." He recoils from her. "I'll get there myself; I don't need your help!" Kota rockets into hydro speed, fuming as he drags his boots across the city blocks.

I can't believe them! How can they call themselves my family??! They're lying to me...my own kin. My own blood. They're deceiving me! Protecting secrets! How could they betray me! I think I know how Darius felt...although he was wrong to punish Kayla for my mistake. Still...it's nothing worse than being lied to by someone you think you know. It's a splitting band aid from the core of your soul...a surreal discovery. A slap in the face.

I can only trust Kayla. I should go to her...but she's had enough stress for one day. She needs to recoup. She knows about whatever my sister was going to say. Kayla knows about this dugout place. I'll ask her at school on Monday. Until then, I'll sail to Oklahoma. It would be nice to be close to my friends. Close to my old home. I need to let off steam. I may return later tonight...if I want to. I can't believe their deceit. My sister is the only one who chose to be honest. If not for her being blunt, I would've never known about the dugout.

Those are used in military bunkers. Ditches dug into the ground to house battalions during war time. But that isn't enough to steer me in the right direction. America has fought many wars, within the country and outside the nation. I won't be able to guess it right.

His hyperactive legs dash through the state of Illinois. Into the farmlands of Missouri and Oklahoma. Just as last time, Kota's nose dissects the air...scrutinizing it for the foul, glacial aroma of his adversary *Nothing...he must cloak his odor somehow. I did get a whiff of the fragrance at the beach, but now it's completely hidden. Do vampires harness the skill to camouflage themselves? Can they become undetectable? That must be the reason behind the sudden lost trace of my enemy.*

The super green fields of his home state are beginning to fade for the autumn. The lack of saturation reminds him of the soulless city. Although Kota's seen this occur all his life, the fall aesthetic is ruining the perfect image of home. *I want here to always be a paradise for my lost mortality. An untouched dreamland. At least the mountains are still vibrant with green.*

He's on the opposite side of the enclosed town, where a waterfall sprays a crystal river. The lake in Chicago isn't as see through, or as clear. It's so polluted and cloudy. He appreciates this small advantage his home has on the windy city.

The high sun dims behind clouds, showcasing a sky so transparent it doesn't seem real. *I'm tempted to stay here forever. But running away isn't my ideal choice anymore. Not now that I have to guard Kayla from Greyson. Gloria isn't enough; I'll have to watch over her too. I'm not losing another friend to this monster. I won't let him hurt her. I won't fail again. Not again…*

Kota does a half circle curve of his body to double around the mountains to the town of Tahlequah. The place is still very deprived but full of unity. The dilapidated village is nowhere near Chicago's poverty. It's more so a beautiful disaster as opposed to detached harmony.

The main entrance of the reservation is secured by the same tribe officers. Bly and another, Chasse. The same cops who watched him and his family from their cop car…as they were exiled.

CHAPTER 31: EVIL ONE

KAYLA

After training, she goes to her room. She's not in the mood for leftovers for dinner. Instead, Kay takes a lavender bubble bath, holding the radio in her hands. Long droplets stream down from her eyes. Her face is frowned and emotional.

"Darius…I need you. Please talk to me." Her light voice cracks with strain. She releases the talk button and waits. Anticipating his creamy, pleasurable voice to answer. Nothing. Nothing at all…not even static. Kay holds the button down again. "I still love you."

Once again, there's a dead line. She rests the radio on the ledge of the platform tub and sinks her body low into it. Until the bubbly water reaches her chin. Kay puffs out air and closes her eyes, allowing heavy tears to fall fast from under her lids.

I should eat. But…I have no hunger in me tonight. No strength to chew…no reason for nutrition. The pain is good enough to hold me over. I deserve it. This is all my fault. Kayla remains in the tub until the water turns cold…until the bubbles disperse. Until her skin wrinkles. *I hope Darius still loves me. I made a mistake. I know I have. If he'd just let me explain. I would tell him the truth…but my boyfriend has shut me out.*

Kay slips into a gown and goes to the kitchen for fudge ice cream. Slouching onto the couch like a zombie. She radios her loved one last time. "Darius." He doesn't reply.

There's a growling storm outside that intensifies second by second. All the rectangle windows go silver and blue from the lightning. Everything shakes. The walls, the chandeliers, the glass staircase, the floor. Even the power sockets click on and off, a brief outage.

The thunder roars so loud it shakes the house. Another flicker of lightning pales the penthouse in silver. Everything appears colorless. Gloria emerges from the guest room, zipping up her coat. She spots Kayla on the couch, slumped in the spot…the radio pressed to her chest; a defibrillator that's failing to restart her heart. The ice cream carton is in her lap, untouched. Her eyes are glass. Staring straight ahead at endless space.

"Sweetheart," Gloria begins. "The Ahokas need us." Kay doesn't blink. "It's about Kota…he knows about the dugout." Gloria steps to her. "You don't have to speak. Just…be in the room." No words. No shift in posture. Just a hollowed-out girl trapped in her own skin. Her Gran kneels in front of her. "Do you want to come along? It'll be good for you…"

Kayla's lips part. But no sound comes out. She looks beyond her grandmother. Past her. Through her…as if seeing a ghost and not caring it is there. *Why won't she leave me alone??!!! I don't want to go to the stupid meeting!! I don't care anymore! She can go and help by herself…just leave me alone!!*

Gloria sweetly touches her granddaughter's knee, bidding her farewell. "If anything happens…call the car phone. Your parents should be home soon." She leaves.

The elevator dings soft. The doors pull inward. The golden glow dies out. Kayla is alone. But this time, it doesn't scare her. This time… she welcomes it. She goes to the fridge to open an ice cream carton. Her finger scoops the cookie dough flavor into her mouth. It's tasteless…bland…not different from water. Her eyes drift to the glass windows. Lightning blinks against the skyline; a dying lightbulb. Severe thunder cracks through the city of glass.

I used to love nights like this. I used to pretend I was a lost princess fighting my way home. Not anymore. Now the thunder sounds like Darius slamming the door in my face. Now the lightning looks like what her touch does to Kota.

Her focus land to her bookbag slumped against the wall. The flap is half open. Inside it is Kota's letter to his father. The one he let me borrow to make amends with my dad. It's still folded in my bookbag. Still unopened. She treads to open the flap, unzips the compartment, and withdraws the letter.

I was supposed to write my own. A letter to fix everything. But what's the point?? Dad won't listen. He put this tape between me and Darius. This is his fault! Why should I apologize? He doesn't deserve an apology. He made this breakup surface.. Not me!! If I was seeing Darius, Kota would have just stayed a friend. This is all on him. NOT ME!!

Her mopey brown irises scowl at the letter. "You don't deserve a letter. I was going to write an apology…but you don't deserve that!! You ruined everything!! You made this happen!! I'll never say sorry!! And Mom?? Where are you?? Too busy working. Too busy to notice me…to help me! I need you! Where are you when I need you…? Where are my girls? Why did everybody leave me…."

She sets the ice cream aside and goes to the sofa to curl into a fetal position…like an infant. The lights pop off with a zap. Kay is unfazed…usually she's a scaredy cat, but now she has no reaction. As impassive as a tomb. Sleep creeps up…she prepares to tap out…to hibernate if she can. *I want to avoid the sun…avoid the fake thrill of life. Avoid humans.*

Just as her lids drift shut. She sees Greyson Mcintyre. Across the way…..perched on the edge of a neighboring rooftop; is a real-life boogeyman. Scarlet eyes. Fire eyes…scarier than the horrendous storm. A long, vintage cloak swipes at his side in the wind…same as his blonde hair. His long mane obscures his face as an enemy's flag would. As a cursed pirate flag would. He's locked on her…utterly fascinated and enraged all at once.

The fury outlines his eyes with harshness…a cruel eyeliner. Deeper than a metal rock band. His irises mark her as if she's an abomination. As if God smiting down Lucifer with just his eyes. She shoots up from the couch and backs away to the wall, holding her chest.

IT'S HIM!!

Kay doesn't know if Greyson shares a mind link with her or if she orders it herself. Another premonition corrupts her:

An underground castle. A massive gothic, estate carved into the earth. Candlelight flickers gold on black stone. Greyson stands in the center of the castle's foyer, circled by 10 Spell Benders, who are buckled at the neck, wrists, and ankles. In chains. Kayla knows them. Not their names…but their blood. Their ancestry. They are her coded DNA, same as her grandmother.

Greyson wears Regal robes and crown…symbolizing a king…or prince. The hem of his black cloak marks the murky marble floor. His eyes burn as coals that never die out. He raises his hand; cherry colored cracks spark from his fingertips. Crystallizing outward from his palms, an inferno beam frozen in time. The beams stretch far…long, pillars of crystal fire.

The spellbenders are linked to his magic beams, which latch to their foreheads in magical lines. Connecting them all as one. All 10 of the witches decompose on the spot, their flesh burning down to the bones. Burning to gray ash…same as cigarette droppings. Melting from their flesh…..acid eating the skin away. The screams are nails on a chalkboard. Desperate. Ear winching. The screeches are dooming. Each of the casters revert to the opposite way of birth. To the shell, we all begin in, to skeletal remains…..to ash…until all are nothing but dust in the air. No corpses. No mercy.

Greyson ciphers the life essence of the benders. His veins glow ruby; his head back—absorbing all of their bodily remains. Swallowing every speck of their bright dust. A burst of something similar to red glitter jets into his chest.

The earthquaking thunder brings her back to real time. To the eerie sight of Greyson penetrating her with his cerise eyes. *HE WANTS TO DRAIN ME!! WANTS TO KILL ME!!*

But his mind is far away…Kayla sees through his vision…through his third eye. Greyson's thoughts are on the State of Oklahoma….fixated on a graveyard. Kota Ahoka.

KOTA

Under the cover of night, he sneaks into his hometown through the loose park gate. The streets are still; most residents inside watch TV or snore peacefully. He races at light-speed to the newsstand posted outside the ice cream shop. The very same place where he killed the Waya family. Flashbacks: tearing off the car door, the father pulling a gun, the mother's blood spilling. His animalistic groans. Their screams. The shredding bullets that marked holes in his clothes. His slicing teeth.

Kota lowers his head in shame. *I'll bring flowers for them... and apologize.* Tears flood his colorless irises… he wipes them with his sleeve. At the newsstand, he sifts through back issues of the local paper…five weeks ago. Their funeral article is easy to find. Tahlequah rarely sees violent deaths.

The cemetery's close—less than a mile. On the way, he snatches a string of sunflowers from a floral shop. It's just past 8 PM; the grounds are empty. Headstones stretch across the field, mostly belonging to those lost to illness or accidents—not murder. The Waya graves stand out, adorned with painted golden feathers. Their relatives must have carved the headstones by hand. Kota gently wraps the sunflowers across the four stones and sinks to his knees.

"I'm sorry. I didn't mean to hurt any of you," he whispers. "Please don't doom me the way the Great Spirit has. I wish I died instead." His tears soak the soil below. "Atsawesolvsdodi hawinaditlv adanvdo igohidaquugesv, (Through teaching, they listen and learn. Spirit—this is what we have become)." The words flow as a lullaby. "Donadagohvi, (Til we meet again)."

He wipes his eyes and bolts toward Stilwell. It only takes seconds for him to arrive. On the roadside, he plucks dandelions. At the Stilwell welcome sign, a map shows the cemetery near the high school. It chills him to pass the lifeless building. *It's like Liz, Jim, and Mike are watching me through the windows…from the gym room. Their ghosts are still in there.*

He rounds three corners to a large open field. A black metal arch labels the graveyard. The gate is locked. He leaps, more like floating, over it, weightless as a drifting star. Using his nose, he finds the newer plots by their fresh, rich dirt. Elizabeth Scott. James Monroe. Michael Sinclair. He sits cross-legged and uses his nails to rake tiny holes into the soil.

"Hey, guys… Sorry it took me so long. A lot's happened. You wouldn't believe it—but maybe you already know." He presses the fluffy stems into the earth. "The vampire that took your lives…is me now." He moves to the next grave, raking more divots. "I wasn't lucky enough to die. I'm dead… but…not in the right way. If I was there, on the other side, you all wouldn't be alone." He sets down the last of the dandelions. "Donadagohvi." He leans in to blow the stems…when a sudden breeze sweeps from behind him, scattering the fluff away.

A smell hits him. Cold. Rotten. Chemical. His nose crinkles. *He's here…* Kota quickly stands and twists around. Far in the distance, by the graveyard archway, is his nemesis. Maroon Irises. Shiny blonde hair…a calculating grin. GREYSON! *HE'S HERE…JUST FEET AWAY!* Kota's mouth spreads wide; revealing sharp teeth. His nails grow into talons. His eyes flood dark. A barbaric growl produces from the core of his spine. Guttural and aggressive. He lunges, his claws out, his canine teeth sharpening.

KILL HIM!! LET'S KILL HIM!!! The reckless fiend snarls in a song.

Kota attempts to fly right into the creature and pin it down to rip its skeleton from its spine as planned. Inch by inch…until the thing knows true pain. But his rival disappears…into thin air. Mist. Made of fog. *WHAT???!! WHERE DID HE GO???!* He notes how the scent still dawdles. *No, he was here! His smell is active. But how did he vanish like that??!*

He reviews the starry sky, scanning it for a flying figure. Evaluating the treetops where it once hid to spy on him. *Nothing's there!* He grits his jagged teeth and snarls as loud as a malicious dog. Another fierce breeze comes from beside him, knocking him down. As he falls, he spies the man jetting away into the distance. Kota's shoes boost forward, throwing dirt in all directions.

GET HIM! GET HIM!!!! The possessive entity dances with joy.

"I WILL GET HIM!"

The evil one is faster; he has to use all his force, all his might to get into close quarters with it. But Greyson is wickedly skilled. He does a vanish act once again, glitching miles ahead within seconds. *How does he do that??! Can I do the same??* He squeezes his eyes and pushes himself to accelerate as swiftly as possible. All of the skin on his body ripples intensely with insane velocity. Houses and roads distort into nothingness. He only sees his target…nothing else exists in the speed vortex.

"COME ON!! COME ON!!!!" He hisses, bullying his legs and arms to stress his command.

Both of them voyage outside the norms of any being, so much that Kota doesn't feel his limbs…or the wind on his skin. He has no sense of his body…no consciousness of his vessel in the impossible turbulence. He draws closer to the vampire. *He's just feet away*!!! He outs a hand and prepare to pounce, but Greyson is aware of his actions without seeing them. He evades him once again by glitching miles up.

Greyson toys with Kota, knowing he has an advantage. The man glitches as an insult this time…to show off his skill. Swaggering. This doesn't discourage him; he keeps high on the man's tail. *I can catch him! COME ON!* The two vamps venture between states, easily avoiding cars, trucks, buildings, even humans. The mortals have a delayed motion in the vortex, slowed and easily predictable. The two swerve, fly, and dart past them, all who have no idea of their presence.

Into the Texas desert they go. On the dusty, wide road. Across grass and sand patched land. Through vacant western settlement towns. Through underground caverns. Caves of insane stature, made of complete stone and thorny ceilings. Kota's nearly exhausted. Just as last time, he's losing energy, but he stays vigilant. Determined to not fall weak.

The underground pathways connect to the Arizona desert. The starry sky streaks as alien travel would; similar to hyper drive in Star Wars. The balls of gas sway, zipping as fast as they are. Kota grows weak, sickly with exertion. His eyelids droop, his body fires up with fatigue. He strains himself one last time. One last attempt.

Kota jumps, flying high into the dark sky, advancing forward with antigravity. "AHHHGH!!!" he warrior yells, amping his body to push itself harder. He closes the distance, diving, his arms so close to wrapping around its head. Inches from skin-on-skin contact. His talons nearly graze the golden head of his rival.

The taste of victory builds…only for Greyson to disintegrate into a cloud of air. Gone. Kota loses his footing, tumbling, rolling on the ground, skidding the desert sand…and crashing into a cave wall…head first.

KAYLA

Kayla is at the wall phone, her ears muffling out the world. Her chest drums. She yanks the receiver off the hook and dials Odina's number from memory. Fingers trembling. The plastic cord tangles around her arm as she drags it to the living room. The skyline blinks with distant lightning, a cracked film of blue. Her eyes scan the rooftop across the way—the same one where she saw Greyson. Where those glowing irises pinned her in place. But now…he's gone.

Oh no. No, NO, NO!! She grips the phone tighter. "Pick up… pick up…come on!!!" Three ringing slugs on forever. *He's in trouble…he needs help. My Kota is in danger, and I'm too far away to help!!!*

Finally, the click. "Hello?"

"MS. AHOKA!!" Her voice is all over the place. "The vampire was outside…on the roof!! He's gone now. He went after Kota in Oklahoma!!"

"OH!!" She drops a glass…the shattering is piercing. Odina's breath catches in her ribcage. "DEAR GREAT SPIRIT!!" She prays. "Greyson has gone after Kota." Odina's voice wavers in octaves as she informs Elu and Gloria. "Mato and Dy went out looking for him. I hope they're back soon. We need to open a portal to see if he's…alive." The word aches from her core…even saying it is difficult for her.

"I know what he wants. He steals magic from Spell Benders. He siphons until they're nothing but dust!!" She vividly imagines her flesh melting from her bones, blackening and converting to ash.

"Oh, my spirit…" Odina mutters everything to Grandad and Grandma. The stolen magic from the spellbenders. His true motive. "That will not be your faith, Kayla."

There's scuffling on the other end. Urgency. Then Gloria's firm voice chimes in. "Kayla."

"Gran!"

"You're safe. You're safe, you hear me? He can't reach you."

"How do you know that?!"

"Because I marked you with protection. A binding. It's been on you since you called me. I know the dangers of being a speller…I know how our kind gets corrupted. Nothing will happen to you. Trust me."

"And Kota?" Kayla's stomach sinks. "What about him? He's in danger!"

"Elu has done the same charm for him as well…"

"What if it doesn't work??" *I can't lose Kota…he's the only one I have. Not my parents…not my friends….not Darius. All I have is him.*

"He doesn't have magic, sweetheart. There's nothing for Greyson to take."

"Maybe we were wrong." Elu's input is a little unsettling.

"How exactly?" Gloria is peeved by his words. "In my entire timeline, my mother's and grandmother's, there's never been an enchanted vampire. That's over a century of proof…proof that vampires can't possess magic."

Wait… Kota had magic before? Was he like me before the curse?? He never said anything about it to me. I thought he was just…a normal boy before death.

"We assumed Kota's powers left. But maybe the gene is still within him. Greyson must have a reason for hunting him down. There is a reason behind this." Kayla presses the phone harder to her ear to hear Elu. "Grayson must have advanced his practices since the 1930s. Back then, he used us as puppets…now somehow he can siphon our power. Times have changed, Gloria. We missed the shift."

"McIntyre has always been a vampire. Nothing more. We have validation of this through the spirit world. The ancestors have told us nothing of his magic. This is a farce…a delusion made of decoy casting. Vampires cannot cast!" Gloria's dismissive tone is thick. "The other side would have alerted us of this truth."

"We need Kayla to access the other side for a deeper understanding. We need answers."

Kayla's breaths are narrow. Her gaze snaps back to the windows, where the roof lies empty. She can still sense the Satan irises of Greyson in the darkness. Still feeling the phantom weight of him. *I don't want to mind link with him again!! It's too scary…too full of gloom. Is everything I see destined to come true?? I saw Kota transformation at the campsite. Saw the dugout. Saw Greyson in the lake preying on Kota. And just minutes ago…I witnessed Kota in Oklahoma…at the graveyard.*

My third eye is accurate about what it sees. Everything comes true. Meaning my skin may melt from my body…I will die like my people did. I can't let Greyson get me!!! He was so close…why am I the only one panicking over how close he was??? None of them are concerned about my safety. This leads me to believe that this isn't the first time Greyson has been near me. This has occurred before.

She clutches the phone with both hands. "How long has Greyson been tailing me?" There's a beat…a long pause, a waiting to exhale. This is something they don't want her to know to avoid hysteria. "GRAN….HOW LONG?!!"

Gloria blows out long air, knowing the secret is out. "Since your first spell…that's when he detected you."

The walls of the room rollercoaster, swirling in a blur. Dizziness buckles her knees; she slips down the wall, half standing. Her forehead slinks into a bunch…the blood of her brain frosts over. *WHAT??? NO WAY!! IS SHE SERIOUS!!!* Kay nearly yanks the phone cord from the wall jack ."YOU KNEW?! YOU KNEW SINCE THEN AND DIDN'T TELL ME?!!"

"I was protecting you—"

"NO, YOU LIED!!! LYING ISN'T PROTECTION!! I have the right to know that I'm in danger!" She gasps roughly. "I…I…I can't let someone get hurt because of me. Does he follow me to school??" She has an eye-opening catharsis. *Gran did start dropping me off at school all of a sudden, despite me telling her that my dad does it. She insisted…I thought it was just her kindness….and her wanting to bond more with me. But it was so she could guard me!!* "Is that why you started escorting me to school??"

"I didn't want you to be afraid, so I didn't tell you."

"Well, you failed! I can't believe this! I can't go back…I can't have him kill someone there too. I CAN'T!!"

"You're fine enough to go to school."

Kay thinks back to Jia words: *"That's not a good idea…we wouldn't be safe. None of the students will!"* Jia *was right about that…just wrong about Kota. He'd never do that…but Greyson will…and has.* Next she recalls Kota and their very first meeting:

"YOU'RE NOT TAKING THIS AWAY FROM ME!! HE LIKED KILLING MY FRIENDS!! YOU DIDN'T SEE WHAT I SAW!!"

I never asked him about that day…because I know his friends were massacred. Greyson has executed teenagers before…why wouldn't he do it again???

An insight blooms her inner eye:

The school hallways. The fluorescent ceiling lights flicker, strobing creepily. All of the lockers ooze carmine lines from the vents. Leaking blood. The redness streams in rivulets on the floor, a hellish waterway. Desks are overturned in all of the classrooms; the top of each is marked by red handprints. Chairs are knocked sideways, puddles of crimson. Lifeless bodies…empty shells. Her classmates, teachers…all dead…all corpses.

"No…NOOO!! I CAN'T GO BACK!!!"

KOTA

He wakes at dawn. Kota hit the rock wall severe enough to knock himself unconscious. If he were human, he'd have a concussion. His sight is hazy and doubled. His weakness is absolute. Kota sits up against the wall, sluggishly holding his head. *I won't be able to catch him if I don't have fuel. I'm too frail! I need to feed…but I won't use humans as a source. I need another solution.*

He rises from the ground, losing his balance so much that he has to grip the cave wall. Kota blinks repeatedly, trying to clear his dizzy, double eyesight. The impact is somewhat like a migraine. Flashing blinds his eyesight and impairs his brain. A liquid, needling effect trickles down from the top of his head.

Kota huffs, squeezing his thumps between his eye sockets. "I need to feed…"

He can't run as blazingly as before, so he does a power walk. Delirious from the heat…and lack of substance. His staggered walking worsens the longer he goes on. His knees buckle from fatigue, sinking him flat to the sandy terrain. He gazes ahead. There's nothing but sand for miles. He's stranded…and starving. The thought of blood flattens his lungs to his ribcage like glue. Kota grips his stomach, groaning hard at the punching dehydration.

A large cooper hawk sails the patchy sky above. Its scratchy song piercing the desert. The nasally noise would panic a human…but it invites Kota's inner hunter. *I have to get it…or I might die. I have to jump up and grab it. I can do it.* He pep talks himself. His arms and legs burn…his knee bones clamp up. Every inner organ smashes flat to his ribcage. Kota gasps from the scrunching sound effect from his deprived body. "Come on…jump. I can do it! Jump!"

The hawk singsongs again, circling around him, assuming he'll become a deceased snack any moment now. Its shadow sinisterly overcast the golden sand…waiting for his death. *It wants to kill me…that's why it's circling. I need to be as ruthless as it is. I have to live. I have to for my family…for Kayla. I thought I wanted to die…but now, being so near to it…I'm fearful. I don't want that.*

Kota wheezes out a huge heap of oxygen, his lungs bite in response. He listlessly gets to his feet, bending his clasped knees, enduring the horrid throbbing. He keeps his eyes on the hawk while bungee jumping upwards without the use of strings. Without the reality of gravity.

The sand below his feet generates a mushroom cloud due to the force. An atom bomb interaction jerks the gritty sand high. The vigor of his takeoff breaks the sound barrier as a supersonic jet does. Kota soars hundreds of feet, lengthening his talons, hugging his arms around the hawk. A predator to prey. His fangs puncture the bird. The blood rains into his mouth, soaking the compressed organs with liquid. Second by second, as he drinks, Kota's strength recovers.

He drains the hawk of all its blood until it crushes in on itself, as trampled as flattened roadkill. Kota drops the lifeless bird to the ground. The bird plummets far and bangs on the sand. The corners of his mouth are stained burgundy, dripping with syrupiness. He swipes it into his mouth using his thumb.

He realizes that he's still floating in the sky. The height he's at is airplane level. *I didn't know I could stay midair like this. Interesting.* Kota views the shallow clouds that are leveled with him. He's hidden by the cover of the fluffy whiteness! *I never thought I'd be an actual Skywalker!* His inner nerd peaks out and fanboys. *I have to get home. I have to tell everyone that this thing has a glitch trait….and that its faster than we could have guessed.*

His boots glide the sky, as if he's suspended on a line. He tracks along the invisible floor. The hidden forced that upholds him in place is trippy. Almost psychedelic, as if he's on a drug journey. He sweeps along the top of the clouds. Sky running. The clouds puff into a mist, creating a foggy exhaust underneath his boots. Kota tastes the essence of each fluff bubble. The acidic, mineral flavor is saccharine; he revels in the flavor while galloping home.

Kota slithers down the treetops in front of his house, not even rustling the leaves on the way down. No sound. He lands softly…stepping to the door to knock on it.

The door is flung opened by his mom. "You're alive!" She slings him tightly to her chest. "We couldn't see you through the portal! Where did you go??!!"

"Portal??" He's perplexed. Wait…they opened a portal to find me?"

"We needed to find you; something happened. Come in." She pulls him inside. "He's home!" She alerts the others, who hurry to the front door.

Mato's face is sentimental…the weakest he's ever seen it in his life. Tired eyes…dark circles, extra creases under his lids. *Wow…was Dad crying?? I never seen him do that…he's always the rock!* His father locks his arms around him in a bear hug. "We thought we lost you."

Dyani blubbers like a baby. "All I heard was you wishing you were dead…I thought it came true!"

"Aww, I'm sorry, *kamama* (butterfly)." Kota embraces her. "I went back home to pray for the dead…I got interrupted."

"We know…" Dy says, separating from the hug but keeping her arm around his shoulders.

"You could've been killed!" Odina nearly chokes on the words.

"Huh…? Wait…how do you guys know about that?? Did you find out from the portal?"

"No…Kayla informed us," Mato reveals. "She had a vision…and found the motive behind all of this."

Oh, really…wow, I know grandad said she's learning fast…but this is faster than I imagined. "What is the motive?"

"The evil one steals magic from spellers to use for himself…"

Kota eyes grow in size…wild and surprised. *So…he's a magic thief…that's what he's after?? But why is he tailing me?? I don't have any powers.*

"There's more," Odina inserts. "Greyson is choosing between two targets. You…or Kayla."

"That's stupid." Kota shakes his head, laughing dryly. "He's going after her. Obviously. She's the Spell Bender…not me."

"You're not wrong…his first choice is her, but she's out of bounds…Gloria has her cloaked. That leaves you as a promising backup for him, son. You're far more accessible than she is," his dad expounds.

"I don't have magic. I used the last of it, breaking your seal…"

"You may still have the gene in you," Odina counters.

Dy bobs her head in agreement. "We all think you do…Grandad is preparing to test this out. To see if you can do a spell." She points to the backyard, where Elu gathers herbs across the ground. A large symbol that crisscrosses into many points at the end. The 13-star symbol from the spell book. He chants odd words under his breath.

Kota takes in everything. *I think this is too much of a stretch. I carved the symbol into the ground because I knew it meant freedom in my culture…not because I knew I had magic. This is all unnecessary.* "Kayla was born with the gene and never had to do the initiation." "Neither did you…" Odina contests.

His insides twist. Everything is backwards. Is this true…if this is true…*why me?? Why the hell would this psycho want me over her? Kay is way above me, training and learning fast…all I did was break a seal. Even grandad said:*

"That was the bloodline's final attempt to guide him to the light."

Was he wrong? If I have magic… then what am I? Not just a freak. Something worse. He stews in deep thought…opening up to the possibility that he is on Greyson's list.

His sister tugs him closer. "I know it's a lot, bro. But it makes sense why he left Kayla's place to aim for you."

What is she talking about?? He left Kayla place….as in my enemy was at her house?? He was at her place??!! When?? And how?? "WHAT DO YOU MEAN??!"

His mom is irritated by Dyani for not keeping that hushed up. "We were getting to telling him that, Dy."

"Were you?? Because that should have been the first thing you told me!" His nostrils flare ferociously. "How close? When??"

"Last night…but she's safe." His father says nonchalant. "She's rattled up, but Gloria is with her, don't worry."

Kota's head sinks towards the floor, full of guilt. "I should've never left…she could've died because of me."

"She has a safety charm on her just like you do."

"Mom, he's out to kill her for her power, and is more than we thought he was."

"We know…Kayla confirmed that he wields magic." His father assumes he knows what his son means.

"Noo….this thing can glitch!" He digs in his mind for the rest of the sentence. Recalling Kayla mentioning dimensions. *That's what it looked like he was doing. I know I felt that way running, but I never literally vanished out of reality.* "I mean, he can phase in and out of dimensions. It can glitch in and out of time. And can evaporate to thin air, like it's nothing! There's more to this devil." He jumbles out the words.

The three share alert glances; Dyani is speechless and fearful, scanning the windows as if Greyson will pop inside at any second. Odina and Mato communicate through eye language, dissecting what this means. As of now, they thought they had this figured out, but this adds another puzzle piece. Another mystery.

"He's   more   than   we
thought…dimensional teleporting…manifestations? What are we dealing with here??" Odina is deeply disturbed.

"My father needs to hurry in….now." Mato states gravely.

"What about Kayla?" Kota wonders.

"She's been through enough…let her rest." Dyani's words sound regretful.

Was it that bad? I guess…I guess so. She's so pure and new to violence. Too delicate for this hardship. If the monster made me and my friends revert to little, helpless kids…it did worse to her. Way worse. She doesn't deserve any of this.

"I need to check on her." None of them have time to protest because he's gone so abruptly that Dy's arm, which was across his shoulders, is still supported mid-air.

It's almost noon by the time Kota is hopping the rooftops of downtown…since she lives so high up. He doesn't land too close, knowing this will cause some PSTD for her. He knows better. *She saw him there.* He deems the roof across from her as the place. He can make out the foul order of the beast.

The living room curtains are closed, but the side ones have no covering. *Aww…she's blocking out everything.* He notes…spotting her unboxing blankets and sheets to nail to the exposed glass. *Why is she by herself? Where are her rents? It's the weekend…are they in? She can't be alone.*

He loves the way she tucks her hair behind her ear, her bushy mane of bouncy curls. *I wish I could touch her…be with her…but I have to be invited in. There are barriers to homes. If only I could hear her voice. I need to be with her…comfort her. The breakup…losing her friends…now this…it's all too much.*

CHAPTER 32: STILLNESS

KAYLA

All the windows are covered in sheets, blankets, and towels. Even the thick tapestry from the guest bedroom hang in jagged layers, tacked with tape and thumbtacks. Blocking out every inch of sky. Every inch of sun. Every trace of the world. The penthouse is a cave. Hollow and gray. The fridge hums too loud.
The floor creaks under her. Every sound appears staged—deliberate. As if someone is trying to trick her into thinking she's alone.

Kayla curls herself into the couch, arms tight around her knees. The shadows are thicker here. Safer. But her muscles won't relax. Her back won't uncurl. Her breathing won't slow down. She flinches at a car horn. Jerks her head to the windows even though the glass is covered.

What if he comes back? What if Grayson comes back? What if my charm stops working? What if this isn't enough?

Her fingers dig into her hoodie sleeves. Her body shakes even though she isn't cold. She looks at the door. Locked. Chained. She looks at the window. Covered. She looks at the knife on the kitchen counter. *Would it even help if he came in?*

Kayla rocks back and forth frantically. *I need him.* She presses her forehead to the couch. *I need Kota. He can protect me. He's the only one who can. Granny means well. Her hexes work, yeah. But even the greatest spell can't stop the way Grayson looked at me. Like I was already his. Like I already belonged in a cage. Kota would keep me safe. I know it in my bones. In my heart.*

She imagines him walking through the door…calm and solid. Friendly and fun. She pictures his arms around her. The coldness of him is inviting and stops the overheating paranoia in her body. Then something flickers. She feels him. There's a wiretapping them as one. A telepathic chord. A live feed of temptation. Her body goes still….her lungs hitch.

A premonition—no, a memory. No… something new. Not a dream. The future:

They're kissing. Her hands are around his neck, and his arms are looped tight around her back. Her lips part his. Not gently—desperately. Urgently. His mouth illuminates under her touch, his jaw is a flashing jigsawpuzzle, breaking his skin wide open. This isn't like before…this time it's possible that he might go extinct. Combust. Ignite. Kota may just metamorph into pure energy. A soul made of only brightness. Without a physical form…an entity of heaven.

Kayla reels on the couch, pressing both palms into her temples. *What did I just do…?* Her breaths stall. She's still sitting in the blanket-draped fortress of the penthouse, but everything inside her has changed. Her pulse jumps beneath her skin; electricity waiting to arc.

"I didn't mean to do that," she whispers. "I didn't mean to…" She hugs herself, arms wrapped tight around her folded knees. "That was wrong… I'm wrong," she mumbles. "Darius still wants me. He's just mad. That's all. Just mad." Her throat thickens. "I need to give him time."

But the kiss—she presses her hand to her lips. The kiss. Her fingers shiver. *What if I hurt Kota? What if a kiss… hurts him?* I transformed him into pure energy…into death! That's what it had to be. The cracks…the spider-webbed pattern of his mouth. Kay's touch had peeled him open. *I think I'll kill him…*She clutches her forehead to her knees, trying to crush the thought out.

"Stop!" she breathes out loud. "Just… stop!"

The hours blur. The sunlight fades behind the barricaded windows. The amber edges disappear to indigo, and then to an inky color. She doesn't move. She stares into the darkness. The silence is buzzing louder than any static. By midnight, her body is stiff and sore. Still folded. Still locked on the couch. Eventually, she drifts off, cheek pressed to her knee, curled in a ball; a wounded animal.

Sometime in the night…her parents came home. Finding it strange that all of the windows are covered up. Her father advances to the window and grabs a tapped sheet from the glass. The moment he yanks it down…everything fractures. Light floods in…a hard beam of moonlight.

"DON'T TAKE IT DOWN!!" Her voice splits the silence like a gunshot. It's so loud, so raw, so distressed—it doesn't sound like her. It sounds like something feral. Something trying to survive death. A dying banshee. She rockets off the couch, eyes blown up, pupils pinned in fright. Her lungs seize mid-breath. Her diaphragm clamps. Her body wobbles so hard that her arms flap against her sides. She lurches forward and doubles over to hold her gut.

Flash. Grayson. At the glass. Russet eyes. Fanged grin. Tall as the skyline. Her heart convulses. *No. No. Not again. He's back. HE'S BACK!!!* Her skin crawls. Her breath stutters in short, shallow gasps. Her throat constricts a noose.. A high-pitched, wheezing sound escapes her lungs. Her hands clutch at her hoodie. At her ribs.

At her throat. Everything's closing in.

Mary gasps. "KAYLA?!"

Kay drops to her knees with a thud. Her forehead slams the carpet, her body folds inward, a dying animal. Arms wrapped tight around her skull. Her whole frame trembles. Her teeth chatter violently. *I can't breathe. I can't breathe. My heart's going to pop. It's too fast. Too loud. TOO LOUD!! IT'S GOING TO POP!!*

A   textbook panic attack detonates through her nervous system, dizziness, choking, tightness, cold sweat. She scrambles across the floor like a creature, clawing at the curtain James pulled down. Her hands shake so hard that she can barely grip the fabric. She throws it over the window again, haphazard, pressing it back onto the strips of tape on the frames.

"Don't open it," she mutters…while dropping to the floor, hugging her knees. "Don't open it, don't open it, don't open it!!"

Mary rushes over. "KAYLA, SWEETHEART, WHAT'S HAPPENING?! WHAT'S HAPPENING??!!"

But Kayla doesn't look at her mom. Her eyes are on the glass. The window. Her lips quiver as she whispers, "The monster…is right there…outside the glass. It knows I'm in here!!"

Mary pulls her gently, but Kayla jerks away. Her legs press tighter into her chest, bones locking together.

James stands frozen with the curtain still in his grasp. His mouth is slacked open. He's never seen his daughter like this before…ever. Never seen anything like this…ever. "What the hell is going on?"

"My baby is having a panic attack! Put the damn curtain back up! PUT IT BACK UP!!"

Kayla's body lurches with every hiccup of breath. Sweat droplets bead down her temple. A fountain of fear.. Her skin is cold as ice…cold and clammy. Lacking heat…void of temperature. Her fingers clamp her knees so tight that her knuckles turn bone-white. *It's not enough. The tape isn't enough. The safe charm isn't enough.* "I can't… breathe…" she rasps thickly. "I can't…"

Mary strokes her back with trembling fingers. "Breathe with me, okay? In through the nose, out through the mouth. In.."

"No." Kayla curls tighter into herself. "It will get in!!"

"What will get in, baby?"

Don't say it. Don't say his name. If you say it, he's real. If you say it, he comes. Her thoughts are muddy; thick and heavy. Drowning her. *This is my fault. I should've never opened that spell book.. I should've never done that hex.* "It's waiting," she croaks. "It's watching me."

Mary drops to the floor beside her daughter, eyes full of tears as she pleads. "Kayla, I need you to come back. Come back to me, baby. Okay?"

But Kayla isn't there. She's stuck in the in-between. In the memory of Greyson's eyes. Of the night. Of the rooftop. Of the air turning cold. The moment time stopped, and all she could feel was him watching her from the shadows.

James steps forward and slowly pulls the curtain all the way back into place. The light moonlight disappears. Kayla breathes a shudder. Another rasp. Her eyes roll toward the window again. It's covered now. She's safe....for now.

She mumbles softly, still dazed. "...don't open it..." Kayla lies there...shaking in the dim light—breathing unevenly, muttering the same three words, "Don't open it. Don't open it. Don't open it."

Kay doesn't sleep. Not at all. She's curled in the corner of the couch like a broken doll; her body stays still, but her mind spins. Each blink feels like a trapdoor...to him. To the demon behind the glass. *Don't open it. Don't open it. Don't open it.* The words play on a loop in her head.

The house is dark now. Her parents have gone to bed, tiptoeing past her like she's a madwoman. They left her in silence, hoping she'd get better. Left her alone. Her pretty, jumpy eyes survey the curtains, which seep the city lights through their taped cracks.

I can't go out....I won't go outside ever again. I can't! It's too dangerous! I'm a target. If I go back to school. She doesn't finish the thought. She saw what would happen.. The school massacre...all of the dead, bloody bodies...and lockers. The horrible crime scene.

Jia. Mya. Fred. Izzy. Chester. Even Vanessa. Kay sniffles. *I don't even like her... but no one deserves to be torn apart by a monster. To be murdered at school....our second home. And it would be all my fault.* The vision made that clear. Her third eye doesn't lie. *If I go back...it'll happen. It's too dangerous.*

The scent of coffee drifts in from the kitchen, sliding under her nose. It's morning, but she doesn't want to wake up. Kay remains in her mind...awake but not ready to move.

"She was quivering all night," Mary murmurs.

"I know," James pours his coffee slowly. "But she's fine now. Probably doesn't even remember it."

"She looked like she saw a monster."

"She was dreaming, Mary."

Kayla is motionless. Her limbs are limp beneath the blanket. She lies on the living room couch as rigid as a zombie.

"She just had a nightmare," James goes on calmly. "She's done this before with the squirrel monkey." There's a pause while he sips the hot joe. "Where is Gloria? She's not in her room." "She's probably out running errands."

Kayla's eyes stay draped. *They don't know she's with Elu.* She's preparing for something….with him. Kayla doesn't know what exactly since she skipped the meeting last night. *I'm glad I stayed home. Glad I didn't go. I would've had to mind-link with Greyson again. I want to stay away….I need to stay away.*

The elevator dings, signaling that her parents have left. Even though it's a Saturday, they have to work. The penthouse is grim as a tomb…the curtains shielding out all light don't help much. If anyone walked in, they'd assume this is a loony bin. Taped up curtains…no brightness. A lair. A dark cave. The quietness is welcoming this time around. *I used to hate it…all the eeriness…but now I only want that.*

The couch cradles her body in a hug. Her limbs are heavy. Her breaths are thin. The blackness of her lids take her away. She tunnels into a world that isn't hers:

An underground fortress. No… not a fortress. A kingdom beneath the earth…carved into an endless cave. A castle. Black stone towers twist upward into a ceiling so high it disappears into shadow.

Where am I? She wonders. But the answer comes before the question finishes forming in her thoughts. Grayson McIntyre's palace. A curved masterpiece of dark stone and gothic gates. Regal. Ancient. Columns of obsidian line the hall. A grand hall…a vacant hall…all except for a throne. A throne chair meant for a graveyard. Jagged…full of earthy roots, which intertwine in harsh loops. Not gold. Not iron…or silver…..it's the color of space. Polished and reflective.

Where am I? I don't understand this. Why am I here…and where is here?? A flaming glare answers her questions. One she knows. One she has seen before. Lava-like energy beams…shooting rays of glittery magic. This is his throne…but who is he? Kay nears the throne, spotting bold letters covered in dust. There are inscribed words on the back of the tall chair. She gets close enough to blow air from her mouth to clear the thick dust away. This vapor muddles her sight; she waves her hand before her face, coughing from the old germy dust. Kayla stops swaying her hand, now able to read what the fine print on the throne says:

Greyson Macintyre XXV.

The 25th…? The 25th what? King? Ruler? If so…of what?

The floor below her crackles. An earthquake. One that bubbles lava from the core of earth. Hundreds of clawed hands dart from the hellfire…digging their nails deep into the stone. Growling. Snarling. Sounding no different from demons. Kay backs away as the ground continues to cave in on itself. The creatures hoist themselves up from the depths of hell…a weird mix of gargoyles and vampires. A mutation of Satan in giant form. Bloodshot eyes…like Greyson…like their master. Only they are abominations. Abnormalities.

The army spills from the pit, climbing the walls like insects, flooding the throne room like a plague. Their faces are sunken. Emaciated. Undead. And just as vicious as their master. The army has its radar on the throne beside her. Looking through her like glass.

The glow of Greyson tints the room in a terminal hue. An old timey man…one who doesn't belong in her world. Let alone her era. His essence is burdened and liable. Leisurely…yet tactful. Computed and reserved. Even the way he holds out his hand of flames to command the horde…is…so… celestial.

KOTA

He sits on the billboard latter, his legs dangling over the edge. Kota has been posted in place since nighttime. All this has done is spike his nerves. *Kayla had a panic attack…I wished her parents stayed with her…they left her alone. She's all alone in that place…without a friend…without me. I want to see her.* He zooms from the high structure down to the sidewalk, where he mocks the human way of walking to fit in. *I don't know her floor number…I should ask the receptionist.*

Just as he turns to the revolving doors, he recognizes someone. A problem….a competitor. Someone who has Kayla heart. Darius. *He must be coming to apologize for treating her so bad. It wasn't her fault. That was all me…I got too close. I crossed the boundary. I caused Kayla pain.* He's doesn't use his rapid run….since he's around dozens of city goers…he doesn't want to splat them into red mush from his velocity. He's stuck…and caught.

Darius lingers in his tracks…both of the boys linger by the entrance door. One is uncomfortable…the other is highly frustrated. "What the hell are you doing here?!"

Crap…here we go. Kota stays calm…not wanting to overstep. "I'm just checking in as a friend….she's going through a lot."

"As a friend??"

"Yes…that's what I said."

"No…you're not." Darius clears the space so that he's face to face now. "Fred and Chester are friends…and they never came onto her."

"That's not what I was doing…"

"Yes, it was!" Darius says with building rage. "Stay away from my girl…next time this won't end nice."

Is he serious…?? "Well…we go to the same school, so that's not happening."

"WHAT??!"

Kota doesn't flinch at his loud shout. "Yeah…you heard me right." He swaggers. "You can't stop us from hanging out."

Darius mean mugs him. "I'll tell her to stop…and she will."

I don't want to go there…but he's pushing me. I want to wait for my time to have her…but this jerk is asking for it. He can't control her.. "Well…she made the first move, not me. So maybe you need to dial it back…some."

This has his rival in a mute stage for a good while. The words sink in…so does the denial…and panic. There's a quick glimmer of weakness in his eyes. "You're bluffing…"

"Then go on up and ask her…she's a bad liar. But you know that already."

Darius shoves him hard…but Kota barely slides back…not even an inch. But the ferocity in Darius doesn't allow him to take in this abnormal truth. He doesn't pick up on Kota being an immovable object. "LISTEN, I'M WARNING YOU!"

"Thank you for stating the obvious."

"Stay out of my way!!" Darius balls up his fists and scowls. "Walk away…final warning…or else."

As much as I want to show him that I'm stronger. It's not worth it. If I hurt him…I hurt her. She'll hate me. Kayla chased after him for a reason. It must be love…has to be. I'm not there yet with her…not now, at least. He wins this round.

Kota slowly back peddles, surrendering for the greater good. "Tell her I said hi…" He walks off. His heart hurting; his soul collapsing. He rounds a corner and dips into an alley way…checking if anyone is there. The alley only holds rats and trash filled dumpsters. It's safe enough. No one is here. He glides up to the rooftops so fast,…vanishing from the human eye.

At home, he slinks down from the cloud filled sky, climbing fast down the treetops. The backyard lusters with herbal dust. In the center, the thirteen-pointed star is etched deep into the soil. Odina, Mato, Gloria and Elu stand around it. Their heads are bowed and their hands interlocked. The wind responds, swirling colorful leaves in a perfect spiral.

Dyani, who sits on the back steps, beckons him over. "Welcome back…I think they're ready for you."

A bowl of cedar water sits in the middle of the symbol. Burnt sage curls the air. Elu begins the mantra in Cherokee. "ᎢᎬꭴᏧ ᏛᏗᎾꭴᏧᎢ... (Bloodline, manifest.)"

"Sharabta ethgaly (Bloodline, manifest.)" Gloria cites in old Ethiopian.

Mato and Odina follow the song, their voices folding into the ritual. The phrase repeats on a loop, a loud broken record. Each of them sing, calling to something greater. Calling for answers.

I'm guessing I have to be in the center like last time. Kota steps into the circle. He's apprehensive…with doubt…with angst. *Am I still mystic? Are they right? Is this why Greyson wants me?* He eyes the center of the star symbol. *Am I wrong? Do I even care if I am or not? What does it matter…I'm still cursed? If I still had magic… I'd be like her. Like Kayla. We'd be the same.*

The possibility slams into him like a freight train. He swallows hard. *It would give me a reason to stay in her life. To belong there. To not be some dead thing.*

The chanting goes on. The syllables wrap around him like a cocoon. He stands in the center, waiting. The last hymn leaves their lips. Kota scans the sky, the cloudy sky. The ground. The air. He waits….waits for the wind to howl. For the stars to shimmer in a new formation. For the herbs to burst celestial flames. For the ground to rumble. For anything. But nothing occurs.

No mystic energy. No dimensional veil is lifted. No ancestral voice calls out. Nothing. The circle is noiseless. The thirteen-pointed star lies inert beneath him, as dead as he feels. He waits another minute. And another. Just in case….but it's useless. *It's gone. If magic was ever there in me, it's gone…now.*

KAYLA

I heard the doorbell ring 3 times…but I didn't get up. It's not my parents or Granny…they have keys. I don't care who it was…leave me alone….until….well. I don't know until when. I need a mental break…from life, from school…from witchcraft. She sighs…huddled up on the couch. *But…that's not fair to Kota…I agreed to help him. It's just going to be some time to adjust to what I saw.*

A vampire army…underneath the dugout is a fortress. Greyson's kingdom. He's a king…there was meaning behind the dream. My third eye only shows me what's important…and this is very important. I'll tell granny…when she's in. But I'll say no to attaching to Greyson's mind….I know he wants to kill me…and my friends….and everyone at my school.

But why? Why my school?? He's bringing innocence into the mix for no reason when I'm his target. Is it to hurt me more? And why the army? I'm just one person…just one speller. Even if I am chosen…it shouldn't take an army to handle me.

Gloria is back by 5pm. Kay musters up enough willpower to defeat the slump she's in. But not enough to take the curtains down. Her gran-gran notes the lightless penthouse. "What's all this?"

Kayla stands with her back facing the windows due to paranoia.. "Nothing…just ignore it."

Her granny sees through the excuse. "You have nothing to be afraid of. I know you think you do…but trust me. He won't get near you."

"Even if that's true…the visions won't stop…" Kay hugs herself for comfort. "I gotta tell you something." She relays the hidden kingdom, the castle, the army, the throne. She spills it all.

Gloria crosses her arms and perches her lips. "This is strange….me and Elu can't see any of this…even in the spirit realm…we're blinded. Why aren't you?"

"I don't know…"

"Your tether to him is deeper, for some reason. We need to get into your mind to figure this out."

"No mind linking….I can't….I won't!!"

"I understand….since we know where he dwells; we won't need you to do that. Elu and I can suppress the link so your mind can be free of Greyson."

Kay is put at ease some much by this that her shoulders drop and her neck slouches. "Good…" She grins jadedly. "When can we do that?"

"The next meeting is on Monday; we'll tackle these issues."

"Issues?" She picks up on the double meaning." "What is the other reason??"

Gloria stares off to the side. "We did a séance for Kota…it turns out he has no magic anymore."

Hmm…so why is Greyson after him? "That doesn't make any sense…why is Kota a target then?"

"Who knows…it could be something else. Maybe he wasn't supposed to survive the attack." Gloria shrugs. "Elu did say his magic revealed itself…I think Kota's legacy may have resurrected him."

"Magic can do that?? It can bring back the dead?"

"It depends on the spirit world."

Kay scratches the back of her head. "I missed a lot last night, huh?"

"Including that Greyson can glitch in and out of dimensions. The mystery doesn't end with this one."

Kay is as mum as a mummy. *Oh, no…why did she tell me that?? Now my paranoia is worse. Can he shift dimensions like me??? What if Greyson was in the house last night and it wasn't just my nerves acting up?? What if he's here now…listening…watching with those scarlet irises?? All while cloaked away…all while on the other side?*

The chiming phone croaks her spinal cord; she quakes. "Geez!"

"Relax, child…"

She gives a faulty chuckle. "I'm trying." Kay goes to the phone to pick it up. "Hello?"

"It's me…"

She beams wide, happy that her boyfriend is finally talking to her again. "Hey….I missed you." Kay drags the corded phone all the way to her bedroom down the hall. She closes the door halfway, not wanting to damage the looped, wire cord. "Look, I'm sorry about what happened. Kota is just a friend." *Although I did think about kissing him…but my boo doesn't need to know that.*

"But you let him come over when your parents are out?"

Huh…? What does he mean?? "I don't know what you're talking about?"

"So now you're playing dumb?'

"I'M NOT!!"

"I came to see you earlier…and he was outside…on his way up."

Why would Kota do that?? He's never visited me before. Now he does? "I didn't know he was outside…I swear, Darius." She connects the dots…*the doorbell did ring….was that him? I should've answered…but I was in a rut. God damn it! I could've been with him. Held him….kissed him….like old times.*

"Well, he acted like it was normal….like he does it all the time."

"No…we only hang out at school and…" she stops herself from mentioning the meetings they had together.

"And what?"

"And…that's all." There's doubt in her voice.

"You can't make a swear…then go back on it!" Darius strains in frustration. "Not once did you mention that he goes to school with you….or told me about him. Why didn't you?!!"

Kay facepalms, emphasizing what she's about to say, "I was going through something…I can't explain it."

"And you talked to him about it and not me?? I'm your boyfriend! Is it your dad? Or the ballet stuff?"

"No…"

"Then what is it? You need to tell me!"

Okay, I told my girls…but they dabbled in superstition with me before. We all called on spirits on Halloween. Jia and Mya were the best-case scenario compared to him, and they still lost their wits. "I…I need more time…but I'll tell you, just give me…."

"I gave you time…I was pissed, but I gave you time because I love you. But you won't tell me the truth…"

"I'm trying too!"

"Then say it!"

I'm up against a wall…I just can't speak it. Not over the phone…I need to tell Darius in person. "You'll have to come over…"

"When?"

"Can you make it…" Kay reads the clock on her wall. "By 5?"

"I can."

"Okay, I'll see you soon, bye." Kay hears the deadline tone…but   keeps   the   receiver to   her

ear,

hoping…wishing…dreaming…that he says; "I love you."

KOTA

The clouds cloak the sky…mimicking night despite it being 5 pm. Kota sits cross-legged, like an oversized child. He plants seeds in the barren garden. He digs using his palms to scoop up the dirt and adds parsley seeds in tidy rows. His mind is far away from the soil. *Greyson followed me to Oklahoma for a reason.*

Was it to mock me? To tease me? Does he want to kill me again? Maybe that's it. I know grandad has a spell on me that guards me…my foe must know this. But why get so close …knowing he can't interact with me?/ Even how he ran off…as if provoking me to chase him.

Why? And chase him where? Where…? He recalls what his sister says, *"Dugout in Zon…"* Only his mom hushed her.

Dugout…Zon…something. I wanted to ask Kayla about this…but I never spoke to her about the secret letters or where else Greyson had been. The beach is one….but I need all his whereabouts. I want every last update my parents have gotten..

Mato comes to assist him with the planting, kneeling down beside him. "You can't stay out here all day."

"I know…"

"You want to talk about it?"

"About what?" He grumbles while dropping seeds.

"I know it's hard to let go of our legacy…"

"I'm fine, Dad…"

"I saw how disappointed you were. I'm sorry I let this happen to you…" Mato grabs his son's hand to stop him from sprinkling seeds. His face is riddled with sensitivity. Sorrow. "You'd think I would have known….or have had some sort of sense of the attack."

"Don't beat yourself up about it…you didn't even know my kind was real."

Mato shakes his head. "My dad mentioned them a lot…"

"Yeah…in bedtime stories. How could you have known?"

"True…" He lets go of his son's hand. "Still…I won't stop until this is corrected. Maybe Kayla is strong enough now to pinpoint a cure."

"I hope so." He grins softly at his father. "We'll see."

"Yes…on Monday."

Kota halts from laying down seeds. He deems this the time to sway his father into giving him more info. *I could at least try to uncover the hidden places of my enemy.*

"Can I ask you something?"

"Sure, son…go on."

"What was Dy about to say?"

"What do you mean?"

"Dy said something about a dugout in Zon….something. Is that what was in all the letters from Gloria?"

"You agreed to let us deal with the monster."

"I need to know."

His dad gets up from the kneel. "Don't stay out too late…"

KAYLA

Darius is at the penthouse fast, already boarding the elevator. Granny must be resting in her room. I wonder if last night was hard on her. But then she had 3 anchors to help with the casting. Maybe she's alright. Maybe she's just sleeping early to recoup. It's unlike her to call it a day in the early evening. She must be so exhausted.

Her thoughts are cut short by the dinging. Darius is here. She runs to him as soon as the lift parts open. She's unsure if she can kiss him, due to all the craziness, so she hugs him instead.

The hug he gives her back is lackluster. Distant. His arms don't rope her in like they've done so many times before. He steps out of the hug immediately. "So...?" His hands shoot to his pocket. "Tell me. Did you kiss him?"

"No..."

"No...never. I love you."

"Stop hanging out with him."

"That's not fair....I don't see you stopping Fred and Chester-"

"Because they know their place...this guy doesn't...." Darius looks her up and down, a little offended. "Did you really make the first move like he said?"

"Kota...said that??"

"DON'T SAY HIS NAME!!" He hits the wall to express his bruised heart.

"Darius...chill....it's just a name."

"No...it's not...you don't hear how you say it. It proves that you're lying!"

Uh oh....do I say it like a crush? Full of obsession and admiration?? I guess so... "Okay...I'll stop." The lift rolls back up, dinging. Kay spins to peer at it in dread. *Oh, no...my parents are back!* "You need to hide!"

"No...I'm sick of your dad....it's his fault this happened. This never would've happened if we were still together."

"I know...I know...but please!" *I can hide him on the balcony and sneak him out later.* "Please!!"

"No." Darius faces the elevator.

Kay turns away as the doors depart, wigging out over what's about to happen. *Dad is going to throw Darius out!* There's a long pause....a stark change in the house's aura. Kay reads it well...hostility and disobedience. A ghostly atmosphere. The tint films over the room , much like a camera filter. As dreary as haze in a graveyard.

"What the hell are you doing here??!"

"James, wait!!"

"Did you sneak him in?!!"

"Don't yell at her, I have the right to see my girlfriend!"

She's too scared to whip around to see what's going on. But she hears heavy steps...a fight is coming. *I don't want them to fight each other.* Kay is brave enough to face the drama.

James is charging at her boyfriend. "Who do you think you're talking to??"

Mary speeds after him, holding him back by the chest. "Relax."

"What do you mean, relax?!! She broke the ultimate rule, Mary!! Are you serious?!!" His eyes are beady. "He's no good for her!!"

"You don't know what's good for her, old man." For the first time ever....Darius calls her dad out of his name. Slights him. Belittles him in a rude slur.

"If you open your mouth one more time!!"
"Or what, asshole?" Darius rebukes James...which is a big mistake. A red flag. He pushes his wife to the side and hammers over to Darius. Amped up for an altercation.
"No...no...NO, STOP!!!" Kay shouts violently, enough to trigger her abilities. Enough to summon her inner air goddess. All the curtains on the windows fly off, rippling hard. The glass of the windows shatter into shards, exploding. Bursting. Creating long, icy daggers.

These daggers float, twisting upright in a weird, uniform pattern. The tiny, bead-sized glass fragments hover the air, same as stuck snowflakes. Similar to a snow globe motion. The air glides her body upwards, off her feet, placing her midair like an angel. Her eyes radiate blinding white, without pupils or irises. Just light. Radiant. Terrifying. Holy. White fissures tear across her body...and her veins protrude, thick, unnatural rivers under her skin.

Each vein forges waves beneath her flesh....much like when she touched Kota. The same splitting skin...but all over her body. Bright. Moving. Expanding. Twisting the same as shimmering tree roots.

Mary stumble backwards; her legs giving out. She falls to the floor. Her hand clutching her mouth with disbelief... eyes are wide...too wide. She gawks at her angelic daughter, who resembles the coming of Christ.

James scrambles into the coffee table hard, nearly tumbling, catching himself against the wall with a long yelp that shatters all of the tension. His hand extend out to defend himself from his own daughter. He shields his face...no different than forfeiting to a scary mugger on the city streets. Shocked. Speechless.

Darius lets out raspy pants, too loud, too fast. His shoulders jiggle from the force of his exhaling. His pupils are blown up a size. "Kayla???" His lips part, astounded by his floating girlfriend.

Kayla is mid-air...hovering without wings. The light all around her bending through her body by her command. The stop motion shard of glass, obey her orders…stuck in place; as robust as stars in outer space.

CHAPTER 33: MARKED

KOTA

FLASH FORWARD

Monday's meeting arrives and is full of news. Kota sits in his chair at the table, all tuned in. *Kayla had a busy weekend.* He politely listens to her rundown of the crazy events.

"Are you sure you saw an army?" Elu inquiries.

"Yes, I'm one hundred percent sure."

"And the throne…."

"Yes."

"Was there a sigil?"

Kay rambles in her mind, thinking hard. "I don't think so."   "I thought the same thing…" Gloria chimes in. "There had to be one. If we knew which empire Greyson belongs to, we'd be closer to the truth."

"Empire?" Kota enquires.

"Yes…there are five that date back past B.C. Some even bypass the creation of human life." Elu lectures.

Dyani shudders from this news. He imagines her mind flying past cavemen and Bigfoot to the dinosaurs. Maybe even before those individuals. "How far back?" He speaks for his sister, who is buried in her mind.

"One of the five dates back to the creation of Earth and nature. Depending on the sigil."

"I don't remember seeing one….just the throne….and the army."

"I'm more concerned by this army." Mato strokes his chin. "We need to get to the bottom of this."

"Yes, we do." His wife seconds.

"We will not understand any of it until the sigil is given." Elu simplifies.

Gloria locks her eyes on Kay. "We could venture into your mind and review the scene to get the answer."

Odina wags her head side to side. "You need rest, Gloria…our last conjure was substantial…you took a large draw."

"I had to…the spirit world is temperamental…Elu

couldn't lead, so I did. We found what we needed, didn't we?" "But at what cost? You'll lose all of your strength." Kay's eyes glint with understanding. "You did sleep in for a whole day, Gran. That's not like you. She's right. Don't hurt yourself."

"I thought we wanted answers?"

"We do…" Mato plays neutral. "But not at your health's expense. Let's allow a few days to pass…just to be safe, before we try retrieving the sigil. Just a few days…that's all we're asking."

Gloria stews in annoyance. "I'm well enough now." "Even grandad had to recharge." Dy sides with her

parents. "We don't want you to deplete yourself."

True….I remember that. I was scared for his life….but in the end, he turned out alright. Gloria seems fine…although Kayla said she slept for an entire day. Maybe this time will be different…they haven't used our weapon yet. "Unless you all let Kayla guide the way." He suggests. "I really want to know what sigil was there…I have to know."

Kay nods to agree. "I think I'm stronger now…after what I did."

"Which is?" Gloria…who was hibernating at the time, seeks out an explanation.

"Umm…while you were out…I sort of…kinda became the air spirit." She clenches her teeth.

"YOU WHAT??!"

"Dad and Darius got into it….over the drama…I lashed out and broke the windows. I think I was flying. There was this brightness. It's all kinda blurry….I was mad and kinda lost it. But I swear no one got hurt…I cleaned up the mess with a reverse spell." "That explains why your mom was so strange…she didn't

say a word. Her aura was off."

"Yeah…dad too…they're processing it. I didn't want to tell them that way…but it's done. They know what I am."

"If you were flying…and producing a source…that means your spirit form has advanced." Elu grins.

"That sounds like good news!"

"It is." He praises her. "It is what you call an upgrade… you have entered terrain lessons."

"Meaning you can detect a possible cure." Gloria applauds. "Brava, my butterfly."

Kayla blushes at the clapping, not just from her Gran, but from the whole table. The triumph is electrifying. Dy hugs Kota, caging him in her arms and tugging him halfway off the chair, enough to get him snickering. Odina kisses his cheek. Mato bends over the table to grasp his son's forearm. Elu outstretches his sweet, aged hand to hold Kota's in his. Kayla smiles big at him, scorching his core with her beauty.

Wow…this is it. This is what I wanted from the start….a cure…a way to be normal again. Even if this is a fantasy, I want to keep believing, *to keep having something to look forward to…because of her.* He beams her way. "Thank you."

Kay eyes dart away in shyness. "No problem."
The clapping dies out little by little, fading away happily, not sadly. Kota swears he can still hear it in his head when it's gone. A good time trapped in his ears.

"Now…on to the tough stuff, now that the good news is out of the way." Gloria starts. "We need to undo the tether between Kayla and Greyson. His access to her…or her access to him is a weakness that may exploit our plans."

"Yes…mind links can work both ways, depending on the connection. Since he shared the massacre of the benders with you…that means he has latched to your soul." His grandad informs. *He's what…? Latched to her soul.* "I didn't know that was possible." Kota observes Kayla, who is mortified, after just being full of delight.

"Greyson marked her after her first spell…since she was not guarded by Gloria yet. There's an access point that we need to close." Elu goes on.

"After the meeting, then?"
"Yes." He assures Gloria.

This just keeps getting more and more of an enigma. According to grandad and Gloria…the wiretap of their minds isn't normal. Kayla is at risk….without knowing. And she's possibly allowing him to hear and see what we're doing. Like a spy…without bad intentions. "What if he knows we're after the cure?"

"That's not a far-off assumption." Gloria utters. "But with Kayla on our side, he can try to intervene all he wants; he'll lose." *I believe this…even grandad says, 'He would be a fool to confront a young bender; Kayla is in her prime.* This guarantees him that Gloria is right.

Odina takes in all of the information. "The sooner we close the gap, the better."

"Is there anything else before we end the day?" Mato looks to everyone at the table.

Kay ups her hand as if she's at school. "Grandma made a good point; Greyson only hunts casters…Kota." She eyes him. "You're bending might be gone, but it could have resurrected you back to life…instead of letting you die. That could be why he's after you."

The table is quiet, calculating this theory. Mato narrows his eyes to the floor, brooding. Odina seeks out Elu to give his comment. Dyani chews on her lip in deep thought.

"I'm sure that this oddity has Greyson intrigued with you." Gloria pulls all of her attention to Kota. "Think about it…the beach…Oklahoma. No telling if his radar is on you at this moment. He steals magic to be better….all while you naturally had it in you without being a thief."

Holy crap….wait? Maybe…just maybe. It doesn't make sense at all why he's going for me when Kayla is the ultimate power. Not me. It could be my blood. My legacy could still course strong…even though I'm undead.

KAYLA

After the conference, Kayla is taken to the backyard by Gloria, Elu, Mato, and Odina. Dyani and Kota stay floored at the table. Piecing together the possibilities. *I stand by the theory. Greyson did prey after me, then leave, going states away to Oklahoma. For Kota. Gran and I aren't wrong.* There's a 13-star symbol drawn deep into the soil. The same one she recognizes from the grimoires. The late morning sun blazes the ground. Unlike the gloomy days before. The herbal dust drifts up into the air like the glass she broke from the windows, only smaller. Micro.

Her gran-gran sets her in the middle of the circle then join hands with the coven…bowing their heads to cite the words of Cherokee and Ethiopian to form the words, "Vincla Nascura, Udanalenvdodi Agisd, (tether unborn).'

This time, unlike Kota's séance, wind isn't the responding element. The earth is. The wobbling reminds her of jelly shaking on a spoon. There's no sound, no rumbling. Noiseless. As delicate as a surge in the ocean.

Kay senses pressure on the side of her head, as if she laid down on a sharp object that cut her temple. The pain is unexpected. *I don't know if I can move to rub it. THAT HURTS!! But I can take it. I'm pretty sure I need to stay still.*

There are flashes of ruby in her eyesight. The same shade Greyson calls upon. She's thankful that that's all she encounters. *Good…I didn't see his face again. I was worried about that.*

The stabbing in her temple ceases; so does the fire-colored glare. The earth goes lazy from its rocking. The mystic dust sinks to the ground. No soon after…the cadence wraps to an end. She's free of the bond with Greyson, free of being monitored. Free of the weight she never knew was on her chest until now.

They all bid each other farewell until the next meeting. Kayla goes inside to say goodbye to Kota in person. She overhears him conversing with his sister.

"The ritual had to be wrong then…" "Rituals aren't wrong." Kota replies.

"I'm sure they can be…human error and all. Even grandad and Gloria are blind to parts of the realm."

"I can't cast."

"You may need to initiate first. Grandad said I have to do it too…so do you too. We aren't born with it like Kayla. What if you have to say a chant?"

"Hmm…" Kota mumbles. "Maybe."

That's an interesting thought…one I think he should follow through with. I can invite him over to borrow the book. This time I'm not scared of the backlash from my dad. I think I put him in his place. He hasn't said a word since my outburst. I won the battle…finally.

The silence between Kota and Dy grants her the right to interrupt without rudeness. "Hey…we're heading out."

"Nice, you're all fixed up?" Dy ups her palm for a high five.

"Yep." Kay slaps her hand. "You guys are a life saver…I was flipping out over all the dead people."

"Yeah, the spellers…that sucks for them."

"No...from my school…" She corrects Dyani. "I can't go back…students will die…everyone will die."

Kota squints. "You're skipping school?" "That's not wise…you'll get caught." Dy adds.

"It's better than causing death."

"How certain are you of that?"

Kay huffs, a little peeved. "Everything I see happens or already happened. Why should this be different?"

Dyani pinches her mouth to the side. "Fair point."

"No, it's not…" her brother quarrels with them both. "You moved up a level, Kayla, meaning you're more powerful now."

"What if I'm not…?"

"You are…why do you think the bastard keeps his distance?"

"Because of the protection mark." Dy inputs.

"And the fact that you're a new bender…If you don't believe me, ask Gloria." He expresses this belief with all his might. "You're safe at school. If you think you aren't…just know that I'll protect you." His affectionate presence speaks to her heart. There's a heated numbness there. She fights her hand from flying to it.

That will only give me away...plus I have Darius. No matter how...tempting Kota is...I can't hurt my boyfriend. She fixes her sight on her feet to steer clear of the sugary sweet moment.

"Yep, my baby bro won't let any danger your way." Dy gives a laugh. "Agali gasgo jigesv!, (ask her out already!)"

"Yitsasdi hi'a, asgaya unadulisvi, (butt out of it, she has a boyfriend)."

She's clueless about what they just said. "Huh?"

"I told him to-"

'NOTHING!" Kota hops from the chair. "She's just being a dumb-dumb."

"His nickname is *walela* (hummingbird)." Dyani embarrasses him. "You can call him that anytime you want."

"DYANI!!" He grunts in humiliation as his big sis jets from the room, giggling.

"Ignore her."

"You do call me princess...so fair is fair."

"Don't say it, please." He pleads....covering his face with both palms to hide from the awkwardness.

"Fine...your saved...for now...I'll call you it at school."

He drops his hands, feeling heat on his cheeks. "So, I got you to not drop out??"

"Maybe......"

His pupils enlarge for her substance. "I meant what I said ...I'll protect you from any and everything."

Her eyes drop to the floor again, her hips swish side to side with unhinged fondness. Overflowing with shy yearning. "I know..." Her voice is barely audible, but he picks up on it just fine. Gloria beeps the horn from the front. Calling her with the blowing. "See you at school...maybe."

"Take out the maybe..." he flirts effortlessly.

"I'll think about it." Once in the Volkswagen, she takes Kota up on what he said. To ask Gloria about being a new bender. "Does me being new make me stronger than Greyson?" Her granny looks her over good, a little suspicious.

"Yes...your source is untapped...unlike his. Why do you ask?" "I saw the school...and...everyone was dead inside."

Gloria turns the key in the ignition. "Everything isn't an omen...or has a rite of passage. Fear can cloud the third eye...and emotions are complex...and can warp reality."

"Greyson killed Kota friends…so it's not crazy to think he would do the same again."

"It's not…but you can be cautious without being paranoid." She drives off, leaving the curb full of autumn leaves. "Plus…your crush might die before he lets that go down." Gloria winks. "It's all in his aura…he's golden when you're around."

"Is golden a good thing?" Kay knit her eyebrows as one, unaware of color meaning.

"I don't think you're ready for that answer…try asking in a few years," she simpers while turning the wheel onto a two-lane street.

Morning traffic is building just before the lunchtime rush. The west side is a dream compared to downtown, where they inch like worms in the sand, making little to no progress. Kay doesn't complain; she's still speculating on what a golden aura means.

KOTA

Dad takes me to school this time. I know he's curious of what a city one looks like. He attended on the rez, a small one-story building with limited windows.

When he pulls up to the school, his mouth is hanging. 7 levels of windows and modern steel extravagance. Surrounded by high rise restaurants and designer outlets. A lottery ticket to high class society. Mato whistles his impressiveness, "you're making the ancestors proud with this one!"

"One of the perks."

"The other one is her, If I'm not mistaken?"

"We're friends." He's spoken this fable so much that he's starting to believe it.

"For now…" His dad unlocks the car. "Have a good day at school."

The Golden Leaf Dance is this Friday. The bronze streamers and balloons, even the banner with the corny leaf and glitter décor, is familiar. *I went to a dance before…and the fun was worth it…but the anguish of that night overshadows it. I'm not ready. It's a good thing Kayla and I are only decorating the gym. That saves me from another round of survivor's guilt. All I'll think about is them…and the dancing…the faded happiness.*

He passes on to his locker. His special hearing is on and wires him to the current 411 amongst girls and boys. "I heard the new boy won't be there…"

"But everyone is going…even the geeks are down. What's his deal?"

"He's trying to make a statement….a lame one at that."

"Nobody wants him there anyway; the dude's a creep."

"Vanessa probably had him banned from going after rejecting her."

"OH, MAN, YOU MIGHT BE ONTO SOMETHING!" A stoner guy over-exaggerates this theory.

"Spread the word, people, spread the word."

Dozens of lockers clink, as the first bell rings. The warning bell. But Kota opens his locker to waste time while waiting for Kayla. *I pray she doesn't drop out…she's the only reason I'm here. The only reason I care.*

Then from the back of his locker door he hears, "Hey, wa..le…la??"

Oh no, she said it! Why is she doing this to me?? Kota deepens his face into the locker, noting how his heart vibrates and his lungs fill up. There's a molted sensation. A melting effect.

"Did I say it right?" She circles around to the other side to peer at his face…which is inches deep into the locker. If his whole body could fit…he'd be completely in. "Nice place you got there…how's the rent?' She hangs her head upside down, her bushy mane draping towards the floor to view his face. "Earth to Spock, come in."

"Hey…" His voice ricochets on the metal door.

"You can't live there…this is a school, sir."

"Give me a minute." He collects himself, inhaling and holding for five seconds. Kota gathers his wood shop book before shutting the locker. "Hey, princess."

"Hey, walela…" She snickers at his quick scratch of the head and eye avoidance. "What does it mean."

"My mom gave it to me…it means hummingbird."

"How did you get it?"

He starts the way to homeroom; she walks beside him. "Umm…something about my voice when I was born. It was super high pitch."

"Higher than it is now?" She jabs.

Great…I'm reliving the teasing from my old life. "Yes…higher than now." He gives a deadpan expression.

"I don't believe it…I need proof."

He facepalms, sliding his hand down very melodramatically. "This again…"

"Oh, so you've been told this before?"

"By my old friends…the ones that…" he cuts himself off from completing the sentence.

Her amused expression diminishes to stoic sadness. "I'm sorry for bringing it up."

"Don't be…I said my farewells."

Her eyes are pitiful…sappy…vulnerable. Kota stops in his tracks, studying her. "I don't want that…with….my…girls."

"Kayla…" He holds the small of her back, not shying away from precise eye contact. His words match the promise in his eyes. "I'll die before I let you…or anyone here, get slaughtered. I'm not letting that repeat. Never!" He wants to embrace her…and almost does, but stops halfway. This has him in a position where it seems he will kiss her. Since he's taller, he has to hunch over a little.

Kayla's chest is motionless…her breaths are gone. Time is an illusion in this bubble. A whirlpool of fondness. One that will surely add more content to all the school rumors.

In wood shop, the assignment is a chessboard, which they have to stain black and white. It's a very aesthetic look….and correlates too well with the supernatural world. Kota moves slothfully…to not be seen as an attention seeker, so his tempo is mediocre and expected. His finished product is still leagues above everyone else's.

Vanessa peers him down in biology, still burned. But Kota pays her little mind while working out the prompt on the chalkboard:

NON-LIVING, YET IT REPRODUCES INSIDE EUKARYOTIC CELLS.

USES HORIZONTAL GENE TRANSFER TO JUMP BETWEEN SPECIES.

CAUSES RAPID ORGAN DEGENERATION, PRIMARILY IN THE LIVER AND BRAIN.

WHAT IS IT?

He bumps into Kayla at her locker. "Oh…I was wondering when we can practice French…I can't keep getting D's."

"Yikes…"

"Yeah…it's sooo bad."

She brainstorms…knowing that inviting him over will get Darius mad. "Ummm…I'm not sure about you coming over…after the Darius issue."

"I'm sorry about that…I was worried. I didn't know Greyson got so close to you."

"It's fine…I know you were just looking out for me." *I need to clear up everything else. I'm sure Darius told her what I said.* "The argument was silly…can we just forget it?"

"Did you really say I made the first move?" Kayla is irked. He picks up on how peeved she is by the way a line works across her forehead. And how her eyes harden.

"It was silly of me to say…"

"It was…" She takes out her history book and clicks the locker closed. "We're friends."

"I know."

Kay studies him close…trying to detect any signs of falseness. Jitteriness…a twitch …a higher pitched voice. But nothing gives him away. Kota buries his longing far and deep…not wanting to lose her. "Good…" She's satisfied with what she finds. "I guess we can start tutoring on Thursday…after decorating the gym for the dance."

"Sounds like a plan."

"A solid plan, man." She jokes with a rhyme.

KAYLA

He follows her to lunch, where they gather the same attention as last time. Everyone treats them like a celebrity couple. *If they had cameras, I really think they would snap photos. Speaking of photos.* Kayla eyes go to where Jia is sitting, singling her out. "I'll be back." She leaves Kota in the lunch line. Her friend is busy writing in her ballet journal. Isabel assigned all of the ballerinas a planning book for their routines. Jia maps out a list for her new choreography.

"I miss that…" Kay breaks the ice. "I don't even plan routines anymore…after everything that's happened." She sits, looking sullener than a zombie. "I miss you…"

"I miss you too…" Jia stops her writing.

"Then why don't you sit with me in photography?? You're at the back of the class. Away from me."

Jia drops her voice to a mutter. "He's not alive…I get he's a victim and all, but….he's dead." The chill in her tone wiggles down her back. "Sorry, but I can't get behind this…I tired."

"So…that means we can't work together in class anymore? You blocked me out…that's not fair!"

"I don't know what else to do….my gut is telling me to stay away."

"Wow…Jia!!"

"Kayla…what does he eat to survive!" She hisses softly.

Unbelievable….is she really implying that Kota drinks blood?? He told me the necklace helps with that. He doesn't drink blood. "I doubt he drinks it…he's too normal."

"Did you ask him??" Kay digs around in her brain for the answer, coming up short. "How about this…ask him if he ever drank blood…if he says no…then…then." Jia twists her face in difficulty. "I'll sit with you…"

"You'll sit with both of us?"

"Kay…" Jia whines. "Just…one step at a time, please? I'll sit with you in class…let's start with that."

"And at lunch…or I won't ask him."

Jia munches on the inside of her jaw, debating, adjusting…computing. "I'll try it out…tomorrow."

"What about Mya?" She jerks her head to the lunch line, where Mya is stacking food on her plate.

"She won't sit by herself…she'll go along…even if she's halfway off the seat."

"Okay…it's a plan." Kay nods, all businesslike, then goes back to the lunch line. Kota is gone. *Huh??* She halts in place. *Did he go to the restroom?? But vampires don't have to use the toilet. They're dead.. Hmm..* She skips the lunch line, going out into the hallway. "Kota??" Where did you run off to??" She passes nonstop rows of lockers.

Suddenly…out the corner of her eye, the glimmer of blood drips out of a locker. The ridged vent at the top leaks red goo. Kay turns her head to view the horror scene. Just then…every last locker, on each side, oozes blood. A gore fest. She's plastered in place…unable to move. A force field holds her there…binding her to the spot.

The red glare washes over her irises…in the shade of evil. The same hallucination from before emerges. Only it takes place right before her. The hall lights strobe over the lockers, which pour out maroon lines. Blood streams in rivulets from the top to the bottom of the doors, flushing out to the floor. The hall transforms to a sea of crimson.

NOO…NOO!!! THE TETHER WAS BROKEN…I FELT IT. I KNOW IT!!

Kay screams internally…that's all she can do…she's suspended in motionless. Not able to move her mouth, limbs…just her eyes. She's splattered by the blood from the lockers and from the pond of gore below. The sprinkling effect douses her hands, arms, and legs. Ruining her clothes. The liquid sinks through…hot and grotesque… rotten smelling.

Greyson zaps in and out of reality. Same as a bad reception on an antenna TV. Static in and out. Pixelating. Blurry…ominous. Freddy Krueger in the flesh…here…while she's awake. The fluorescent lights pop in and out. The red river swooshes. He creeps closer and closer. Glitching in and out.

Her mind recalls the tune from the backyard…the one that severed the soul bond. She cites exactly what her granny said…only as a thought since she's locked in place. **Vincla Nascura…(tether unborn)**. But the slaughter scene remains there…the pond spills taller…more than two feet off the ground now. The lockers are completely painted over red gore. The lights go out for good. Fizz. Fizz. Fizz. The vampire king's demon irises spark…coming closer and closer.

VINCLA NASCURA!!! The booming thought is useless. **VINCLA NASCURA!!!**

Damn it!!! No!! I can't let him kill! them! No…no!!" Greyson's claws grow out far…far from his nail beds…to her. The glitching is slower…slow enough to zip him into this realm. A carbon copy…a solid figure…that can touch her.

Out of options…Kay attempts a final incantation. **GRROC COUM!!!!** She battle cries internally. The floor below sinks inward…dividing as mountains struck by lightning. An earthquake. Snapping. Banging….as it swallows Greyson whole. This releases her from the body barrier. Kay flees, her wet hair slapping her face, her arms over-working to her destination. The exit.

KOTA

He finds himself at Juneway Beach, Far North of Rogers Park., just before the Evanston border. The very tucked away part that he visited for fresh soil. Very quiet. No tourist…or traffic. A lake outlined with huge rocks. And trees. The same trees Greyson were in. But his mind is far off from that now.

Kayla thinks I'm better than what I am…thinks I never killed. She doesn't know about the monster I was…the monster I can still be. The voice in my head…the possession. The family I killed…even if it was the fiend in my head. I still did it. So…her confidence in me is wrong. I wish it wasn't. I don't want her to ask me…she'll be sickened by the truth.

He walks the beach…kicking sand under the sunlight. Luminous in the shine…in the warmth. *I don't think I can take that. I can't take her revolted at what I've done.* Kota stops…his hand pressed to the chain around his neck. *I wouldn't want to exist…I wouldn't want that image of her in my head.*

His pale eyes survey the sun…mesmerized by the torching momentum. Tempted by the afterlife. Tempted by justice. *I asked before…why am I not dead. But my friends are…the family and the kids are. The little children. Isn't it justice if I was dead too…on fire in hell?? That way I'll meet the Great Spirit…and all will be as it should be.*

His fingers clutch around the wooden chain…*all I have to do.*, he curls it once…twice…around his fingers, ready to snap it off of his neck. *Is take it off. All I have to do is*…he yanks slightly…then goes in for a heavier pull.

"KOTA! KOTA!!!" His hand falls…his neck whips to the sound of her shouting his name. Desperate for him…believing in him. He trails along the path…in her direction. Back to the school…but that's not where she is…Kay is farther away. Not in the building. He blasts off again…passing an entire city block…where she is. Kayla scurries off…glancing behind her shoulders. Full of shock. He zips in front of her in a millisecond.

"AHH!! GET AWAY!!! NOOO!!!"

"It's me!! It's me…"

Kayla pants hard, whipping her head the opposite way. "I wanna go home!"

"Tell me what happened…"

"No…just…I wanna go home!" She sobs. "There's blood all over me…everywhere…" She rakes her fingers through her hair. "My clothes…my…" Her hands pat over her body randomly.

"Kayla…there's no blood on you…" He's perplexed. Her blouse and jeans are normal…spotless. Clean.

"The school is full of blood!!"

"No…the school is fine."

"I KNOW WHAT I SAW!!"

She's so sure…so certain. Kota double checks this…flexing his nostrils to test the air closely. The odor of atomic nickel…of plasma…is nowhere in the vicinity. "I don't smell it…I don't smell anything. If there was blood, I would know…trust me."

"It was there…so was Greyson; he was in the hall! I opened the ground up to trap him in…he fell in! He was so close!" "The tether

is fixed…your mind is making this up. You said yourself that you saw dead students. No one is dead….and there is no blood."
"What about the broken ground?? I said the chant and the floor cracked open!"

"I'll check and see…but believe me…his stench is not here. I know it well…I know when he's around."
Kay stops her weeping. "No…in another dimension…he was there…but not there. I'm not going crazy!" *Okay…she could be right…but the blood and sunken in floor bit isn't adding up for me.* "I just wanna go…home."
I don't agree with her blowing off school…but I get it. I support it…for this. She's crying…and shaking. I need to help her.
"Alright…umm…how do we do this?"

"Do what?"
"I never vamp ran with anyone…I usually go solo." "Oh…" She looks down at his waist, wondering if that's a good spot to hug. *Oh…what is she thinking….does she want to grab me there? Out of all the places for support…there is where she chooses?* "I…umm …I'm not sure about touching you."
"Yeah…the dryer effect." *Right, that…the triboelectric effect…the static zapping of my skin..* "It won't be for long…less than 5 seconds. I'm fast."

"Brag much?"
"You started it…miss earthquake." He gently hold her by the elbows. "Hold still….one…two….three."

The vortex is a blazing blur, a whirlpool of zigzagging lines. He hears her suck in air…and hold it, as if plunging from a roller coaster. Then nothing. They're at the penthouse. Kayla staggers: he steadies her by the elbows. His hands are on her long enough to scorch his skin wide open with a holy shine. His veins gravitate outward, changing to a wiry state, all over his body. Kota chokes on air…and that's when he sees it.

A silhouette made completely of smoke and stars, cloaked transcendentally. Radiant and everlasting. A presence of comfort and healing. Faceless, but familiar to him. Gigantic, but minor enough to be understood with ease. An atmospheric figure of closure…of divinity…and afterlife. The Great Spirit.

CHAPTER 34: BECOMING

KAYLA

She stumbles away…all abashed. 'I'm sorry…I…didn't mean to…" Kay hurries into the penthouse…loathing what she just did. *That looked worse than last time. I was suffocating him…ki…killing him!! Ugh!!! I can't deal with that and the school dilemma too. I'll worry about that tomorrow. I can't right now!*

Once upstairs, she glimpses over the living room. *One would think it never gotten trashed just 2 days ago. But it did. I lost control…and could have hurt my parents. Hurt Darius. The glass from the windows were active weapons. I made it right…I had to clean up my mess. I can't let go like that again. No matter how angry I was.*

FLASHBACK

There's no sound. Mary is on the floor. James has an arm on the wall to support him upright…yet he's scrunched over. Darius is amazed. *Did I just do that??* Kay eyes reverted to normal; her angelic body lowers to the floor. The airborne glass still hung mid-air. *Oh…no…this is not how I wanted this to go. Look what I did!!! I need to put it back…put our house back to how it was.*

"Ummm…don't…don't move, I can fix this!" She conveyed this command with a stop signal with her hands. Kay sprinted to her mom's room. Taking out a witch book…and browsed for a repair incantation. "I can fix it!" She sorted through the pages quick for a symbol…for a repair charm. Not finding it there…so she tried a second book, and repeated the skin through the pages. Nothing. "Come on…come on!" The third book held luck for her. "YES! THERE!"

NARA'TEL ENRUS :
A CRACKED CIRCLE RECONNECTED
AT THE CENTER, DEPICTS THIS SPELL.

Kay hustled back to the trashed living room, where glassless windows and curtains thrown awaited her. She sounded out the words in her head before she spoke it. *Nara tel enrus? I think that's how it's spoken.* "Nara'tel Enrus."

As soon as she spoke, the glass dangling in the air shot back to the skyrise windows. Piece by piece, reconstructed. Whizzed the air and clinked back as one. Even the tiniest, rice sized shards returned back to where they belonged. When all fixed up, the place appeared to had never experienced a supernatural disturbance. Even the curtains reattached back to the window; the frames accompanied by the tape.

"That's not how I wanted it to go…" She addressed them all. "Talking it out would've been better."

Crickets. None of them moved an inch…or said a thing. Their small minds couldn't compute. Their utter plausible deniability. The boxed in logic all humans have…even she had it. Doubted it. Discharged it as nonsense. As a myth. The inner workings of their brains sought out a natural reason…and failed. Despite what was before them. Regardless of the proof before them.

Mary scrubbed at her eyes and gave an intense stare to the windows. James didn't make a peep, same as Darius. They were just fighting and now had nothing to declare but emotionlessness.

"I know this is a lot…" Her view landed on her mother. "But mom…you knew about this…grandma told you." Mary just gawped at the windows…unable to form words. "It's in our blood…" What she said didn't register to her mom…who was stumped by the witchcraft she has just seen.

Darius…whose body rocked back and forth with the gravitational pull of Earth, was the only one who moved a fraction. Only a bit fraction…not even an inch. "What…w…w…what did you just do???!!"

Kay inclined her head to her mother. "Ask her?"

Darius rotated his head to Mary. "Mrs. Harris..?"

"I don't believe it! Nooo…" Her mom shielded her eyes with her palms.

James was as directionless as a puppy. "Mary…what just happened???"

Mom never answered him…but Dad knew. He knew about the books…the ones he slept just feet from. Knew it…but had to fib to himself and anticipate that Mom would say something other than a Spell Bender. But she never did. Dad stayed permanently welded on the wall by his arm. Darius left without another word, leaving faster than ever.

No, he didn't leave…he fled to the elevator…rattling the button over a dozen times….never looking back at me. My boyfriend couldn't handle it…couldn't face me being a witch. A non-human. And this time I don't know if he'll give me another chance.

I spent the night in Gran's room while she hibernated, regaining her strength from the untying charm. It took a toll. I've never seen someone look exactly like Snow White in her see-through coffin. How Gran lied there…straight as a board…as if she was a dead corpse. But I knew she wasn't…her chest moved up and down…producing oxygen. She's breathing. As much as this creeped me out…I never left the room. I sat at the footboard; my legs folded …and wished my Granny was awake to tell me what to do next with my parents.

Kayla leaves the living room, away from memory lane…going up to her art studio. An old relic she abandoned when life got too strange. Too real. Too deadly. The room is full of her canvas sketches…including old ones on the wall, propped up like museum art. On full display. But she doesn't clear the canvas…or grab a pencil. She flops down onto the floor, arms around her knees and head resting atop them.

I knew going back would cause this. I let Kota and Granny convince me that it was a good idea to play teenager with a killer on the loose. Why? Why did I? I should've gone with my gut.

KOTA

The school has no sign of hell opening to eat his enemy. *The hall is…average…clean…as always. I know there's no blood, but I still observe the floors. Nothing. I think this was all in her head. Greyson got in her head. Even if I didn't run off…which I hate myself for. How would I have defended her?? This was on a mental level…not physical. I hoped she told Gloria…because I'm off to update my parents on the opposite matter. I hate to ditch school…something I've never done…but this is essential.*

I saw the Great Spirit…the creator. The merger of the afterlife…was all through her…she was the vessel. The vessel of the afterlife….a true anchor for redemption. One I can utilize without removing my necklet and melting in the sun. Without killing myself…without succumbing to ash…and bone. I can access death in a safer way.

He exits the school; glad that it's still lunch break…or he'd be yelled at. Students are allowed outside to eat; some do so on benches, and the stone ledges of ponds. Unaware of who may have been or not been, just pass the doors. An evil they'll never understand.

I have to walk around the corner before racing off…if I do it now, I'll be noticed as vanishing from thin air. I don't need any more rumors going around about me.

Kota bypasses batches of students on the city sidewalks, who chat it up about the dance. He keeps his focus ahead to act as if he doesn't realize the flirty looks from giggling girls. Once at the corner, and ready to flash off, he hears:

"Vampire dugout…I haven't finished the illustration of what's down there."

"Why are we still on Zonnebeke anyway?? There's better history to learn here in America…not that Belgian place." His thoughts erupt:

Dy words, "Dugout in Zon…"

Mato speaking, "You agreed to let us deal with the monster." When he interrogated Dyani's meaning.

The letters Gloria delivered in secret…well, not secret anymore. Now I know…the moment I lost to ask Kayla before her boyfriend came between us….isn't lost anymore. The time of planning the next attempt…is no longer needed. I know where he lives. The words my sister tried to say were, "like that dugout in Zonnebeke. Somewhere hidden in Belgian is his fortress.

He blazes home…relieved and pissed that this was kept from him…and if he never overheard the students…it would've remained kept from him. What just occurred with Kayla is put out of his mind. *I'll leave it for some other time…this has priority over that.*

No one is home, not even grandad. He hears no one…picks up on no one's fragrance. He checks each of the rooms upstairs. No one. Kota goes to the backyard…empty. *They must have gone shopping for the garden.*

He treads to the living room to recover the map that they used to pinpoint Kayla. He knows it's under the end table, collecting dust on the dark wood. *It's still stained with blood…but that's unimportant.* His mind is set overseas as he unfolds the world map to view every measure of planet Earth. His fingertip dashes over the blue of the map, going away from America, clear across the North Atlantic Ocean. To the Celtic Sea.

Passing Ireland. The United Kingdom, Netherlands, before stopping. *There….right below…it's there!!* His finger descends to Belgian. *I found it…I found his Lair! This must be where Kayla saw the throne room. But isn't it too public??? I mean….my school has assignments on it. That's too accessible. It can't be…*

A flashback to his mother's words to Chief Ridge, right before the failed ritual back home: "I conducted a locator spell. The animal fled far enough to escape the charm. The beast is most likely underground…."

Underground…has to be. That would make the most sense…if it's a known landmark, it would have to be beneath the surface. Kota measures the distance. *That's thousands of miles away. I could barely go states away without frying myself out…no way I can do thousands of miles…and over the seas to Belgian.*

I need to plan this right. It'll take days…I'll need to hunt for fuel. It won't be easy. I'm out of my league here…but I won't give up.

The wagon door shuts. He hears his family piling out, with what sounds like bags of seeds. Kota puts away the map, just how it was, folded neatly on the American side.

I'll keep this hushed up…I won't blow it up….I won't make a scene. I may be bounded to the house again…probably for good. Jailed by magic. Not happening…not again. So, I need to be cool about this and play my part. After all, I did promise to leave it all in the past. I swore to my mother…and my father to let them handle it. Playing my cards right is the only option…not raging over this and awakening my inner villain. No…this time I will be smarter.

KAYLA

"I'll be out tonight; I have to gather crystals for the next meeting. Will you be okay until then?" Gloria waits for her reply through the phone.

"Yeah…I'm used to soloing it." Kay brushes off the alone time. "Crystals? What for?"

"Mind traveling. We have to review the sigil, if there was one in the throne room."

"Oh…right.." *Should I tell her about school?? I think so…only she'd tell me I'm fine, and it's all in my head, like Kota did. She believes that the tether break was successful., not a bust. Even I believe it was. Maybe I am going crazy.* "How does that work?"

"The crystals will reflect your memory…like a projector."

All Kayla thinks of are the school projectors that teachers use. "Kinda like a slide show?"

"Precisely."

"Will you be alright enough to assist with this?"

"Yes."

Is she saying yes to pacify me?? I saw how deep in a slumber she was…just like a coma. I never seen one…ever…not in person…not even on TV. But I am very sure that it looks like that. "You were…hibernating…for…a day."

"That's expected when exerting so much power."

"Will that happen to me??"

"No…dear…not in many years…decades even. I envy your youth." She chuckles low, but it's bittersweet, not jubilant. "I'll see you later, dear…be safe."

"I will."

"No more breaking windows!" She scolds with an amused laugh.

"I can't make any promises." Kay grins before hanging up. The kitchen is bare…as the rest of the house.

My parents don't small talk with me anymore. In the morning before work, they would chit chat…now they're gone so fast, I don't hear them leave. They're at work super early to evade me. As if they weren't already tied up in what I am. They have seen what I am…and are acting odd.

Her feet guide her upstairs, away from the abyss of a home. The cold house is even more frigid. This time is worse than before….because for a fact, she knows her parents are choosing to not interact with her at all. Treating her as a stranger.

Up in her studio, she opens the balcony doors…to let in fresh autumn air. Well, semi autumn air. The middle of November is a strange blend of winter…too warm for frost. The last of the vibrant shaded leaves begin to fall from skeleton trees. Kay analyzes the trees below…zoned in on a dark purple one…only three leaves are there. Barely clinging on…barely alive. She pities the long descend to the ground more than the poor nature dread their end.

End…will this end well? My parents know I'm non-human…so does my boyfriend. Can this chaos end well and go back to how times used to be? Or have the good times ended? Just as the artistic fall season has wrapped up??? I hate being here alone…and not knowing if my mom and dad will return home…or pull an all-nighter to be far away from their freak of a daughter. Who used to be their pride and joy.

A recurrence peels from her inner eye:

FLASHBACK

Five-year-old Kayla sits in the lobby of Studio Doll, swinging her short legs back and forth, humming Mozart's Moonlight Sonata in a chipmunk tune. James is on one side of the bench holding her tiny hands….and Mary is on the other side, holding the other. They both read over the pamphlet for the summer program:

TUTU & TIARA'S INITIATIVE. APPLY NOW.

"We really shouldn't ignore her skills…"

James rubs his chin while reading. "Are you sure it wasn't just a coincidence?"

"Honey, she did a pointe pose...on tiptoe! Yes, she was already playing around...but this is impressive. We can't overlook it."

"I did like this, Daddy!" Kay's helium balloon voice declares as she stands up on the bench to jump off the edge of it.

"Whoa there!!" Her dad stands.

"Careful, baby!" Mary uses her arms to cage her child in.

Kayla is too blind to be afraid of hurting herself. Her naïve brain just wants to demonstrate what she did...regardless of hitting the floor face first or not. Her tiny pink, dress shoes with a cute buckle, are on tiptoe. Perfect posture...no dipping, no slacking. No struggle. She holds it for 5 seconds, then goes flat footed to the floor. "LIKE THAT!!"

Mary holds her chest, strained by the reckless stunt, "Good job...but next time, no jumping."

"Wow, princess...where did you learn that?"

Kay mumbles, "I don't know," in a nonverbal mumble. "My shoes do it, Daddy." She bends to touch her shiny shoes. "They move like me!!"

"Somebody's seen the moonwalk..." James smirks. "That's all this is. She's imitating what she sees on Tv."

"Even if she is...you gotta admit, that's impressive!"

"It is."

Kay does a silly wobbling arm dance while on tiptoe, strutting her talent. "No...I'm surfing." She explains. "I'm surfing in the ocean." They crack up at her goofy, flapping arms, knowing she was special.

Waterworks fleet down her cheeks, curving to her chin and staying put. *If only I stayed that kind of special....not this kind. If only the good times never stopped. If only.*

One leaf sails off, plummeting in a swirl to the watercolored ground...with the rest. The second one follows suit, air surfing, looping the brisk winter wind. Now only one remains. Alone. She doesn't eat dinner...hunger is a stranger.

The sad nostalgia has her in bed by 6pm. She's in her room...her grand palace of a room, for the first time in days. Her sheets are fluffy like her parents hugs, but the dark overcast has their long distance written all over it.

Gloria isn't in yet...no one is in. Like old times, the penthouse is lifeless. A graveyard...all because she shared her secret with her mom and dad. *I really wanted it to go better! Why did I have to lose my temper??? Why didn't I keep my cool and give a better confession?*

KOTA

He offered to collect more soil for the garden and is off. This time the beach isn't his destination. His nose has coined a better grade…far away from Chicago. Salt Creek Forest Preserve. Kota slips through the trees just before sunset. The sky is bruised lavender. A fitting shade for the winter. The forest hushes around him as he arrives, cloaked in stillness. Here, the earth is old. Untouched. Moss carpets the roots like velvet; the soil beneath it thumps with quiet animation.

The pure soil smells deep and ancient. Wet bark, crushed leaves, rain soaked into roots. A dark, earthy musk. He kneels near a bend in the creek, fingers slicing through the rich black dirt, cool and dense and perfect. He presses his palm into the earth, feeling gentle vibrations. Tranquil frequencies. So delightful. So still. Until it's not.

There's a disturbance…a deeper…harsher…wicked frequency seizes the peace of the earth. Miles away…Greyson booms the air, clashing anarchy with harmony. The one with a nauseating aroma. Ice. Peroxide. Kota immediately hurtles in the direction, without a moment of hesitation. Knowing where his foe is going.

The November sun bleeds violet. The forest vanishes behind him in a blur, his boots scanning over frozen leaves and cold dirt. He cuts across fields, neighborhoods, and rail yards, unseen by the world, a shadow in motion. Kota missiles all the way back to Chicago, in pursuit of Greyson. The hunt is on.

The city is a steel crown. Smoke, frost, and concrete. He weaves through alleyways and rooftops. His legs and arms cutting the air. His eyes grow beady with determination. By the time he reaches the river, the sky is dark, and the lights of downtown act as coronas. The yellow streetlamps haze in a portal.

Just as he enclose the distance to the penthouse, the evil king hauls him hard. Kota is knocked upwards. He tumbles backwards, in reverse, falling upside down. Reaching the murky night sky, breaking through thick clouds, and out. Way out.. to the other side. Out into the stratosphere. Buzzing past the ozone. The outer limits of Earth. Into outer space.

The slow, crystallizing arctic of space rims over his clothes in less than a second. The dimension is hell turned frozen. The absolute darkness of the universe. His lungs block up. There is no air. No pressure. His chest caves inward, desperate to inhale what doesn't exist. The blood vessels burst in his eyes and under his skin. If human, they would leak crimson, but instead his sockets squeeze…ready to pop.

His skin swells, not from heat, but from the vacuum of the cosmos. Kota's body doesn't blow up like a balloon, but the fluids within swell up his skin, a puffer fish. All moisture evaporates from his eyes. The silence is total, deafening. Kota drifts in space…stuck in stationary mode. He glides in black infinity, stiff limbs, skin ashen and puffed. Caught between two worlds.

What drives him to fight is the idea of kissing Kayla. *I can't die yet…not now. Not when I haven't lived for her. Loved her. Owned her as mine.* The image of their lips touching…the chemical reaction that almost consumes him into sunlight. Into an angel. The feeling of resurrection….of human pain and fragility. *I need her…I need to get back…to her.*

The globe of Earth is outlined hazy…far away from him. From his touch. *Save me, my fiend.* He internally speaks to his savage alter ego. *LET'S GO HUNT!!!*

"HUNT…HUNT…HUNT!!!!" It croons.

And then—he moves. Gradually at first. Then promptly. The paused motion of his body regresses, along with the puffy skin and enlarged inner organs. Kota jerks his limbs to crack off the shell of thick ice, crushing it to snow flurries. He's pulled downward, not by gravity but by his own willpower. The stars spin just like a disco ball light pattern. The void blurs to a swirl of stretched gas beams.

"SHE'S MINE!!!" He roars selfishly, directing himself in a soaring position, aiming for Earth. His pupils spike bloodshot. His teeth morph to fangs….his claws span out long… animalistic, all while he skydives down.

KAYLA

Kay jerks awake from her slumber, mounting herself onto her elbows. *It's nothing. I need to sleep.* The radio clock on her nightstand reads 7:33 pm. She lies back down, snuggling into the blanket. The oddest noise fill her ears…the sound barrier is broken…as if a jet ramping up the night sky. *Huh?*

She sits up, going to her window. Her attention is ahead. Kay follows her line of sight, finding the evil one standing on air…between the spaces of neighboring penthouses. Still as a statue, placed on what she thinks is a wire. One like in the circus….but the vampire king is up mid-air, by himself…with no tricks or gimmicks. Standing in the sky. His royal robe made for a true king, gold cursive lace…black velvet gemstones.

The bitter wind sweeps his long blonde hair. The carmine eyes of his has her recoiling and gripping her chest. Greyson latches his creepy eyes on her with devious delight. The upward tug of his mouth blocks her blood from flowing in her veins. Images flash in her mind:

Spellers…chained to the floor like animals. Their hands interlocked together in the restraints. The veins under their eyes are enlarged and bright red. The 13-pointed symbol designs their distorted veins as the benders cry out in unison. "RELEASE US!!! RELEASE US!! SLAY GREYSON MACINTYRE!!"

He strides between the glass towers, sauntering to her with ease…as if sky walking is normal. He comes closer and closer. Slyly stepping to her window. Kay doesn't move…she doesn't think. She's too dumbfounded by how he defies gravity. Even when he's at the glass…right on the other side. The stuff of nightmares; sharp teeth and a seething expression.

Grayson places his palms to the surface of the glass…the window of his bedroom. His long talons scratch the window, which glow with burgundy witchcraft lines under his touch. The glass splinters, cracking lines in all directions; the weight of his summance is a hammer on rock.

Kay's feet sleek forward to the window, ready to combat him. *I can keep him out!!! I just have to do the opposite of what I did to the living room. I have to reverse the breakage.* And that's exactly what she does when the jagged shards push outward, glowing bloodshot. Pointed, blade-esque pieces aimed to slice her up her skin. *I CAN FIGHT THIS! NO WAY I'LL LET THIS THING IN MY HOUSE!* "NARA'TEL ENRUS." She visualizes the reversal of the shards of glass in her head.

This prompts gravity to fracture the shards in on themselves…a weird, spiky artwork. The frozen icicle daggers bend away from her and back his way. Greyson counteracts this, rewinding the deadly daggers back at her. Only his mouth doesn't move. Greyson doesn't have to speak any words to produce magic.

Her eyes blaze over…going all pure….all powerful. A goddess. She rewinds it back at him. Kayla undoes it with no straining….commanding the window to seal itself back up completely. Just how it was before.

The king lowers his hands…accepting the defeat. His demeanor is cautious. Beaten. Bested. Greyson assesses his next move carefully. *If he wasn't so cruel…he'd be somewhere in a model magazine. A foreign flavor of simple…yet striking beauty. A sunken face so peculiar that it's unique, jaws so deep set like a zombie. A suggestive appearance that rewrites traditional attractiveness. A petrifying gorgeousness.* The nonmoving motion he's in right now trumps all of his threatening ways.

Greyson sails in place, outside her window. "I'm not your enemy…Spell Bender 13." He speaks for the first time. A profound note, the last chord of a bass, a sound belonging to blues music…not a person. His accent is Scottish…not too thick to understand…but heavy enough to notice. The rolling tongue, the elongated vowels. The dialect in which he speaks his words…is a homage to the Transatlantic accent of 1950s America. Old world famished….the great depression in the flesh. A time traveler.

Just then, from beyond the clouds, Kota free falls, soaring down to building level, to the high rise. His maroon eyes steaming bright. He cannonballs into Greyson, slamming him into the side of the building. The brick siding is bombed into a cavity, a huge dent in the exterior. The skyscraper shakes in place, going back and forth, bobbing; the metal structure rings.

Kota's teeth snap at his foe's neck. He submerges Grey's wrists deep into the dull brick with all the strength of his inner fiend assisting him. The vampire king angles his neck up, exhaling through his mouth, summoning hellfire airwaves, all from his organs. A living dragon…with breath made of combustion.

The fire expels far out past his mouth, conjuring a hell storm of utter destruction. His goal is to scorch Kota alive, even if it means Chicago has to singe with him. The searing element blackens the sides of not just the penthouse but spans out to torch every building in a three-mile radius.

A live flamethrower from video games amplified to the max. Killing all the trees…boiling the branches on down in a flash, including the last leaf…still clinging Still a message of her life before…and her life now. *NO…NOT…NOT HERE….NOT INNOCENT PEOPLE….NOT MY CITY…MY HOMETOWN!!!*

Kay outs her hands, thinking of water…of the spell from the book. WATER SUMMANCE. **Aqwav coum.**

Kota screeches, smashing Greyson's whole body into the brick high rise, a few feet in depth. He injects both of his hands into Greyson's chest cavity…going for his heart….or his spine. Whichever is closest. This ends the breath of dragon fire from the king.

"AQWAV COUM!"

The water of Lake Michigan uproots, splashing a high tidal wave over 100 feet. The lake is a wet tornado….spilling itself onto the horizon. Spraying rain, so hard that it dents the top of car roofs like hail. Indenting concrete and the rooftops. The city goers run for cover, shrilling in terror. Many shriek from the sidewalks, fleeing into stores to shield themselves. Many cars hit the gas to escape the aggressive liquid; others press the brake pedals, long, and abruptly.

The tropical rain droplets increase in harsh impact when Kay orders the water funnel in the sky to clear away the fire engrossing the city.

Kota has Greyson's heart in his grip. He digs his other hand deeper for the spine….to do what he promised. Rip his spine out….slowly….to torture him. His sharp nails curled, he starts to pull. Individual pillars of red disperse from within Greyson's chest….charging up…powering up.

Kota is blasted away by the beaming pressure…traveling all the way to the lake….hundreds of feet. Rag dolling, skidding. A rock skipping over water, flung miles away. Out of the city…to farmlands and cornfields.

"NO…KOTA!!!"

Greyson gives a fleeting look to Kayla, whose eyes are still heavenly lit, whose hands are still out. She gives a flick of her wrist and bullets the water tornado his way. The funnel sweeps him up. Kay tilts her hands forward, instructing the rotating tidal wave to eat him up…and transport him to the lake, where she sinks him. Drowning him in all of the 925 feet of mini ocean. Trapping him down deep below.

He struggles, swarming, shooting violent rays from his hands. But not for long; her power should be stronger than his…but he counters it. Grey sprouts out from the depths of the lake. A rocket ship of water, straight up, whizzing high above the surface.

Kota wheels in the air, landing on the skyscraper across the street. He's ready to attack again. But Greyson teleports out of existence…pixelating to nothingness. Vanishing to smoke and mirrors. Kota growls…a long, brutish sound. A demonic anthem that rattles her bones. His shady ego has obscured him, making him a void of mercy. Possessed.

The essence of a good heart…of a good being…of a person….is gone. The kindness and humanity he once had…is…absent. His mouth expands to the max, baring canine teeth, shark teeth in the mouth of a kind boy.

He's a demon! A monster….not my…not my Kota. Kayla gulps so hard that her stomach stings…that her knees numb. Even in her powerful form, he terrifies her. Even her heightened pupils fizzle off, heartbroken at what he's become. *That can't be him….that's not him.*

CHAPTER 35: ROUND ONE

KOTA

I hear her cower from me…and it shames me…even from how far away she is. From her window….the trepidation is skin deep. In my bones…in my flesh. His dark eyes seek her out. Kayla slinks to the center of her bedroom, shaking, at how his appearance is way worse than Greyson's.

I'm a friend…a familiar face…and now I'm riddled with a spooky corruption. The doom in her is glaring, so much that he can taste the emotion of her sweat. *Now…she has met the real me…the one I hid from her. The one who killed and drank blood. The one she thought I could never. But…I am…exactly that. Inside…deep down…I am this thing out for blood…only I'm out for Greyson's this time around. Not humans.*

She shakes her head…sniveling at his dark side…the alter ego…the fiend. "Kota…?" The tears in her eyes are his kryptonite.

He shuts off the rage…the murder….the vengeance with a tug of a light switch in his head. *Oh, no…I'm a monster to her.* Kota swiftly but slowly make his way over. Not wanting to go as rapid in pace, *she might retreat to her bed to hide under the covers…and treat me as the monster I am.* He gradually hops building from building, taking a few seconds to move. 1.2.3.4.5. Next. 1.2.3.4.5. Last one. 1.2.3.4.5. Then he's there…at her window.

"Let me in…I can explain." His brows convey a high form of sign language and anguish. "I can explain."

Kayla slinks further away, closing in on her room's door. Never turning away, never taking her eyes off of him…not even when she's out the door. In the hall….bathed in the night's cloak. Even when she is swallowed up by the dark…he still feels her.

Did…did…she just?? Did I just…lose her?? She's gone….forever?? He groans low in despondency….*I don't blame her.* He hears a click from up above. The balcony door…just opened. Kota climbs up the side of the brick wall, to her…his princess in the glass tower. The railings are easy to cover; he's over them quick…but not too quick to have her running off. He drapes one leg after the other across the railing to not scare her more than she is.

Kayla is half hidden in the art studio. It's lightless…but his super vision makes out the shape of her body and the gracefulness of her face. "Explain…."

He tiptoes to the door frame, knowing that a barrier is up blocking him from entering the penthouse. "Please let me in...I can't come in unless I'm invited."

She hugs herself. "Right there is fine..."

"You know I'll never hurt you."

"What was that with your eyes...and mouth...your teeth!" She eyes his lips...where the round, piercing teeth were...just moments ago. "And that noise...you made!"

He shamefully lowers his head. "The price of this curse..."

"You were a....you were a killer!!" She shudders.

"Let me in...Kayla."

"You should go."

"Don't hate me! I didn't want to be like this! I can't control it! Whatever is possessing me-"

"Possessing??"

"Yes..." He faces away from her, viewing the other side of the roof's railing. "I'm not in control of myself...and that's made me do...things I never wanted. I...I..." Kota stammers before admitting his worse deeds. "I...killed before."

She sucks in air, coming to terms with why he was in the lunchroom one minute, then gone. "Is that...why you...disappeared?? Why you left lunch??"

I already said it all...I might as well be specific. "I drank blood before...and killed humans. This voice in my head... it takes over. It makes me kill when I don't want to. My parents saved me from it...and grandad gave me the necklace to stop it."

"And...is it helping?? Is the necklace helping?"

"Yes."

Kay moves up a bit to the balcony door. "But...it took you over."

"I let in. this time...I need it to help me when I'm hunting. The bad side gives me the boost I need to hunt."

Kay stutters, finding it hard to compute words. "But...you...I....I...I thought you said it stopped with the necklace?"

"The thirst...and the sun curse stopped...not the voice. I still have to live with it."

"How many people have you killed?"

The past replays. The sedan parked on the curb. The parents and the two kids. The four vanilla cones. The sloshing river of desire in their veins. The delicious flavor of hemoglobin. Old coins…copper dessert. How he ripped off the side door to slaughter the poor family.

SLICE THEIR NECKS!!

The parents choking on blood. The kids pulling at their door handles. Kota's claws cutting their throats. The gory cones…sweet with death's flavor. He sheds a tear for the family. "4…I killed 4 people." *It's best that I don't say I slaughtered a family. Little kids…and their parents…out to enjoy sweets. Out to see a movie…out bonding…as families should. I stole the night from them.* "And I hated every second of it…"

"Jia was right…I was wrong!"

"I'm not like that anymore." He swirls around to meet her soaked eyes.

Tears slide down her heart-shaped cheeks. "I vouched for you…I had a read on you….and I stood against you being bad. I said you were safe…."

"I am safe…"

"Even with it in your head?? Even with it still living in there??" She points to his head….then drops her index finger to the jewelry wedged to his neck. "If you take it off…"

"Something I'll never do."

"You don't know that."

"I do…"

"What if it comes off?!"

Why is she stuck on this?? It's irking me. How many times do I have to answer?? "You're projecting!" He shouts in annoyance. "You're making this way worse than what it is!"

"Like the school….the hallway!!? I didn't imagine it!" She bites back, getting loud. "I'm not over-exaggerating anything!"

"With this, you are!"

"You just told me you killed 4 people! How can I trust you?!!"

"BECAUSE!!" He yells…then goes silent. *Can I say it? Is it true? Will she laugh…and shoot me down. Or say she'll never love me back…over what I am. Over what I wasn't born to be??*

"Because…what?" *I love you…but you think I'll turn bad, is* what he wants to say. The knowing silence is the key to getting her out of the studio. She steps past the doorframe…walking out onto the balcony. To him. "You can say it…" Her puppy dog eyes loosen him up, her soft voice, light as honey…clear and thrilling.

"It'll ruin our friendship."

"It won't…I care about you too."

"You have a boyfriend…" Every ounce of agony, every syllable of forbidden love, every meaning of temptation marks his voice with longing. Marks his eyes with pain. "I can't have you…"

"We can still share our feelings."

"What's the point of that??" He scoffs. "Sharing and not letting it play out? That's pointless."

"It's not…letting it out helps."

"No acting on it…helps."

"We…we…can't."

I want to…I might as well pour it all out. Waiting for Darius to mess up isn't the key. My dad is out of touch…and wrong…I have to fight for her. Convince her to choose me…pick me. She has to leave her boyfriend. "You don't understand….you brought me back to myself…made me myself again. The sound of you …your halo…your voice." He goes in closer, not shy of ruining the friendship. Not this time. His fingers tenderly strokes her bushy hairline, in a loving side-to-side dance. "Before you… I was nothing. All hope was gone…my life was gone. I didn't feel anything…until you."

Kayla is a deer in headlights. Her eyelids slack, her lashes bat wildly, flustered. She pulls away. "W…w…we can't."

"I need you to know."

"That's enough…" Her legs peddle her back inside; she clamps her hands to her forehead…breathing vigorously. "Don't…"

His fingers twitch at his sides…rendered useless without contact to her skin. Missing their pair…their mate. "You…tricked the curse and made me mortal again. My heart…my lungs….my soul…it all- "

"You're not making any sense!" She goes farther away into the art studio, disappearing into the darkness. "…you need to go…before-"

"Before what?"

"….something…happens…"

So, she knows what I mean? She knows….she knows…yet she is making me go. "Like what?"

"Please…don't do this…don't make me say it!" Kay pleads, elongating the words into more syllables than they have. Fortifying the request with a vigorous tone to shoo him to comply. Wishing him to leave.

Or maybe not…I guess I misread it. I guess this is one sided. So…this is what unrequited love feels like? This is what a fool in love means?

"I'll go…" In a dash, he's at the railing, balanced atop it in a crouch. Too scorned to look int her eyes, so he watches the street below. "Sorry…that I misread it.…my fault. I held you above the cure…that was my fault."

KAYLA

He's gone. My bipolar emotions…my erratic mind…wants him back. *What are you doing to me, Kota? Your signal.…your sound. The buzzing frequency. I can't stop hearing it…even when you're gone. It's faint, but there. A reminder that you're around. I miss it. I miss him. But we can't go down that road. We can't be together. Even with how Darius took off…doesn't mean we're over. He's given me another chance already. Why not again? I do love him.*

I could love them both. Darius makes me flightless…high in the clouds on bliss. I get all the butterflies, and all the intoxication. My first boyfriend. That all seem minimum when Kota is around…I forget I have him.
That night we met. The crowd full of strangers. The way my eyes sought him out. Those ivory eyes. He saw me…and hasn't stopped seeing me since. All my daydreams about his world-shattering beauty…and how his voice would sound when he spoke.

All of my fantasies about loving him…when I was taken already. All the invasive thoughts of kissing him…choosing him. How he burned into my retinas…stained my sight…even when I shut my eyes. I saw him…wanted him…craved him. Kota was.…and still is stamped behind my eyelids; I blink for him…just as he lives for me.

I burned him by sending him away. I needed him to know too…needed to confess too…needed to lay myself on a live wire…even if it blew up on me. Kota did it…I should have too.

"OH, THANK GOD!!!" Gloria yells from the glass staircase. "There was a disturbance…what in the world went on outside??!"

"Oh, you know…the usual overlord out to get me." She tries to use comedy to save face, but the sad sniffles expose her.

Her gran-gran hugs her tight. "Aww, sweet child! I'm sorry…I should've taken you with me to for the crystals! Did he touch you?? Are you hurt??"

"No…" Kay expresses ragged wails, blubbering like a baby.

"Then…what has you so-"

"It's nothing…just drop it." Kayla pulls away, wiping her eyes with her sleeve. "I handled it."

"And the mess outside??"

"I'll repair it…I know the incantation."

"Too many people saw the showdown, drivers, late nighters, planes! Everyone on the ground and in the sky…saw everything! I felt the strength...the cosmic read is off the charts!! This story will be on the news channels within an hour...and on the radio. We have to do better than a reversal charm!"

Oh...okay.....so this isn't an easy fix like I thought. "I don't...I don't know anymore!" She cries. "I just wanna go to bed...I wanna go to bed!"

"Okay...okay..." The jazzy voice of hers is heavy with strain. "I'll work this out, perhaps a time-lapse. It'll be tricky...but the most suitable route. You still have to fill me in on everything." "IN THE MORNING, GRAN!!" Kay is in hysterics, seizuring her body while bawling droplets from her injured eyes.

"What in the world???"

"Why did you say I can love more than one boy?!!"

Gloria is put off...caught off guard. "Umm...are we still talking about Greyson...don't tell me you're-" her granny's mind is all jumbled up. "How close did he get??" She stammers. "His kind can plant traps in your head...and make you see...feel...and believe anything, just to get to you. Including being in love."

"No! Not him! Kota!" She howls. "Greyson didn't get inside. I had it under control...I kept him out of the house."

"Did you cause the fire?"

"Greyson did that, not me...so I used the lake to put it out."

"Oh, no..." Gloria leans against an easel to steady herself. "This is bad...very bad...worse than I thought. Kayla...you did a water summance over a city of millions!" This ticks her off and boils her up all at once. She truly is a fed-up grandma, the wrinkled face of disapproval and all.

"I HAD TO!!"

"I GET THAT BUT YOU NEED TO BE CAREFUL!!"

"Oh, right like you??" Kay claps back just as lively as a hissing kitten. "Don't give me good advice now...after what you lied about."

"The heart is complicated....that's no lie...it isn't trained on one person."

"Mincs was before all of this!" She waves her arms dramatically. "All of this is destroying my life!! I don't want it anymore!" Kay stampedes to the staircase and down, using all her might to trudge her fluffy slippers as a weapon.

She lies on the fuzzy carpet of her room. A bedroom devoid of a light source other than the faint city ambience. "I'm sorry, Kota...I'm sorry, Darius....I'm horrible...evil...selfish." Her creamy voice go up an octave. "I can't have you both…" She wipes away falling droplets. "I can't…"

Sleep never comes; she is dead set on the ceiling for hours. Blinking less than she should….her eyes sleek with desolation. The droplets haven't ceased…each one punctures her eyeballs…dulling them gray.

Her parents aren't in at all; she listens out for them, knowing all hope is gone. *I'm a freak of a daughter…a flaw. That's why they're away. Far away…definitely at one of Mom's properties. That's where I bet they are. How can they sleep in a bedroom with sorcery literature just feet away??? Or be at ease in a house that was totaled by their gifted daughter? Not even the right kind of gifted. If they stay away…in a condo somewhere forever…I understand. I'm a letdown.*

I might as well keep letting them down by never going back to school. I'm swearing it off…all the money they pumped into my education is down the drain. I'm not normal…not their princess anymore…I'm something else. Mom and Dad may not care anymore…all their expectations may be out the window. Even if this isn't true. I'm never going back to school. I'll stand by that, if it takes my dying breath…I'll stand by it.

Time blends as one…in a loop. Night blurs into dawn. In a peculiar way. There's a thick electricity in the air. A voltage that stands the hairs of her arms high. She swears a huge magnet is tugging her skin forward…tugging every hair on her body. She sits up…looking to the nightstand at the clock. 6:34. She counts to 60 seconds. Sensing that the minute won't change without knowing how she's aware of this.

Is this Granny's doing? Or I could just be deprived of rest and am imagining this. But Gran did say something about a time lapse.

Kay is on second 10. She goes on counting as she hoists herself up from the floor and out into the corridor. The door to her parents room is open. But Mary and James are not there. She doesn't smell coffee…or the Chanel perfume she sneaks from her mom. She doesn't smell her dad's Old Spice spray. As she enters, even the bed is made up neatly…not messy from them rushing out. She looks over the barren room.

When will they come back?? I was kidding…I don't want them away forever. I wouldn't be fine with that. I want my mom and dad back.

The 60 seconds are up; she zooms back to her room, reading the clock: 6:34. Still. *The batteries are not dead…Dad replaces them every month….every clock here works as normal. My grandma has done something.*

Up to the balcony she goes…finding her gran citing words

from one of the sorcery volumes. "Velora Tenebrix, (Time, unwind thy thread and weave the lapse)." The words are so majestic and tuneful, her Gran all but breaks out in song. "Velora Tenebrix. Velora Tenebrix. Velora Tenebrix."

Kay goes to the balcony, feeling guilty about last night, how she ended things…how she put all of the drama on her granny…on her legacy. None of that is to blame. *I was being overdramatic…Kota was right…sometimes I do that. Now I need to do better….be better. My gran didn't lie…I just never knew the heart can't be trained. Not until now.*

She takes hold of her granny's hands. "You shouldn't do it by yourself…it's too much."

"You're right…I need you."

"And I need you." She replies sentimentally. "I don't hate being a part of this…I take back everything I said."

"I know…I was a teenager once…we…blow things out of proportion."

"I'm so sorry…"

"No…you're confused…that's normal when in love. It's best you prepare for that ache." She admits morbidly, then cites the words. "Velora Tenebrix."

Kay follows suit…despite her mind soaking up what she just heard. "Velora Tenebrix."

Magnetism ignites the airwaves intensely…not only does the hair on their arms stand, but so does the hair on their heads. Same as a provoked balloon held close. Straight up hair strands, pointing to the sky…like porcupines; every follicle on their body is bone straight.

The watch on her grandma's wrist is still stuck at 6:34…and doesn't move…not the seconds arrow, or the minutes one. Time is still…time is an illusion…time is lost.

KOTA

I should've kissed her…that was my chance too…but she pushed me away. Told me to go…to leave. She also told me we could share our feelings. Feelings…as in plural. Kayla wanted to let it out…yet, was so confused she told me to leave. She does care. Her actions are proof of this. Our first coven meeting…she was captivated with me…she all but slobbered over me…crushed on me. My parents saw it. Their chat from the backyard blossoms:

"How did he look at her?"

"As if she was the only girl in the world…she gave him the look too."

"She did?"

"Sweetie, learn to use your eyes." Mom knew...

Even how impatient she was to walk up to me at school. Waiting for the crowd to thin...to get to me. Counting the seconds...fed up with the wait. The distance was devastating. Her thoughts were so clear...so intolerant. Annoyed...by the students for keeping us apart. Even how she hid that she had a boyfriend from me...saying the topic didn't come up. The truth is, she didn't want it to come up. I made her forget...made her drop him to an afterthought.

Kota walks to school...at a normal pace...no vamping there; he wanders leisurely same as humans do. The distance isn't a problem. He's mind entertains him from the impoverished area. The zip code of the poor....of the unfortunate. The homeless sleep out on cardboard boxes...some on benches....some in tents. The same boarded up church. The stained glass. The multicolored hues portraying artwork of angels. The parking lot is bare...the same broken glass is there.

She wanted to be mine...on the balcony....her mind fought it off...but her words were real. "I care about you too...talk about our feelings." He plays the words through his head on a loop, all the way to school, 23 blocks away. *Did Kay tell her friends about me...isn't that what girls do...chat about boys? I may have been a topic between them. I had to be.*

"It's not pointless...you said so..." He flashbacks to her mini meltdown on the balcony...her hands on her forehead to open her airways...open her lungs. *I made her breathless...that's why she sent me away.*

"...you need to go...before-"

"Before what?"

"....something...happens..."

"Like what?"

"Please...don't make me say it."

The way she begged me...shooed me away...it wasn't rejection...it was too much to deal with. The fake coldness in her voice...wasn't her heart speaking...it was her conscious. The tension in her tone....wishing me away...to keep us from acting on emotions. I should've kissed her....not caressed her beautiful hair....I should've shown her.

At Jones Prep, the morning filing line is abundant. Some many students are here early...20 minutes in advance. A colorful mob of teens. Bold and layered fashion, punk-meets-pop edge. Girls rock off-the-shoulder sweatshirts, miniskirts over leggings, and lace gloves. Chunky belts, oversized bows in their hair. High-top sneakers and ankle boots.

The boys wear graphic tees, parachute pants, Converse Chuck Taylors, customized with random marker art. Bulky, headphones are draped from their necks and cassette-players attached to their bookbags, and jean loops. To his surprise…Darius is at the entrance, chatting with Jia in a hushed voice:

"How is this possible??"

"I don't know…she said something about it being a part of her family." She mutters low.

"But how is it possible???! I saw her use…use…"

"Superpowers…" Jia completes the word he can't say.

"This is fake…I'm dreaming…this isn't real." His denial is stubborn enough to sound true. "This isn't the real world!" Darius drags his hands down his face, rough and lazy.

"I know it's a lot; me and Mya are still…processing it."

He repeats the face rub. "No…witches aren't real…we're dreaming."

"Then when do we wake up??"

"I don't know…soon!"

Jia huffs out low. "You should talk to Kay."

Darius is iffy on this. "I can't right now…'

"Okay…then take your time…she's not here, anyway."

"Where is she?"

Kota goes unnoticed, herding into the pack as stray cattle does. The long line slugs on. Up ahead, there's commotion. "What it klutz!" Vanessa bullies a bumpy faced freshman boy.

"There's no room…what do you expect me to do?!!" The boy stands his ground.

"Yes, there is…over there with the scrubs." She demeans him with privileged class.

"No…"

"Yes…you don't have a date for a reason! Skuzzball. Bag your face…that should work."

"Neither do you…the new boy told you to kick rocks."

There's an uproar of insults from her pink minions. The mindless robots who only exist to restore her ego. The three even dress like their leader, feathery tops, puff ball earrings, bags…all plastic and pink.

"As if? The queen has a date…."

"Yeah, and 5 are from the football team."

"And Francis Parker High…our arch nemesis."

Vanessa tosses back her blonde hair, pleased by their praising of her. "Exactly…so…watch where you're going!"

The horde of teens slinks ahead….but not quick enough. The argument caught Jia's attention….but not Darius's. His is on

Kota. The deep wrath in him overshadows the superstitious grudge he was just battling. "YOU!!"

The pack of students shush their side chats...now panning their heads in Darius's direction. Some are ready for good drama...others are scaredy cats and move out of the way. All eyes are on them.

I don't have time for this...he better back off. I'm in no mood to be nice. He needs to back off.

'I told you to stay out of my way!"

"...last time I checked, I go here. You don't...so you're in my way." Kota voice seethes with fierce ire.

"I'm this close to knocking you out!"

"For what...?"

"You know what!"

The students near Kota divide, same as swarms of bees do in formation. "I don't...you need to chill."

"Trying to steal my girl...but you lost."

BREAK HIS NECK...BREAK HIS NECK...PROBLEM SOLVED!!! His violent ego suggests.

"Be quiet!" he tells it off aloud.

"You first!!"

"I said we're just friends!"

"And that's a bogus comeback!" Darius is amped up on testosterone. "Accept it, loser...she loves me, not you."

"Look...I'm trying to be respectful.'

"Screw that...you trying to rub one out on my girl. Take a hint, she's not into you!"

Alright...I'm done....done being a saint!! "She confessed to me last night...and wanted to talk about our feelings. So, who really lost here?" He struts with a smirk.

That's it...that's all it takes to have him swinging. The motion is slow tempo; Kota swerves his head to the side with ease. Darius keeps throwing. Lick...diverted. Upper cut. Missed. Blow to the gut. No contact. Elbow to the groin...pointless. None of them make contact. Kota matrix maneuvers, showing off his skills...his abilities. His all-knowing reflexes.

"Stay still you, PUNK!!"

Kota simpers, still dodging each fist and elbow with slyness. "Speed up, you square."

"WHAT IS THE ISSUE HERE!!!" Mr. Hamilton howls from the steps. 'BREAK IT UP!! NOW...BACK OFF!" He plants himself between the boys and shove them apart with both hands. "What is the deal here?!"

"Nothing…I'm on my way to breakfast, sir."

Mr. Hamilton sizes up Darius. "Well…what about you?"

"Nothing…" he repeats what Kota just said.

"Well…it's something, so start explaining why you're fighting." The two boys are mute…the bald man scrutinizes them both. "Alright…to my office…since you both are lying."

I'm ratting him out….Darius doesn't even go here. He's not a student of Jones Prep. "He doesn't even go here, Mr. Hamilton…"

"You don't?" Darius eyes throw daggers at Kota while he walks off down the sidewalk. *Good riddance….to him. I'm not a pushover, like he thinks.* "I still need answers." Mr. Hamilton rests his hands on his hips, the lime dress shirt of his tucked in his belt.

"He picked a fight with me over his girlfriend."

"Which is whom?"

"Kayla Harris."

The principal is indifferent. "That doesn't sound like my valedictorian. This is too…low for her to cause." He assures himself more than anyone else. "I'll make a call…there has to be something going on at home."

Oh, there's a lot going on at home…if only he knew. Her folks know what their daughter is now….and must he losing it. Their reality has flipped upside down. Kayla is…overwhelmed. That's why she's not here today. The reveal to her family…my confession…the boyfriend drama…the showdown with Greyson. There's a lot going on.

KAYLA

Wednesday. This is day 2 of me cutting school…and not for cool points. Not that I would ever be that shallow. I'm dropping out for a better cause. I'll bring death to everyone there. Kay paints on a canvas…glad to be with an old friend. Her passion. Her drive. Her calling. The blank slate board is her first true companion. The pencil…her first session of therapy. Everything her parents were supposed to be… represented by inanimate objects.

For the first time in weeks, she outlines the silhouette of a ballerina…shoes….tutu,…leotard. Relevé in fifth position, legs crossed, heels high, arms in a V shape. Fingertips reaching upward like wings drawn from the chest. Shoulders relaxed, spine elongated, power and poise.

From downstairs, she hears her granny on the phone. "Hello, this is Gloria Cooke for Mary Harris. I need to speak with my daughter."

She's calling into Mom's office. I support her for doing this choice. I do miss Mom and Dad. It's been 3 days…Sunday was the last time I saw them. Monday morning is when they snuck out for good without me knowing. I'm not what they want….but I'm what they have.

"I can't believe this! What is the matter with you two?? The both of you took off, the same as teens under pressure. Your own daughter didn't drop all responsibility like this!!" Gloria exhales like a bull in a mean lecture. "Who's the adult here, again??" She waits for an answer, stepping in the kitchen, covering the girth to the windows on back to the phone set. "So come back…I expected you not to know what to do…but this is poor parenting!"

Geez…she's really letting Mom have it. Kay sets down the pencil, and flanks to the staircase ever so softly. *I need to stay quiet before I'm her next outlet. She doesn't know I skipped school. Gran drove me there…and I came back home. I beat her here…morning traffic is always jammed…and school is only a few blocks away. I hide up here until hours are over…then I go back to school and act as if I just left classes. I don't step a foot inside…I stand right by the curb until granny shows up.*

"No, this is childish!! I didn't raise you to buckle and runaway when life gets tough!! Stand your ground! Your daughter needs you! It's been 3 days! Come home." She allows her daughter to speak from the other end…very briefly before she interrupts. "Oh, yes, I am…James is gonna hear it too. His number is in the book; I'm calling him next! Get your behind back here right now!! You're not too old to be discipline, little girl!"

Kay covers her mouth to hold in a laugh. "Wow…"

"This is not how parenthood goes. My mother didn't pack up and leave when I triggered the gene. I was younger than Kayla. 8 years old…and my mother stayed by my side." Mary has only a few seconds to speak before Gloria lets loose on her again. Chiding her. Penalizing her. "You've always known, don't be an idiot! You knew the truth of the Cooke family since you were little! Stop the excuses because they're weighing thin! Correct yourself now! Or so help me, I will come up there and give you worse than a whooping! How can you be so WEAK!!"

"Get her, Granny…" Kayla chortles silently.

"I AM NOT KIDDING AROUND!!!" She snatches up her car keys from the counter and walks over to the elevator. "You have one more time to tell me no. I dare you…" The calm scariness of her voice is tenfold. "Then get your behind back here, or I will do exactly that…embarrass you in front of your boss." *Holy crap! Is she really going up there???*

"I will count to 3…if you say no one more time, I'm taking this address book and driving your way. Be an adult…this is ridiculous of you!"

Mom must have bowed down…..she has to say yes. Gran is going back to the kitchen. That's good news…..very good. I do feel like a chore…an unwanted child…a shunned daughter. All because of our family curse.

"Think about how this disappearing act has her feeling…you may as well have given her up for adoption. Think before you act…you hurt your little girl. By the grace of the spirit, I will make you fix it!" Gloria slams the phone to the receiver. "UNBELIEVABLE!"

Kay hears her unhook the phone and punch in digits. *Uh oh…dad is next. Darn it…the other receiver is in their room…I can't hear anything from the other line. I need to hear what my parents are saying. From what I made out from Mom's call is that she said no…and that she doesn't know what to do. Everything else is missing context. What else did Mom say about me???*

"Hello, this is Gloria Cooke for James Harris. I need to speak with my son-in-law."

Oh, this is gonna be good. In her eagerness, she moves closer to the stair railing, only to lose her footing. Her body flings in a clumsy slip. She catches the stair railing to save herself. But the thudding of her feet heaving the floor to stop her from tumbling? That's what gets her heard.

"What in the world…?"

Kay looks for somewhere to take cover…even though there's no use. She was loud as an elephant…a circus elephant….all she needed was the trumpet. *There's nowhere to go. Just paintings and easels. The artwork can't conceal my whole body….ballerinas are petite but not miniature.* "Crap…why didn't I look for a shrinking charm…I need to shrink!" She yells at herself in a meek volume.

"Kayla, is that you???" Her gran-gran strikes up the stairs. "I swear if it is…you're in a heap of trouble!"

The balcony??? Maybe….? She jets to it…opening the door, going to the tall sofa…to scope it out. "No…she'll see me under there. *I'll be seen behind the high furniture. I…I'm caught. The jig is up. It lasted long…I fooled her for days. I had a good plan….I just spoiled it.*

Her apologetic eyes hold on the stairs as her grandma makes it up in a severe mood. Set on punishing her just as she just done Mary. "Explain yourself, young lady, before I put my shoe to your backside!"

Kay does exactly that...breaking down the encounter from school. The river of blood, the leaking lockers, and how it proved her sighting of dead students and teachers. "I told you about it...in the car. You said fear made me see it. But Greyson was actually there."

"The mind tie is undone...we disconnected him from you." Gloria is less peeved now...and more so bamboozled.

"I don't think so... he was there...glitching in and out. Coming for me! That means the death I saw was real! He's killed people my age before...why wouldn't he do it again??? He will do it again at Jones Prep!"

"This doesn't mean you can miss school."

"SERIOUSLY??!" She puts out an exasperated moan. "That's exactly what it means...I tried to go back...I listened to your advice."

"I'm calling a meeting for today...we need to try another way to cut him out of your mind." She strokes below her chin. "Elu may have a clue on this...hiccup."

"Okay..."

"I'm telling your parents about this...you're not getting off free."

Kayla smashes her mouth into a fine line. "Alright..." she pouts with a frown. "I didn't do it on purpose."

"I know....still...this is bad...never do this again. School is important."

"I know...it lays out my future...and gives me a fighting chance...I heard the lecture before."

"Well, you're hearing it again...your education is important...and a luxury...one I couldn't have. But I was hell bent on your mother having that privilege over me."

Wait...she couldn't go to school as a kid??? How come? That's something everyone has in their childhood. "Was it the...cost of the school...or something??"

She titters coarsely. "No...I didn't attend school for safety of my classmates. I couldn't mingle with kids my age because of magic. My powers were...tied to my emotions. I lashed out in...evil ways...because of it."

Evil...what does she mean by evil...?

CHAPTER 36: ROUND TWO

KOTA

"Pop up meeting at 5, baby bro." Dyani opens his bedroom door. Her brother is laid like a plank on the bed…his eyes hooded. "Oops…sorry…keep sleeping."

"I'm not…" he speaks sorrowfully.

"It looks like it." She comes in to sit on the side of him and pokes at his nose.

"Stop it."

"What's your deal??"

"Nothing…"

"You're moping."

"I'm not!" She nudges his nose again to get him all revved up. "Gadóuli igaehi! Ukatv!, (Stop it right now! Back off!)."

"Gagohi ugesgiga digalvquogisdi?, (who peed in your cornflakes?)"

"I don't even eat food…"

"Someone has you all in your moody phase."

"Hi-a Ukatv!, (get away!)"

"Yigiga, (make me.)"

"Screw off, Dy!"

"Oh, my!" She laughs. "Such naughty language…" Kota glares her down when a mean mug. "This is definitely about Kayla…you never act like this."

"Just leave…"

"What did you two lovebirds get in a fight about??"

"We're not lovebirds."

"If you say so." Dyani hops from the bed. "You have 30 minutes until they're here."

"I can listen from here just fine."

Dyani eyes pop wide. "Oh, yeah…you two had your first fight…aww…so cute."

"I'm getting a lock for this door."

"And I'll get a key…or have Mom un-cast it open." She blows raspberries at him on her way out.

UGH…WHY DO I HAVE A SISTER??!! He blankets his lids over his eyes again. *I wish I could sleep…or hibernate like Gloria did. It must be nice to fast-forward the day. A real-life VHS tape player….only for unwanted encounters….not movies.*

His mom is cooking Three Sisters Casserole, an earthy dish. Roasted squash, sweet corn, and savory, simmered beans. Garlic, onion, and sage. So woodsy. He knows this dinner well, the golden top, bubbling gently at the corners, the crust crisped with toasted cornmeal. The creamy softness of squash melts on the tongue; the corn pops. The taste of home….right here in the city.

His ears make out the rest of them situating the table for dinner. Plates…bowls…silverware. Glasses for Sassafras Tea. Real roots from the small tree Odina planted out back. Lightly spiced, naturally sweet with a hint of licorice added in.

Mmm hmm…it's calling to me…I wish I could go down and have a glass. My dead tastebuds won't steer me from the scent…I'll taste the flavor through my nose. He sits up, throwing his feet to the side to touch the wood floor. *I wanna go down…but we left off so…bad. What do we even say? Hi? What's up? Sorry for breaking your heart? Sorry for over-stepping? Sory for pushing our feelings away??*

5 pm arrives, and he's still sitting on the edge of his bed, stuck between the want of going down and joining his family for dinner. To share a piece of Tahlequah with them…and reminisce the simple days of normal living. Normal problems. Just to be normal even for a little bit.

"Where is your brother?" His mom queries.

"He's not coming down…him and Kayla had a fight."

"They did??"

"Yes…it's obvious…he's all wimpy."

"Don't call your brother that, Dyani!" "What was it about?" Their father wonders.

"I don't know…"

"It's not serious…just some teenage angst." Mato minimizes the impact as if he knows the root cause.

The doorbell rings, and the slow-motion feet of Elu head over to the door to greet the guests.

KAYLA

The food smells so. Yummy. I can't wait to dig in. I'm not against eating my feelings away. I'll focus on that…and not Kota. He'll be at the table…possibly mad at me. I can't imagine him treating me bad…or ignoring me. But then again…I had that same belief with Darius. That was a wake-up call. Boys can be nasty…when they're wounded. He won't look my way. I won't look his way. I'll ogle my food…and keep my head down.

Elu slides open the door and smiles adorably. "Welcome back, dear friends."

"Thank you…old friend." Gloria smiles back. "Hi, Mr.…Mr.…Sr. Ahoka??" Kay scuffles with how to properly address him.

"Call me Elu…formalities are not needed. We are good as family. Come in, dinner is ready. Let's discuss the dilemma."

"Yes…"

The two are escorted to the table by Elu, who points out seats at the end. Kay goes to one, and prepares to sit, but her gran holds her by the arm. "Wait…Elu has to sit first…then myself."

"Huh?"

"It's tradition."

"None of that, sit, everyone, sit." Elu waves his hand to dismiss this custom of respect. "We have a flaw to smooth out." Everyone does as he says, sitting.

"The food needs to cool…we can talk it over while we wait." Odina grants Gloria the spotlight.

"Thank you…Odina." She looks over the table at everyone…aware that someone is missing. "Where is Kota."

"He's sitting this one out." Mato replies.

Gloria peers at Kayla. "What exactly happened?" "Nothing…." Kay's view is set on the plate and bowl before her.

"Whatever it is, they're acting weird." Dy starts. "He doesn't want to come out of his room…the emo king." "Dyani…enough!" Her mom snaps.

"Just teen hardships…nothing we all haven't experienced. Let's move on." Mato gives the spotlight back to Gloria with a slight hand beckon.

"I would have liked him to hear this."

"He can hear just fine." Mato reminds her.

"Oh…right." Granny recalls his vampire abilities. "Very well…I'll continue. Before we begin with the crystals." She pats the satchel around her shoulder, full of the hard, long, spears of clear gems. "We need to discuss the school sighting." "School sighting??" Mato is lost.

"And the downtown ordeal." Kay adds, her attention still on the dining set pieces.

"What downtown ordeal?" Odina is muddled as well. Elu gives a grave expression. "The war of fire and water…the one wiped away by the time-lapse spell."

"Time-lapse?" Dy joins the train of misunderstanding. Elu breaks it down further. "As in time rewriting…time travel …of the present into the past."

"I had to…the fight was too…public…too many saw it. There was too much damage." Gloria beats Mato to the next question. "Greyson came to Kayla again…while she was at home. The war Elu is talking about is the one he started with Kayla. He forged fire…"

"From his mouth…" Kay cuts in, her eyes are up, but her head still points at the table in self-consciousness. "Like a dragon…he almost burned down the whole city. So, I…did a water summance…using the lake."

"The lake??" Dyani is stunned.

"I had nothing else to call on…I had to…"

"Damn, that's badass!"

"Yes…it is…" Her granny tweaks her mouth to the side. "That's why we needed to rewind time…reset the present. Good thing it was only for one night."

"I helped her…so she didn't tire herself out." Kay adds.

"Which made it far easier on me….so much easier that we can memory walk with the crystals. I'm charged up enough for the journey."

"And the second unlink." Kay reminds her Gran.

"Oh, yes…our ritual didn't work, Elu…Greyson can still invade her thoughts and fool her senses. He did so at her school a few days ago."

"No…that was real."

"We're not sure of that."

"I know what my eyes saw! I felt him there…I had to run! He locked me in this…type of…limbo…I couldn't move until I broke the ground to get free. It wasn't in my mind."

"If you had broken the ground, the cosmic reading would be offset. I know when catastrophic extremes are taken, so does Elu. The downtown incident was real…but the school incident wasn't real! I sensed no signals from the spirit world."

"You said he glitches from dimension to dimension, right?? I get that there was no proof of my school being rocked in…but that's the only explanation I can think of!"

"Listen to the child…" Elu mellows the mood before it heightens to a bigger argument. "We were wrong once, Gloria. And may be wrong many more times to come in the future. It seems Greyson was there in a sense…not physically, but interdimensionally."

"No...there would still be a mark...there's nothing. The school meta realm is intact. Kayla is mistaken by his trickery. That's all...we both know very well that reality can be bent by his compulsion."

I'm so done with her....she doesn't know everything. Even Elu said they could be wrong about it. I can be right. Why can't she be more like him?? Open minded. She's so skeptical and unmoving. Like a brick wall. Why can't she believe me??!!! Kay slumps back in her chair, with much attitude. "It wasn't fake..."

"Then where is the proof....not in this realm...but on the other side. The astro reports all terrain damages. This was in your head!"

Mato, Odina, and Dyani have no input...since they never been inside...or even faced any realm...other than Earth. Odina shares a glance with her husband and daughter, then looks to Kay. "I'm sorry...we can't take sides on this...this is beyond our knowledge."

Elu nods. "This may be beyond all of our knowledge." "The rules don't change, Elu." Gloria drills on. "Solid proof is our answer...and there is none when concerning the school."

"Fine...whatever." Kay moodily blows off the topic. "Can we just...go on to the next thing."

"Can we re-examine the ritual...Elu. We need to learn mend this issue of the mind link."

"Yes, we can attempt to do so after the ceremony. Until then, we need to eat."

The cooled off serving bowls are passed around, beginning with Odina. Then, one by one, around the table. The casserole, then a side of wild greens, and hot skillet bread. Each handoff is gentle, friendly. Kayla scoops carefully, feeling the weakened heat on the serving spoon, adding small portions of each dish to her plate and bowl.

The Sassafras tea is in a pretty teapot, which is also passed around and poured into each glass. Soft, spiced sweetness. *The goodness of the food is the only reason my mood is building towards the better. The appetizing taste keeps me mute.....keeps me from going at my granny again. She can be a bully sometimes. Even with mom...I found it funny...until now. I found it loveable...until now. She doesn't meet you in the middle...she drags you to it...moving her post up to be the smart one. I never thought I would hate my grandma.*

Kay turns her mind off, diving into dinner as her peace of mind from all of it. The food is her comfort. The corn hits like sunshine. The squash, rich and milky, on the tongue like butter. The herbal beans settle it all. Heavy in the best way...filling her gut.

The tea is divine…a liquid anti-stressor. All the combativeness from the spat with her granny vapor away with the steam from the glass. To her, the taste is holier than a baptizing, especially the licorice.

After dinner, Gloria and Elu draw a circle on the living room floor. Dyani sprinkles herbs atop the white chalk as they finish the lines. Mato and Odina, who unload the crystals from the satchel, place the 13 shiny gems in the same pattern of the star symbol.

Okay…this is it. I'm returning to the throne room to identify a sigil. Although…I don't recall one there. Just the chair…the crown….the evil army of demons. There was nothing else there. Or was there…? It's time to find out. It's time to place Greyson to one of the 5 empires. Elu mentioned that there are 5 that date back past the B.C. era. That there is one that's higher than the rest.

One from the creation of earth and nature…from the beginning of time. Before humans. Can the vampire king belong to the worst of the worst? Or am I making him more of a boogeyman than he really is? No way he can belong to the first vampire kingdom…the first immortals. No way…it can't be. That would be insane…and too…unbeatable. Not that this king isn't already unbeatable….but if this is true…then, there's no winning.

The crystals spark long and bright. There's an opening in the oval in the middle…perfect for someone to stand. "It's time…" Gloria points her to the spot. "Stand there." Kay does so, wanting to be obedient…so she can get answers.

As soon as she's inside. They all cite a song of sorcery. "Liora Venemar Udalvlev Udatlisdodi." The two different languages distort as one. This time, they aren't said separately…everyone chants both of the words…both tongues. Cherokee and Ethiopian. All of them speak the same message. **MEMORY MANIFEST.** "Liora Venemar Udalvlev Udatlisdodi."

The crystals are transparent….so inviting. Kayla is entrapped by the celestial aura. Burning clear hotness. The steam spread in all of her veins, all over her body. The overwhelming aura takes her back. Only she is still conscious…she doesn't view her memories like before….like all the other times. No…not at all. Each gem extracts from her brain…a projector on a screen…imaging brainwave video to each crystal, each spear combines the throne room as one picture, despite being disconnected from one another.

Candlelight flickers gold on black stone. The fortress. The kingdom beneath the earth. The castle. Black stone towers spiral upward to the ceiling, beyond shadow.

I'm back here…but…there is no…army…no Greyson. No sign of anyone else but me.. The Columns of obsidian line the grand hall. A throne, jagged…full of earthy roots the color of space. But only that. Nothing else. Not like before. This manifest took away from the memory…so it's just me. So that I can channel all my attention on the sigil.

She looks behind the throne…hoping it's there…it's not. Where do kings hang their sigils?? Kay browses the walls of the hall; only black stone is there. The walls are bare. I don't think he has a sigil. Her legs move forward…out of the throne room…to new territory. To an atrium of endless columns.

The void space goes on forever in this limitless foyer of infinity…of no end. So much that darkness eats at the shadows. The dark side of space. The gold candles wrap fully around the columns…providing some light…but not enough to view far. I don't know where to go…it has to be here, somewhere. In this vicinity…although the walls are empty. The whole throne room is empty…just like the first time. Where do I go?

UGH!!! I need help. Someone should've come with me…I don't know what I'm doing here. She tosses her head back in anxiety. Do I go back into the hall? That is where I was sent the first time…my magic sent me in there for a reason. The sigil has to be in the throne room. I'm going back in.

That's when she spots it…the clue…the task of the mission. The sigil. Not back in the hall…but tacked above the colossal archway leading in. Not inside at all. I found it…it's there…above the arch. Shaded…visible by the glaring candles. Somewhat hazy…but comprehendible. On a texture that's not of cloth…not of cotton…but on parchment. Old parchment. The kind from Old Testament times. Biblical artwork, even the borders of the sigil, dusty gold, faded, worn out.. A relic.

Thirteen fiery tree roots—no trunk, only the underside. Each root springs far below the surface. Above the odd piece of nature, there are no leaves on the tree roots. Just bare branches forming to a monstrous, clawed hand. Sharp talons.

Elu's voice sounds from beyond the vision. "The Skaith Empire…the first kingdom…oh, dear…"

Kayla can't look away from the crystal to see his face…she's locked in…and only meant to view ahead of her, not the rest of the room. The first empire….meaning the one that predates human life. It's just as I thought…unbeatable…there's no winning.

"BRING HER BACK…THIS INSTANT!!" Elu warns in haste. "Liora Venemar Udalvlev Udatlisdodi." They all quote the magical song.

Her eyes are not hers…suddenly her view is teleported past to the columns in the golden tinted foyer…past the cutoff point of no return…until she is in the void beyond the shadows. To the unseen. To the other side of the Skaith

Empire, hidden in the depths. There, in the darkness…there is a silver ripple. A pond of angelic waves.

"WHERE IS IT TAKING HER??? THE SPIRIT IS TAKING HER!! BRING HER BACK!!" Gloria is distressed…this wasn't a part of the plan. "HURRY. "LIORA VENEMAR UDALVLEV UDATLISDODI."

"LIORA VENEMAR UDALVLEV UDATLISDODI." Odina, Mato, and Elu chant desperately.

The teleportation places her at the pond, right above it…where there is no reflection…the water isn't water….it's a solid liquid. The consistency of clay…but it's animated so falsely.

"LIORA VENEMAR UDALVLEV UDATLISDODI." Their voices break through to the realm she's in.

In the strange pond, devoid of shallow transparency, are memories. Not from her mind…not from anyone's mind. This is a manifestation of the earth's memory. The surface displays a vision…a video…from ancient times. Before humans.

"Liora Venemar Udalvlev Udatlisdodi." The quoting fades away.

The birth of Earth…the terraforming of the bubbling lava planet to the green blades of grass. To flowers that nature births. To tall trees in plain fields. There is no human innovation…no roads…no houses…no pavements…no cars…no cities. Nothing but the garden of heaven…the garden of Adam and Eve. Only the red tree from the sigil is off by itself…away from the others. Isolated. An outcast…a misfit…a defect.

None of the others are red…and leafless…none are rugged with age as this one. All the rest are young…smooth…ageless…untouched by deep lines and large holes. But this one is scarred…battled worn…already dying at birth.

The claws, same as on the sigil, punch out from the ground. The taloned hands of monsters tear through the virgin land of God…assassinating the roots of flowers…assassinating the blades of grass from the sockets. Until multiple divots, the size of human anthills, are the only version of the land. The beasts aren't vampires…or an army. These are 13 giants…with skin of red stone, scaly…serpent like in texture. Some are wounded…stabbed…battle bruised. There are deep gashes belonging to swords in their flesh…deep wounds that bleed silver…same as the pond Kayla is looking into. Silver blood.

I don't understand…why am I being shown this?? I'm lost. I don't know what this is…or what it means!

The visual time jumps from B.C. to the 1700s…to a vampire standing exactly where she is. A weeping woman in a lace dress, her ballroom gown all drenched in blood. The old timey pale blue is devoured by gore. The yellow haired lady in the cupcake gown weeps drastically. Her eyes are red…she's a vampire. Long, clawed nails…pointed, canine fangs. Her feet are full of bloody lines…as they plunge, one by one…into the silver liquid. The cursed woman sinks into the pond; as she lowers, there is a sudden enormous blast. Rumbling…booming…quaking.

The silver liquid bonds to her skin like goo; her feet…arms…chest…face. Maneuvering with intelligence…with purpose. And that purpose is to strip the lady of the horrid curse. To revert the demonic appearance and hardship. To reverse the scarlet eyes…the jagged teeth…the monster claws….the thirst…the deadly hunt of survival.

To cure all of the devils of earth just as the woman who is gifted back her blue eyes…human eyes…teeth…hands…and sun kissed skin. All normalcy is returned…by the pond…by the holy grail in water form. The answer to correct all of the damned souls on earth…is within The Skaith Empire.

CHAPTER 37: NEUTRALIZE

KOTA

He's out of bed in a heartbeat. He was trying to kill the urge to run to her…but her clamping teeth…and erratic hands are concerning him. *Is she seizuring? Is she that frightened? Will she pass out? Fall to the floor? Will her heart go out???* *It seems so*…He swallows his pride and puts his moping off to the side.

"FIREFLY!" Gloria starts.

"Is she okay??!!" Dy is trying to stabilize Kay, who may just be having a real-life body spasm.

"She saw him…I told her she wouldn't…I didn't know, sweetie! Please relax. "I'm here!"

Kayla sobs, her eyes tightened so rigid that it hurts. "YOU SAID NO MIND LINKING!!"

"I know…I know…I'm sorry that you saw-"

"I didn't want to see him…" "I'm

so sorry…" Gloria hugs her.

Dyani slowly releases Kayla from her hold. "What is the Skaith Empire??"

Kota is down the stairs in an instant and in the archway of the living room. No one notices him…that's how fast he is. He enters the room very slowly to not panic Kayla more than she already is.

Elu is fatigued but manages to speak. "The war has begun…"

"War has begun…?" Mato echoes his father. "What war??"

"This is as I feared…Greyson Macintyre is a direct descendant of the Elders. The first of everything…and the last of nothing. The end of humanity as we know it."

"Wait…" Kay succeeds to mumble, despite her nerves being all over the place. "I thought…Gran said…but…" She fumbles. "I thought Spell benders were one with the first immortals?"

"We are…but only one bloodline descends from the Celestians. We are one with the elements and senses, not one with the giants of old."

"The what?" Dy asks.

"The giants of old…the birthers of vampire life."

Kota sees Kay's eyes spark. "I saw them…they come from a tree…but not a normal one. It looked…all wrong."

"Yes...that is the sigil of the Celestians." Elu states gravely.

"But what do these giants have to do with the cure? "And why does Greyson have it...in a pond? In his kingdom??"

Cure? Pond? What?? Did she just say that my foe has the answer I want in his possession?? Why? Why does he have that?? Why is my salvation in Greyson's kingdom??!!

It becomes known that Kota is at the archway. Kayla spies him first. Her sappy eyes tug him in...she looks through him...not in a bad way. In the best way possible. Seeing to his core....seeing him. But at the same time, he knows about the dugout in Zonnebeke and is torn between two paths.

I have to make a choice. Do I choose love....or the cure? Do I head there and seek it out? That way I can come back and be normal again. Be magical again, as I'm supposed to be. Or do I stay with her? Protect her? I'm split between being her savior...and saving myself. Heading to Belgium right this second is a choice I have. Do I choose duty over love...?

He rips his eyes from Kay and says. "I know where the dugout is...you all kept Zonnebeke from me on purpose. That was a mistake." Kota beady eyes glare at his mom and dad. "I'm going, and there's nothing any of you can do to stop me."

"No! Don't go there! Not by yourself...there's an army. You'll die!" Kay is strict with him regardless of her wobbly knees.

"Son...you can't do this alone."

"I wouldn't have to if we worked as a team!" He growls at his father.

"I promise to start...we all promise to do better. We have to work as one now...to save you from this life."

Should I believe my father?? Or is this a trick? Will he spell me to my room?? Take away my voice? Punish me again? I need to do this on my own...by myself. For myself. Away from everyone, Even Kayla...she made it clear that she doesn't want me. I'm the one still holding onto lost hope....to a lost cause. She has a boyfriend. I'm not hers...and never will be. So why do I need to stay here?? I have to go....

"No..." He calls on the inner devil...pitch-colored eyes and cutthroat canines. Kota expects to go through all of the motions of his other half...the predatory rage...the blindness...the danger. And is ready to feel it all...that is...until Kayla's hand is on his forearm. He doesn't recall her walking over to him...doesn't recall if she ran...or walked to him. He was too preoccupied with leveling up his wrath.

The triboelectric effect activates. His skin splits whiteness in searing bolts. The hue crackles through his entire body, dazzling.

Only this is the lightest it's ever been…this is angelic halos in real life. The room is nearly engulfed out of existence. The Great Spirit unites with Kota. The silhouette of the afterlife. Smoke and stars of everlasting. Divinity. And just like a switch…the dark pupils of his drain away…the voice never comes to rile him up. It's quiet….dead quiet in his head.

All of the rage is gone…all of the pervious thoughts of being a loner and going off by himself. Are gone. He hears himself gasp for air…as if drowning…and feels his shoulders slump forward. All while his body is shooting rays of sizzling lines just like a disco ball with a million holes in it.

"KAYLA!!" Gloria yelps. "WHAT ARE YOU DOING??!"

"I'm calming him down…he can't go there alone!"

"RELEASE HIM THIS INSTANT…YOU'LL KILL HIM!!"

"I won't!" Her stubbornness is solid even as his ears muffle with high ringing; he hears her. "I know what I'm doing." That's the last thing Kota hears. He passes out.

KAYLA

EASE THE DEMON! The thought comes rapidly to her mind. Kay is fast…and doesn't want him to hit the floor, even though his pain tolerance is high. She outs her hands to create an invisible sort of hover board that he plops onto with as stiff as a falling plank. The pillars of bright ambiance power down…fading. Everyone's eye…everyone's attention is on her.

"WHAT DID YOU JUST DO TO MY BROTHER?!!" Dyani jets to her little brother to hug her arms around him.

"He's fine…I promise I asked the spirits to ease him." "I didn't see you call on the spirits??" Her Gran replies.

"I did…" Kay disputes.

"You didn't…you said nothing, you just did it!"

Kay goes mute. *Wait…did I? I thought I did…right? I swear I spoke. Or did I think the words ease the demon?? I swore I said it aloud.* Kay look to Odina and Mato, who she hopes will back me up on this…and make her not seem crazy. But they are too caught between their son; who she turned into a floating body.

"Am I wrong??" Granny asks. "She didn't cast…right? "Elu?" Gloria looks to him.

"I do not...recall her performing any enchantments." His sight is still on his grandson, locked in a tangled stare. "I am more worried about the inner glow from within his body. It appears to be painful."

Mato joins Dyani at his son's side. "He's breathing...that's the important part."

"I swear I didn't hurt him...I made sure to tell myself not to. I think it did hurt him the first two times...but I got better at it. I promise."

"He was going to blow up...Kayla!!" Dy yells at me. "If you held on longer...he would have blown up and died!"

"No...I promise...I...I..." She goes silent. *What if they're right?? Maybe I thought I could safely deter Kota from going off all alone. Maybe I was about to kill him? Am I wrong for saving him from a war with an army?? He's outnumbered. I had to do something to stop him.* "I couldn't let him go to Zonnebeke by himself; he won't be safe! I'm sorry."

Odina shakes her head. "I understand...we understand...you did the right thing."

"She did....Dyani...now apologize right now."

"But Dad...she-"

"Enough!"

"He's not waking up!!"

"DYANI! ENOUGH!!"

Elu scuffles forward, barely raising his feet in his house slippers. His steps have weight...from exhaustion. "This is nothing but a simple stupefying incantation. Nothing too severe. All is alright; Kota will wake in a few hours. As for the source working in his veins...we must de-code it-"

"We need to decode how she casted without speaking."

"The spirits answered her thoughts...dear Gloria." He speaks politely. "Yes...this is beyond her training...but she had assistance with this spell."

"Without tapping into the realm?? That's impossible!"

"Not impossible...but yes...it is rare...let us just suffice it to her youthful range." This catches her Granny's tongue...rendering her speechless.

Is this true? I know I've been told that my youth grants me unlimited abilities. I've been told I'm the ultimate weapon...because of my age. So, I go along with this excuse and go on to the next issue. "The triboelectric effect. It's just a side effect of my magic...right, Odina??"

She is jammed in a hard place, desiring to rush to her son, but too terror stricken to move...and if something taboo will happen if she does. Her long face and dark eyes sets on Kay. "I thought so before…I told Kota it was a triboelectric effect…but I didn't think he meant this. I thought he meant a little static shock…that he oversimplified things."

"This is far past triboelectric…" Elu seconds.

"Then what is it??" Kay observes Kota…who lies bone straight…a plank of wood laid flat out. Stuck in the air…hovering.

"Let's save that for another night…" Elu is a little winded from expelling so much energy tonight.

"I second that." Gloria is just as out of breath.

"Yes…we've had enough excitement for one night." Mato responds.

"But…" Kay is still focusing on Kota. "But…I want to stay until he wakes up…so he knows I didn't attack him. It may have looked like I did."

"He knows you would never do that." Mato reassures her.

"But…we had a fight…he might assume I was being mean. I can't just go….without him knowing."

Mrs. Ahoka peers at Gloria. "The choice is up to you."

Kayla grimaces. "Please, Gran."

"He may be out for hours…"

"I don't want to go home…" She whispers.

Granny sighs. "You can't avoid your parents…they're home tonight."

"I know…that's why I don't want to go."

"The house will be a home again…you can count on me for that."

Kay huffs out air, pining over this demand. "Just a few more minutes….please?" *I wish I could stay the night here instead…and stare at him until he's up…and back to normal. Please, Kota…know that my plan wasn't to harm you…just to stop you. Please…you have to know this.*

"Very well…ten minutes, then we're gone."

Kayla makes her way over to Kota, levitating five feet above the floor as if this is his bed. As if he's asleep. *I heard him gasp rigidly…how aching is this for him? Does he scream on the inside? Does his head set on fire? Does his skin throb??* She outstretches a hand…very gradually. Debating on if she can jolt him conscious with another touch…or if that would be too dangerous.

"DON'T TOUCH HIM!!" Dy is livid. "You've done enough! Leave!!" She shield her baby brother from Kayla in protector mode.

Mato pries his daughter off of Kota's body. "Off to your room…we'll have a talk later! Now…young lady…this instant!"

Dyani shoots daggers at me with eyes that used to be sweet…now they hate me. Kay hangs her head low…avoiding eye contact. His sister is out, but not in peace. Every step on the stairs is a hammer to wood. *A dislike of me…a warning. I should just go. I'm sure they all feel the same way. His mom must be just as upset with me. I knocked her son out. Doesn't she want to yell at me too? Isn't that why she's keeping her distance from me?? Because it'll make her spaz out on me for revenge??*

"I'll just go…" Kay rubs the back of her neck, embarrassed for causing all of this tension.

She's out the door and to the car in a dash….moving almost like a vampire. Faster than normal. When inside…Kay rests her head on the glove department on the dashboard. The chilled leather helps her high temperature. All the fear from the mind walk…and from what she inflicted on Kota has her body writhing.

Gran isn't in the car yet…she's taking her time to come out. This is most likely done so they can talk about me. Chat about how much of a freak I am. Discuss how I'm a threat to him. That I'm far worse for his wellbeing than Greyson is. WHY COULD I HAVE NOT KEPT MY HANDS OFF OF HIM?? WHY DID I TOUCH…WHEN I COULD HAVE FROZEN HIM IN PLACE?! I COULD HAVE ASKED THE SPIRITS TO FREEZE HIM. INSTEAD, I HARMED HIM! I'M SO STUPID!! I KNOW WHAT I DO TO KOTA…WHAT MY HANDS DO TO KOTA! STILL…I DID IT!! I TOOK HIS BREATH AWAY!

Gloria is buckling into the car now, right at her side. She adjusts the heat on for the November wind chill. The vents whoosh out heat…which only doubles Kay's feverous body temp. She buries her head deeper into the leather compartment.

"Kota will be fine…"

"Will he…?"

"Yes."

"Then what took you so long to come out? You were talking about how bad of an idea it was…."

"No…" Gran leans over to hoist her from the critical slough she's in. "You did what was best…he would've gotten killed at the dugout site if he went there alone. But…if you held on longer…Kayla…"

"Dyani was right…I would've killed him."

Gran cups her granddaughters face in her palms. "No…not quite…I'm not positive of how true that is…Elu isn't either. We'll work this out at the next meeting. Until…forgive yourself. You saved him from a horrible mistake.”

“He was in pain…I heard it.”

Her Granny sighs toughly. “You did what you thought was best. You’re not evil…what you did wasn’t evil…or mean. I thank you for acting so fast…and calling onto the realm for assistance.”

KOTA

There’s no darkness…not like before. Not like when my parents rescued me and I fainted. No. This is the opposite. Kota stands at the edge of himself. The sharp dimension he’s in tilts—not with chaos, but vast clarity. Illumination pours through him, not from above, but from everything around him, thick and shimmering like the surface of a river in sunlight. Shapes of golden warmth and soft, flowing silver move through the air, not solid but alive, curling around him. Gentle wind.

The presence of the Great Spirit is active…not as a figure with form, but as a living radiance, flowing in currents that rise from the ground and settling in the river. It is patient, immense, and constant, holding even the parts of him he thought were lost. Mortality. fragileness. Balance. His deepest fractures are woven into holy joy.

"Child of shadow," the grand voice speaks through him like thunder, pulsating every atom of his being. *"You are lost no longer. The pulse of creation has not abandoned you. The Silver River. Step in with courage.. Let it cleanse, let it restore….your legacy."*

Kota bounces straight up, heaving air, clutching his chest, which is a ton of bricks. There’s a sting…in his chest. There’s a shiver…as if he’s cold. And in need of a blanket.

“KOTA!!” Dyani rushes down the stairs. “Are you okay?? OH, GREAT SPIRIT!! You looked like you died!!”

He drops his hand from his chest…all muddled by the vision…and the fact that Kayla touched him. *She knows what it does to me…why would she do that??*

“You never told us how…hazardous her touch was.”

“Yes…I told you…mom…and dad.”

“You didn’t explain it like this, Kota…you were on fire…but not! It’s hard to explain. White fire…like the burning herbs…from magic! How do you feel?”

He doesn’t know how to answer this…his chest is weighty…and the prickle is still there…right in the middle. Not to mention the frostiness firing up his core. Kota hugs himself for warmth…fighting off a similar temperature as if out in a blizzard. "Where is Kayla?"

"Don't speak her name…she did this!"

"Where is she, Dy??"

"I made her leave…"

"You what??" He slides off of the translucent hover bed.

"I. Made. Her. Leave." She draws out each word. "She attacked you!!"

Kota's evil eyes her. "Why would you do that??"

"Last I checked…you two were fighting…and now she did this to you??"

"I caused the fight…not her….and this has nothing to do with that!"

"She's dangerous."

"No…"

"Yes…you didn't see what I saw…what we saw from the outside looking in."

Hmmm…is that true? From the outside looking in…the whole light up show of my body must be…frightening for those who never seen it in real time. "I'm fine…"

"Are you serious??!!" Dy croaks. "You are not fine."

"Actually, I am…I'm more than fine." Kota treads to the hallway…in search of his parents and grandad.

"Umm…noo!!" His sis trails after him. "What makes you say that?? Honestly…you need to lay back down….maybe even sleep in for a day or two."

"There's no need."

Dy takes her little brother's arm to persistently escort him back to the strange, clear air- bed. "Rest. Now."

He wags his head side to side. "I don't need to…I saw the Great Spirit…it spoke to me."

"YOU WHAT??"

"I've seen it…" He bares all of his teeth in a large grin. "This is the second time…last time Kay did this…I only saw a cloud."

"…Like….from the teachings?" Her mouth forms a dramatic O shape.

"Yes…only last time it was just a cloud with a shadow…"

"And this time??"

"….this time…I saw the river…and The Greater spoke."

"And said what…" Dyani is amazed and terrified at the same time.

"Child of shadow. You are lost no longer. The pulse of creation has not abandoned you. The Silver River. Step in with courage.. Let it cleanse, let it restore your legacy." He returns to the hall to summon the others. Knowing that planning a trip to the Skaith Empire will go smoother if they all pitched as one…as a team. *I have to cure myself…and my family has to be there with me when I do so. I need them there…when I fix my damned spirit and revert back to human life.*

CHAPTER 38: BLOCKED

KAYLA

Once out of the elevator, the penthouse is still an empty shell. Worse than before…at least before Kayla knew that her parents would be home, eventually. Now she isn't so sure. She glides to the kitchen…hoping to see Mary and James there. Her mom cooking…and her dad filling out application tickets. But…the place is a ghost town.

Gran bites the inside of her jaw. "Their supposed to be here by now!"

"I don't care…I'm going to bed." Kay's voice is etched with anxiety.

"Firefly…I really am sorry…we brought you back as soon as we could. Greyson wasn't supposed to be there."

"I know…it's no one's fault…he's just stalking me."

"And he won't drain your essence…I'll die before I let that happen."

Just then the lift beeps a ring. Someone is boarding from down below. Her parents. Kay frowns, caught between happiness and burden. "I don't know if I can deal with this…tonight."

"Then let me do most of the talking."

Good…my mind is free for a few seconds. Although it really isn't free. I still have to mentally tap in on this conversation…Gran can't do all of the talking…I have to speak too. Ugh…why couldn't this be tomorrow?? I'm still hung up on the throne room…on the vampire king…and Kota.

The wooden doors depart, clearing a deep gap…revealing her parents. Mary's eyes are sunken…dark circles…even her always perfect, coily hair is all over the place. Untamed.. Yet she wears a cream power suit to somewhat hold herself together. Like a band aid…one that hangs off because it can't stick right. And the bruise it's covering…is a critical strain. Beyond stress…beyond nerves. She's fried, same as the end of a matchstick.

James is tense…his shoulders set back in uneasy tension. The dress shirt he wears may rip at the seams at any second, and not in a cool way…such as Superman…more like the Hulk on the edge of expanding. His face is just as sleep deprived…jumpy…and restless as his wife's.

"Sit… the both of you." Gloria directs them to the sofa.

Kay looks to the floor, not wanting to meet their eyes…their terrified eyes…so jittery…so dull…vacant of love. *What*

"No…here is fine…" Mary begins. "Tell us what you need to tell us…so we can go." The robotic tone of her words is the nail in the coffin.

"You won't stay??!!"

"Mom…"

"Don't "mom", me!"

"Can we not shout, please?" Kay holds her hands over her ears…experiencing a delayed headache from the mind walk. Needles shaking in her head…piercing her temples.

"What's the matter with her?" Mary inches up, her heels catching friction on the carpet.

"Let's not overwork her…we know what happened last time." James pacifies the moment. "Just breathe, baby girl." Kay meets his eyes, finding a glimmer of daddy's love in his troubled irises.

"Then have a seat…if you don't want to overwork her." Granny begins to walk, taking Kayla along with her, navigating her shoulders to the couch. She sets her down, while she stays standing. After all, this is her meeting. Mary and James share an iffy glance, communicating voicelessly. The translation is clear as day…let's go….away from this. Gloria has had enough of them two; she mumbles something under her breath…something

Kayla doesn't understand. Whatever enchantment she just used has their feet peddling forward while they try to move backwards, try to walk backwards from the unwanted motion on their legs. But they lose…and near the sofa unwillingly. Puppets…under the master's control.

"WHAT IS GOING ON??!!"

"MOM, WHAT IN THE WORLD?!!"

"I told you twice…I won't say it a third." She jabs her index finger downward, at just that slight motion, James and Mary drop to the couch…nothing but rag dolls. "Now listen…and be quiet.

"I knew this would be a lot to swallow…but you two are horrible."

"But…"

She cuts her daughter off with a raise of her hand…no magic needed. "But…nothing!! I expected this from James…he's not of our bloodline…but you!" Her nostrils flare at Mary. "I've told you of our legacy…countless times."

"AND I ASSUMED YOU WERE JOKING!!"

"I WASN'T!!"

Kayla cringes at all of the shouting, ramming her shoulders far to her neck, just like a turtle in its shell. James, on the opposite side of his wife…is far away from his daughter. His arm absentmindedly stretches her way, to comfort his baby. The simple touch to the backside of her palm is all she needs. Her doe eyes water like a broken hose. "Are you alright??"

"No, she's not…she needs her parents." Gloria spats with James.

"Kay still has us."

"Oh, really??"

"Yes."

"Then why leave??"

"We needed time…this is too much to take in." He combats her respectfully…never yelling.

Mary peers at her child…the middle of her forehead denting inward, distressed. "How do we fix this??"

"There is no fixing it…this is for the rest of her life." Gloria advises.

Kay is crying more now…mad that her mom wants to fix her…instead of accepting her. "I'm not something to fix, mom! This is me! This is our family! You know this!"

"I don't…"

"You do…why keep the books? You had to know deep down that they were part of you. You had to know!"

"I had no clue…"

Gran kneels in front of her daughter; the compassion in her replaces the irritation. "Asitawisi, (remember)."

Mary brown eyes wash over going colorless…no pupils.

"AHHH!!" James springs from the sofa.

"Relax, James."

"WHERE DID HER EYES GO??!!!"

"Shhh." Gran shushes him.

"NO, TELL ME!! WHERE DID HER EYES GO??!!"

"Dad no screaming!!" Kay violently massages her temples and goes for two tiny pillows on the couch to shield her eardrums. The needles are now grains of sand swirling her brain. Agony.

"I remember…" Mary speaks in a trance…far away, despite her sitting right next to them. Her mind travels back in time, memory walking.

Kay knows the exact look in her mom's eyes. *They look just like the crystals …the ones that sent me back into the past. Diamond clear…and hazy. What does Gran want her to remember?? I want to know...*

KOTA

"The Great Spirit doesn't speak…" Mato strokes his chin.

"Then what did I hear, father??" Kota rallies.

"You may have misread the experience…I don't doubt that you met the soul…"

"There were no misreadings; I know what I heard! And it wasn't directly…it spoke through me…like-"

"A vessel…" His mom beats him to the description.

Dyani is planted on the bottom of the staircase, her legs folded while sitting. "It's normal to hear the spirit, dad."

"Yes, it is…but not so directly. Feeling the connection to life and the protection is normal. This isn't." Mato is pushed to his limit. The night has him depleted. "Let's put a pin in it…tonight has had enough adventure."

"Yes…please, son, go rest…you've been through a lot."

"So has Kayla…mom. You both need a time out." Dy mumbles.

"Oh…so you're being nice to her now?!" Kota barks at his sis. "You made her leave for no reason!"

"Well, you hid in your room, now you want to care about her again??! Kota, she took you away from us!"

"For a good reason!"

"DO NOT START, YOU TWO!" Mato threatens in a snarl. "Enough is enough. Goodnight!"

Kota scowls at his big sister …hoping that she can sense all of his disgust in his mind. *I hate you for this, Dy…you were wrong for this!* Then he passes her by so speedily that not even her blouse flutters from his body's pace. The creaky stairs don't even sing in his weight. He slams the door once upstairs, pissed at himself.

My goal was to check on her…to soothe her…and I failed. I saw red. I heard where the cure was and went haywire. I'm thankful that Kay brought me back to myself. Dyani is wrong…Kay didn't take me away…she restored me back.

In a millisecond, Kota is out of his window, dashing the November painted streets. The leaves are layered in thin snow...barely visible. Winter is coming. The loose flakes drizzle down in circles around him. None of them graze him...the tempo of his legs don't allow reality to dance on him.

The penthouse is somewhat normal. The coverings on the windows are still up, blocking his view from the top of the roof. He tiptoes to the ledge, not afraid of falling dozens of stories down to solid concrete. This provides him a way to see in...through a crinkled line in a curtain. *I wonder when Kayla will take them down?? When will she be ready??* He glimpses all four of them gathered around the sofa; only Gloria is still in a stoop right ahead of her daughter. James is standing but will collapse from the white eyes of his wife sooner or later. *Wait...white eyes...?? Mrs. Harris has empty eyes?? Why?*

"Asitawisi, (remember)." Gloria chants.

"I remember."

Remember?? Remember what exactly??

As if hearing the inner workings of his mind, Kay asks, "Remember what exactly??"

Her grandmother never blinks...never glances away from Mary, her daughter. "Your mother performed a summon before....at five years old. I found her playing in the books, as children often do with things."

"Mary has magic??!!" James is startled.

"We all do...son."

"I never seen it...she never opened the books...never even held them. Not in the 18 years I've been with her! She's never..."

"My daughter suppressed the memory once she was old enough to recall it. Mary buried it deep in her subconscious. That is why you've never seen her use the grimoires. I'm certain you've seen her staring at the bookcase...longer than normal."

James ponders this. "She daydreams sometimes...I assumed it was work related."

"No...that was a calling. Same as Kayla was drawn to the scriptures."

"My mom has said a spell before??? But...But how?? I remember her saying: *"Those are just words dressed up to seem magical. Just a prank. Just a prank. If that was a lie...and mom made herself believe it...that means she activated her gene. So...mom is a spell bender too?"*

"No...your mom is a second-grade caster...the genes skipped her. Think back to our first call...and the first meeting."

"Oh…right." *Kay must have forgotten the info. It was a while ago…and a lot has occurred. So, a muddled mind is expected.*

"When will she be…normal again?"

"Dad…none of this is normal…you and mom need to stop saying that word!"

"Princess…"

Mary shrieks to the top of her lungs, snapping out of the stupor she was in. The sound is nails on a chalkboard. Kota shrinks into his neck…affected by the noise. A noise that is heard by their neighbors below. He notes how the three floors just underneath theirs, pop on the lights. *They probably think someone just got murdered. The cops may get called.* Mary screams on.

"MARY!" James hugs her tightly.

"Dear…relax." Gloria comforts her daughter.

"NO. NO. NO!"

The floors below are still lit up by inside lighting. The residents near their large windows, some looking down at the street for a crime scene…others looking straight up…locating the source. Kota wants to stop a woman in oversized pajamas from scuffling to her kitchen for the wall phone. But he isn't allowed inside the dwelling. *If only I could stop the lady…the cops will come…and more burden will be on this very long night. This endless night.*

"I COULDN'T HAVE DONE THAT! I COULDN'T! YOU PUT IT IN MY HEAD!"

"Something I would never do…" Gloria is so composed regardless of the shouting. "You played in the books…you summoned initiation…"

"No…" Mary hides her head in her hands, muffling her voice.

"And called on fire…nearly burned down my house." Gloria is more so amused at this than upset. "You called on fire…you know you did. Mary…it's in you."

"Then take it out of me…I don't want it!!" "It's too late for that, dear…you're in the war now." "What war?" Kay wonders.

Grandad said war too…he said it had begun…but never explained. Will Gloria explain it?? I need to know…what this means.

She finally rip her eyes from Mary to land on her grandchild. "The war of good and evil. Our kind is easily corrupted…and have hidden from this Greyson for a reason. You've seen the ashes of our fallen…the torment…and the disregard. He will round up our people once again…and use us as batteries. We're all in this now…including your mom."

"No…mom can't go through that!"

"It's not your choice…"

"Batteries???" James only picked up on this part. "What do you mean, use you like batteries??"

"It's a lot to explain, Dad…"

"And what war??'

"I'll tell you tomorrow at the meeting...after school."

"GRAN! You honestly expect me to go back to school after this??"

"Yes."

Her father is processing all of the supernatural world…still alarmed and oblivious of the magic world…yet he agrees. "Yes. You're going to school tomorrow."

YES!! Kota celebrates all too happily from the rooftop. I'll see her in the morning. Hopefully, we can go back to being friends. I want to forget the stupid stuff I told her…I want to forget my confession…It's not like she wanted us to be that way, anyway. I won't mess up a good thing. Starting now. I should leave…and give her privacy with her fam. She's better now…less panicky. More herself.

KAYLA

James is still a rock in a hard place but has enough courage to say, "No skipping classes…that's at least one thing I can control." "You control way more than that…" Kay grunts.

"You're allowed to see Darius again…and I'll call Isabell in the morning to re-enroll you in practice."

Her mouth vacuums all of the air from the room…the shockwave is massive in her lungs. "REALLY, DAD?? THANK YOU! THANK YOU!" She hops up to hug him. "You have no idea how much this helps!"

"I'm pretty sure I have a clue…" He chuckles. "Just don't break the windows anymore…no magic inside the house. That's a new rule. Don't break it."

She giggles tautly. "Okay…I won't."

"No more temper tantrums…I can't handle it."

"I'll calm myself down next time."

James looks to his wife…who is still hiding behind her palms. "Mary…baby?"

She shakes her head. "Just…give me some space! All of you!"

Gloria straightens from the crouch she's been in this whole time. "Yes…take in the information…because there's more to come. I'll be sure to expose the truth slowly…a sort of drip feed…so you two don't lose your heads."

"Too late for that…" James jokes dryly.

"All of you need to get some shut eye, sleep tight, and don't stress out." Gloria bends to hug her displaced daughter. "That includes you…dear. Don't lose sleep over this. There's nothing to be afraid of. You can trust me." She tugs her tighter before going to the hallway to the guest bedroom.

"I don't want you by yourself…come to bed." He holds a hand out…his wedding hand, to his wife. The gold band is sleek and shiny on his mahogany skin. "Please…for me."

Mary lets loose a laboring breath…then drops her hands. Her eyes are extremely red…warped with disbelief and apprehension. "Not in the bedroom…not the bookcase…I'd rather not be by it."

Her husband peeps at the hall for a few seconds, mulling things over. "I'll…bring out the pillows and the blanket."

"Can I sleep out here too…mom.." Kay's tiny voice begs for bonding time…for missed affection….and is ready to rekindle.

"Sure, baby." Mary beckons her over, arms wide open, drenched in unconditional love. Kay hurries into her arms.

"So…I might as well bring the mattress out then?" Her daddy chortles.

YES! My mommy and daddy are back! They're home….they're really home! And we're having a slumber party! She rejoices as she climbs between them on the mattress laid in the middle of the floor. James and Mary sandwiches her in the center, just as protective as bears. Their body heat is welcomed on this semi winter night. Kay revels in the cuddling…the type she hasn't had since she was a little kid.

The close contact reminds her of how the womb would feel…comfy and never-ending relief. The last image she sees before falling fast to sleep is the soft flurries of snow kicking up outside the glamorous skyrise windows.

The morning is bitter…worse than the night was. But the scent of hot chocolate rectifies the situation. Kay yawns big and gets up from the mattress on the luxurious floor. "Jumbo or mini marshmallows?" Mary asks from the kitchen.

"Mini." She replies…yawning again, only this time with a stretch. She drags her feet to the kitchen and scoots onto a bar stool. "Morning mo-" Her voice falters…at what's before her.

There are at least fifteen cups of hot chocolate on the counter. Some with jumbo and mini marshmallows, some with both mixtures, and others with too much whipped cream. The fluffy clouds drip over the sides. The counter is messy…so filthy….in the pristine house.

"We can try them all." Her father is trying to make a dozen and a half of mugs seem typical for four people. "Right?" He signals to her to go along.

"Yeah…I can down 4 by myself." Kay jokes nervously. *Mom is kinda losing it. Last night was…a breaking point. Maybe that's on me and gran…we never should have off-loaded so much at one time. That was a bad idea. The normal human brain can't handle that much unrealistic truth.*

"Oh, really…well, I'm gonna have to make more." Mary's apron is all dirtied with cocoa powder and cream…also liquid caramel and sugar pebbles.

"Oh…it has sugar…remember, mom? I can't have it."

"Of course you can." Her frantic voice is off tune and forceful. "Drink." She pushes a mug her way.

"But ballet…this will bloat my feet."

"COME ON…LIVE A LITTLE! I ate tons of sugar at your age!" She waves a dismissive hand. "Go on…drink up."

James, who's beside her at the stove, grabs a mug and sips. "Hmmm….delicious."

Kay sips hers too, while chewing on the mini marshmallows. An explosion of tingling hot pleasure scratches at her jaws. "OH MY GOD!!"

"I KNOW RIGHT!"

"I haven't had this in forever!" Kay downs two more gulps.

"Right?" Mary aggressively pours more cocoa powder from a jar into the wide rim, deep set tea kettle. "We're gonna need more."

James rubs on her back. "Maybe a few more…then that should be enough."

When will she stop…? How many will she make?? 50?? 100?? Doesn't her hand hurt from whisking the kettle?? Dad must have been trying to stop her…but this is how mom is coping with the night's news.

"I missed you, mom…I missed both of you."

"We know, princess, we did too. It felt…off…being away from home. The hotel was nice and all…but. It wasn't home. We're back now…and will never leave again."

Mary stares angrily at him. "Oh…stop bringing up the past…let's move from that! Anyone wants French toast??"

"You've been at it for 2 hours…baby. The coco is good enough."

"We need breakfast." She's at the giant refrigerator in a blink of an eye. "French toast…French toast…French Toast." She sing songs sporadically while outing all of the ingredients. Nutmeg. Cinnamon. Butter. Eggs. Mixing bowl.

Gloria is heard down the hall. *Good. Gran is up…we can tag team this. 3 against one is better than 1.* "Morning, Granny."

"Morning, firefly." She greets…then takes in the endless mugs on the counter. "Oh…that's a lot of-"

"Ugh, ummm." James clears his throat, speaking to her through the non-verbal intellect…signaling her to pacify the craziness.

"That's perfect…we need a coco party!" Gloria swipes a cup and blows on the beverage. "So…about last night."

"NOO!" Mary claps her hands together…only they aren't empty…so the round, glass bowl in her hand shatters to the floor. James shoves her out of the way….away from the loose shards of glass. Kay shoots up from the stool.

Gloria speaks a charm. "Bek'elalu, (at ease)." Instantly, Mary goes blank in the face…and stands there quiet.

"What did you say??"

"I put her at ease….she's having a meltdown. The relax stupor will wear off in fifteen minutes."

"Good…" James heaves. "She wasn't going to stop cooking."

"My daughter has a habit of being a busybody in a crisis. When her dad passed…she wouldn't leave the flower session at the store. She wanted a shade of yellow that didn't exist…so she tricked her mind that it did…to waste time. I had to drag her home to say goodbye to him."

"I…never knew that." James sulks.

"Suppression is her closure…erasing bad moments is her method."

"Will…whatever you just did…fix her…?"

"For now…the only permanent fix is acceptance of what she is. Give her time to learn her true self." She grins slightly at him. "As for you…" She gazes at Kayla. "Balcony…now. I need to show you something."

The balcony is sheeted in snow on the verge of icing over. The banisters are frosty…so is the furniture. *Mom forgot to bring the chairs and sofa inside into the studio. She never forgets to do this when the winter is near. Her mind really is spiraling.* Kay hugs herself from the cold air. "Can't we do this inside??"

"It'll be quick." Gran closes the door behind her. "Plus, you dad will lose it...let's hold off on doing any magic around him."

"Magic?? Are we doing a spell?"

"Yes...well...no. More of a demonstration." Gloria's palms blaze pale with flames. From the flames...comes a winged silhouette which manifests right in the center. "Bīrabīro, (butterfly)." The hard to label shadow is now a blue and red butterfly. Flapping its wings in the mid of November...when it should be in a cocoon for safety and warmth. *Birds have flown south to sunny weather...yet this fly is here.* It flutters her way in a sort of air dance, bobbing side to side, above the snowfall. Just within her range...within her space. It disintegrates to gray flames. Ate up by unseen acid. Kay holds her heart, saddened by the death of the pretty fly.

"I fortified your protective charm to kill on the spot if any vampire nears you."

"But what about Kota....?"

"I excluded him...you have a good enough hold on him to keep yourself safe. He isn't a threat. I trust you to fight off his darkness. As for Greyson, this is an almost lethal outcome."

"Almost lethal...?"

"If not for the mystic abilities he has, this would kill him...but he can counteract it...in time. A curse like this will delay him for about a month...so I will have to re-apply it very soon. Until then, you are safe from his astro physical attacks."

"Good..."

"Please forgive me for last night."

"I forgive you...gran, I need to be better. I hate how scared I am of him."

"With good reason...he's your enemy."

Enemy...I heard Greyson say that from the other side of my window...on that dreadful night. He said something before that...but I couldn't hear. My world was crashing...he was a monster at the behind the glass...looking right at me. Out to kill me. I had to save myself...and save the city from his evilness. So, of course, I can't recall his words. What did he say before the word enemy?? Was it important?? Or a ploy?

CHAPTER 39: REACH OUT

Photography class has a new assignment. Kayla has missed 3 days and is not in tune. Ms. Ruby has a sticky note for her, with all of the missed assignments and homework. She's styling in an oversized yellow jumpsuit with the only function being to heat her up. It's a fuzzy fest just for winter. "Morning, Miss. Harris. Where have you been?"

Ummm…hurry up with a lie. I need to make it believable. "I've been…under the weather." *That's a good save…and isn't a complete lie. I've been under the influence and the weather…and have fought fire with water. That counts…right??*

"Oh…well…it is that time of the year. I hope you're all better now."

"I am."

"I guess Jia moved her desk to not get sick from you?"

"Umm…yeah, she has a weak stomach." Once again, this isn't a lie. Her misdirects hold a piece of the truth.

"At least she knows herself…I stayed sick when I was in school. It was very…annoying. Anyway…welcome back!"

"Thanks."

Ms. Ruby goes to the chalkboard. Kay peeps over at the empty seat…where Jia is supposed to be. Her bestie isn't there. *Jia said she'd sit with me.* Kay twists in her chair to peer at Jia, who is all alone at the back of the class. Next to the second chalkboard that Ms. Ruby never uses.

"Jia." She mouths the words more than she says them, then points her hand at the chair beside her. "Come on." Jia shakes her head, a little mean this time. Rough and stubborn. *Huh?? What is going on??* "Hey, Ms. Ruby? Can I get notes from Jia so I can knock these off the list?" She waves the yellow sticky note like a flag.

"Sure, you can, just be sure one of you record today's instruments in your notes."

"We will." Kay hustles to the back, passing semi full desks. A lot of kids are out today…either sick…or skipping because of the change in weather. No one is near Jia. She's completely isolated in the back. Her friend has a composition book open and a pen ready to transcribe everything the teacher has to say. "We agreed!" Kay hisses lowly.

"Yes, we did…and you didn't hold up your half! I told you to ask him if he ever drank blood…and that if he said no…I'd sit with you…" Jia is enraged, her brows curve and her sweet eyes are steel. "You avoided it on purpose!"

"No, I didn't! I was…busy with other things." She oversimplifies.

"With what exactly??"

"I'll tell you later."

"There won't be a later!!" Her harsh tone is undeniable.

"Why are you being like this??"

Jia ducks her head to speak louder while staying low in volume. "Because he's killing beachgoers…and you won't admit it!" "Pay attention girls!" Ms. Ruby calls back to the two. "Today we will take portraits of a fellow peer…and will frame this said photo with a meaningful border." On the projector screen is an example from their teacher. A photo of a long-haired orange cat who couldn't be bothered with having their picture taken. The bad attitude of the pet is clear through the lens. Appalled sourness. "That's Ginxy…with a G. and I selected the bubble frame because he loves to chase them when I'm washing dishes."

The girls pretend to take notes of the lecture. Kay slips out a pencil from the side of her backpack and scribbles on the opposite page from Jia. "There's nothing to admit…Kota isn't doing the killing." Kay keeps her eyes straight at the board, same as Jia.

"Then who is killing?? We don't get that many cougars in the city…not all at once. It's rare. I looked into it."

"Kota isn't the culprit…there's…" Kay drops her voice a few more octaves. "There's another vampire in the city…"

"2!!!"

Ms. Ruby halts her speech to squint at them. "Is everything alright back there?"

Jia gulps hard. "Yeah…I just forgot to bring another…" She slyly yanks the pencil from her friend's grasp and hide it under the desk. "Another pencil…for Kayla."

"Oh, I have one for you, just give me a few moments."

"Okay."

"As I was saying…the frame dimension must be 10 by 8 inches-"

"When did another one come to town?"

"About a week ago…

"And you're sure some of the killings aren't Kota?"

She makes to answer but snaps her mouth back shut. *I can't say yes 100%...not after I found out Kota killed 4 people. Those deaths could have been here in Chicago...for all I know. Aside from where he killed...I know he's done it. He has blood on his hands. Lots of it.* "I...don't know."

"Then stop hanging out with him!"

A table full of girls, just a few feet up, glare back at them for interrupting the note taking. "SHH!!"

"Some of us are trying to work!"

"Be quiet!"

One curly-haired guy raises his hand to Ms. Ruby. "Could you tell them to take that out to the hall? I can't concentrate!"

Ms. Ruby is yet again stalled from her presentation. This time, she is exasperated; her chest sinks deep to her ribs. "Now, you know that I dislike writing demerits....so handle whatever is going on in the hall. You have five minutes."

"Thank you, Ms. Ruby." Kay tags Jia's arm along the way to the hall, pulling her out past the door to the lockers. She allows the classroom door to close with a click before speaking. "That's a little extreme, Jia."

"It's not...you yourself know that he's killed, just say it."

"Kota has killed...he told me."

"AT THE BEACH!!"

"I can't say if it was there or not."

"Then dig deeper...ask him until he tells you where and when."

Kay rubs the back of her neck. "It's a touchy subject."

"So what?! You owe it to me...to Mya...and yourself-"

"I know..."

"So, what's the plan here?"

Do I really need to uncover this? Do I even want the truth?? I'm half afraid to find out. "I'll work it out."

"By staying away from him!"

"No...by helping like I promised." Kayla grips the nape of her neck intensely. "There's a cure...I located a cure...and that will fix him. If he's killing anyone...it'll stop soon."

KOTA

Kota is done with the miniature hair comb before everyone else. The wood is marble patterned, striped both brown and black in a glossy finish. If this was in the hair session of a store, no one would hesitate to purchase it. His project is flawless ...as usual. Since he has nothing to do, and the bell is five minutes away, he decides to turn in the assignment to the old man.

"Marvelous as always!" He grins, then offers Kota a flyer. One promoting an upcoming wood shop contest: **SHOP CHOPS.** "Look into it. I have an eye for talent…trust me." The man inclines his head to demonstrate the sort of skills he has to endure in this school.

One guy cradles what appears to be burnt, twisted rubber…full of elasticity…no structure. As flimsy as laffy taffy. Another guy mean mugs a distorted hanger sort of project…only it's missing the bottom half. One girl is somewhat better…if the assignment was a fish bone depleted of a ribcage.

"Some of them have potential." He cracks.

"For a boneyard…yeah…sure." Kota accepts the flyer. *This may be the distraction I need. Kayla and I are still …rocky. She's turned me down. This is a one-way connection. Although I still want her…but I can't have her. This will be a good distraction for me. I don't know how to deal with rejection….so I'll hide behind this competition.* "I'll sign up."

"Lovely!"

Out at his locker is the same old, same old. This time the vent of his unit is stuffed tight…unable to hold together for long. The date mail will fall out as soon as he scrolls the lock-pad numbers in. *I'm speedy enough to snatch and close it before anyone sees…but I shouldn't risk it. Too many eyes are on me.* Kota studies the locker, even the bottom is compact; the metal is bent out from numerous hands tugging it back to jam in envelopes.

"Not even the cream of the crop."

Oh, no…her. Vanessa Skye and her brats from hell. The irony of how I'm labeling humans as being from hell…when I am? That's how unsavory they are. As expected, the plastic pinks are in…pink, obviously. But not skirts and dresses this time…thick leggings, a few inches of padding for the cold, and tops with puffy sleeves with twinkles of diamonds.

"And you are?" Kota has an edge to his voice.

"Oh, you know it, no matter how much you deny it." Vanessa gloats.

"Isn't it a tell of insecurity when someone brags about being the best. Instead of just…I don't know…being the best?"

"Oh! He's sour today!" One laughs. "Did Kayla reject you for the dance?"

"No…I just see-through the façade."

"Umm…hello….I'm the queen…voted by the people."

"Out of force."

"Okay…then who should be queen…little miss Kayla?" Another of her minions tag in.

"That wouldn't be a bad choice."

"Only it would! Geez…you need to demand power to get anywhere here…not sit around being a delicate princess." Vanessa spits, and that's when he sees it. A break in her seamless, porcelain persona. A fracture in the decoy of a babydoll's ceramic. Jealousy. Envy. In her eyes and voice…which she usually keeps cold and emotionless. Now it's all exposed. The weak point in her high voice cracks, giving out…going croaky with despise and envy.

I almost feel bad for this human girl now. She doesn't know who she's trying to live up to. Kayla isn't human…maybe Vanessa knows this and is over projecting her dislike on purpose. Over-exaggerating the hostility because that's all her human brain can compute it as. High school politics…not supernatural competition. Not an otherworldly contest.

"You think you hate Kayla….but you just don't understand her."

"No, I understand her…it must be nice getting everything without working for it."

"I thought you were the queen…don't queens have everything already??" This catches her tongue right in her mouth; her voice leaves her body, struck by what he just said. So, her minions jump in for her.

"Go find a date for the dance, leave loser!"

"Yeah, bye bye, get away from us!"

"How dare you question what she has. Queen Skye has everything and everyone!"

"You all came to my locker…" Kota chuckles just as the bell rings, finding the humor in the empty threats and selfconsciousness. They're just shallow, self-annotated heirs to a fake queen. Anxious of rejection…and of being bested by Kayla…which they are by tenfold. He strolls to second period still tittering at their bad attempt of overruling the school. "…there's still some room if you want to drop your names in." He refers to his locker full of date submissions.

KAYLA

In law, Kay and her trio, Izzy, Chester and Fred, team up. The topic is to add to a justice balance scale. Each student has one on their desks. The infamous golden weigh scale, which tips to one side or the other depending on what is placed in the trays. The class has to place law books over the gavel. A depiction of justice over bias. Kay has the books high on the scale and the gavel low.

Fred is salty, so much that his pencil nearly pokes through the notepaper. The led tip leaves dents in the parchment.

"Whoa, easy on the pencil…?"

Fred doesn't look from the paper. "So, you're back?"

"Yep, I am."

"Where were you??"

"Just…away."

Fred's red eyebrows tighten. "What's really going on with you?? Jia and Mya won't tell me anything. They're acting weird….not sitting with you at lunch…not even chatting it up."

"It's a lot to explain."

"Is it about him?"

Kay decides to be a little honest. "Kind of."

Fred's green eyes swipe sideways at her skeptically. "It's true then…you're dating the creepy guy." He says more as a statement, not a question.

Izzy stops weighing on her scale to butt in. "I like his style."

"Of course you would…it's right up your alley."

"True." Izzy, in a dark crochet sweater, shrugs. "Plus, he's all mysterious…so I'm for it if Kay wants to switch it up."

"I'm not switching it up!"

"Then who's your date to the dance tonight?"

"Nobody."

Izzy isn't convinced. "Lies."

"No…I'm not going."

"Okay, don't tell me the juicy boy drama…" Izzy flips her ink-colored hair back with nails of deep purple.

Kay huffs, frustrated. "There's no juicy boy drama…I won't be at the dance!"

"Because she's grounded." Fred clarifies.

"Shit…still??" Izzy rolls her eyes "Your dad needs to give it up…you didn't blow up the school or anything."

Hmmm…blow up the school…if only she knew. But regular humans can't see the astro world. But still…she's spot on without knowing it. I did cave the school in on itself…practically blew up the floor. "No…he finally let me off the hook. I'm not in cuffs anymore."

"Then come with us tonight." Fred requests. "We can go as 4…right, Chester??"

Chester is invested in the convo, but is too nervous to tag in. Mr. Smith is glowering at their table. They are the only ones speaking; the rest of the class is dead silent. He marks points to take away from their attendance score, sneakily deducting tallies without their knowledge. Well…Chester knows what's going on and doesn't let out a peep.

"See…even he agrees." Fred Jabs, making fun of how tongueless Chester is. "Let's be a wolf pack tonight…and travel in numbers. Please come."

If I go to the dance tonight…I'll have to tell Darius…but he's staying away from me. I'll try to call and see if he picks up. If he does. That's a good sign …. That means we can go out to the dance tonight. Then Kota would be out of bounds. Yes…I evaded his feelings for me. I let him down easy…only because choosing is harder than saying yes. Good thing we can decorate the gym together…that is, if he wants to still do it.

"I'll think it over." She declines the outing. "Maybe…it depends on what Darius says."

After class, she takes a detour outside the school building for the first time ever. *I never leave the school between the bell…but this is important. I don't have my walkie talkie…I wish I brought it to school with me. I'll have to use a pay phone.* Kayla locates one easily. After all, this is downtown…the business district, so pay phones are on almost every corner.

She pats around in the pockets of her loose jeans for a dime, finding nothing. *Crap! I don't have any change.* A glint of silver from the top of the booth grabs her eye. *AHH YES. A good Samaritan. Thank you!* She takes the dime and inserts it, punching the keypad to call her boyfriend's house. *His dad will pick up. I'll tell his dad to pass on the message for me when Darius comes home from school.*

My boyfriend made up with me at the penthouse…but…that was before I used my powers in front of him. He ran away from me. I ran him away. I need him to love me again…need him to take me to the dance.

The line clicks. "Hello?"

"Hey, Mr. Scott. It's Kayla."

"Oh…hi."

"I know this is a random call…but Darius needs to call me…." She rubs the back of her neck to make up a lie. "Can you tell him to call me when he gets home from school?"

"Of course I can. I've been wondering why he's so quiet lately. I figured it had to be something with dating." He laughs. "What happened?"

"Umm…" Kay bounce her eyes side to side. "I think I scared him…with my words."

"So, you two had an argument?"

"Kinda…"

"Well…don't stress over it…I'm sure this is an easy fix."

"I hope so." The bell rings from within Jones Prep. "Oh…that's the bell. I gotta go…but thank you for picking up."

"No problem, have a good day at school."

"Thanks, bye!" She hangs up and runs back inside, to her next period.

KOTA

Lunch is Ravioli and Alfredo. Kota grabs a mixture of both with fresh baked bread. The lunchroom isn't full at all today. He counts the tables easily. There are 15 tables out of about 50 that are full. The rest are bare. *Hmm…everyone took a snow day. I mean I don't hate winter…Oklahoma has brutal snowstorms just like here. I'd never missed school over it. I doubt that parents are just letting their kids miss school.*

My peers definitely skipped classes to have fun. They must have orchestrated a ditch day walk out in secret. Most likely to hang at the mall or hit up a gaming arcade while their parents are at work with no idea.

He notices the eyes of Kayla girls on him. Mya and Jia are at the back table, watching him guardedly as if he's going to kill them and drink their blood at any second. Kota gives a slight smile…waving nicely. But they don't return the niceness. They stare hard and long with mistrust…their minds are made up. He awkwardly drops his hand. Her girls observe him all the way to the table. *I hope they come around soon. It'll be cool to have more friends.* His pale eyes find them again. This time Mya and Jia shiver away from his gaze…even though his glance is pleasant.

"Soooo…." Kay is already seated. "I need to apologize."

"They just need time to get used to me."

She looks up from her pasta. "Huh…? Who is they?"

"Your girls. " He tilts his head.

Her brown eyes swivel to the back of the cafeteria. Jia and Mya look away fast…hiding from her gaze. But she saw them glaring. Kay frowns. "I don't think they will."

"Don't say that…my family was the same way…just give them time."

"Jia knows you killed people…and judging by how the two are staring at you, she told Mya. So, they both know now." She peers at her plate of food, playing with the fork in the pasta. "I need you to be honest with me…"

I should have saw this coming just from their looks towards me. "I'll never hurt anyone here."

"I know…I believe you….you proved it. But…Kota…did…you-"

"Did I what??"

"Did you kill those people on the beach…I know you said you killed 4 people before-"

"Back home…in Oklahoma. That was the only time, and I couldn't control myself."

"So…you're not hunting for blood in Chicago?"

"No."

"But…how are you surviving? Don't vampires need it to live? Like water? Isn't it essential??"

"In the beginning, it was…"

"And now?"

He recalls the bird in the desert…how he needed the animal for fuel, or he would have passed out. "I only need blood when I exhaust myself from hunting. The last thing I fed on was a hawk….and I wish I didn't have to kill it…but I probably would've fainted or…maybe died."

"A hawk??"

"Yeah, I was tracking down Greyson and ended up in Texas…I wore myself out and needed to eat."

"So, you don't feed every day??"

"No…I haven't had blood in weeks."

Kay flattens into her chair…relaxing her arched back. "Good…I was worried that you were drinking from the beachgoers and might have accidentally killed them."

Kota shakes his head. "No…I'm never killing innocents again." His sight catches the back table…where her girls are inspecting him again. Mya is almost off her seat…she's on the very edge of it…and could tip over and fall over so easily. "Can you tell them they don't have to be scared?"

"I can…but I don't think that'll make it better."

"It might…never give up hope. I trust you."

She quivers at him using the word trust…shaking as if she's outside in the snowy weather. As if she's standing in the cold with no warmth. "About that. Umm….I'm sorry about what I did at the last meeting. I just didn't want you going halfway across the world to get wounded or killed." Her puppy dog eyes are somber and tugged downward. "I'm sorry for hurting you."

He grins sweetly. "You don't have to apologize for anything. And it's not really pain I'm in when you touch me. The feeling is more so…" He searches for a word that can describe the emotion he has when in the heavenly blaze of her hands. *Floating? Godly. Angelic. Redemption. After Life. But none of those label the experience completely.*

"When you gasped…it wasn't pain?? I heard you suck in air."

"No…not at all." He assure Kay. "I told you before how you make me feel. I'm cured…just for a little bit…I feel normal. It's happiness and calmness whenever you do it. More than you know."

"More than I know??"

He nods. "I'll tell you the rest tonight at the meeting."

"Okay….I'm just glad it isn't causing any discomfort."

"Don't fret about it." He forks a ravioli from his plate and chews, soaking in the aroma as if he's tasting the Italian dish. "Anyway….um…could we still decorate the gym after school?" "As friends?"

These words stab…but he made his move and has to accept that Kayla doesn't want anything else with him but companionship. "Sure, just friends hanging out." The bell rings; Kota actually hates that he has to face French class, a period he's about to fail. "Also, umm, can we study French after school? I'm at a C – Minus. If I get a D, I'll hate myself forever. I need straight A's" "You trying to be valedictorian??" "You bet!" He beams big.

"I have the spot on lockdown; if I help you that will mean war!"

"Shall the best one win!"

"You're on!" She gives a competitive squint.

Kota count down the seconds until they hang out after school. His mind is shut off…but his ears are on auto pilot. He doesn't need to pay attention to all of the teachers lecturing their students. His ears automatically store the lessons without his brain computing anything. The class periods fly by, even though every now and then a teacher calls on him to answer a question, believing he's not paying attention. Kota answers all questions with the correct response every time, while simultaneously thinking about her.

The last bell chime of the day is a freedom anthem. He gets up so fast, slightly jogging from the classroom to get to her. *Finally! That took forever!* His destination is the gym room. There's already a line at the door. Kota has to buffer in an assembly line behind the students. He leans his body over sideways to see the front of the line. His homeroom teacher has each and everybody signing a list before assigning them sections.

"Streamers." He directs 3 girls into the gym. The next to sign are given the duties of "table setup. Next in line." Things go on like this for a few minutes. "Glitter. Confetti. DJ booth. Posters. Chairs. Rugs. Flowers. Silverware."

When Kota is up next, the teacher has his assignment fast. "Seems like you and Ms. Harris applied in advance."

"We did."

"Balloons…there's a pump station right over there." He points to a corner where a rusty, dingy green tank is posted. "Try to aim for 200 within the hour."

"Will do , sir." He glances behind his shoulder for Kayla. She isn't there yet. *Hmm, where is she?? We planned this…I hope she didn't bail on me.* He heads to the pump and bends to snatch a pack of gold balloons from a tall stack on the light wood floor. Kota peers behind himself, checking if any eyes are on him. Obviously, everyone is observing him…teachers included.

Will I ever get used to being gawked at?? I'm not a test subject that escaped from a lab. When will this be over? When will I bathe in the pond of freedom and revert myself to mortality?? How long do I have to wait?? I don't want to be a freak show anymore! I just want to be human. He turns around to give his face some privacy, not wanting everyone to see his eyes water and his gloom take over like a ton of bricks. He cries silently…facing the wall. Still not understanding how he can produce teardrops as if a human boy.

Tonight's meeting will set our journey to Belgian, Zonnebeke in motion. *We need to pack and prepare a strategy for traveling across the world. Will we all take a plane? Or go by boat? Or could I just vamp ran everyone overseas to cut the route in half?? There's so much to hammer out tonight.*

"Hey, Walela." Kay is behind him. "Why are you facing the wall?"

Kota, in a millisecond, wipes away the tears on his cheek. Kayla doesn't catch onto this action; he's too fast even for her; the supernatural witch. "Just working on the balloons." He faces her.

"You know you can have this done in like 5 seconds??" She points at the stack of balloon packets on the floor.

"The same goes for you, Miss Shadow Breather."

"I guess so…I mean I can breathe out for 15 seconds. I'm working my way up to an hour." Kay brags.

"Show off."

"Look who's talking?" Kay clears her throat to mock his high voice. "I can run blah blah many blocks in blah blah many minutes!" He uses the balloon in his hand as a sling shot, cocking it backward, pulling the rubber to flick it at her. Kayla ducks to avoid his assault. "Oh no, you're making all vampires look bad."

He chortles. "I'll get you…just watch." He hands her a balloon so she can begin filling it with air. "What took you so long?"

"I was trying to explain to Jia what you told me…"

"And?"

"I think her and Mya might need a break till the end of the year."

"Yeah, don't rush it. It's easier for us because we come from weird family stuff, so we can adapt fast. It's in our legacy."

"Speaking of legacy." Kay steps over to the air pump tank and connects the rubber end of the balloon. "I didn't know you had magic before being a vampire."

"Well, I didn't have magic…I didn't unlock the ability. But I did produce a spell at the very beginning before I transitioned. My grandad said that was the last time I could ever cast."

"What spell did you say?"

"I didn't say a spell…I drew the symbol for freedom. Bird wings. That freed me from being trapped by my dad's locking charm. He tried to cage me in so I couldn't hunt for my first blood…but I broke the spell."

"You drew a spell?? I haven't even gotten that far yet. That's advanced."

"I guess."

"I'm jealous."

"Good, princess." He flicks a balloon her way, whacking the side of her puffy, curly hair behind her like a gush of wind. "Got you!"

Kay cracks up and counteracts him, slinging 5 balloons his way. Kota swerves side to side, displaying his best dodge ball dance. "Ah, missed me. Missed again. Good try! Oh, come on! I thought you were a royal warrior…did you miss your arrow training??"

"Keep talking!" She fills her fist up and toss the entire handful at him. Kota can't dodge them by using his powers; too many people are around so he gives up and welcomes defeat. "HA! LOSER!"

"I let you win…I can't do my skill around people."

"Sure, sure, make up excuses."

Someone clears their throat. "Excuse me." The two look to see who it is.

KAYLA

I know this girl. Vanessa and her clique pushed her down to the floor a few weeks ago. All of her books fell, and she stumbled down to collect them. A mousy, brown-haired girl with bangs. *An extremely quiet, shy girl. She doesn't speak much. She's smart and a loner. No friends, no one to talk to. I wonder what she has to say…and wonder how much anxiety she's holding back.*

The fear of socializing is in her eyes…eyes she keeps on the floor to keep her confidence from fading   "Hi…I remember you. Hannah, right?."

"Yeah, you helped me pick up my books." The mousy girl's voice is barely a whisper. Her face is flushed red; this chat is tormenting her.

"What's up?"

Hannah shifts her body towards Kota…just her body. Using it as a communication   tool….physical   language.   "I   was hoping…wondering…if Kota had a date to the dance?" She rubs the back of her ear to calm her nerves.

"I'm not sure…you could ask, he's right there." *I know he doesn't have one, but I need to play it cool and be oblivious.*

Hannah pivots her body more in the direction of Kota, using this motion same as making eye contact. "Do you have a date to the dance?" She mutters virtually inaudibly.

He shakes his head with a faint grin. "No, I don't. I'm not going tonight, but thanks for asking."

Come on, Kota. You're not going with me; that doesn't mean you can't go. Why is he turning her down? I'm going with Darius…he should come along too. "Come on, you just can't stay home when there's a party."   "You're staying home too." He rebukes.

"Actually, I changed my mind. I'm going with Darius. You two should go together and have fun. Live a little. It'll be cool. We can all go as a double date." Kay wiggle her brows at him. "What do you say?"

Kota considers this…going deep into his mind and taking longer than what's needed. Hannah is far more uncomfortable by him dragging out the answer than she was when speaking to him. A few seconds…a good moment of time passes before he makes up his mind. He looks Hannah over, smiling nicely. "That would be fun! Why have a boring night in the house?"

Hannah neck jerks upward, her eyes finally shoot up from the floor, stunned and big eyed. "You'll…go with me?"

"Yeah…let's not be prudes; we're too young for that."

"Oh! Okay! Wow!" Hannah smiles with all of her teeth. "Good, I'll be here around 6. My parents are dropping me off."

"I can't wait to see your dress!" Kay activates her girly mode.

Hannah giggles. "And I can't wait to see yours!"

"I actually haven't picked one out…this is all so last second. I'll have to raid my closet for a good fit." Kayla grits her teeth together. "But still, we'll both be pretty, regardless."

"Thank you!" The girl blushes hard at Kota. "And thank you for saying yes."

"You're welcome." Kota grins politely. "See you at 6."

"Okay!" She squeals. "See you at 6!" Hannah powerwalks out of the gym; her head held higher with true confidence. Chin lifted, eyes straight. Liquid courage.

Vanessa Skye has a murderous scowl aimed on the sweetheart of a girl. Green with envy. The queen bee scoffs and folds her arms. Kayla is entertained by her sourness. "A good thing already came out of this. The queen is mad. She wanted to go with you."

"Icicles aren't my type…too cold and off-putting."

"Now that's a burn!"

He smirks at Vanessa. "I have a better burn."

"What is it?"

"Let's just smile and wave."

Kay titters at the idea. "You are pure evil!"

"Maybe a little."

"MAWH HA HA HA HA HA!" Kay evil laughs. "On 3. 1.2.3." The two beam wide flashing their teeth; waving fast at Vanessa, who sticks out her tongue and swipes her long blonde hair at them as a weapon.

The balloon blowing is finished in an hour. Not because Kota and Kayla cheat using supernatural methods; because of the air tank. They have a good system going. Kayla cranks the air pump rapidly, adding air to each balloon in 8 seconds. Kota ties the knots of each balloon she passes him in 7 seconds. This record speed never slacks off….not once. One after another, just like clockwork. 15 seconds turnover time. In 1 minute, 4 balloons are blown up. In an hour, 240 balloons are on the floor, filling up a good chunk of the gym.

"Piece of cake!" She celebrates.

"Took you 8 seconds…only took me 7."

"You don't play fair."

"I was going slow."

"Still…you have an advantage." Kay rolls her eyes.

"Slow poke."

"Give me a few more weeks, and you'll be eating your words." She snaps her finger sassily. "Now…time for French studying.

"Where do you have in mind?"

My newfound escape spot is the rooftop. This became my de-stressing spot ever since the fight with Mya. It would be a good pick, but winter is here and it's too cold outside. There's snow on the way. The cold season is upon us.

"I guess the library….it's very cliché, but quite effective."

CHAPTER 40: COUNTDOWN

The library is close to empty. Kay can easily count the students on one hand. "Not too crowded, that's good." She chooses a round table set up by the long windows. The snow flurries outside are still falling. Not thick…very tiny flakes that will melt as soon as they hit the humid ground. "Tell me what you're struggling with?"

"Pretty much everything in French II…back home we didn't learn this language, so it sounds alien."

"Good thing I'm an alien."

"I'm not surprised."

"Where's you book?"

Kota unzips his bookbag to set his French II textbook atop the table. "Ta da!"

"Nice magic trick."

"Could you actually charm me to learn this whole book?" "That would be cheating!" Kay is only a little offended. "I haven't got that far in the grimoire, but I bet a knowledge cheat spell exists. I may seek it out if I get too overwhelmed."

"Overwhelmed how?"

Kay slides the textbook her way and opens it to the first chapter section. "Casting trainings…dating drama…missed assignments. I'm also back in ballet class." She exhales. "I'm a captured fish."

"You're destroying the cast trainings. You can take that off of your workload list."

"For now…I'm in the beginning phase…of course it's easy. But will I be this good when I have to master everything else?? I'm only on shadow breathing. I haven't even touched water, earth and fire."

"But…the face off downtown you pulled all of the water from the lake."

"Due to emotion…I was going off of my feelings not my mind. Just because I called on water doesn't mean I have it in the bag. I have a lot more to learn. Everyone is counting on me."

"You can do it."

"And if I can't do it?"

"You can."

"I don't know…this is all so much pressure. Yes, I'm having fun with my lessons…but it won't always be fun. It'll get serious. Then what will I do?" Kay groans. "Be honest…if I fail getting you the cure…if I can't get it for you. Would you still talk to me?"

Kayla…" He leans forward on the table with sincerity. "Yes…we'd still be friends."

"But you want the cure."
"I do…" His white eyes land on the floor. "But don't stretch yourself thin. Or go too far because you think it's what I want. This isn't just about me."

'It is…the whole reason I'm involved is to help you."
"I'm better now. I know how to live with this curse…I'm doing it right now. Aren't I? The worst-case scenario is I'll have to stay this way. And that isn't a bad thing. If you fail, I won't hate you."
"If I fail, you'll go evil." He doesn't have a comeback for the solid truth. "You know you will…you'll go after Greyson for the rest of your life…and lose yourself in revenge. I know you will…and it'll be all my fault. I can't fail…I can't. "

Kota has misplaced his tongue. Not a peep. Not a sound. He's muted. *He knows this is true…he can't sugarcoat me and say I can do anything. I can't do anything. Half of everything I do I don't understand why and how I did it. Everything I do is done on impulse. No rhythm or reason. Just spontaneous casting. Being wild and unprepared has never won a war…not a single war in history has reached victory this way.*

This topic is dropped because Kota knows it's true. He'll go on a rampage if the outcome isn't to his liking. Kayla clears her throat uncomfortably and says, "let's get to studying."

Kayla tutors him in French II, instructing him to repeat phrases after she speaks them, to act as a parrot. Correcting his pronunciation repeatedly as he stumbles over nasal vowels, silent letters. Words that sound completely different from how they are spelled. Whenever he finally assumes he comprehends a sentence, liaison confuses him. Normally silent consonants suddenly appear in the French dictation and blend words too quickly.

Kota keeps relying on English grammar patterns, trying to translate word for word, but French structure is all wrong.

Once 4:30 hits…they call it quits. A coven meeting is set for today, and the dance is at 6. They are cutting it close when it comes to time. The two descend the steps down the endless school staircase. All students are gone home…no one hangs out in the main lobby. Not a single kid.

"We should put a hustle on it." Kota says.
"Yeah…we both have hot dates tonight. I'm happy you had enough courage to not be shy."

"Well, technically she asked me out…" He shrugs. "I'm still pretty bad at approaching girls."

"You're getting better."

The last flight of stairs is where a headache is waiting. *Oh…I did ask his dad to tell him to call me! I lost track of time. Decorating the gym for the dance…and the tutoring session left me late to pick up his call. He must have called once…or twice…maybe even more than that.*

"I'M GETTING TIRED OF THIS!" Darius shouts at Kota. "I'm done repeating myself!"

"DARIUS STOP!" Kay pushes on his chest to stop him from bulldozing over to Kota to start an altercation. "Stop…it isn't like that!"

"You wanted me to call you….I thought this was important, but you're here spending time with him!"

"For French class, nothing else! And what I need to talk to you about is important." She keeps her hands on his chest using all of her might to hold him back from a fight. *They can't fight! I can't take it. I wouldn't know who to help or who to hate…choosing who to support will break me. I can't break anymore. I want to stay in one piece…I can't break!* "We were catching up for French class, that's all! I really need to talk to you. Let's talk."

Darius mugs down his enemy with intense dislike. "He needs to leave."

KOTA

I won't complain…I won't make this what it isn't. Kayla will never be my girl…I came to terms with that. So, I'll leave and respect her boyfriend. "I'll see you later." He strides off, away from the couple. Regardless of the distance that his feet carry him, his ears hear every word spoken.

"Yeah…bye."

"You're not seeing her later! What is he talking about??" "Darius, he's talking about the dance! He's going with a date; he has a plus one. I want to go too. That's why I called your dad. I want to go with you instead of being at home missing out."

"He has a date?"

"Yes…her name is Hannah…she's sweet. I was hoping we could have a double date."

"No, I'm not hanging with him."

"Just to break the ice…please. Do it for me. This is all just a big misunderstanding."

Darius mulls over the intel he just learned; he's silent. No more yelling….no more anger. "I'm not doing a double date with him…just me and you." He gives her an ultimatum. "I'll go with you to the dance…but you can't be around him…speak to him…or look at him."

Kota shoes plummets across the concrete sidewalk, burning with speed, going home. This crazy demand doesn't bother him at all. *His request is silly…and won't hold up. I'll see Kayla in a few minutes at the meeting. Her gran will pick her up in a little bit and bring her to my house…bring her straight to me. Darius can think he has control of us all he wants. He can believe the lie…I'll let him keep believing he has power.*

His mom and dad are baking up bean bread, black beans, mashed up. Flour. Sugar. Butter. Sweet Potato. Eggs. Vanilla. Pecans. The main dish is pumpkin soup, which Dyani is stirring in the pot. He takes in a big whiff before opening the door and going inside.

"You were gone for a long time." His sis addresses him.   He goes over to take a spoonful of the soup, sneaking a taste of dinner. "Kayla and I were decorating the gym for a dance tonight. Then, after we went to the library. I needed help with
French class. I'm almost failing."

"Oh, no…" His big sis peeps over at the stove at their parents who roll bread together in perfect sync. "Don't let them know."

"Way ahead of you."

"Are you going?"

"I didn't want to…but Kay talked me into it."

"I'm sure she did." Dy has a harsh undertone.

"Look can you let it go…she stopped me from doing something stupid."

"I know she did…still I can be mad about how it was done." She stares at him vigorously. "I'm supposed to protect you…you're my problem. We have a sibling pact…bonded for life. I was doing my job."

When she puts it that way…it seems less horrible. I did pass out…I did fall…I probably looked like I was dead. My sis…my family probably thought I died.

"I'm sorry…I took your caring as being rude."

"I'm sorry too! I know how much you like her. I bet you're over the moon about the date."

"I'm…going to the dance with someone else. Kayla is going with her boyfriend."

"Hold on, I thought you would've asked her with how smitten you are."

"She has a boyfriend."

"And she can still go to a dance with a friend. That's not against the law. The two ain't married, you know??" "They may as well be…" His somberness is dense.

"Don't give up because of him. Keep at it."
"You sound like dad…he told me to wait until the two breakup."
"I get my smarts from dad…he's right and I'm right, too." 5pm is when Gloria and Kayla show up. She waves at Kota trying to ease things over from where they left off. Even she knows the demands her boyfriend gave are useless. They're still close buddies, best buddies. "Hey."

"Hey." He replies lightly.

"Hello all!" Gloria greets. "We have a lot to discuss."
"That we do." Mato agrees. "Let's start with Kota…he has something to say."

"Guest please have a seat, have some food." Elu sits down at the dining table, so does everyone else. They pack into the dining chairs. The dishes are laid out on serving platters, hot and delicious dinner.

"Wow, this looks yummy!" Kay all but licks her lips.

"Thank you, dear," Odina expresses sweetly.
"What does Kota have to say?" Her granny requests. "It's about last night…the strange coma I went into after the accident with Kayla. I meant to bring this up before…because I went through this before."

"Went through what before??"
"The great spirit…I saw it clear as day." He updates Kayla and her Granny. Rerunning everything he told his parents and sister. The godly dimension. The illumination pouring through his body in the realm, the shimmering sunlight. The shapes of golden warmth and flowing silver in the air, alive and breathing. The presence of the Spirit active,…a living radiance of holy joy. The words from the majestic god, *"Child of shadow. You are lost no longer. The pulse of creation has not abandoned you. The Silver River. Step in with courage.. Let it cleanse, let it restore….your legacy."*

Gloria is stumped. "Legacy…what legacy?"

"I…think…I mean we…think the spirit was assuring me that I can still have magic if I cure myself. That's the only legacy I have." Kota explains. "Meaning we need to arrange the journey to the dugout fast. As soon as possible….as a team. Could we go next week?"

Gloria is opposed to this; her tightened lips flatten to a thin line. "Kayla isn't ready yet. Her shadow breathing is still a work in progress. We can't travel to Belgian, Zonnebeke until she masters a duration of 1 hour. She has to stop her oxygen flow for 1 hour. This will allow her to locate the precise location of the dugout through remote viewing with the wind. We can't go in blindly. We know the empire is there…but not where exactly it is. We will be lost without a clue. We only have the country and city…not the true location." Elu is on board with her words of wisdom. "Unfortunately, I have to back Gloria on this, Grandson. The entrance to the fortress is a mystery still. Let us all be sure of the gateway to the empire and not waste our resources. This will be a costly venture…the point of transportation has not yet been decided."

 Mato has no choice but to side with his father. "That's a smart point. There are 7 of us….we haven't chosen if we arrive by plane or boat…or a portal incantation. Whichever one it will be. Yet this is still a wasteful discussion if we don't know where we're going."

 "Even if we summon a portal…transitioning 1 person will take a toll on Kayla. It will exhaust her." Odina worries. "When we called on the portal for her, we lost a lot of energy. Elu, myself and Mato. We fought through it…yes….still the exposure was severe." Kay grimaces at Kota, hating herself for being against him. "I'm sorry…I don't know how to do that yet. I can't go too fast…and be reckless."

She's told me something like this in the library when we were studying. I thought she was downplaying herself…underestimating herself. Now I'm not so sure. I'm out numbered. 5 against 2. What does my sis think? "Dyani??" She twists her fingers together due to the sudden spotlight of eyes watching her. "I…I want you to be yourself again."

"So, you're with me?"

"Yes…just not next week; the timing you want is too unrealistic. Walela, (hummingbird)."

 "I get that the means of getting there are tricky…I could carry everyone there 1 by 1. I can do it. I already ran 17 states in the US in less than 10 minutes. I could speed us all overseas, trust me."

"You'll tire yourself out, son."

"I won't, dad!"

Kay cuts in. "You told me you needed blood…that last time you had to feed on a bird because you wore yourself out and needed to eat." She reminds him in case he forgot how fatigued he became once before.

"We don't need you relying on blood…of any kind, son."
"I could visit a butcher and get some bloody meat I don't have to

kill for it like you think. And I'll just need the blood for the journey. After we're done with the mission, I'll be fixed."

"You say that now…but you will get hooked on the source."

"I know myself better than you!"

Odina peers between her son and her husband, upset about a bad argument arising. "Walela, (hummingbird)." His mom reaches across the table to hold her son's forearm. "I believe you can do it…I do…just don't harm yourself to reach the goal.. I prefer you not to drink blood. Not when we're so close to ridding you of depending on human's for substance."

You all act as if I'm not a vampire!"

"We know you are son…"

"No…you don't! I can't avoid blood…especially with a war on the way. I can't defend myself against Greyson or his army without blood!"

"You battled him downtown…" Kayla speaks calmly. "You didn't need it then."

"That was 1 versus 1…and isn't the same. I'll get tired…I'll probably faint. I almost passed out…that's why I used the bird as food. I needed fuel to keep myself going. If I run low on energy, I might die. I don't know what will happen to me if I give my all and lose strength. I'm sure vampires can die from lack of blood." He revisits the very first conversation he had with his dark side…his unwanted subconscious…and what the demented voice said:

To survive, do as I say. You will lose; the lack of blood will defeat you. Defeat…means death…vampires can die from blood withdrawal.

"None of you understand this. Going to war without the ammo is pointless."

Silence. No one has anything to say to combat him. None of them have knowledge on blood and how the absence of it can kill a vampire. Or that if not for the hawk in Texas…Kota would've died in the sand…no different than a human dying from heat exposure. He would be dead….not here…not alive. Dead…for real this time.

The steam from the food sizzles on the platters, stuffing up his ears. Only he can hear this sound. Rising mist…crackling. The only noise in the dining room for some time is audible only to him. *Have I won them over?? Will they all agree now? I suggested a butcher shop, with bloody meat ready to sale to customers. No killing involve….just me going up to the counter and paying for meat; same as normal humans do.*

His father expresses pity instead of a bad temper. "The butcher shop could work….that's a very clever idea." He rewards Kota. "We are the ones who are outside looking in after all…and shouldn't question how you stay alive in this condition." Mato examines the table. "All of those who agree, raise your hand. Votes are needed."

Votes…that's a first…and it's fair and not just one sided. I'm not boxed out and treated like a kid anymore. My father is actually listening to me? My dad is actually being fair with me?? All hands go up. No one is protesting. The thought of Kota facing death due to deficiency of the red liquid is enough to tug on everyone's heart strings.

"Thank you." Kota responds to their positive voting.

"As for your plan of being a physical passenger vehicle for us all…" Elu tags in. "That is a plausible strategy."

Gloria bobs her head up and down to approve. "It is…but only if a pinpointed entrance is accessible. I need a month longer with Kayla. Just give me a month with her, Kota."

A month…that's doable. "Okay…I'll chill out until then."

KAYLA

That was a crisis averted. I feared a word battle would stem from Kota and his dad…like it had last time. Kota has gotten better with his impulsive temper. I'm proud of him. Her stopwatch on her wrist sounds off. The time is 5:35. Kayla hops up from her chair. "I'm so sorry…I wish I could stay for dinner, but the school dance is in less than an hour. Kota and I need to get ready."

"Oh…right." He eyes the grandfather clock from across the hallway. "Yeah…time is something else today."

"Tell me about it."

"Have you prepared a dress?" Her gran asks.

"I'll just throw on something in my closet. I have plenty of gowns to pick from in my stash. My main task right now is makeup and my hair. I'm not sure what to do. "

Gloria stands slowly. "Now…this is a real crisis!" She pokes. "Excuse us for the night, have a blessed sleep. Until next time."

"Bye for now…until next time." Kayla bids the Ahokas farewell.

"Donadagohvi, (Til we meet again)." The Ahoka family replies in perfect unison. A smooth, watery Cherokee tongue.

"Huh??" Kay rotates her head to one side, intrigued.

"Til we meet again." Kota translates.

"Be sure to take loads of pictures." His mom assumes they are going as a pair to the party.

Oh…he hasn't told his mom that we have separate dates??? Does any of them even know I'm going with Darius, not him?? Odina is too happy to know this truth. Mato is too proud of his son. Why didn't Kota share this?? "We will…" Kay plays along.

 She and Gran-Gran pile into the Volkswagen. Kay is deep in thought about why he lied to his mom and dad…and possibly his sister. Gloria is amused. Her tittering is hard to miss. "What's so funny?"

"You're in for a very interesting night!" She says. "It looks like Kota couldn't tell his folks that you weren't his date." "I don't know why he didn't."

"Oh…you know why." Gloria laughs on, applying her seatbelt strap across her body. "Just keep the two away from each other. You'll be fine. Play it smart."

"I'd rather not play at all…why does it have to be a game?"

"Life is nothing but competition, firefly."

"Do I have to compete??"

"Unfortunately." Gloria twists the keys into the ignition and roars the car engine to life. " You're locked in for good." She drives off, pulling away from the curb, in the direction of downtown. To the penthouse.

 Her mom is pacing in the lobby of the penthouse. James is beside her, very tensed up, Tight forehead wrinkled and a deep-set grimace. *Oh, no…did something go down when we were gone?? Why is mom power walking in circles?* The front desk receptionist is wondering the same. The woman is noisy, taking in every action of Mary's body, while speaking over the phone. Multitasking on the job, clocking hours while being entertained.

"Mom…what's up?"

"THE BOOKS!"

"Shhh!" Kay shushes her mom. She can't talk about this in public…the receptionist is right there hanging onto every last word. For all we know, the lady is faking a call to appear busy…just to gain some gossip for the day. "Mom…we have ears on us.." She murmurs.

"Let's retire upstairs." Gloria waves Mary in the direction of the elevator.

"I'm not going back up there!"

James rubs his forehead. "Baby…not here, we need to talk about this in private."

"Why?? Stop behaving as if this isn't crazy! No one will believe this nutty shit! Let everyone hear the craziness. I'm not going back up there! The books are speak-"

"*Tse Tta*, (Silence)." Granny does a charm to lock her daughter's mouth shut. Similar to a mummy…without the gross mouth stitching threads on the lips.

"GRAN!" Kay peeps back of the receptionist, who is wide eyed at what just occurred. "She saw!"

"I'll perform an erase incantation; no need to fret." She snaps her fingers at James. "Son, carry her upstairs. I don't care if she kicks and scratches as a big child. Handle her."

James shares an apologetic gaze with his wife. "Sorry, dear." He lifts her over his shoulder as if a pirate stealing a princess bride away to his ship. With ease and pure muscle.

Mary does exactly what's expected; kicks and screams. Her words are closed off behind her lips yet are easily made out in muffles. "LET ME GO!! LET ME GOOO!!!" She throws a tantrum all the way to the elevator…even when the doors close.

"Mom please! The house is still okay…the books won't do anything bad to you. If you hear the grimoires speaking, that's okay. The books are your friend."

"AHHHH!!!" Mary mumbles a terrified scream.

"Don't think about it! Just help me. I'm going to a dance. You can help me pick out a dress. You can help me with my hair and makeup. This is a fun!" Her mom kicks and yells on, not at all in the mood for a makeover session.

Gloria is the first one out of the metal lift. "If you don't behave yourself, I will lock you like glue to this damn house until you learn to relax! You've had enough time to come to terms with this family and our meaning! Pull yourself together this instant!" She scolds. "Tanagaro, (speak)." The quiet lock on Mary's mouth diminishes away entirely.

"MOM! I HEARD VOICES!"

"GET USED TO IT! STOP COMPLIANING! NOW WE'RE GOING TO GET HER READY FOR THE DANCE. THAT'S AN ORDER!!!" Mary sews in fury like a big kid put in time out not daring to challenge her mom. Gloria could trap her to this house for years if she wanted to.

"Please, mom…help me get ready?"

"Fine…" Her mom trains her tongue to agree in order to keep her physical freedom. "What do you want to wear?" She forces the words out hoping to sound excited, yet it comes off frazzled.

"Ice cream, anyone? Ice cream will help." James makes his way to the kitchen with this remedy of restoring normalcy. "Sweets always help."

"Cookie dough." Mary requests her go to flavor for stressing out. "Lots of it."

"Me too!"

"Me three." Gloria joins the dessert train. "How are you visualizing your hair, dear?"

"Up…I'm thinking a nice wrap updo with bangs out…fringe type bangs."

"Like a beehive style from the 50's??"

"Not exactly that, but something close. What do you say about that, mom??"

Mary sight is on the hallway, where the witch books are…in her bedroom…just feet away. Frightened at the thought of being in close proximity. "A bit more modern…kinda like Cindy Lauper."

"YES!!"

"For makeup…bronzer and glitter set in silver highlights."

"WHOA! LOOK AT MOM GO!"

Mary smiles genuinely, returning a bit to herself. "I can be a fashionista when I want to be."

"What about your dress?"

"Gold…it has to be gold, mom. That's the theme."

"Okay…we have to work out a gown. The gold has to stand out."

"Can't I just have a little gold? Like as an accent color to my dress."

"No…not at all. Themes are meant to be followed. You're wearing all gold."

"Your mommy is right. All school dances have to be spot on…even if it's cringey. You have to be on theme to make the memories count. So, you can look back and hate how you look and what you wore. That's a successful life lived."

Kay is so happy that her mom is joking and serving personality and not a dead-pan input on the girly activity. "You would know best; I'm on board for it! Right, granny??"

"I am…only if you stand out from the crowd. You just can't wear a simple dress that any girl can throw on. That'll lead to a copycat duplicate."

"AVOID COPYCATS! You can't have on the same dress as another girl. That's a total meltdown…a big no-no!"

"So, what should I wear??" Kay pivots her head between her mom and granny, seeking advice.

"Don't freakout, Mary."

"Mom! What are you about to do??!" Mary backs away towards the wall for dear life, nearly melting into the drywall.

"I have an idea."

"No magic!!"

"Hush!" Gloria ups a hand to dismiss her daughter. "Come, firefly. I know exactly what to do. You don't have time to guess on what outfit to put on. You have 15 minutes to get there. Let me do my work."

Kayla steps to her granny, full of joy. *Is my gran about to do what I think she's about to do?? Is she about to cast a dress onto my body. Is she about to become a real-life fairy godmother and give me a real princess treatment makeover? Am I Cinderella?*

"Habesha Kemis, (dress)." Gloria says an incantation.

Immediately, the fabric of her ordinary clothes dissolve into glowing particles, shapeshifting off of her very skin. Her body is engulfed in wavelengths gold dust. The sleeves disappear first, unraveling into golden sparkles drifting upward just as fireflies do. The material of the dress is a chain link, gold looped circle texture. The shoulders of the dress have looped chain links as well Something an Egyptian queen wore centuries ago, old fabric, chic. An old-fashioned love letter.

The shimmers of glitter etched into the texture patterns are silver twinkles. Dazzling dust trapped within the gown itself. Any slight move she makes will flicker as stars of outer space do every second of the day.

A gold, thick belt is spiraled across her waistline, applying warrior goddess vibes. The smooth, glossy belt is a mirror reflecting all around her. The dress's neckline is slightly draped to her chest…just enough without revealing any cleavage. Elegant. Poised. Tasteful. The hem of the dress is a mermaid; the a-line shape is flared near the bottom. Modern charm. Marilyn Monroe living in the 1980's. Slim and flared perfection.

CHAPTER 41: DARK TANGO

KOTA

His mom and dad drives him to school, overjoyed by him mingling with kids his own age. "I'm sooo happy you're going!"

"He's even more happy." His father chimes in. "I'm sure he's holding back all of the excitement."

"I thought you'd be more elated…you're going out with Kayla!"

I dug myself into a hole here. Why can't I just say I'm going with another girl? Why can't I bring up Hannah?? Is it because I know this is a onenight thing? Hannah looks lovely…still…I have no interest in dating her. I'll have to let her down easy…and put up a friendzone. "I just got a lot on my mind."

"We all do…" Odina twists to look back at her son in the backseat. "Just put it all out of your mind."

"Look at the bright side of things…you got the girl. Mato is impressed. "A lot faster than I thought you would."

"I thought you said Kayla had a boyfriend."

"She does, mom…" He swallows hard. *Let me end this before it goes too far. I can't keep lying to them…Kayla isn't my date.* "Kayla is going with her boyfriend, Darius. I'm going with someone else."

His dad peeps at him through the rearview mirror. "Why didn't you say so before??"

"I…was trying to avoid it."

Odina rubs his kneecap to soothe him. "Oh…we're so sorry…we just assumed that you two were going as a pair." "Even she made it seem like a date." "I know…we both did." He sulks.

"Hang onto hope."

"Your mom is right… no matter how much it hurts, please try to have fun tonight. Don't think too much about it. Take as many pictures as possible." His dad prep talks his son. The wagon parks on the extremely clean curb of downtown Chicago. The polished school of 7 stories high… a miniature skyrise.

Kota's mother bends back to him for a quick embrace. "Have fun."

"Yeah, live a little…pun intended."

"Good one, dad." Kota snickers. "I'll be ready at 8."

"See you then." His mom kisses his dead, cold cheek, never wincing at all from the subzero touch.

"See you then." He leaves the wagon, adjusting the silver and gold, elegant outfit he has on. A silk, gold dress shirt trimmed with silver and straight legged dark jeans. Semi formal as always. Yet his hair is different, no longer straight down but in a single, triple knotted long braid down his back. A very native touch.

The gymnasium is a walk to the past…only the tacky under the sea dance from back home in Oklahoma was corny. This golden leaf party is sophisticated and regal. Gilded sparkle leaves hang from the very top of the ceiling from strings. The theme is somewhat like psychedelic beads a hippy would deck their home out in…only this is on steroids.

The dangling leaf petals form a circle around the dance floor, a dense curtain which students have to part with their hands to pass through. The clink of the hanging art is metallic and authentic. The balloons are tied around flower centerpieces on every table. The back of each chair holds 2 balloons sort of like makeshift pillars for a king's throne. The DJ booth is decked out with gold confetti…which also riddles the entire gym floor, stuck in place and shining; a strange seaweed décor approach.

There are wall length posters covering the gym room in a 360 circle; artwork of the autumn season, which is coming to an end. This is a farewell to the fall season.

Kota searches the faces of all of the teenagers in the gym. Browsing for Kayla, hoping to see her so he can get through the night with ease. *I don't have any other option but to let my eyes enjoy her. But Kayla isn't here yet…is she late? Fashionably late…? Must be….I don't see Darius anywhere around here. I wonder when they will show. I'm sure he said yes to her proposal.*

"Hi, Kota." Hannah wouldn't have been heard by a normal boy. A normal boy would have asked what she said. He has no need to confirm her tiny words.

"Hi." He takes in her simple, sleek black dress, a watery material. Cut short at the hem in a poodle ruffle and a boxy neckline. Plain and pretty. "You look really nice."

"I wasn't sure what to wear, so I just threw on the first thing I saw."

"You did good."

Hannah tucks her flat, hazel hair behind her ears. "Thank you…you did good too."

"I just threw on anything."

All of the scorned girls he turned down through a quick convo or by not responding to their letters, scowl. Mad, hurt, and jealous that he showed up with the quiet girl. Their rude remarks are clear as day:

"Really, her!!"

"She didn't even stuff up his locker; I wrote him 5 times!"

"I asked and got turned down, and she just wins the date??"

"Hannah doesn't even talk…why would he go with her??!"

"Wait until Vanessa sees this…'

"The queen bee will be royally pissed off."

"Wasn't he supposed to be here with Kayla."

"Hannah is his date?? That doesn't even make sense!!"

"I told you they weren't dating."

"Where is Kayla?"

Good question. Where is Kayla?? He reads the giant gym room clock above the main door. *It's 6:25.*

"Do you want to get some punch?"

"We can do that." He leads the way to the banquet tables. Hot dogs. Nachos. Burgers. Chips. Soda. Brownies. He and Hannah bypass the main entrees to bright green fruit punch, the sour kind. He's a gentleman; he pours her a cup using a deeply hallowed wooden spoon.

"Thanks."

As he passes her the red cup of sweet, a strong aroma flames up his nostrils. A poisonous flavor is in the punch. Someone spiked the bowl with alcohol. There's liquor in the bowl. Kota stares over at 3 more bowls shaded with blue, red, and orange liquid, sniffing. Finding the same fragrance there. *Uh oh…some rebels want us all to get hammered tonight.*

"Umm…wait!" He yanks the cup from her hand. "I wouldn't drink that…someone added alcohol to it."

"REALLY??" Han peeks into the cup as if her bare eyes can pick up on the adult drink. "How did you know??"

"I just remembered there were a group of guys looking pretty suspicious. They were hanging here before you showed." He fibs a cover story for his supernatural nose.

Hannah sets the cup down, very disturbed. "I have to tell the chaperones. I'll be back." Her voice volume is stronger no longer a pipsqueak mouse. The bad action of boozing up the punch has her courageous enough to reveal her outrage in a strong voice.

"Good thinking.…I'll make sure no one gets a cup." Kota observes Hannah walks off to locate the teachers. *There are 3 here patrolling the dance. None of them spotted the crime of giving all the students a banging hangover in the morning??? Whoever slipped the alcohol in did it fast and slick. Under the radar.*

A song sounds on. Wind chimes. Crystal singing. An ethereal orchestra. But the DJ isn't set up yet. The middle-aged man is still connecting a mixing keyboard and cassette tape to two tower speakers through a soundboard system. The DJ isn't producing any remix beats. Kota knows where the song is coming from. Kayla has arrived.

His attention cuts everyone out of the gym, tunnel visioning to one person only. *Where did she get that dress from? How does the fabric exist?? How is the material just as enchanting as she is???* A chained crochet, warrior princess gown fit for battle. Old age Egyptian cloth. A design fit only for her body, a glove made only for her. The gold jewelry; earrings…necklace…bracelets. The gold knitted slippers on her tiny feet, adjacent to glass slippers in real life. Her coily hair in a half updo with fringe bangs framing her forehead in thin lines.

She's…incredible! He slobbers over her. But his bliss short lived. His admiration for the super model goddess standing a few feet away, is interrupted. A repeat of the past kills off his craving. Darius is agitated by the attraction Kota has for his girl….so he blocks Kayla. Standing his tall body before her to wedge an end to Kota's ogling. *I've seen this before. Macy…Macy's jock boyfriend from back home. The blonde guy made the same chess move on me. A knight piece on the chessboard game…protecting his queen…the most valuable asset worth redeeming.*

Darius dark irises are cautioning him. Translating to the same phrase he used before, *"stay away from my girl."*

Kayla tiptoes, without any true progress, he's about a foot and a half taller than she is. Her head barely goes past his shoulder. "Stop it."

"I'll stop if he stays put."

"We talked about this already!"

"He keeps looking."

"I don't want to argue anymore…let's go dance, okay??"

The DJ bumps up the music, playing the hit song Total Eclipse Of The Heart by Bonnie Tyler. A piano prances softly and mournfully, each note falling epically. The synthesizers hum beneath the distant thunder in the background of the dark, atmospheric, track. A caressing midnight love. Doomed loved. The drums; heavy, and theatrical—thumping a desperate heartbeat. Electric guitars. Aching background vocals. The bass line; a shooting a war cannon in an open battlefield.

"Turn around. Every now and then I get a little bit lonely. And you never coming 'round. Turn around. Every now and then I get a little bit tired. Of listening to the sound of my tears."

Kota automatically takes Hannah by the hand, not thinking it over. He just wants to get out of sight of Darius and Kayla. His mom was right…it hurt…so bad. The rejection. The punishment of having to endure them dancing together on the floor…right in front of him.

"Every now and then I get a little bit restless. And I dream of something wild. Turn around. Every now and then I get a little bit helpless. And I'm lying like a child in your arms." The gloom lyrics of the song are haunting.

Kota chooses a spot on the other side of the gym…close to a corner by the window. Private and far from who he believes to be the love of his life. His soulmate. His twin flame. A romance written in the stars. His hand parts the heavy curtain of leaves to enter the dance floor. The oval is full of teenage bodies and feet, moving limbs swaying to the beat.

"I like this song." His date starts conversation.

"I never heard it before." Kota covers up his sorrow, trying to enjoy the night like his parents want. He respectfully hold her by the shoulders, not the waist; that would imply that he likes her. So, Kota holds her there and slowly dance to the music. They two-step in a slow tempo, side to side, back and forth.

"Bonnie Tyler is my queen…I'm saving up to see her in concert."

"That's nice." His interest is weaker, less energetic.

Hannah isn't dumb…she feels the distance. "I know you like her more than me." She stops the two-step dancing to get serious.

Kota frowns down at her. "I'm sorry…I really not big on dances. I didn't want to be here. I was-"

"Forced to choose me as your date??" Han shrugs. "I know…I'm quiet…I'm not stupid."

Kota grins with life. "Most quiet kids are the smart ones. I'm glad you're one." He jabs. "And thanks for understanding. I didn't mean to be mean just now."

"You don't seem mean at all…you seem more so sad."

Is it that obvious?? Is my depression that easily detectable?? "I try not to be."

"So, let's not be gloom and doom…at least for one night."

"You seem happy…to me….just a little shy."

"Looks can deceive."

"I guess so." He returns to the standard slow-motion dance with his date. "What has you so sad?"

Han follows his lead…turning in a half circle prance along with the DJ sound board. "I never been to a dance…and I never asked a boy out. I almost died walking up to you. But…I needed to face my fears. I can't be scared for the rest of my life."

"So, you went after the boy who every girl wants to ask out?"

"That made it even more of a challenge…which is a good thing. I needed the push to get myself out of my shell. So yes…I went after you, the heartthrob who turned down the most popular girl in school. Now, what do I have to be afraid of? That's the scariest thing any girl can do…and I did it."

KAYLA

"You look like a fairy princess." Darius flirts while holding her by the waist in a romantic waltz.

Kay swoons at the compliment. "Aww. How did you know that was the look I was going for?" Her hands are on his neck, applying a sweet, caressing hold to his skin.

"I know how to connect the dots."

Kayla smooches his lips. "I didn't think you would say yes to me. After the last time…"

"I still love you…I just don't really get what's going on?"

"There's so much I have to tell you…"

"You have to tell me everything."

"Maybe not all at once…you already ran away from me."

"You can't blame me for that."

"I know…"

"How could you tell Mya and Jia…and not tell me? I could have taken it well too."

"Because they didn't take it well…at all."

"Looks like they did…last time I saw Jia she seemed on good terms with you."

"It's all an act…she hasn't been there for me lately. It sucks…I hate it. Mya is worse…she hasn't talked to me in days. They barely speak to me anymore…all because my world got too dangerous to handle."

"Dangerous?"

"Yes."

"How do you mean??"

Here isn't the place or time to drop the bombshell on the existence of vampires. Although I need to give him something to win his trust back. "You already know that magic exist…but there are more supernatural beings out there other than me." *Dare I say there are giants who gave birth to vampires? And that a wicked, vampire king has an army of dead demons and will try to kill me because I'm his target?? Or will Darius run screaming again…and losing his shit???*

"Supernatural beings??" Darius stops their gentle tango to read her pretty eyes closely. "Not just witches?"

"No…there's more."

"Like what??!"

He hasn't even gotten used to me being a witch…so how can he take in all of the other information?? "Let's take it one day at a time. I'll start with telling you everything about me…then we can talk about the rest. Deal?"

He debates on whether to challenge his girlfriend for the information, only to compromise. "Deal…I don't want to get all spooked again."

"No…please not again…my heart can't take you being scared of me." Kay slides her hands from around his neck and down to his chest. Seductively giving her boyfriend a siren gaze. Her eyelids hooded with lust and ache. "I love you."

"I love you more…"

The song Tainted Love by Soft Cell is next up. The embodiment of neon dripping onto wet pavement. The synthesizer stabs the air, mechanical, obsessive, emotionally poisoned. The drums parade dead-eyed precision, loud, free, and relentless. A heartbeat trapped within a chrome shell of toxic desire. Crawling bass, sensual vocals, smoke curling through a nightclub in the sky.

"Sometimes I feel I've got to run away. I've got to get away. From the pain you drive into the heart of me. The love we share seems to go nowhere. And I've lost my light. For I toss and turn, I can't sleep at night. Once I ran to you (I ran). Now I run from you. This tainted love you've given I give you all a boy could give you Take my tears and that's not nearly all Tainted love (oh-oh-oh-oh). Tainted love."

"HEYY….YOU'RE HERE!!" Izzy shouts from a few feet down. She and Chester are dancing in all gothic black getup…tight leather and tazed hair full of frizzy fluff. They're the only two who chose an emo dress theme, complete with jet black eye shadow and makeup bronzer on their cheeks.

"YEAH, I GOT IT TO WORK OUT!" Kay bellows over the brain crushing music.

"GOOD! LET'S PARTY!!!" Her leather dress is a one piece connected to a choker necklace set with a large diamond in the center. The bottom is super straight with tiny ruffles at the very bottom.

"WHERE IS FRED??" Kay asks.

Izzy points to the far middle of the dance floor, where Fred and Marla are paired up as dates, in all gold from head to toe. He's vogueing like a drag queen on the runway; hitting the perfect hand gestures of artwork in rhythm to the beat. Marla tries to keep up; her arm language is goofy and rushed to be in tune with Fred.

He's too much…how can he move like that…better than I can move. Kay snorts like a little piglet. "FRED!!" She waves him down, hopping up and down to get his attention. His sight lands on her almost immediately. Fred's big, childish smile gives her life. "GET DOWN TO THE MUSIC!!!" She cheers him on.

"Tainted love (oh-oh-oh-oh). Tainted love (oh-oh-oh-oh). Touch me, baby, tainted love. Touch me, baby, tainted love." The party song drones on, hyping up all of the teens to jump into a mosh pit. Bodies leaping. Some bounce and fall down, landing the wrong way. Some stumble backwards when dropping on their feet. Only a few teenagers actually stick the landing…appearing to be worthy of gymnastics gold medals.

"I'm thirsty." She says to Darius. "Let's go get some punch." The lovebirds claw themselves from the depths of the tight knitted crowd of frantic teens, traveling a sea of chaos to get out of the pit of jumping fury.

"You okay?" His protective eyes examine her arms for any form of harm from the mob, scratches included.

"I'm good."

"Perfect." The pair continues onward to the refreshment table…unaware that, while they were dancing, a group of biker boys added alcohol to the bowl. Unaware that the teachers were too distracted by the mosh pit to spy this rudeness occurring for a second time.

But Kota is aware…he knows about the bad boys pulling a sick prank. He excuses himself from Hannah's side to give yet another warning to an innocent bystander.

"Which flavor you want?" Darius snatches two red cups from a tall stack.

"Hmmm….I want to say orange…then again…green is nice and sour…then again blue-"

"Think twice about drinking that!" Kota alerts her.

Huh…what?? Why?? Why would I think twice?? What is Kota talking about?? Kayla inspects the colorful bowls of sugary liquid.

"What do you mean??" Darius contends, growing impatient. "What's wrong with it??"

Kay peers at Kota. "Yeah, what's wrong with it?" "Did you spike the punch??" Darius wrongfully deduces.

"No."

"You did!"

"Some other guys did…I saw them."

"No, you did!"

"Why would I do something that silly?? Come on, think a little, man."

"I don't know you, so I'll assume you're the culprit! You're trying to get Kayla to loosen up some so you can have your way with her."

"Please stop!" Kay is embarrassed…there are ears on them as the song fades out to cross blend to the next. These few seconds are endless. *Darius needs to stop…he's making a bad scene. He's drawing the attention of everyone here. Everyone is watching the show. I don't want this to be gossip for later on.* "I don't think he did that. How about we forget the juice? We can go back to the floor."

"You actually believe him?" Darius scoffs.

Kota is exasperated beyond annoyance. "If I'm the culprit, would it make sense to tell on myself. Would I even be warning her if I was trying to be so slime?"

"You don't need to warn her about anything…that's why I'm here??" Darius shoves Kayla to the side, away from the close distance of his enemy. "Go back to your date…I'll worry about mine."

"Darius…I wanna go back to the dance floor." Kay slinks low into her neck, humiliated more by the second. *He needs to listen. I don't want all of this drama. He's turning this into something completely false.*

Billy Idol's White Wedding plays next. Cathedral echoes. A snarling guitar riff, fast, sharp as a switchblade. Endless deep chords orbiting a holy chant. The drums stomp with militant force, heavy boots on the floor, exploding. The backing vocals are full of a ghost choir blessing something beautiful and doomed. Seduction and accusation. The punk melody; a rebellion of the law. Velvet corruption.

Kayla tugs at Darius's shirt harder, attempting to pull him away…all the way back to the paradise they were just in minutes ago. Her eyes can't help but take in the room full of people. Some of the dancing is resumed by the teens; who are close to breaking their necks mid dance to view the spectacle. Other students are boldly noisy, not caring that they are seen as peeping toms. "Drop it, okay?" She pulls at his shirt harder.

"Just don't drink any of it…that's all I'm saying, dude."

"Don't tell me to do anything!" In the blink of an eye, Darius connects his fist to Kota's jaw. This time the hit is solid. Kota was unprepared…caught off guard.

"NOO!" Kayla covers her mouth…her feet slide under her weight, tumbling in a reverse walk. "DON'T DO THIS!" "STAY BACK!" Darius growls at her.

Kota is flabbergasted…bested…not believing that his quick abilities were just rendered useless to respond properly. His head is sideways from the lick to his jaw….stuck in place for a few seconds.

"Don't do it. Don't do it KOTA! Please!" She begs him.

"I want him to!" Darius goes in for another lick, all cocky about the first one landing. He assumes Kota will stand down like a good boy. But he's wrong. His rival grabs his arm, flipping him over in the air like a doll. Body slamming Darius straight onto the juice table; a pro wrestler move seen on TV…or a video game. The bowls of colorful juice shoot up and drench everyone in close vicinity; mini waterfall splashes. Ruined clothes. Ruined hair. Ruined shoes.
All spoiled green, orange, blue, and red. Real life water coloring. Teen after teen are infuriated over the mess, whining and fuming:

"MY HAIR TOOK HOURS!"

"NOT MY KICKS, I JUST BOUGHT THESE!!"

"MY DRESS!!"

"WHOA! WHAT IN THE WORLD!"

"NOOO, MY MAKEUP!"

"WHAT'S GOING ON??"

"AHHH!!"

The DJ station outputs the lyrics: "It's a nice day to start again. It's a nice day for a white wedding. It's a nice day to start again, ow!"

"Are they fighting over Kayla??"

"It figures; she likes drama, so obvious."

"Attention whore!"

"Don't look like she's that perfect."

"I don't get the deal…she isn't worth all of that!"

The 3 teachers step in unison to correct the dilemma, navigating past the teenage mob to the front of the gym. Students clear a path for the authority figures.

"Everyone get back!" Ms. Ruby "What is the matter here?"

"What are you boys doing??! Kota is that you?!" His wood shop teacher is disappointed in the violent actions of his star student. "Get up from there boys, this instant. Mr. Ahoka!" His French teacher is upset as well. "UP! UP! UP FROM THERE!" Her broken, thick accent is clearly audible when enraged. "UP NOW!!"

Kota still holds Darius down in place, on the broken table. Pieces of wood, stained tablecloth…dripping juice and all. His grip is overpowered; he turned it on just to one up Darius; who is unable to move beneath the supernatural weight. He squirms, using his hands to pry Kota off of him, but the locked paws of his vampire side won't let up. He has him pinned down in puddles of wasted juice.

The wood shop teacher tugs Kota by the shoulder. "Mr. Ahoka…let him go. Be easy." Kota doesn't budge…his white, furious irises are fixated on Darius. His snarled mouth is vicious…and his palms are immoveable as dried concrete. "Mr. Ahoka??" Still no response…not a twitch…not a blink…not an inch of movement from him.

"Let go of him!" Ms. Ruby begs.

The French teacher puffs out air. "He is not listening!"

Why is Kota doing this to me? Why is Darius so bad with his temper?? This was totally avoidable. I HATE BOTH OF THEM. I HATE THIS! This is so embarrassing! Do they care how this makes me feel?? No. Not at all. They're just stupid boys. SO STUPID!!! Kayla stomps away from her crush and her boyfriend. Her shiny slippers pound away from the party of thousands of students. From a thousand eyes…judging her choices.

Her eyes fuzz in and out, water droplets of mortification. She's at the entrance of the gym, passing a walk of shame, her peers evaluate her all the way there…all the way out into the school's hallway. She turns the corner in her warrior gown…weak…not strong like a goddess. Crying. Hyperventilating. Sniffling. Her knees buckle and shake; she clutches the wall for support. Holds the wall to stop from collapsing face first to the floor.

This is the worst night of my life. The both of them are careless…selfish! How could Darius?! How could Kota?!

"Miss goody toe shoes is just a player!" *Nooo. Nooo. Not here! Get away! I can't right now. Not now!* Vanessa curves around the corner with a vengeful smirk. "Such a shocker! You played the part well. I give you that. I never expected the valedictorian to be so scammy."

"Get away from me!"

"You led both of them on…and now it blew up in your face."

"Go away, Vanessa!"

"I appreciate the master plan. It took you far."

Kay glowers at her nemesis. "You need to leave!"

"Oh, don't be so touchy; it's not your fault you're not smart enough to keep them in check. You should've done better with your boy toys. Learn how to keep them in check."

"BACK OFF OF ME!!" Kay stands up straight from the wall and bellows, putting her arms into the hostel yell.

"If you weren't a loser…I would tell you my secret. Too bad you're not popular. You're just a selfish wanna be queen."

Kayla's scowl loses power. Doubt sets in. Her fierce mood degrades to a blank slate…a regretful state. She's speechless…too speechless to even throw out a rude retort to the mean girl. *Vanessa is right. I am selfish. I knew it would end like this. I knew it would all end badly. I can't have them both. Still…I led Kota on…when I said we should share our feeling and that it would help to talk it out…together. I led my boyfriend on…told him; "just friends,". Told him, "I loved him." I'm the bad guy…I'm a user. I'm…the selfish one.*

She directs herself down the hall…without a single word. Letting Vanessa win the shakedown. Her glass slipper shoes of enchantment carry her to the main stairs of the lobby. Her feet guide her more than her mind does. Kay shuts her mind off. Step by step up the staircase, she goes. Numb and dead as a zombie. No thoughts…no words. Not even breathing. Her lungs stop producing air…no inhaling or exhaling. Just…gone. Switched off oxygen. The last step of the 7-level staircase leads to the rooftop. Her escape. The weather is frigid. Downtown Chicago is a thin sheet of ice flakes. The winter storm is still kicking up flurries. This time the snowflakes are thicker. Falling faster…oval icebergs in medium size.

Her legs lead her out onto the roof full of 3 feet of snow. Her fancy slippers crunch on the puffy ice. Kayla's makeup is wrecked by tears. Her dark bronzer is smudged in zigzag lines down her cheeks. The gold highlighting contour is a caked up, wet mess. Kay's hands cup her face in a therapy bear hug. She can careless that her palms are dirtied with makeup foundation. Or that her dreamy appearance is all soggy and ugly. Or that the blizzard is dampening her entire body, and bare arms, in wet cold drops.

"I need to go..I want to go…away." She pleads out a murmur. "I want to go away from here." Her mind isn't set on running home…or racing to her bedroom to hide under her covers and pine. No. She wants to stop existing completely. Her request is granted by the force of the other side. Kayla's words come into fruition. Casting an escape. "Take me away…from here." She sobs.

 Kayla whitens to nothingness. Wiping out of reality itself. Thinning where she stands. Light leaks from her vessel; luminous, bright fire. Beneath her skin, her veins burn; pale line patterns in her veins. All over her skin, from her head to her toes. All that she is erased away from the world. Tiny particles peel the skin of her body to hot, clear colored dust. Her hands lose definition; fingers dissolve to silvery static. Flickering in and out. Translucent, glass in human form. An inferno made of bright, hot heat. Kayla hollows away…her physical matter losing the shape of a human. The outline of her body; billions of radiant bursts—releasing into the snowy, night sky. Within moments, there is no solid form of her left on earth….no trace at all. Only a bloom of drifting, pixie dust where Kayla Harris once stood.

EPILOGUE

1918

18-year-old Greyson Mcintyre positions army figurines atop oil cans, which act as a table. Three handheld lanterns light the area; shading his chin and eyes in a shadowy undercast. The bunker he occupies is made of mismatched wood, oak, and cherry. Eighty soldiers lay on thin beds stacked atop one another, sporting white shirts and pants. Chipping, tunneling noises sound from a narrow hall, growing louder and louder. He arranges the twenty figurines against sixty others.

"Any luck?" One British man queries from a bunk bed.

"No."

"Of course not." Another one says, a Frenchman. "That is karma telling you to lose your green eyes and respect our commander."

"I'm not jealous of the man." Greyson retorts angrily. "I just managed to draft up a better strategy." Greyson pushes the make-shift table towards the beds. The noise of the scraping cans interrupts sleeping soldiers. Many of the men groan, covering their faces, and turning away as the lanterns brighten the sleeping quarters.

"Vyklyuchi svet ili zhopu porvu margala vikoliu!" (Kill the lights, or I'll rip your ass and poke out your eyes!) A Russian growls.

"Rasslab'sya, Vasil'yev, pust' mal'chik unizhayetsya." (Relax, Vasiliev, let the boy humiliate himself)."

"I know what uniz means, Nicolas...I'm not here to humiliate myself." Greyson slides a lantern closer to the figurines; the height of the mini soldiers dance and elongate on the wooden walls. He knocks the oil cans free of the tiny men in uniform. "Listen."

Nicolas, who rests with both arms under his head, surveys as Greyson places one soldier by itself. "Wonderful plan. We all die, and you are the only survivor. Lovely teamwork."

"No, this will not be a soldier." He picks up the piece. "This will be a decoy, a dummy board posing as one of us. If we allow Belgium reentry to the trench, their guards will be down. We could swat them one by one. The side of the dugout being drilled leads to a treeline. Us men can take cover there until the battalion exits."

"Like cowards? You want us to hide like cowards?"

"No, I want us to bide our time, be a predator, a lion. The commander's plan of charging out blindly will kill us all. We need bait…and an ambush."

"I like what you're on about; that way is much more clever." The British man compliments.

"Thank you for realizing that, Charlie…now the commander just has to."

"I wouldn't be so keen on that." Nicolas hustles from the bed and salutes someone behind Greyson. Charlie exits his bed too, shaking it enough to squeak the cheaply made frame. He does a salute as well.

"What aren't I realizing, trooper?" A tall, emotionless man in a green uniform, asks.

Greyson swings around and salutes him. "Nothing, Commander Rossi."

"I heard different." His deep, Italian accent is thick. *"Thank you for realizing that, Charlie…now the commander just has to."* That is what you said, isn't it?" The man chastises him using a disciplinary tone. "I'm not fond of fabricators on my team, McIntyre. Would you like to go home and maybe get some attention from your Mommy? You're not getting enough from me?"

"No, sir!"

Rossi looks down at the toy soldier and grimaces. "Do you have an advance you'd like to share, McIntyre?"

"No."

"Then…why are these here?" The leader points to the ones on the dirt floor. "Return them to the war room and think twice before you orchestrate a plan of attack. You're not here to lead, boy! Next time you attempt to do so, you're on a ship back home. Do I make myself clear?"

"Yes, sir!"

Nicolas lets out an enormous hooting titter. "No laughing, you're not at a show! Half rations for the both of you and every bastard that slept through my words!" Rossi shouts, waking the resting troops. Each of the men stumble out of bed and salutes. "You have three minutes. Go!" The men stampede from the quarters, rushing to a meal counter to slop rice, barley, and biscuits onto grimy, dirty plates.

Greyson collects the figurines and walks the tunnels of the dugout. The rocky ceiling drips, accumulating puddles of mud which his boots slosh through. *Humiliating! Why did I cower like that? My plan is a sure shot! Rossi is old and small-minded; same as all war chiefs, he follows a predictable pattern.* He steps on, passing a drilling team that hammers a gigantic cavity into a wall.

The dust from the spades and shoveling tools hooks his attention. It turns in a perfect curling motion, almost as if being controlled. An odd chitter from the gaping hole causes him to stop walking. *What's that?* The picking tools carry on, breaking chunks of rock little by little. He stands there for some time, listening to the chittering morph to cryptic whispers.

When his peers are done eating, they suit up in various uniforms, red and navy, olive, and pale blue. The words of Rossi travel down the way; he orders troops to get their helmets; lay sandbags and carry barbed wire. Then barks at the slow movers to "pick up the pace!"

The dust from the cavity flows thicker now. One of the five handymen stop to wipe his sweaty face and stretch his hands out. This man accidentally streaks a long scratch across his forehead. "Oh, bloody hell…"

Greyson, still trapped in place by the odd dust, eyes the man's wounded forehead. The red liquid sleeks down the man's nose and curves to his mouth. Thrashing from the other side of the wall echoes the underground fort. This rattles the men of war to flock to the back for rifles, snipers, machetes, manual machine guns, and bazookas.

"You think they've been digging in while we've been digging out?!" Nicolas asks Commander Rossi.

"Ready yourselves!" Rossi unclips a bomb from a side pouch and waves the diggers away. "BACK EVERYONE, BACK!"

Charlie snatches a hypnotized Greyson away from the hole. "You alright, mate?"

He doesn't hear the words; his eardrums drown out all normal noises. Everything, besides the hushed voices, is muted. Rossi throws his bomb to blow the hole to smithereens. "ATTACK!"

Bullets are fed into the mounted machine guns; blasting sporadically out the other end. Dozens of explosives and gas bombs are tossed far into the crevice by the army men. The firing squad pumps rounds into the black pit ahead. The industrial, bazookas cannon out mini missiles, sparking explosive rockets down the tunnel.

Dark and tall forms flash from within the hole in an unnatural motion. Grey is the first one who spots this. *What?* He pants, slinking away slowly. A hot-coldness chills his head;

goosebumps slither his arms. The dark shapes grow closer, seeming twenty feet tall and unfazed by all the ammunition.

The metal beaded bullets, bombs, and rockets pass through the giant, shadow creatures as they spread out to the lantern-filled dugout. The immortal force slaughters the army men, engulfing their shells, bombs, and tear gas. Unfazed.

The men near the back runoff…so does Greyson, now covering his ears to block out the unbearable whispers. The pack of soldiers races past the sleep quarters, past the food counter, to a single latter that leads up fifteen feet. One after one, the men fling each other from it, scuffling in a brawl to climb up. Greyson is at the very back of the line. He glances over his shoulder when hollering and slashing noises arise from the distance.

"IT'S DEMONS!"

"BELGIUM HAS THE DEVIL ON ITS SIDE!"

"MOVE!!" The men fistfight.

"OUT OF THE WAY!!!"

Grey notices the blaze of gun rounds lighting up the darkness behind him. Screams, ammo, growls, and beating prompt him to dash to the latter. As his mates duke it out on the ground, the sounds of agony and fear cease. The left behind men are now all dead…now all are slain. Killed. Dead. Including the Commander. The soldiers pause their brawls and lock their sights on the towering shadows coming their way. Dozens of red eyes burn into theirs.

"IT'S DEMONS…IT'S DEMONS!!"

McIntyre runs to the latter just as the next attack kicks up. Blood splatters everywhere. The cracking of bones and the sound of slurping are behind him as he climbs up. The freakishly long claws of the vampires pierce skin, rip out hearts, decapitate heads, drinking blood. Ripped out human organs fling all the way up, spilling past him to the top of the tunnel. Spraying his uniform dark red.

Grey is completely soaked in guts and gore. With every step of the ladder his boots make, he yells. Screams. *I NEED TO GET OUT. GET OUT!! I WILL DIE HERE!!!* The rest of his crew mount the latter bars below him in haste, yelling when the sinister, demons creatures yank each of them down.

"HELP?!!!!" One squeals, gurgling on blood.

When Grey is three feet away from freedom, claws slash through his pants and dig past his skin to muscle. "AHHH!!" He almost falls. He grips onto the last plank of the latter, hanging on for dear life, heaving himself onto the dull grass outside. He hurriedly closes the tunnel's lid, locking the metal bolt. The last of the massacred survivors bang on the lid for dear life. Helpless.

"OPEN UP!!!"

"PLEASE??!!!"

"HELP!!!!"

"NOOOOOO!!!!!!!!!!!!!"

"AHHHHH!!!" The cries for help are silenced by gagging.

He eyes the lid, sweating up a storm, weak to his stomach. A decreased heart rate corrupts his ears, slowing to a drum. The mysterious whispers overtake his brain, calling him, summoning him…welcoming him to the kingdom.

Grey whacks the ground, wheezing, his heart rate give out. Dead heart.. The green of his eyes toggles to red demon irises. His chest stops pumping air…choked by death. His human teeth, squared and short, now transformed to razor blades. A deadly gift from his ancestors. The Celestians. The giants of old…invite him to the afterlife.

ACKNOWLEDGMENT

A big shout-out to Wattpad and Inkitt for motivating me enough to complete this book. The comments and likes I received are what made this book launch possible. If not for the fanbase I built there, this book would still be in draft...and there for good.

I also give thanks to Stephenie Meyer for introducing me to the Twilight Saga at such a young age. Twi-Heart for life. Those books and movies were the driving force for this story.

Thank you, Queen.

REVIEWS NEEDED

Your words hold magic….share your powers below.

If Blood Rose left a mark on your heart, would you consider leaving a review? Did you fall for Kota's curse? Did Kayla's magic give you chills? Did the darkness inside Greyson steal your breath?

BOOK 2: BLOOD SOUL

THE STORY ISN'T OVER YET….

READ LIVE, WEEKLY
UPDATES ON INKSTAR

BLOOD
SOUL
KESHA D. ELY